dheart

ction Copyright © 2020 Argyll Productions

a work of fiction. All characters are fictional and anybody who says
tly is itching for a fight.

ht © 2018 by T. Kingfisher

w.tkingfisher.com

by Argyll Productions

xas

productions.com

61450-522-8

Softcover April 2020

SWORDHE

T.KING

Swor

Produ

This is
differe

Copyrig

http://wv

Published

Dallas, Te

www.argyl

ISBN 978-1-

First Edition

To Kevin

CHAPTER 1

Halla of Rutger's Howe had just inherited a great deal of money and was therefore spending her evening trying to figure out how to kill herself.

This was not a normal response to inheriting wealth. She was aware of that. Unfortunately, she didn't seem to have many other options. She had been locked in her room for three days and the odds of escape, never good, were growing increasingly slim.

Her relatives were going to be the death of her.

She had always believed that this was true in a metaphorical sense. Her two aunts and her assorted cousins would have tried the patience of a paladin or a saint. It was only in the last two days that she'd realized it was probably true in a literal sense as well.

Halla rested her forehead against the diamond-shaped glass in the window. Uncle Silas had been reasonably wealthy, partly because he never spent a single penny he didn't have to. All the windows were made of many tiny panes, inexpensive to replace if one was broken. He would have used oiled paper if he could have gotten away with it, like the poorest houses in the village, but as he aged, the damp got into his joints. When not even a roaring fire could drive it away, he finally gave up and put glass in the windows.

It was cheap glass, full of bubbles. The reflection it threw back to her was distorted, so she could see only an oval of pale skin, pale hair, and respectably dark mourning clothes.

She wished Silas had spent more on glass and saved less. Or at least had the decency to leave the money to his other family members, and not to her.

The look of shock on Aunt Malva's face when the village clerk had read out the will had been gratifying for an instant. Then the rest of Silas's family had turned to stare at her and it had sunk into Halla's brain that her great-uncle had really and truly left everything to her.

He'd probably thought he was doing her a favor.

Now I have something they want, and they can only get it by going through me.

Married or buried, I suspect it's all the same to them. So long as the marriage comes first.

Cousin Alver had proposed that first evening. She rebuffed him, claiming that she was still much too distraught to think of any such things. The conversation hadn't gone well after that.

"Your husband is long gone," said Aunt Malva, setting her knife down on the table with a click. "You cannot possibly still be in mourning for him!"

Halla narrowed her eyes and set her own fork down. "My great-uncle passed away *yesterday,* madam!"

Aunt Malva flushed. Her skin was whited with powder to an unnatural shade, which matched the whitewash on the walls. It made her flush of anger all the more vivid, coming out in red blotches around her eyes and her ears where the powder hadn't quite gone on correctly.

Great-Uncle Silas had not believed in wasting money on

tablecloths, even if it made the kitchen look like a poor crofter's hall, so Malva's hands were very white against the dark wood of the table. She reminded Halla of a ghost or a ghoul.

Mostly a ghoul. Coming along to gnaw the corpse before Silas is even cold.

Hmm, perhaps a ghoul would prefer a warm corpse, now that I think about it. Maybe it's like fresh bread out of the oven, if you're a ghoul.

"Well," said Aunt Malva. "I suppose I am simply surprised that anyone would mourn Silas, that's all."

"Mother," said Cousin Alver quietly.

"I'll speak the truth, Alver! I always do, no matter how it costs me. Silas was a strange, wretched, tight-fisted old man, with no proper affection for his kin or clan."

"He is not even in the *ground*," said Halla, abandoning her thoughts about ghoul diet. "And he was very kind to me when I was young."

"And even kinder now that you aren't!"

"*Mother.*"

"In fact—" Malva began, and then a guttural voice interrupted her.

"Into the pit, the pit, the black pit, when the souls scream and the worms coil..."

Halla seized on the excuse gratefully and rose to her feet. "You've upset the bird," she said.

The bird in question was a small, finch-like creature that could have perched easily on Halla's smallest finger, had she been foolish enough to stick her finger in its cage, which she wasn't. It had a red beak and red eyes and most of the time it sang a repetitive three-note song that went, "tweedle-tweedle-twee!" Occasionally, its eyes would flash green and it would begin roaring in an impossibly deep voice about the end of the world and the screams of the damned.

Great-Uncle Silas had been extraordinarily fond of it. Two priests and a paladin had certified that it wasn't possessed by a demon, although they also all said that there was clearly something very wrong with it and had recommended a great deal of fire followed by a great deal of holy water. Silas had instead put it in a cage in the dining room, because he was that sort of person.

"Hush," said Halla, pulling the tray with the bird's food out. It was built so that you never had to put your hand inside the cage. She took a bit of chicken off her plate and put it in the tray, then slid it back in. The bird leapt on it, cackling in a voice like a very old man heard through a drainpipe.

"Nasty creature," said Aunt Malva.

Normally Halla would have agreed with her, but she didn't want to give the woman any satisfaction. "Silas was fond of it," she said.

"Silas was fond of a great many useless things," said Malva, giving her a look that left no doubt who she was referring to.

"If you'll excuse me," said Halla, "I find I have no appetite." She stalked from the room, angry and shaken and secretly relieved that she had a perfectly good excuse to flee from Alver and his mother.

Cousin Alver had caught her on the stairs. She might have felt the smallest twinge of respect for that, except that she had clearly heard, as the door swung shut, Aunt Malva saying, "Well? Go after her!"

You know that she is wrong, but you feel no need to smooth things over unless she orders you to do it.

"Halla," he said from the bottom of the staircase. He curled his hands around the banister. He wore large gold rings set with stones. The servants said he never took them off, not even to bathe or sleep, and Halla knew that the skin around them was always clammy with sweat.

She could imagine, far too easily, those clammy, ringed hands on her skin. Her stomach turned over and she was glad that she hadn't eaten much.

"Halla, my mother doesn't mean the things she says. She just wants what's best for you."

"She means every word," said Halla. "It's just a shock to her that I'm not her nephew's penniless widow any longer."

Cousin Alver gripped the knob at the base of the banister, not looking at her. "You know she's always been fond of you."

"She's got a damned strange way of showing it!"

"Yes, she does." His voice was so dry that for a minute Halla was forced into unwilling sympathy with him. However hard it was to deal with Aunt Malva in small doses, being her son was probably an entirely different circle of hell. Then he destroyed that instant of sympathy by saying "She'll be better if there are children. She's always been very good with children."

"I have *not* agreed to your proposal!"

"Well." Cousin Alver still didn't meet her eyes. "We'll discuss this tomorrow, when you're less tired."

Halla wanted to be the sort of person who yelled at her cousin and forced him to acknowledge that she had a choice in the matter. Unfortunately, it seemed that she was the sort of person who ran up the stairs to her bedchamber, grateful for the reprieve.

This was a depressing discovery.

But not, I suppose, an unexpected one.

At least I am the sort of person who slams the door. That's worth something.

She collapsed on her bed, the echoes of the slam still ringing through the house.

The money was useless to her. She knew that she would never be allowed to touch it. They would marry her to Alver and take it away so that it stayed in the family and everything would be just as it had been, except worse because Alver was alive and Silas was dead.

Why couldn't it be Alver who was old and had bad lungs? Why couldn't he have died instead?

Well, but if Alver was old then he wouldn't be looking to marry me, and presumably there'd be someone else to fill the Alver-shaped hole in the world, and I'd be right back here except with a different obnoxious person trying to wed me.

Although at least that person might not have clammy hands.

She got up and stared out the window into the dark, thinking about all the ways a woman could die.

Even if her cousins did not actually poison her or push her down the steps, there were many ways to make an unwanted relative's life shorter. Medicines administered for her "health" that left her docile as a milch-cow. Wonderworkers whose talents ran to harm.

Childbirth.

Halla shuddered.

Her late husband had been more dutiful than passionate, but at least he hadn't made her skin crawl. They had gotten along tolerably well for a few years, until a late spring fever had swept the land and carried him off. His estate had gone to his brother and Halla had found herself nearly penniless after the death duties.

A young widow, she might have remarried if she were wealthy, but there was no market for widows of no particular wealth and no particular beauty. Her mother's family was far too poor to be burdened with another mouth to feed. Her husband's great-uncle, Silas, had taken her in and she had become a middle-aged widow in his house, running the household and seeing that his old age was as comfortable as she could make it.

He had been a strange, erratic, maddening man, but she

had always been grateful. He put up with her, and Halla knew that could be difficult.

She knew that he had saved her from the convent, or worse.

There was a click at the door. She knew without turning that someone had bolted the door to her chamber.

It seemed that *worse* had finally caught up with her.

CHAPTER 2

She had naively assumed, that first night, that they would unlock the door in the morning. In retrospect, she wasn't sure why she had assumed that.

I thought I was being punished like a naughty child who misbehaved at dinner, not being held prisoner in my own home like...well, like an extremely unwilling potential bride...

In the morning, the door had still been locked. She had rattled the knob and hammered on the door until Malva came through, glaring at her. "Stop making all that racket! People are trying to sleep!"

"Well, if you hadn't locked the door—" Halla began.

"The door," said Malva, drawing herself up, "will remain locked until you have learned how to conduct yourself in a manner becoming a woman of this family."

Halla should have said something clever. She'd eventually had three days to think of all the clever things that she should have said. But it was such an incomprehensible thing that in the moment, Halla's first thought was that she had misheard or misunderstood, and then she said, "Excuse me, what?" and then Malva made a disgusted noise and pulled the door shut and locked it.

They'd brought her food. Alver came up to say, politely, that he was sorry about all this. Halla stared at him and said "So why aren't you letting me go?"

"Mother, you know," said Alver, wringing his clammy, ringed hands.

"Get out," said Halla. To her moderate surprise, he obeyed.

She was extremely tempted to throw the chamber pot at Malva the next time she arrived. The only reason she didn't was because it would get all over the floor and the doorway and then she'd be sitting in the stink of it, and she was increasingly certain that they weren't going to let her out.

"You'll change your mind," said Malva airily, bringing up dinner. Her sister waited in the hallway, which meant that even if Halla had overpowered her, the door would simply get slammed in her face again, and they'd come back in greater force.

"About what?" said Halla.

"Marrying Alver, obviously. It's the only sensible thing to do. You just need some time to think on it."

"Or what? You'll keep me locked up here forever?"

Malva shrugged.

"You'll have to let me out for the funeral," said Halla, through gritted teeth.

"No, I don't," said Malva. "You'll be overcome with grief, that's all. Although if you'd stop being so stubborn and simply agree to marry Alver—who is better than you deserve!—you'll be able to attend as you ought." She set the tray down on the cedar chest at the end of the bed. "Really, Halla, if you had any feeling for Silas at all, I would think you would do whatever it took to attend, but I suppose such family loyalty is simply beyond you."

Halla hated that she had never been able to get angry without crying. It meant that her vision was too blurred for her to actually hit Malva with a flung candlestick. Fortunately, the other woman's expression was also too blurry to make out.

"*Really*, Halla," she said, and swept out of the room.

Midafternoon on the second day, there was an ungodly commotion downstairs. Halla heard shouts and a scream, and for one moment thought that someone might be coming to rescue her. She half-rose from her seat by the window. Then she heard a guttural voice shouting, "*Hellfire! Hellfire and burning for the worm, the worm that gnaws the roots of the world!*" and realized that the bird was loose.

"Blast," she muttered, dropping back into her chair.

The thumping and shouting went on for some time. She hoped they hadn't killed the bird. She didn't like the bird, but at the moment, she had a certain amount of fellow feeling for it.

"*The veins of the earth run fat with rot!*" shrieked the bird.

"Get a broom!" shouted someone, probably Alver.

More thumping, followed by cackling, followed by silence.

One of the cousins brought her food that night. Halla couldn't remember her name, but it didn't much matter, since they were all fairly interchangeable anyway. Sayvil, Aunt Malva's sister, lurked on the other side of the door, watching them through a crack.

"What was all that noise earlier?" she asked.

"Malva told Roderick to wring the bird's neck," said the cousin.

"He opened the cage, didn't he?"

The cousin nodded. "Fastened onto his face like a leech," she said, with a certain amount of relish. "He was screaming and hopping around like anything. Then he got it loose but it flew up into the rafters."

"Oh dear." Halla composed her face to look as innocent as possible. "I'm good with the bird, I could probably get it back."

The cousin looked blank. "Do you think we were born yesterday, girl?" snapped Sayvil from the door. "Anyway, the bird's gone out the door, and good riddance."

Halla sagged. Well, it had been a thin hope.

It was that night, as she sat brooding, that she realized that she was probably going to have to kill herself.

HALLA HAD no great desire to die, but she had even less desire to remain living among her relatives. This did not leave her with many options. She had run through every possibility in her head and no matter which way she turned it, her continued life was about to get very, very bad.

If I could just break out of the house and...and what? Be penniless on the street on the edge of winter?

This was a daunting prospect, but she'd been willing to try. It wasn't the worst situation she'd ever found herself in. If she could get to a convent, she could throw herself on the mercy of the nuns, like so many other unfortunate women did. It would probably mean a lot of scrubbing floors, but Halla wasn't afraid of hard work.

If she could get to a priest, things would get easier. She could throw herself on the mercy of the Four-Faced God, whose priest currently inhabited the village church. He wouldn't let her be dragged to the altar unwillingly.

But that assumes I can get out. And that's the tricky part.

Well, the windows are right out. Even if they weren't these stupid diamonds, I'm two floors up. I'd fall in the street and probably break my legs, and then I'd be in pain as well as betrothed. And then I couldn't run.

The notion of being at Alver and Malva's mercy and unable to escape...she couldn't imagine.

No, wait, she could imagine it very well, since it was apparently happening *right now*.

Once they start locking you in your room, it only gets worse though. I'm going to be kept in an attic like a mad aunt. And Alver seems to think we'll have children, which... Halla shuddered. *Locked in a room, pregnant...gods above and below...*

She didn't even dare to think about what else could happen. There were rumored to be drugs that could render someone docile or wipe their mind as clean as new snow. Death was undoubtedly preferable to *that*.

No, the future is not looking very good at all. Unless I do something...drastic.

There was a sword over the bed, in a tarnished silver scabbard. One of Silas's prizes, no doubt. He had collected strange objects and left them scattered haphazardly around the house. She'd found a manticore skull in the pantry once. It had just stared eyelessly at her and eventually she rearranged the sacks of flour and jars of spices to make room. It was still there. The cook had screaming hysterics when she found it the next day, but you got used to things. She'd never been quite sure if Silas had gone senile or just enjoyed leaving things where they would shock people.

And then, of course, there was the bird. It had been sold to Silas as a dwarf parrot, which it certainly was not, and while you could argue that it did talk, it did so in a way so unnatural that it raised the hair on the back of your neck. Two servants and the cook had quit on the spot. The cook had to be rehired at twice her previous wage and one of the servants had refused to come back for any price.

Halla took the sword down and stared at it. The hilt was wrapped in leather and the crossguard was plain. The scabbard was the only ornamented part, the metal etched with interlocking circles. The grooves in the etching were black, with paint or tarnish, she didn't know.

It looked old. She wasn't even sure if she could pull it out of the sheath or if it had rusted in place.

She tried to hold it by the hilt and her wrists immediately began wobbling with the weight.

How *did* you kill yourself with a sword? People in ballads and sagas fell on their swords, but what did that mean? If she fell over on the sword, presumably she'd be lying on top of a sword and then what? If it was lying flat on the ground, nothing would happen, and if it was lying on its side, she might get cut up a bit. Were you supposed to wait for infection to take you?

No, no, don't be stupid. Obviously you have to prop the thing up on the floor somehow so it goes through you when you fall on it.

...however the devil you do that.

Obviously, guardsmen and soldiers killed each other with swords all the time. It was just that it seemed like it would be much easier to kill someone *else*, when the sharp bits were all aimed away and you didn't have to worry about whether it hurt. In actual practice, Halla found herself looking at the sheathed sword and thinking that she could probably hurt herself quite badly, but what if she *lived*?

Aunt Malva might try to nurse me back to health. Dear sweet merciful gods, please, anything but that.

And they'll post the banns while I'm in bed and when I wake up, I'll be wed to Alver.

She put the sword on the bed and made another circuit of the chamber, looking for usefully fatal objects. There weren't many.

Why couldn't Silas have left bottles labeled *Deadly But Conveniently Painless Poison* lying around?

She could make a rope of blankets and try to hang herself,

but there weren't any exposed rafters. And her bedchamber had quite low ceilings and was stuffed to bursting with furniture that Silas had needed to store somewhere, so even if she'd somehow managed all the rest, she could have just put her feet onto the bed once it got hard to breathe.

Even in her most dramatic imaginings, Halla didn't think she could beat herself to death with the chamberpot.

It was going to have to be the sword. Halla sighed.

No use dithering. Roll up your sleeves and get to work.

Her mother had always said that, although to be fair, not usually about killing oneself.

The sword was just so *unwieldy*. If it had been a knife, she would have had no problem, but the blade was so long that if she held the hilt in her right hand, she had no way to get the point actually into her chest.

How marvelously stupid. Give me an enormous piece of sharp metal and I still can't think of a way to use it. Perhaps I should just wait for Aunt Malva to come in for the night and try to cut her head off.

Tempting as this idea was, she would merely end up in a prison cell. If she was lucky, they would hang her. If she was unlucky, the family would argue that she had gone mad, take her home, and lock her up somewhere. And Alver would probably *still* marry her and her nieces would still not get any money out of the deal.

She left the sword in the sheath while she tried to figure out what to do. With her luck, she'd cut something off while trying to prop everything in place.

Something not vital enough to kill me, but something I'd miss. A thumb, maybe. I would miss my thumbs.

Maybe if she braced the pommel on the wall, somehow fixed it in place, and then got a running start...around the night table and the large ornamental chest and the bed posts and...

All right, the running start was probably not going to work either.

The pommel on the wall was still the best bet though. Perhaps against the windowsill. She had no idea how to make it stay in one place, though. Could she hold the blade?

I could try, I suppose...and there would go my thumbs again...

If I'm dead, I don't need both thumbs.

She stripped down to her shift to make it easier to stab. Stabbing through cloth was already a pain. Through the heart? Yes, that seemed best. People in ballads always stabbed themselves through the heart.

She tugged the fabric down. No sense in getting more cloth in the way of things.

I've already got far too much in the way there, she thought glumly, looking down at her chest. *What a nuisance. Over the top and I'll have to keep the blade angled well up. It would be humiliating to try to stab myself in the heart and get hung up on my own left breast.*

Still, I suppose it's easier than it would have been before I turned thirty and everything began sagging...

Somehow this was not terribly comforting.

Okay, I brace the end there, and then I shove myself onto the sword. Through the heart.

Fast. I should try to do this fast.

There was just barely enough room between the edge of the bed and the windowsill that she thought she could manage it. She was also rather gloomily certain that she would be standing there with a sword in one hand for the next hour and end up not actually stabbing herself at all, but maybe she'd surprise herself.

What other choice do I have? I don't want to die, but at least this way, my nieces inherit everything and I don't end up locked in Alver's attic.

Maybe it will be easy.

She didn't think it would be easy. She didn't want to die. She quite liked living. Even when it was bad, it was interesting. There was always something fascinating going on.

On the other hand, being locked in Alver's attic for the rest of her life would not be interesting. In fact, it would likely be a combination of horrific and horrifically boring. Surely death was preferable to that.

"Well," she said out loud, trying to bolster her own courage. "My mother's clan were raiding cattle and slaying their enemies only a generation ago. Some of them probably still are. Let's go."

Let's go did not seem like very good last words, so she added, "I commend my soul to any god that will take it."

It occurred to her suddenly that the sword might very well be rusted into its scabbard, in which case she'd feel rather stupid about standing here, bare-breasted, commending her soul to the gods.

She drew the sword.

There was a crack like silent thunder and blue light pulsed around the sheath. She immediately dropped the sheath, but the light was faster. It ran over her hands and down her wrists. She clutched the sword hilt in sheer astonishment.

The blue light shot around the room and coalesced into a figure. It was roughly human-shaped, although man or woman or both or neither, she could not tell.

It could be a demon for all I know.

She threw her empty hand up in front of her to ward off the blaze of light. When the light faded, leaving orange afterimages on her eyes, there was a man standing in her bedchamber, in the narrow space between the chest and the night table.

"I am the servant of the sword," he said. "I obey the will of the—great god, woman, put on some clothes!"

CHAPTER 3

Halla lowered her hand slowly, her mouth hanging open.

A man just came out of the sword. I drew the sword and he appeared.

Oh gods, it's magic, isn't it? Something horrible and magicky happened.

It was possible that she'd gone mad with grief and was hallucinating. Halla had no illusions about her grip on reality. But if she were hallucinating, would she really have included a man coming out of the sword and yelling at her to put on more clothes?

Well...yes. That is exactly the sort of thing I would do.

Her possible hallucination had staggered back and thrown his forearm across his eyes, apparently to block out the unexpected sight.

She pulled her shift up so that her breasts were covered. "Sorry! I didn't mean to scare you."

Wait, he just appeared from a sword *and I'm apologizing for scaring* him?

"I'm not scared!" The man in question was trying to scan

the room while not looking anywhere near her. "I'm used to being summoned on the battlefield, not a brothel!"

"This isn't a brothel! I'm a respectable widow!"

"You aren't dressed like a respectable widow!"

"I wasn't expecting company!"

The servant of the sword looked at her cautiously through his fingers. Seeing that she was at least covered by her shift, he lowered his hand. "Sorry," he said, sounding as if the word was getting dragged out of him. "Didn't mean to give offense. I just wasn't expecting to see that...ah...much of you, that's all."

"I'm not offended," said Halla. "I think we...errr..." *Not scared. He got very prickly about the word 'scared.'* "...startled each other."

"You could still be wearing a bit more," he said reproachfully, keeping his eyes very obviously above her collarbone.

Halla looked down, realized that anyone looking at her would know that it was quite cold in the room, and fumbled for her dressing gown.

"I'll take it you were not summoning me deliberately, then?" the man said, trying not to look.

"No! I didn't know you were in there! Err—you *were* in there, right?"

"In where?"

"In the sword. I thought you came out when I drew the sword but it occurs to me that it could have been a coincidence and you just happened to appear as I was drawing the sword..."

"Yes. That's why I'm the servant of the sword. I'm in the sword." He pointed to the sword in her hands. There was a look on his face as if he didn't know whether to laugh or begin yelling.

"This sword here?"

"Yes. That sword. That you're carrying. Which just summoned me. *Because that's what it does.*"

Halla had no idea what to say to that, so she settled on, "That's very interesting."

He rubbed his face. "So we're not in battle, then."

"No. Err. Sorry?" The dressing gown was proving to be a problem. She needed two hands to get her arms through the sleeves and tie it and that would involve putting down the sword. It seemed, for some reason, enormously rude to put the sword down in front of its...owner? Spirit? Djinn? But she couldn't very well hold the collar of the dressing gown in the hand she was trying to put through the sleeve.

I don't think I can hold the sword in my teeth. That would probably be rude.

"You don't need to apologize for that," said the man. "A battle's not...a...oh, for the god's sake. Turn around."

She turned around. He held up the dressing gown so that she could get her arms into it, although she had to swap the sword between hands.

"I'm a warrior, not a lady's maid," he said. "If you're summoning me to help you dress, there'd better be assassins in the garderobe next time."

"Oh, I don't have a garderobe," Halla assured him.

"Or assassins?"

"Well, I don't think there are any. I suppose if they were any good, I wouldn't know, would I?"

She thought this was quite logical, and did not know why he stared at her for so long.

Finally, he looked around the room again, shaking his head. "Not that I see where you could fit an assassin in this place. Under the bed, maybe. Have you checked?"

"For assassins? No, I—"

He promptly dropped to his knees and peered under the bed. "Nothing," he said, sounding slightly disappointed.

Halla stared at him as he rose to his feet.

He was only about an inch taller than she was, but the breadth of his shoulders made him look much larger. He had deeply tanned skin and long hair that curled when it reached his shoulders and was gray mixed liberally with black. His close-cropped beard was shot with gray as well.

Not a young man, then.

Sword.

Being.

He was wearing a leather surcoat which left his upper arms bare, heavy leather gauntlets that covered his forearms, and he also seemed to be carrying quite a large sword of his own. That struck Halla as bizarre. *Why does a sword need a sword?*

He made a circuit of the room. Halla sat down on the bed to give him room. He checked the great wooden wardrobe, lifted the lid on the chest, and then, apparently satisfied that there were no assassins anywhere, turned back to her.

"So why *did* you summon me, then?"

"I didn't mean to," Halla said. "Sorry?"

"Well. I am the servant of the sword. I serve the one who wields the sword."

"Uh. It was my great-uncle's sword, but he died. And left everything to me." Did that count as wielding? The warrior was looking at her like it might. She gulped, remembering suddenly what kind of trouble she was in *because* Silas had left everything to her. "I'm Halla."

"Lady Halla." He inclined his head. "Then I'm to be a lady's guardsman, am I?" The thought seemed to amuse him, but Halla caught bitterness in the quirk of his lips. "I'd draw my blade and swear you fealty, my lady, but I'm afraid it would stick in the ceiling. So we'll wait on a more convenient moment."

"Why *do* you have a sword, anyway?"

He looked down at the blade by his side, then up at her. "To fight with. It's a *sword.*"

"Yes, but you came out of a sword. It seems redundant."

He stared at her as if she had lost her mind. "I can't very well wield myself, lady."

Oh. Perhaps he'd go blind.

It occurred to her that this would not be a very good thought to say out loud, so she plastered an agreeable look on her face.

"Where is this place, lady?" he asked.

"My bedchamber," said Halla.

"Yes," he said patiently. "I had worked that much out. What land is this?"

"Oh! We're in Rutger's Howe. That's in Archenhold."

He shook his head. "I do not know that land."

"Archenhold's outside of Anuket City."

"Anuket—ah! The place of the artificers?"

"Yes." Silas had visited the markets of Anuket City often. She was pretty sure that was where the manticore skull had come from, although he was far too cheap to buy any of the strange mechanical constructs that the city exported.

"I have come far south of the Weeping Land, then. And the year?"

"1346."

He shook his head. "It was the Year of the Ghost Sturgeon in the great god's reign of heaven."

It was Halla's turn to shake her head. "I don't know when that was. I'm sorry. Err...the sword's been on my wall for years. I think it was here before I moved in. I thought about asking him to replace it with something better—maybe a stuffed fish or a portrait of a saint—but he was being so kind taking me in that I didn't want to seem ungrateful and then you know how it is, suddenly it's a decade later and you've stopped even noticing there's a sword on the wall..."

She stopped because the servant of the sword was staring at her again. "Did I say something wrong?"

"A...stuffed...fish."

"You know, with the fins and the sort of..." She trailed off because he was turning an alarming color. "Look, I didn't *do* it. Your sword stayed on the wall. I thought it was quite pretty. Err, I mean that *you* were quite pretty."

He put his hand over his face again. His shoulders were shaking.

"I'm sorry I don't know what year it is. Or what year it was. Comparatively."

He accepted this change of topic gratefully. "Well, that is the peril of being a sword. You have no clear perception of time passing. I suppose we will make do."

"So *are* you the sword? Or do you live in it?" She looked at the naked steel in her hands, then back up at him. "Like a djinn in a bottle? Wait, *are* you a djinn?"

"Most certainly not!" He looked offended at the very notion. "I'm a human man, or was before I went into the blade. Now I suppose I'm a bit less human, but not a spirit or a djinn."

"Or a demon?"

"Definitely *not* a demon!"

"That's good!" said Halla. Goodness, he was prickly. She wondered if he'd been like this before he became a sword or if being enspelled in metal made a person grouchy. "Do you have a name?"

He pinched the bridge of his nose. "It's writ on the blade, my lady."

She looked down at the sword. The blade had what looked like an entire saga engraved into it, in fine, spidery script.

She squinted. "I don't recognize this language. I'm sorry. Could you just tell me your name?"

"Oh?" For an odd moment, she thought he was pleased by that. "Sarkis, my lady."

"It's a pleasure to meet you, Ser Sarkis."

"Just Sarkis," he said. "What lands I held are far from here and long forfeit." He frowned at her, as if realizing something. "So why is a respectable widow drawing swords in the middle of the night?"

"Oh!" Halla waved her free hand. "I was planning on killing myself. By...err...stabbing myself through the heart. On the sword. Which I guess is your sword?"

"You will do no such thing!"

Halla blinked at him. "They'd have cleaned the sword after. I'm pretty sure. It looks like it might be valuable, you see, and Aunt Malva never wastes money."

"The great god give me patience!" shouted Sarkis. "That's not my concern! I'll not have any woman under my protection killing herself!"

"Keep your voice down!" hissed Halla. "They'll hear you!"

He looked mutinous, but dropped his voice. "Who's they?"

"My relatives. Well, my husband's relatives. They—oh, *blast*..."

Footsteps sounded in the hall. "Halla? Halla, what's going on in there?"

"Oh gods, it's Aunt Malva." Halla looked around wildly. "Hide! You have to hide!"

Sarkis drew himself up to his full height. "I'll not hide from—"

"I will get in serious trouble if there's a strange man in my room!" Halla looked around frantically. Could he fit under the bed?

"Oh. A question of honor. Of course. Forgive me." The servant of the sword bowed his head. "Sheathe the sword."

"What?"

"Sheathe the sword."

"Halla, do you have someone in there?" She could hear Malva fumbling with the lock.

"Don't be ridiculous, Aunt Malva!" shouted Halla. "I couldn't possibly!" She snatched up the sheath and tried to jam the sword back in, missed the opening twice, then got it the third time.

Blue light writhed over Sarkis's skin, and then he was gone. The crossguard clicked against the mouth of the scabbard. She dropped it to the floor and shoved it hastily under the bed with her foot.

Aunt Malva finally got the door unlocked and pushed it open. "What are you..."

Halla blinked at her innocently.

The woman's eyes narrowed and she scanned the room as intently as Sarkis had done earlier. *Threats to my life, threats to my virtue...* Halla had gone for years without anyone worrying about people hiding in her room, and here she was dealing with it twice in one night.

It's not like I make a habit of hiding people in my room. I don't know why everyone is so suspicious all of a sudden.

"I heard voices," said Malva.

"I was praying for Silas's soul," said Halla.

Aunt Malva's eyes narrowed even farther. "I heard a man's voice."

"Maybe it was a god answering."

Malva snorted loudly. "Don't be smart with me, girl."

"I am thirty-six," growled Halla. "I am *not* a girl!"

"So you should be well aware of what duty you owe the family!

And well past dithering like a maiden when you're offered a chance at a respectable marriage." She drew herself up and looked down her powdered nose. "You've no beauty and no prospects. And only a year or two left where you might bear children. Don't be a fool."

"I've not the least desire in the world to bear children," said Halla. "And certainly not Alver's!"

"Alver will be a fine husband and a fine father!"

"So bed him yourself, if you're so keen on it!"

Aunt Malva inhaled as if she'd been struck.

"You're out of your head with grief," she announced. "I'll not listen to such talk. Tomorrow we'll have a family meeting and you'll keep a civil tongue in your head and remember what you owe a family that took you in instead of casting you out on the street."

Halla could think of so many things to say in response that she choked. *Silas* had taken her in, not their precious family. Malva had treated her like a drudge whenever she came to visit, which she did as rarely as possible. And they'd never cared much for her husband when he was alive, only to turn him into a saint after his death.

"I—you—how *dare*—"

Aunt Malva slammed the door. The lock clicked again.

Halla stood with her chest heaving, clutching one of the bedposts for strength. How *dare* that powdered old monster talk to her about gratitude? *How dare they...how dare she...*

"What an unpleasant woman," Sarkis said, from under the bed.

Halla yelped and went down to her knees. He lay flat under the bed, wearing a resigned expression.

"I thought you went back in the sword!"

"I did. Unfortunately, I came loose when you kicked the scabbard under the bed." He crawled free. "I didn't think that my presence would contribute much to the conversation, though."

He rose and handed her the sword, still several inches out of the sheath.

"Well, now you see why I *have* to kill myself," said Halla.

His eyebrows slammed together over his nose. He had a broad nose and a scar cut through one eyebrow, which gave him a singularly wicked look when he scowled. "I see no such thing!"

Halla groaned. "Look. My husband died years ago. His great-uncle Silas took me in. Silas left me everything in his will, like an idiot. His family wants that money, so now they plan to have me marry my husband's cousin Alver, which will keep it in the family."

"Which I gather does not please you, lady."

"Alver wouldn't please anyone. He's got clammy hands."

"The great god save us." Sarkis raised his eyes, presumably to heaven. "Death is too good for such a creature."

Halla was fairly sure that he was making fun of her. "You're missing the point! Once I'm married to Alver, my life won't be worth a penny anyway. They'll kill me off so that Alver can marry someone younger and get heirs. But if I die now, *before* I get married, it will all go to my mother's family. I've got a will with the town clerk that says so."

"Where is your family?" Sarkis growled, his voice dropping an octave. "Why are your kinsman not saving you from these grasping maggots?"

She sighed. "They're poor."

"Poverty's no shame, lady, compared to abandoning kin to these jackals."

"Yes, but...well, after my husband died, I didn't want to burden them. They didn't need another mouth to feed. And then my sister died and now it's only my nieces, you understand, and...well."

"What of your father's kin?"

Halla shrugged. "I don't expect a lot of help from that quarter."

"Why not?"

"Because I don't know who they are?"

Understanding dawned in Sarkis's eyes and he looked down hurriedly. "Apologies, lady."

"It's fine. It was Great-uncle Silas who took me in." She sat down on the bed. "And really, Silas wasn't *that* wealthy. But it would be enough, if the clerks could get it to my nieces, that it would help. They'd have dowries. Good ones. They could marry who they wanted instead of who agreed to take them."

Sarkis folded his arms. His upper arms were bare and tattooed in dark blue. He wore leather forearm guards and leather gauntlets. He scowled again. "You've no male kin to ride to your aid?"

Halla snorted. "My niece Erris would ride to my aid in a heartbeat, *if* she could afford a horse, and *if* I had any way to get a message to her."

She expected some kind of sarcastic rejoinder to that, but Sarkis nodded. "A strong shieldmaid is the equal of any man in combat. Certainly equal to an old woman and a man with clammy hands. Have these jackals any guardsmen in their train?"

"I think you're missing a critical point here," said Halla, rubbing her face. "I mean, yes, they've got one. Malva won't travel without a guard in case of brigands. His name's Roderick."

"Will Lady Erris be able to dispatch this Roderick?"

"I—no, we're not—" She set the sword across her knees and put her head in her hands.

My great-uncle died three days ago. His wretched family descended on me a week ago. I vowed to kill myself this morning. And I have just drawn a magic sword with a man inside and now I am discussing whether my fifteen-year-old niece can slaughter Aunt Malva's guardsman.

What in the name of all the gods is going on?

"She's fifteen," said Halla, since Sarkis seemed to be waiting for an answer.

Sarkis frowned. "How much sword training has she had?"

"She's a farmer! She's a very fierce farmer, but she can't—Roderick's an ex-mercenary. I mean, I don't know anything about how he fights. Just that I have to warn the servant girls before they come to visit, because he's got wandering hands."

"Oh," said Sarkis, his lips thinning with disgust. "One of *those* men. Your niece will do the world a favor removing him."

"My niece is a farmer! And she isn't *here*."

"I will undertake her training, then," said Sarkis, nodding as if something important had been decided.

"Fine! I'll write a note saying that the sword goes to her! Then can you *please* kill me so she has a chance to inherit you?"

"Most certainly not!" He looked deeply offended. Halla dug her fingers into her scalp in frustration.

"Then Alver's going to marry me and when his wretched aunt kills me off, he'll be your next owner!"

"I shall *not* be wielded by a man with clammy hands!"

"Keep your voice down!"

"Oh. Of course. Apologies, my lady." He lowered his voice. "I will not allow you to kill yourself, however. Certainly not with my blade!"

"Oh!" Halla had a sudden thought. "Would you feel it? I mean, if I did that on your sword? Would it hurt?"

"It would hurt *you*."

"Well, obviously. But I mean, would you be able to tell it had happened?"

"You would have to draw the sword in order to kill yourself on it. I would be standing right here. I believe that I would notice, yes."

"Arrgh." She wrung her hands.

"And you are my wielder," said Sarkis. "I am bound to protect you. If I tried to kill you, I would be forced to leap between your neck and my own blade."

"That sounds awkward."

"I do not think it would go well, no."

"And if I killed myself?"

"I would try to take the blow myself. I have no choice."

This was getting worse and worse. Halla groaned. "Do you have any better ideas? Other than my fifteen-year-old niece somehow staging a rescue that she doesn't know anything about?"

Sarkis frowned and leaned against the bedpost. "Clearly you must drive these ruffians from your home and then alert her."

"Drive them from my home?" Halla almost choked at the impossibility of it all. "They wouldn't go! Nobody thinks it's really my home, no matter what the clerks say! I'm locked in my own room!"

He inhaled sharply. "You are a prisoner here?"

"Yes! I've been locked in here for three days!"

This seemed to change everything. The servant of the sword was abruptly all business. "We cannot wait on the honor of your kinswoman, it seems."

"...my fifteen-year-old kinswoman..."

"Pack for a journey. I will allow no one under my protection to be held prisoner, even by their marriage kin."

"Wait, it's all right if they're not locking the door, but since they are, now we'll leave?"

He looked at her as if she were daft. "Yes."

"I don't understand."

"Clearly."

She put her hands on her hips. Sarkis sighed. "It would be extremely rude to interfere with your kinswoman's efforts to rescue you. An insult to their honor. But as you are clearly in immediate and present danger, we cannot afford to wait. We must leave this place at once."

"Where are we going?"

"Away from here."

CHAPTER 4

I t did not take Halla long to pack. She had few enough possessions...at least, not possessions that she felt were hers, and not Silas's. Most of those she abandoned without a qualm. The jewelry that her husband had given her, she dutifully packed, feeling that it was the sort of thing a widow ought to keep.

I suppose I could sell it if I have to. It's not worth much, but it might...oh, damn, I'm doing this wrong. I should be very upset that I have to sell my jewelry, shouldn't I?

It's just that I'm fairly certain his mother picked it out. Or he picked it out thinking it was something his mother would wear.

Her late mother-in-law had been cut from the same cloth as her sister Malva. Halla had tried to love her and then had tried to like her, and then had tried to be dutiful and compliant, and finally had settled for not being too obviously relieved when the woman had dropped dead.

All her possessions and a spare change of clothes, the tiny tinderbox she kept for lighting candles, and a few coins piled together. It made a pitifully small bundle.

She thought about trying to find more to pack, then heard

her mother's voice in her head: *No use dithering. Roll up your sleeves.* Very well. She tied it all up, started to heft it, and Sarkis took it and slung it over his shoulder.

He had turned his back earlier while she changed into sturdier clothes for travel. She'd had no idea that an enchanted sword would have such a strong sense of propriety.

Well, perhaps it's different where he's from. The Weeping Lands? I've never heard of them, but I suppose that doesn't mean much.

She slithered hastily into a long woolen habit with somber sleeves. The material was fine enough, but the dark color and lack of ornamentation marked her as either mourning, eccentric, or on her way to a convent.

And I might be all three, for all I know. A convent might be the best place for me. Except that I ask too many odd questions and I don't think you're supposed to do that in a convent, are you?

Well, it probably depends on the god.

"Do you know if there's any god that doesn't mind lots of questions?" she asked.

Sarkis looked at her as if she'd gone mad. "What?"

"Questions. I ask a lot of them, you see."

"I had noticed, yes."

"Gods don't like that."

He shrugged. "Your decadent southern gods might not."

This gave her pause. "You have a less decadent god?"

"The great god is not decadent."

"How does he feel about questions?"

"I don't know the mind of the god."

"Yes, but if I ran away to join a convent, you see, I'd want to pick the correct sort of convent or else they might throw me out and I'd be right back where I started."

He pinched the bridge of his nose again. "Is this the best time to discuss theology, lady?"

"Err...no?"

"No."

"All right then."

For all his claims of not being a lady's maid, Sarkis helped her put on her cloak and then to arrange the sword slung across her back, which might otherwise have taken all night and ended with Halla cutting her own head off. They wrapped the cords of her dressing gown around the hilt of the sword and the opening in the scabbard so that the sword was held in place with an inch of steel still drawn.

"How many people are in this house?" he said, adjusting the buckles that held the scabbard in place.

"Eight. Me, Cousin Alver, Aunt Malva, her maid, her sister, and two cousins. And Roderick."

"Are any of the cousins warriors? Are they armed?"

"Uh...I mean, Cousin Sayvil's got a pretty wicked pinch. And I suppose they have...err...needles? Oh! And embroidery hooks!"

"Embroidery hooks."

"Yes. Do they have them where you're from? They're sort of —err—pointy—" She tried to explain with hand gestures.

Sarkis began muttering savagely under his breath. He didn't look at her while he did it.

"What are you saying?" she asked.

"I'm counting," he said, with marvelous patience.

"Why?"

"So I don't scream at you. My lady."

"Oh. Silas used to do that, too."

"I am not in the least surprised."

When he had reached a sufficiently high number—Halla noted with interest that Sarkis seemed to count by eights instead of tens—he said "The woman's sister? Is she a shieldmaid?"

"She's seventy-three."

33

"I would fear a trained shieldmaid if she were a hundred and three."

"Oh. No, she's not. I mean, she can be annoying asking for her tea to be brought to her at exactly the right temperature, but that's about it." She frowned. "Are we going to have to go through all those people? Err—are you sure you can?"

"Are you asking me if I think I can fight one guard and a group of elderly women with embroidery hooks?"

"...yes?"

"My lady Halla, I have fought *dragons* on multiple occasions."

Halla considered this. "Did you win, though?"

Sarkis coughed, looking suddenly embarrassed. "Well, one time."

"What about the others?"

"It was more of a draw. The point is that they were dragons, not your cousins."

Halla folded her arms. "How big is a dragon, anyway?"

"What?"

"I've never seen one. Are they rabbit-sized? Cow-sized?"

"They're *dragon*-sized!" he started to roar, caught himself, and continued in an angry whisper, "They're the size of a house!"

"All right, but a big house or a small—"

Sarkis turned around and began to beat his forehead very gently against the wall. "The great god is punishing me," he said softly, "for my crimes. I cannot go to his hell, and so he has sent a woman to torment me."

"Hey! You *could* just chop my head off and we'd be done here!"

"I will not chop your head off. I will, in fact, defend you to my dying breath. It is what a servant of the sword does."

"Really?"

"Really." He didn't sound as if this made him very happy. "And after, for that matter. If I am mortally wounded, I will return to the blade," he said. "Should that happen tonight, get away as swiftly as you can and draw it in a fortnight's time."

"You're not going to be mortally wounded," said Halla. The whole evening had assumed a desperately surreal quality. A man in a magic sword? Really? Probably she was having a dream.

Would that be so bad? Maybe I'll wake up and Silas will be alive and everything will be back to normal...

"It is highly unlikely, but if I must fight this Roderick to ensure your escape, then there are no guarantees."

Halla gazed at Sarkis in frank disbelief.

He might be shorter than Roderick, but he was at least as broad across the shoulders. His armor was stained and scarred with use and his gloved hand rested on his sword hilt with the ease of long familiarity. His bare arms were as thick around than her thighs, and Halla was not a small woman. She compared him in her head to her aunt's guardsman and couldn't even fit them into the same mental picture. It would be like a wolf fighting an overfed bulldog.

"What?" he said.

"One of us is very confused," she said. "I won't swear that it's not me. Is this really happening?"

Sarkis frowned at her. "Of course."

"That's what you'd say if you were a hallucination, too."

He held out his gloved fingers impatiently. "I am not made of dream flesh, lady."

She took his hand. It certainly felt solid.

There were machines in Anuket City that the artificers made that felt almost real as well, though. She'd gone to the market there with Silas once and shaken hands with a contraption that had wooden fingers inside a glove.

And would that be more or less strange than a man enchanted into a sword?

"How *did* you come to inhabit a sword, anyway?"

"The usual way."

"I have no idea what that might be."

"Sorcerer-smith," he said, dropping her hand. "Forge the sword, quench the steel in the blood of the one you wish to bind."

"Really! How much blood does that take? Do you have to use leeches?"

Sarkis stared at the ceiling, his lips moving silently. "I was stabbed through the heart, actually."

"Dear gods! Didn't that hurt?"

"A great deal. Are we ready to leave this accursed house?"

"It's not *that* accursed. I mean, the fireplace draws very badly, but you get used to it."

Sarkis gazed up to heaven again, perhaps looking for strength.

"How *are* we getting out, anyway?" asked Halla. *If I am having a dream or a hallucination or if devils are sending me visions to torment me, it is likely best just to go along with what is happening. And on the remote chance that this is, indeed, happening, I will at least be away from Cousin Alver.*

"Through the door. Climbing down from the window will take too much time."

"But it's locked—" she started to say, and then Sarkis kicked the door down.

CHAPTER 5

The lock held. The door itself held. The door frame did not. The door shot open with a sharp splintering noise, the bolt dangling at eye level, scraps of wood still clinging to it. It slammed against the hallway wall and rebounded with a bang.

Sarkis drew his sword and stalked down the hallway. Halla's sense of unreality got even stronger. She'd had sweet herbs strewn on the floor mats just five days ago, she brought the basket up herself, and here they were, crunching softly under the feet of a swordsman who'd come out of nowhere in a flash of blue light.

Very belatedly, it occurred to her that Sarkis himself might be dangerous.

You were hoping he'd kill you anyway, so what does that matter? Your family will still get your inheritance.

And let's be honest, he'll probably make much less of a hash of it than you will. You couldn't even figure out how to stab yourself with a sword.

Sarkis did not look as if he would have any problem stabbing someone with a sword. He looked like the sort of man who stabbed people all the time, possibly before breakfast.

The sound of the door breaking had woken everyone in the house, assuming they'd been asleep. Doors opened. On the floor below her, she heard Aunt Malva's querulous voice demanding to know what was going on.

"We should go," said Halla.

"Stay behind me." Sarkis led the way down the hall, sword at the ready.

Cousin Alver came up the stairs, wearing a long white bedshirt. He squinted up the steps. "Halla? What are you..."

He stopped.

He stared.

"Is this your relative with the clammy hands, lady?" asked Sarkis.

She peered over his shoulder. "Yes."

"Halla, what in the name of heaven is going on?" cried Alver. "Why is this person here?"

"And your niece is fifteen, you say?"

"She is."

Sarkis shook his head in disgust. "She could fight him without my help."

Halla burst out laughing for the first time since her great-uncle had died.

"Alver?" shouted Aunt Malva. "Alver, what is happening?"

Cousin Alver drew himself up as tall as he could. Since he was still about five steps down, this brought the top of his head even with Sarkis's shins.

"There is an intruder in the house, mother!" he shouted. "Stay in your room!"

"We were just leaving," said Halla.

"You'll do no such thing, cousin! If you think that I'll stand by and let my betrothed be kidnapped—"

"We are not betrothed! I didn't agree to anything! I *won't* agree to anything!" Halla started forward, furious, and Sarkis had to shift hastily to one side to block her advance with his shoulder.

"Halla, you are overwrought! And clearly in danger! Go back to your room, and Roderick and I will deal with this...this *person!*"

Sarkis rolled his eyes, took a step forward, and lifted his sword. "Go back down the stairs, little man," he said. "With your head or without it, it's all the same to me."

Cousin Alver's mouth fell open.

"May I kill him now, lady?" asked Sarkis politely.

"Yes! No, wait, that's not charitable of me. Can you just cut him? His mother's really punishment enough."

Alver leveled a trembling finger at Sarkis. "I don't know who you are or how you got in here..."

"*I am Sarkis of the Weeping Lands!*" roared the servant of the sword, in a voice loud enough to shake the walls. "And you are *in my way!*"

Cousin Alver let out a squeak and nearly fell in his haste to get off the staircase.

"It is so gratifying when that works," murmured Sarkis.

"Does it not usually work?"

"Not on actual warriors, no." He started down the steps, one hand gripping Halla's. "Normally they just yell back, 'No one cares, come and die.' Is anyone likely to come from above?"

"The servants go home at night. Silas wouldn't pay for them to stay full time. It's just attics now."

Cousin Alver hit the landing where the stairs met the second floor hallway and really did fall. He landed at his mother's feet and crabwalked backward.

"I knew it!" cried Aunt Malva. She held a candle in her

hand, casting shaky yellow light across the scene. "I knew I heard a man in your room, Halla!"

"He's not a man! He's a sword!"

"I am actually both," said Sarkis, sounding somewhat apologetic. "First one, then the other."

"Sorry. No offense meant. It seems very complicated."

"How long have you been disgracing your dear husband's memory with this man?!" shouted Malva.

"I haven't disgraced anybody's memory! But he's been here about an hour, I think."

"*What?!*"

"You are laboring under a misapprehension," said Sarkis sternly. "I am the servant of the sword. Lady Halla is under my protection."

"Are you *raving?*" Aunt Malva's dressing gown flapped like wings. Cousin Alver had taken refuge behind her.

Sarkis angled his body as he reached the landing so that both he and his sword were between Halla and her aunt. Clearly he had identified the real threat, and it wasn't Alver.

Halla could hear the sounds of the other family members stirring in the rooms off the hallway. Two cousins and Malva's elderly sister. Halla felt no great affection for any of them, but their malice had been mostly in service to Aunt Malva, not to themselves.

"Stay in your rooms!" shouted Alver, trying to sound authoritative but squeaking a bit on the last word. He was still on the floor, which didn't help. "There's a madman in the house!"

"Roderick!" bellowed Aunt Malva. "Roderick, where are you?"

"Go past me," said Sarkis, releasing her hand. "Down the next set of stairs. I'll hold them off." His lip curled as he looked at Alver. "Or...well, I'll hold *her* off."

"She's the dangerous one," agreed Halla. She hastily fled down the stairs. Moonlight fell in a dozen diamonds across the front hall.

"Roderick, *stop them!*"

"Mistress Malva?"

Oh damnation, thought Halla. She'd been hoping that her aunt's guard would be asleep himself.

"Are you in danger, Mistress?" The guardsman's voice was depressingly alert. He barreled in from the back of the house. Judging by his attire, he either hadn't been asleep or was an extraordinarily fast dresser.

"Yes!" cried Malva. "Yes, I am! This—*person*—is trying to abduct my niece!"

"I am not being abducted!" yelled Halla. "This man with a sword is just breaking me out of my room so I can leave and—oh, hmm, when I say it like that, I suppose it does sound a little—"

"*Roderick!*"

"But I want to go! It's not an abduction! Really!"

Roderick started up the stairs. There was a bandage across part of his face, probably where the bird got him. Halla hoped he took care of it. The bird's wounds tended to fester. Then it occurred to her that Roderick was part of the reason she was trapped in her own home and made up her mind not to care if his wounds turned so septic that his nose fell off.

Sarkis muttered something under his breath and went down the steps two at a time. Halla flattened herself against the wall to let him pass, and he halted on the step just below her.

"It'll go easier on you if you just surrender," said Roderick. "I'm not looking to shed anyone's blood."

"I could say the same to you," said Sarkis. "But I'd be lying. Bloodshed is beginning to seem like quite a fine idea. Starting with that clammy-handed fellow there."

"Can't let you do that," said Roderick. Halla was probably imagining the note of regret in his voice.

"No, of course not," said Sarkis. "Your duty does not permit it. Shall we duel, then?"

Roderick groaned.

"Kill him!" Malva and Alver stood at the top of the stairs, neither one quite willing to descend. Unsurprisingly, Aunt Malva was the one shouting for blood.

"Look," said Roderick in an undertone, "this isn't the best job, but it pays well. Do we really have to do this?"

"It seems we do," said Sarkis. "Draw your weapon, man, and defend the honor of your liege's house."

"She's not my liege," said Roderick. He drew his sword anyway. The sound of steel ringing out of its sheath made Halla wince.

Sarkis took a step forward. Roderick took a step back.

The first swing was clearly a test. The guard slapped it away and countered with a swing of his own. Sarkis didn't even bother to counter, simply leaned back and let it cleave empty air.

Another exchange of metal and Sarkis drove Roderick down two steps, apparently without effort.

They're fighting in the dark. On the stairs. This can't be a good idea. Halla wondered if she should be helping. She had quite a large sword on her back, didn't she?

And if I try to swing it, I'll probably accidentally take Sarkis's head off and that will be extremely awkward for everyone. Does that count as a mortal wound? I imagine it would have to be, wouldn't it? Or is it worse than mortal? Would he be able to come back from that?

"Sarkis, is beheading just a mortal wound?"

"*What?*"

"I thought—"

"Great god's breath, not now!"

Roderick swung again and was easily batted back down the stairs.

"Is this how you defend your liege's house?" Sarkis growled.

"I told you, it's just a job," said Roderick.

"If you were a man in my command, you'd be stripped of rank for such half-heartedness!"

Roderick might have had something to say to that, but Sarkis swung at his head and the guardsman was driven back down the steps. His back struck the front door of the house behind him.

A clammy hand closed over Halla's wrist. She cried out, partly in surprise and partly in disgust. "Let go of me!"

"Come on," hissed Cousin Alver. "While Roderick's got him distracted!"

"I'm not going anywhere with you!" Halla twisted her arm, feeling Alver's rings cut into her skin. "You're a nasty little —little—"

She was trying to think of something suitably nasty and little to describe Cousin Alver when Aunt Malva slapped her.

For all her querulousness, there was nothing elderly about that slap. Halla's head rang. She stumbled backward, missed her footing on the stairs, and fell. Alver yelped and released her wrist as if it were on fire.

Uh-oh, she thought, and that was as far as she got before someone caught her.

Her weight knocked Sarkis into the wall, but he kept his feet somehow, holding her up with one arm while she tried to get her footing back. She heard a scrape of steel and a hiss of anger.

"Are you all right?" she said. "I fell on you."

"I fear that I am going to have to kill your aunt's hireling."

"Go right ahead."

"Hey now..." said Roderick.

Sarkis released her and struck out with sudden fury.

The guardsman let out a squall of surprise and fell over sideways. Malva screamed.

As the echoes faded, the sound of Roderick's labored breathing seemed very loud in the house.

"Is he going to die?" whispered Halla.

"He may or may not. But he won't hold a sword again." The servant of the sword looked back up the steps toward Malva. The candle in the old woman's hand shook so wildly that the flame looked close to guttering out.

"Is there anything else you require from this house, lady?" asked Sarkis politely.

Halla had an intense desire to run back to her room and hide under the covers. The violence of the last five minutes had been more than she had experienced in a decade.

But then:

"You'll be hanged!" hissed Malva. "For murder! For abduction! And don't think you're coming back here, Halla. You're dead to this family. *Dead!*"

Oh gods, please let that be true.

She raised her chin. "Just to leave it."

Sarkis stepped over the prone Roderick and pushed the door open. The square of moonlight on the other side looked cold and clear and extraordinarily inviting.

"Then let us go."

CHAPTER 6

The air outside was chilly. The moon blazed in the sky overhead.

Sarkis took her hand again as they left the house. It felt less like affection and more like a rider tugging on a horse's reins, but at the moment, Halla was willing to be led. Her ear still felt hot and swollen from Malva's slap.

"My Aunt'll rouse the constables," whispered Halla. "We need to get out of the town."

He nodded. The cobbled streets were empty as they hurried away from Silas's house, but Halla knew it wouldn't last for long.

He pulled her into a narrow alley. The walls rose above them, shutters locked against the night. This part of town was mostly tall, narrow buildings, sharing walls with one another. The tightly canted rooftops fit together like puzzle boxes, following old lines of ownership. The alleys between them twisted and turned like snakes.

"Where can we steal a horse?"

She gaped at him. "What?"

"A horse," said Sarkis patiently. "They still make horses, don't they? I haven't been in the sword that long?"

"Yes, of course, but... We're going to steal one?"

"I don't propose to buy one in the middle of the night, my lady."

"I've never stolen a horse before."

"That doesn't surprise me."

"You were very concerned with the honor of my kinswomen," said Halla, "but you're not concerned with being a horse-thief?"

He snorted. "Raiding cattle and kine is a fine and honorable tradition. If they cannot hold their beasts, they deserve to lose them."

Halla might have had something to say to that, but a shout rang out from farther down the street.

"Wake the constables! *Murder!*"

"Your aunt has quite a set of lungs," Sarkis observed.

"She always had," said Halla wearily. "She'd yell for her tray in bed in the morning when she visited, and you could hear her clear out back with the chickens."

He stepped to the mouth of the alley and looked both ways, then stepped back into shadow. "Too exposed. Which way do you suggest?"

"We need to get to the churchyard," said Halla. "It's near the edge of town. If we can get into the burial yard, we can cut through. There's a lich-gate at the far end that leads out of the walls and into the fields."

"Will it be open?"

Halla sighed. "Yes. They keep it open for dead bodies. My great-uncle is lying under it."

"Ah. I'm sorry."

She shrugged. It seemed like an age of the earth had passed

since Silas had coughed out his last on the pillow. "I suppose I will not be attending his funeral, so I might as well pay my respects now."

"Will someone be keeping the vigil for him?"

"They damn well better be! I paid the lay brothers to see that someone did!"

Sarkis's lips twitched. "Well, we will deal with that as we must. Lead the way."

Halla plunged into the alley, following a turn to the left. A stray cat looked up at her, annoyed, and scurried into the dark. She crossed an open street and darted down the side of the public house. Light gleamed through the closed shutters, and the sounds of revelry inside drowned out their footsteps.

She started to leave the far side of the alley, but Sarkis caught her shoulder and pulled her back into the shadows. Two men wearing the round helms of constables jogged past. Halla clamped her teeth shut on a gasp.

"Sorry," she whispered. "I didn't hear them over the noise."

"How many constables does your town field?"

"Eight. Two per hundred, you know, to keep the peace."

"Is that how you do it here?"

"Certainly. How do you do it where you are?"

"Each lord has a holding. He keeps the peace."

"What if he doesn't?"

"They string him up and get a new lord."

"But what if—"

"Two constables there means six elsewhere, then," he interrupted. "Hmm. Perhaps we'd best wait on the horse and focus on getting out from under them."

Halla looked out into the street again. It looked clear, but she didn't breathe easy until they had crossed the jagged band of moonlight into the shadows on the opposite side.

Another pair of constables passed them on the next road. "Still going toward the house," whispered Halla.

"They've barely had time to get there," he said in an undertone. "And somehow I doubt your aunt will give a clear and concise report about what transpired."

Halla found that she had a strong urge to snicker and muffled it. She was afraid that if she started laughing she wouldn't be able to stop.

They reached another alleyway. "This way," whispered Halla. "We have to cross the corner of the market."

Sarkis did not ask if there was another way. He simply nodded. "Very well. I see a wall. Toward there?"

"That's the churchyard. Yes."

He took her hand again, looked around, and then dashed across the open space.

In the shadow of the market stall, they paused. Shouts were beginning to come from the direction of Silas's house. Halla could hear shutters banging. "Is it fire?" someone yelled.

"Fire?!" cried someone else in response.

"I don't see smoke!"

"What's on fire?"

They darted to the next shadow, beside the well. Sarkis dropped down and set his back against the stones. Halla crouched beside him, trying to catch her breath.

"I suppose you'd object to actually setting part of the town on fire?" Sarkis asked.

"I most certainly would!"

"Pity."

Halla was beginning to question the servant of the sword's definition of honorable behavior.

She heard running feet on the far side of the market and flattened herself even farther against the ground. When the footsteps had faded, she peered over the lip of the well. "I don't see anyone."

"Good." He caught her hand again. Halla blinked, suddenly noticing the dark lines across his arm.

"You're bleeding!" she whispered, when they reached the safety of the church's walls.

"A fair bit, I imagine. Your aunt's hireling got a blow in."

Halla remembered the sound of steel and the hiss that followed. "When you caught me, wasn't it?"

"I could hardly let you fall down the stairs."

She winced. "Does it hurt?"

"Stab wounds usually do."

"I'm sorry!"

"Don't be." She couldn't see his face, but he sounded amused. "It will heal when you sheath the sword for a little time. I've had much worse."

"Yes, but if you hadn't caught me..."

"If your wretched cousin hadn't dropped you to save his own skin, you wouldn't have fallen. I've a mind to go back and cut his ears off, but it doesn't seem like a good time. Can you get over the wall here if I give you a boost?"

Halla looked up at the stone wall rising over her head. The stones were roughly laid, with plenty of handholds, but still... "I don't know," she admitted. "My tree climbing days are long behind me."

Sarkis knelt down. "Climb up on my shoulders."

Halla gulped.

She was not a particularly small woman, she knew. Heavy hips and heavy breasts and a frame to carry both. A good child-bearing figure, her husband had said, for all the good it had done either of them.

Not, perhaps, the ideal figure for scaling church walls in the dark.

"Are you sure?" she whispered.

"I am not kneeling in the dirt here for my health."

"I don't want to hurt you, though."

"I could throw you over the wall instead."

"Could you?"

"I am considering it very strongly."

Ah...that was a joke, I think. Or something. All right. No use dithering. Roll up your sleeves...

She stepped up, first onto his knee and then onto his shoulder. He stayed as still as stone while she caught at the top of the wall.

"I've got it," she whispered. "I don't think I can pull myself up, though."

"I'm going to stand," he warned her, and rose slowly to his feet.

Halla clung to the top of the wall, feeling her fingernails catch and tear against the stone. Her stomach lurched. She wanted to squeak in terror but that seemed humiliating, so she didn't.

Don't embarrass yourself in front of the magic sword.

She heard more shouts in the streets. Terror fired her muscles and she scrabbled at the top of the wall, flinging herself up with a strength she hadn't known she possessed. Her arms ached.

She lay flat on top, gasping. "Now what? I can't pull you up!"

"Now sheath the sword," he said calmly.

"What?"

"Sheath the sword. Then unsheathe it and toss it down inside the wall."

Halla blinked at him, then grinned. "That *works?*"

"Remarkably well."

She sat up, straddling the wall—her habit was going to be rather the worse for wear afterward, but there was nothing to be done—and fumbled the sword out from behind her back. The cords came loose and she pushed the blade into the scabbard with a click.

Blue light swirled through the shadows and he vanished.

"Eh!" someone shouted. "What's that over there?"

"Oh blast..." whispered Halla, shaking the scabbard loose again and dropping the sword down inside the churchyard.

Sarkis reappeared. Halla flattened herself back against the wall and swung her leg over.

I am the picture of grace.

"Lower yourself down," he whispered.

"I'm afraid I'll fall!"

"Then I'll catch you."

This might be true—the servant of the sword did seem very strong—but Halla couldn't quite make her gut believe it.

"Someone up on the wall!" shouted a voice. "Constables!"

She cursed, swung herself over, and prayed that she didn't fall onto a tombstone and bash her brains out.

Well, here goes—

Arms locked around the waist and Sarkis lowered her to the grass and handed her the sword.

"Out the lich-gate!" she whispered, slinging the scabbard back over her shoulder. "They'll have to wake the priest to get the main church gate opened."

They ran. It was an old churchyard and the graves were uneven, parts upthrust and others sinking. Halla skidded on a mossy stone slab and nearly went to her knees. Sarkis caught her, made three more steps, and then tripped over the hidden edge of a grave and sprawled across the grass himself.

Halla felt a sneaking satisfaction that it wasn't just her.

"What god keeps this place?" said Sarkis, rising and slapping dirt from his knees.

"All of them," said Halla. "I mean, it's not a specific temple.

Traveling priests come through and any of them who want to use it. And we've got the village priest, of course, for the marrying and burying. This one serves the Four-Faced God, but the last was out of the Temple of the White Rat."

"Oh, the decadent south," muttered Sarkis. "All these gods. Which way?"

Halla pointed. "Toward the—"

A loud clanging rang out over the village. Halla winced.

"And that would be the church bell?" asked Sarkis.

"They ring it for alarms."

"That may make things difficult."

"What, only now?" said Halla, and saw Sarkis's teeth flash in the moonlight as he grinned.

The lich-gate loomed before them. A stone slab, shrouded in cloth and moonlight lay beneath the covered roof, and beyond, the iron gates stood ajar.

There was a body on the slab.

Great-uncle Silas. Forgive me, uncle, for not being able to be grateful for the gift you gave me.

"Huh? What's going on?" A young man, heavy-eyed with sleep, rose from the bench beside the gate. "Why are they sounding the alarm?"

Sarkis went for his sword. Halla grabbed his sword hand and shoved it back down. He glanced at her, startled, and she gave him a sharp, hopefully meaningful look, then stepped forward. "Ladden? Is that you?"

"Mistress Halla?"

"There's something happening in the village, Ladden. It's not grave-robbers, is it?"

"Grave robbers?" Ladden looked around for the corpse, panicking. "No! He's still—oh, thank the Four. No. He's still here."

"Thank heaven," said Halla. "I don't know what's happening. I just heard the alarm and someone had said there were grave robbers about the other day, so I came straight here to make sure no one had designs on poor Silas."

"Not while I'm here, ma'am," said Ladden, standing up as straight as he could.

"They steal people's parts and sell them. Although I've never been sure if they took the whole body or just the parts they're going to sell..."

Ladden's eyes went wide. Sarkis made a small noise of despair.

"But you're here!" Halla finished hurriedly. "So they didn't get him. That's good. But something's happening in town, obviously."

Bless the lad's thick skull. There's more holes in that story than in a cheese. But he's probably worried I'll notice he was asleep and not guarding Silas.

"No, ma'am."

"Good. Roderick and I will go out that way and make sure no one suspicious is lurking around. Oh, this is Roderick, my aunt's guardsman."

"Pleased to meet you, sir," said Ladden, touching his forehead and stepping back to let them pass. Sarkis nodded to him as they hurried by.

"I am almost insulted," whispered Sarkis, as they left the lich-gate behind. "I am nothing like that wretched hireling."

"Yes, but it'll muddy the waters nicely when they ask Ladden what happened."

He took a moment to unclench his jaw, then finally said, "It was well done, Lady Halla."

"Thanks."

The lich road led across the open fields into the distance.

There were ditches on either side, overgrown with tangles of blackberry and cattail.

"Are there no houses here?" asked Sarkis.

"Not on the lich road. You can farm it, but you don't build along it. Good way to have the dead tapping on your door at night. Although what the dead want, I don't know."

The servant of the sword frowned, looking back over his shoulder. Pinpoints of light were appearing in the village as people brought out torches to light the darkness. "Not much cover, either."

"Well, no, but if we can get over the hill, we'll be up against another hill and there's rocks on that hill. Are rocks cover?"

"Rocks are cover."

"All right then."

"Then let us hurry."

They abandoned stealth for speed and ran down the lich road. Moonlight blazed on the stubble standing in the fields. The harvest was nearly over, the sheaves drying, making lumpy shapes in the fields on the right. Hills rose off to the left, not high but increasingly stony, unfit for anything but sheep.

After a few minutes, Halla had to slow, gasping for breath. She put her hands on her knees. "Sorry."

Sarkis shrugged, watching behind them. "Do your people have dogs that track men?"

Halla nodded. "Slewhounds," she panted. "But not in... Rutger's Howe. They'd have to go to... Archon's Glory to raise a pack. We're just not...big enough..."

"No lord runs them to bring back slaves?"

Halla stared at him, round-eyed. "My people aren't slavers!"

"Ah. Good to know."

"Are yours?"

"Occasionally."

"That's dreadful!"

"It is. But my people also don't force women to marry their cousins in order to steal their fortunes."

Halla closed her mouth with a click.

After a moment, she straightened and began walking swiftly down the lich road, with Sarkis silent at her side.

CHAPTER 7

S arkis was having a rather odd day.

It was not the worst day of his life by any measure, nor even the strangest. It was simply odd.

He had been an heirloom for years, passed down from generation to generation, the guard who did not tire, the sword that did not break. It was rather tiresome, being an heirloom, but you got used to it, and at least everyone knew what to expect.

Some wielders he knew well. Some he saw only briefly. Most of them he failed, in the end. There was only so much that a single warrior could do to stave off death.

And then there had been another dying: a blade through the chest, up and under, just notching the sternum. His last thought had been, *Hung up on my ribs, you bastard, you're not getting your sword back unless you cut it loose,* and then he had gone into the long, dreaming torpor of death.

In truth, he'd half-expected it. His last wielder had been a boy barely out of the nursery, defending the family lands with no more than a handful of old men. Sarkis had known they were going to die when the enemy came for them. The best he could do was muster a defense that cost the enemy more than they expected.

He had done that, and done it well, but at last he had fallen. Then had come the *snap* of the wielder's death, like a bone breaking, and then he had been alone inside the sword.

He felt the sting of his failures keenly, but this one, at least, he could not blame himself too harshly for. There had been no chance of victory, only courage.

Sarkis knew that a long time had passed after that. Decades, probably. Not the first time that the sword had gone for years without a wielder, but one of the longest.

Fortunately, he had only the vague sense of time passing. The world inside the sword was a place of silver shadows, of darkness and metallic dreams. He could not say if he slept, exactly, but he knew that he never stayed conscious for very long.

To spend eternity trapped in a blade, and to be awake the entire time, would have been a recipe for madness. The sorcerer-smith had explained it all very clearly that day so long ago, perched on the edge of the worktable. She had been a lanky woman with a blacksmith's oversized arms, and a light in her eyes that would make a rabid dog howl and run for the hills.

She had not told them that they would have a sense of time passing, though. Perhaps she hadn't known.

She's been dead for centuries, so I can't exactly ask.

Regardless, he had been content to wait in the blade, dreaming its bloody silver dreams, until someone drew him again.

What he hadn't expected was to finally be drawn by a baffled woman wearing rather less clothing than she might be. Sarkis appreciated a woman's body, particularly a well-endowed one, but he liked to at least know her name and whether she had any relations of a vindictive nature.

He did not at all appreciate learning that said woman was looking for a way to kill herself to escape said vindictive relations and had picked his blade to do it with. The world had few enough good women in it, it needed to keep hold of the ones it had.

Halla wasn't a bad looking woman, either. A solid armful, with pale blonde hair and large, expressive gray eyes. You'd didn't see many women with hair that color in the Weeping Lands, but she had the sort of generous figure he'd always favored. *More curves than the River Scythe*, as the saying went.

But the questions she'd asked! Great god give him strength! He could either snatch an unwilling bride from under the noses of her vile relatives, or he could be interrogated about the size of dragons. Both at once was asking too much. Was she completely daft?

Still, they'd gotten out with minimal trouble. And she hadn't had hysterics over the blood or fallen down in a faint, which was good. You never knew what civilians, men or women, were going to be like. Sometimes they sailed through like hardened campaigners, and sometimes they fell all to pieces.

Halla, for all that she looked soft and kind and wide-eyed, had stepped over the guardsman's groaning body without a second glance. He couldn't very well ask for more than that.

He was fairly sure he'd offended her just now, though. Decadent, damnable civilization. Too many gods and they treated their women like cattle, but mention that their high horse was more like a donkey on stilts and they became furious with you.

Well, it wouldn't be the first wielder who had disliked him. Some of them simply forbade him to talk.

Occasionally, he even obeyed.

There had been the one who cut his tongue out. Sarkis had a bad few weeks until the man had sheathed the sword in a fit of pique and he discovered that even that would heal inside the blade.

The downside to that was that he'd had his tongue cut out three more times over the course of the next year, but it had only been pain. He'd known it wasn't going to be permanent.

That particular wielder had ended up with so many crossbow bolts in him that he looked like a porcupine turned inside out. Sarkis had been forced to defend him—the sword's magic left him no choice—but he hadn't been able to defend against a dozen archers at once. His failure, in that case, had been remarkably gratifying. He'd actually been able to pick the sword up and hand it to the next wielder, who'd been carrying one of the crossbows.

He leaned over and spat. He always had to do that when he thought about having his tongue cut out, he couldn't help it.

Halla did not look like she would order anyone's tongue cut out. Sarkis was really quite happy with that. There came a point in an enchanted sword's life where even temporary dismemberment really started to wear on you.

Mind you, if she kept asking him questions about the relative size of dragons, he might start to remember the old days fondly. Perhaps she was just nervous. Many people talked too much when they were nervous.

He stifled a sigh, thinking that if being a fugitive made one nervous, Halla would probably not quiet down any time soon.

Well. It's hardly the worst way to wake up. At least you've only had one person come at you with a sword so far today…

CHAPTER 8

They traveled in silence for some time, and then Sarkis's head snapped up.

"Horsemen." He caught Halla's arm and tugged her toward the ditch.

We've got to have a talk about all this dragging me about, thought Halla wearily. *A simple 'follow me' would suffice.*

She suffered Sarkis to pull her down into the weed-choked ditch. There was a thin trickle of icy water at the bottom, and the cattails were shedding thick sprays of down into the grass.

"Further back," he whispered. "Into the brambles."

Halla pulled her hood down as close over her face as she could, and crawled on her hands and knees into the blackberry. Thorns stabbed at her cloak and hair. She could hear hoofbeats now.

"Further," he whispered behind her.

"I'm not a rabbit!" she hissed. "There are stems here thicker than my wrist. Unless you've got an axe, this is as far as I go."

He peered over her shoulder, then grunted acknowledgment. "Fair enough."

The hoofbeats were getting loud. Sarkis flattened down

even farther into the shadow of the thorns. Halla reached out and found Sarkis's gloved hand, and was grateful when he gripped hers back.

Don't let them find us. I don't even know what they'd do, but please don't let us find out.

The horse's hooves rang like metal on the cold earth as they passed. Halla closed her eyes. Her breathing was so loud that it seemed like anyone should be able to hear her, like Aunt Malva could hear her back in the town.

The hoofbeats clattered by and were gone.

They lay in the ditch for some time, until finally Sarkis squeezed her hand and let go, then climbed out and looked over the edge.

"Clear," he reported. "They may yet come back this way, though. Be ready to duck."

They kept going. Twice more, they had to dive into the ditch. By the third time, Halla was no longer frightened so much as exasperated. *Why are you still looking along this road? This is ridiculous. Go bother someone else.*

After the second one passed, she glared at Sarkis and said, "You could just say, 'Get in the ditch now.' You'll have my arm out of the socket if you keep this up."

"Sorry," he said. "I don't mean to hurt you."

"I am capable of following simple orders, you know."

"Without having to have a lengthy discussion about them, you mean?"

Halla narrowed her eyes.

"...that's what I thought."

The moon began to sink.

It was cold. Their brief run had left her sweating, and now the sweat chilled her. She shivered violently whenever the wind blew past, despite the weight of her cloak. Her legs ached from walking.

"We've come a few miles," said Sarkis. "We need shelter soon, I think."

He must be colder than I am. He's wearing less. Unless magic swords don't get cold. I wonder if he'll get mad if I ask. He seems rather short-tempered.

Halla realized that he was expecting her to have suggestions. *Of course. He's never been here before.* She stopped, arms wrapped tightly around herself, stamping her feet to warm them.

"Left," she said, and nodded in that direction. "Into the stones. The shepherds keep summer houses up there sometimes, for when the lambs are out. I don't know that we'd want to light a fire, but it'll keep the wind off if we can find one."

Sarkis nodded.

The hills were worse going than the road had been. It reminded her of the churchyard, uneven with hidden stones that rolled and dropped away underfoot. When Halla finally stopped and looked behind her, the road was *right there*, as if she had barely moved at all.

She had been frightened before, but the unmoving road felt like despair.

Sarkis took her arm without asking and helped her keep going.

"Only a little farther, lady," he said.

"I'm not a lady," she said wearily.

"Gentleman, then?"

"No, I mean..." She nearly stepped in a hole and had to grab his arm for support. "Ladies are noble. I'm not."

He shrugged. "Nobility is handed out arbitrarily at best."

Halla thought of the Squire that had owned her mother's land, and grunted agreement.

After what seemed like hours, they had toiled around the edge of the hillside. She was willing to collapse anywhere, between two rocks if it meant they were out of the wind, but Sarkis pointed.

The shepherd's building was roughly circular, made of stones piled together and bound with clay. The roof was thatch, dry and cold and partly fallen in. Half the stones had collapsed in the back and brushwood had been dragged in to fill the gap, but clearly no one had felt the need to effect repairs.

To Halla, it looked like a palace.

Sarkis had her stay well back as he entered the building, but soon turned and gestured to her. "Nothing," he said. "Owls, maybe, but they'll be out hunting now."

"I don't think owls are dangerous."

"Perhaps not the southern ones."

"Are northern owls dangerous?"

"Some of them."

"Which kind? What do they do? Do they eat p-p-people?" Her teeth were chattering.

"You're cold," said Sarkis.

"So are you."

He looked down at his arms, which were covered in goose-flesh. "Fair enough."

"Do you want to go back in the sword?"

"That won't do much to warm you."

"No sense in both of us being miserable."

He shook his head. "I'm not fleeing back to a hunk of metal and letting you freeze. I am your guard, lady, as long as you wield the sword."

She wrapped her arms around herself, and managed a chuckle. "And supposing someone takes it away from me?"

"No," said Sarkis. "It's your sword, until you sell it or give it away, or die. And I am your servant until you sell me or give me to another."

"Or die."

He inclined his head.

"So you're stuck with me?"

"Yes." The way he drew the word out into a sigh made Halla think that he was probably contemplating that fact right now.

"How do you know? If I've given the sword away or if someone's stolen it?"

Sarkis shrugged. "I'd know."

"Is that what happened last time? Someone sold the sword to Silas? Or gave it away?"

"I don't know. No one drew the sword for a long time. I was killed, and the man I protected died very shortly after."

Halla's eyes went wide.

"The sword wouldn't draw for a few days after that, while I recovered," he explained. "Likely they thought it was rusted into the sheath and useless. From there, I suppose, it was spoils of war. I had no wielder until you drew the blade."

"Great-Uncle Silas found many things in the market in Anuket City," said Halla. "I'm surprised he never tried to draw it." She frowned, remembering the manticore skull. "Although given the way he enjoyed leaving strange things around the house, perhaps he didn't think of it. He wasn't any sort of warrior. He just liked odd things."

Sarkis looked over at her and frowned suddenly. "I'm lighting a fire," he said. "As small as I can manage, but I'll be a poor guardsman if I let my charge freeze our first night out."

"Is it safe?"

"No."

He went out of the hut and left Halla shivering.

She was exhausted. The flood of adrenaline from their wild escape had finally faded, leaving her bone-weary and filled with the sense that she had committed some terrible crime.

No. I've done nothing wrong.

So why were you running? And chased by constables like a criminal?

She burrowed deeper in her cloak, seeking warmth. It had all made so much sense at the time, one thing leading inevitably to another, and now here she was, hiding in a shepherd's hut, her only ally a man who had come out of an enchanted sword.

If you say it like that, even inside your head, it sounds very strange.

She roused briefly at the sound of Sarkis returning.

"I'm sorry," she said, as he laid out bits of broken brushwood in the corner and built up stones around them. "I am very dull and stupid right now. I should be helping you."

She expected another sardonic response, but Sarkis surprised her.

"It was a long night we had," he said. "And I have been in a sword for a long time, but you, unless I miss my guess, have been nursing a sick man for some days before tonight."

Halla gave a short, choking laugh. "It's not many men who appreciate the work that goes into that."

"I led a small band of warriors," said Sarkis, taking out the tinderbox she had packed. "Before I am...what I am now. In the early days, if one of us was injured, it fell upon the rest of us to nurse him. It was grim duty, particularly if you didn't expect them to live."

She glanced over at him. He had removed his gauntlets to use the tinderbox. His hands were hard-looking, scarred and callused. It was difficult to imagine those hands tending to the injured or doing any work of kindness.

"I hated it," she admitted. "I know, we're supposed to be...I don't know. Ministering angels. But I'm dreadful at it. I've no patience. I wanted to strangle Silas after half a day. And I love him."

Fire flared up beneath Sarkis's hands. "Well," he said. "The dead aren't saints, merely because they're dead."

"No," said Halla. "And he's a spiteful old beast when he feels thwarted. Which is all the time when he's sick."

She rubbed her hands together to warm them, and then thought, *Was. Not is. He's dead. The last few days really happened, even if they don't seem like it.*

Sarkis didn't seem to have noticed the lapse, or if he had, he did not comment on it.

Toward the end, Silas had been less spiteful and more tired. He would sleep for most of the day, waking only to drink a little and grumble. She'd sat by the bed because that was what you did with the dying, though she doubted he much cared.

"I've always thought," she said, a bit dryly, "that if I were dying, the last thing I'd want was people fussing over me. I'd just want them to go away and let me get on with it."

Sarkis actually laughed. "I have died," he said. "Many times now. But usually quickly, so I'm not sure it's the same thing."

She looked at him, puzzled. He'd mentioned being killed, but somehow she hadn't put that together with the fact he was still here. "You've died?"

"Indeed."

"Is it really dying? I mean, you're still here."

"I don't know," he admitted. "Pain, and then a long silver sleep with dreams. Then I wake up inside the sword again."

"Are you awake inside the sword? You know what's happening?"

"I can be. Usually not for long, though. There is only a faint sense of time passing. I fall asleep after a time, and then wake when someone draws the blade. Sometimes I'll rouse a little, if something is happening outside, but I have no real way of telling what it is."

"And you heal inside the blade..." It reminded her suddenly

of his injury. If he wouldn't go back in the sword, it needed treating, didn't it?

"Let me bind your arm," she said, summoning the last of her energy.

He seemed genuinely surprised, but offered her his arm. The skin was heavily tattooed, the black faded to dark blue, in patterns of stylized rams, stags, horses. There were scars there, too, cutting starkly across the lines of ink. A stag with curling horns ran across his left bicep, its throat sliced open with silver.

It must be the light, she thought, *or perhaps the sword heals him with metal instead of flesh.*

She'd brought a kerchief with her, but sacrificed it now. The blood had dried black across his tattoos, and she wished that she could clean it. Did enchanted swords worry about infection?

Regardless, she folded the cloth neatly and tied it around his upper arm. His skin was human temperature, but the muscle underneath was hard as iron. If she'd banged her knuckles on it, it would probably have rung like metal.

And I am growing fanciful in my old age, or I am very tired, or both.

The fire was putting out a tiny bit of heat now. Halla huddled close to it, barely able to tell if it was warmer or not. Sarkis knelt beside her, feeding twigs to the flame.

She wasn't sure if she slept. It seemed more like she stopped thinking and her eyelids closed.

He never did explain about the owls...

And then it was nearly dawn and the fire was out and Sarkis was shaking her awake.

CHAPTER 9

Sarkis spent the hours while Halla slept wondering what the hell to do next.

It was one thing to remove a woman from a house she very much did not wish to be in. It was another to become a fugitive in a strange land within an hour of meeting.

Possibly I could have planned that better.

If only she'd had some kin to come ride to her rescue. Still, he couldn't very well leave her to get married off to a man who would drop her down the stairs to save his own skin.

He'd been reasonably optimistic until he'd actually climbed the hillside to the top and looked out over the landscape.

Rutger's Howe was tucked into a half-circle of hills. North, the land was flat farmland. South were rolling, stony hills, suitable for sheep and not much else. The lich road meandered between the two, where the main road ran east to west. Obviously if one wanted to move quickly, one would head north.

Unfortunately, the land to the north was well-farmed, well-tended, obviously not at all wild, and that made it difficult for two people to vanish into. There were a few patches of woodland that might be promising, but that was all.

He would have been fine in a wilderness. Sarkis was excellent with wilderness. The south had nothing to compare to a winter in the Weeping Lands anyway.

But where you had farms and roads, you got people and people asked questions. Questions like, "Hey, are you the pair that vanished from that town after killing that guard?"

Halla had, he would admit, handled the young man at the lich-gate well. He had been afraid he'd have to kill him too, and Sarkis disliked killing priests, even priests of soft southern gods. There were stories that a priest's blood would etch a blade that drew it and curse it to never take an edge, and Sarkis wasn't sure how far that curse would extend. It would be damnably inconvenient to be trapped for eternity in a dull sword.

Without a handy wilderness to vanish into, they would probably need a city. Cities were basically wildernesses with too many witnesses anyway.

He contemplated how long it would take to walk down the average city street with Halla asking questions about every single thing that caught her interest.

Great god give me strength.

He scanned the landscape again, hoping that something would jump out at him. Nothing did.

For a moment, he could almost feel the presence of two people behind him. Something more than memory, less than ghosts. Angharad, to his left, a step behind. On his right, the Dervish, moving restlessly, never still. He had looked over more lands and more maps than he could count with those two beside him, and he had trusted their eyes to find the patterns he had missed.

But they were gone now, and Sarkis's only ally in this land was a middle-aged woman fleeing from her family.

He climbed back down the hill and settled into the corner beside the fire, opposite Halla.

It was cold. Not the wracking, bone-chilling cold of the Weeping Lands in winter, but cold enough to make him fold his arms and tuck his hands underneath, cold enough to pull his knees up to conserve what heat he could.

His charge had huddled into her cloak, hood drawn down. He had not had a chance to study her closely in their flight, beyond his initial impressions.

She was a handsome woman, if not beautiful. Her upper lip was thin, the lower one full, which might have looked like a pout on someone else. On Halla, combined with her wide, curious eyes, she mostly looked as if she had just thought of a particularly interesting question and was trying to figure out how to phrase it.

Her hair was pulled back in a thick braid. Women in this country did not cover their hair, as he recalled, unless they were in religious orders. In the heavy black habit, she looked as if she might be about to join such an order.

I suppose if I must escort her to a nunnery, then so be it. Great god help me, then I'll be servant to a nun. Unless she surrenders the blade to her order, and then I'd be in service to...what? Whichever one of her superiors drew the blade?

He put his hand over his eyes. Bound to a nunnery. Great god. The Dervish would have laughed until he fell over.

No sense in borrowing trouble. We haven't even gotten free of her relatives yet.

Her hands, when she bandaged the slash on his arm, had been work-roughened but kind. It had been a long time since someone had touched him kindly. He was more used to people trying to stab him or bash his head in.

Well, it might yet come to that.

Sarkis sank his chin to his chest, and waited for morning to come.

IT WAS A COLD, cheerless waking. Halla was thirsty, and starting to wish she'd eaten more of the dinner they'd brought her the night before.

"From the top of the hill, I see woods to the north," Sarkis said. "Better cover, but are they safe?"

Halla considered for a moment. "Not the nearer ones. That's an acorn wood, and they'll be rounding the pigs up for slaughter. They're busier than a market at this time of autumn."

Sarkis sighed. "All right. I cannot swear we've eluded pursuit, but since no one's breathing down our necks at the moment, we should plan as best we can. Where should we go next, lady?"

"You're asking *me?*" said Halla.

"I am hundreds of miles and a number of years from the lands that I know. You know far better than I do where we might go safely next."

This was true. It was just that the notion of *any* warrior, let alone an enchanted one, taking orders from Halla seemed faintly absurd. She couldn't even give orders to servants without phrasing them as requests, and half the time the servants talked back anyway.

"I'm sorry," she said, shaking her head. "I'm just...not used to anyone asking my opinion, that's all."

Sarkis raised an eyebrow and said, "I don't know why not. You ask too many questions, but you have not struck me as overly stupid. Merely...easily distracted."

"I try not to be stupid," said Halla. "But I have made so many poor choices in my life, so perhaps I must be, after all."

She looked up to find that he had cocked an eyebrow at her. "Then that makes two of us," he said, and smiled.

Halla laughed. It was an odd thing to feel solidarity with an enchanted sword, but the last few days had been nothing but odd things piled together. "I was thinking we might go to the Temple of the White Rat," she said.

"I do not know of them."

"They...fix things. I told you, our priest before the current one was of the White Rat? They find solutions."

"An odd thing for a religion to be good at."

Halla shrugged. "There's a saying about it, or maybe a joke —I can't remember all of it. About how two people disagreed over a cow and brought it to a priest. Priests of the Forge God would take the cow as a tithe for wasting their time, the Dreaming God would kill the cow on suspicion of being possessed by demons, and the Four-Faced God would wait until the cow died and deliver a sermon about how all of us, men and cows, must pass away. But the White Rat's priests would take the cow, breed her, give a calf to each of the people arguing, and then sell the milk for a profit."

"That sounds like plain good sense."

"Perhaps there's so little of that to go around that they had to make it divine."

He snorted. "How many gods do you *have* in this accursed land?"

Halla had to think. "Um. Well, there's the Rat, and the Four-Faced God and the Dreaming God and the Forge God and the Lady of Grass and St. Ursa—although she's a saint, not a god— and the Saint of Steel, but he's actually a god, not a saint, which is very confusing—"

Sarkis put his face in his hands. Halla couldn't quite make out what he said, but it seemed to involve something about putting the entire country to the torch. She hurried on. "There's a big temple to the Rat in Archen's Glory...uh, that's the capital of Archenhold."

Sarkis rubbed the back of his neck. "And how far away is that?"

"Not quite a week, maybe five days on foot. North and east. But wait, that's the thing!" She reached out and caught his sleeve. "Amalcross is on the way!"

He waited politely for her to explain.

"It's a town. Great-uncle Silas had a friend there. Another collector. They used to visit sometimes, and trade objects. I'm sure that if he knew I was in trouble, he'd help me."

"Would he?" asked Sarkis.

Halla spread her hands. "Well, if he wouldn't normally, I can always bribe him with the stuff in Uncle Silas's house."

Sarkis nodded. "That's a fair thought. I do not always trust goodwill, but greed...greed is usually predictable."

"That's a dark way to look at the world."

"The world is a dark place. What is the land like, between here and there?"

"Err...farmland, mostly. Woods along the road in a few places."

"Is your land at war? Do clans raid the road?"

"Uh..." Halla wasn't quite sure how to answer that. "No, the war's been over for years now. I guess there might be highwaymen, sometimes? But they get rooted out if they get too bad. And...err..." She wracked her brain. "There's sheep?"

He gave her a fixed look. "Do the sheep in your land attack travelers?"

Is he joking? It seems like he must be joking... Sarkis's face was so grim and the scar through his eyebrow made him look so stern that she couldn't be sure.

"Yes," she said. "Constantly. I'm surprised we haven't been set upon by attack sheep already."

He did not crack a smile.

"Of course they don't! They're sheep!"

His lips twitched.

She gave up. "Does this seem...doable?"

"Are you asking me if I think I can protect you for a week's walk through pacified farmland?"

Halla threw her hands in the air.

"I believe we can manage, once we've thrown off pursuit. I do not know about the road. If we circled far south, into the hills, we might be safer."

"Ah...hmm. If we go too far south, we'll risk running into the Vagrant Hills."

"I take it that is not a place we wish to be?"

"No. They're...weird. Uncanny. Not natural." It occurred to her suddenly that she was saying these things to a clearly unnatural and uncanny being who lived in a sword. "No offense intended!"

"Not being a hill, I take no offense."

Halla sighed. "I mean...well, we don't want to go there. Strange things happen. And if you get too close, sometimes you wake up and you're in the hills even when you weren't. At least, so I'm told." She picked at her skirt, reluctant to admit that she had never been anywhere near the Vagrant Hills herself. *Or almost anywhere, for that matter.*

Sarkis nodded. "We will avoid the far south, then. Now which way must we go, to find this friend of your uncle's?"

CHAPTER 10

They set out. The sky was gray instead of black and there was frost on the ground instead of dew. The trail they left looked stark against the shining silver grass. Halla knew that it would melt a little after sunrise, but it still made her feel exposed.

They drank from a tiny rill at the bottom of the hill. It was icy cold and set her shivering again.

There were still blackberries clinging to the brambles. She pulled them off as they walked along the side of the ditch, offering a handful to Sarkis.

"Do you eat?"

"I do, if I stay outside the sword for long enough." He took one politely. "These are safe, then? They look like berries in my part of the world, but one is never sure."

"Quite safe. What do the berries in your part of the world do?"

"The ones like this? Nothing. Smaller ones, with a green bloom, that darken from red? You begin to sweat, then you convulse, and then your heart races until it fails."

Halla paused momentarily, a berry on the way to her mouth. "That sounds unpleasant."

"It is over quickly."

"Well, there's that." She examined the berry, then shrugged and ate it. "These don't do that."

"I gathered."

There were purple stains on her fingers by the time she was through, but between the water and the food, Halla felt a little better.

Sarkis was making a wide circle around Rutger's Howe, through fields that did not overlook the road. There were a number of hedgerows, which was good. The direct path ran through much more densely planted farmland, and Halla suspected that she'd get pulled into so many ditches that her shoulder joints might never recover.

"How did you learn my language?" she asked, as they walked.

"I didn't," said Sarkis.

She gave him a sidelong look. "We're talking right now, though."

"Yes, but not because I am inherently familiar with the tongue of the decadent south. The magic of the sword allows me to speak the language of the wielder, that's all."

"That's handy."

"It's essential." Sarkis shook his head. "It's a real problem to be drawn on the battlefield and have to be shouting, 'What? Say again? Do you speak any other languages?' while the enemy is charging at you."

Halla laughed.

"There is also the difficulty that our great-great-grand-mothers spoke differently than we did. If I slept for too long in the sword, I might not even comprehend the tongue of the

Weeping Lands. So the sorcerer-smith corrected for that problem early on, she said."

"You mean there're other swords?" said Halla.

Sarkis nodded. "At least two others that I know of," he said. "My friends. The Dervish and Angharad Shieldborn. More before us, but no one I knew. Presumably some afterwards as well."

Halla stared at him, her mouth falling open. "But *why?* Why would you choose to get put in a sword?"

"Sometimes all the choices are bad ones," he said, in a tone that did not invite further comment.

"Yes, but—"

"You are not good at taking hints, are you, my lady?"

"Was that a hint?"

He started counting in his own language again. Halla waited.

After reaching thirty-two, he said, "I was a commander. There was a war. It did not go well."

"Ohhh..." Halla nodded. "You sacrificed yourself to become a weapon, didn't you?"

He didn't look at her. "Something like that."

"That's very noble."

He grunted.

"Did it work?"

"We lost the war."

"Oh."

Halla bit her lip. Was he one of those people who wanted their heroism acknowledged, or one of those who would gnaw their own arm off before admitting they had done anything heroic? She was getting the impression that it was the latter.

Still, if agreeing to be stuffed into a sword to become an unkillable weapon wasn't heroic, what was?

She settled on the truth. "I'm sorry that it went so badly. But I'm very glad you're here now."

Sarkis looked over at her, his expression briefly unreadable, then dipped his head in acknowledgement. "I'm glad that I'm able to help, lady."

———

IT WAS another day before Sarkis was willing to return to a road, and only then because he knew that his charge could not take much more.

She hadn't complained. Great god help him, she was cheerful the entire time, and he knew that she had to be exhausted. Her hair was full of dead leaves and the handprint where that foul old shrew had slapped her was still faintly visible across the side of her face.

He could also hear her stomach growling every few minutes.

Despite all this, she didn't snap, she didn't demand that he do something to fix this. She...just...kept...asking...questions.

"So how far can you go from the sword itself? Do you have to come back?"

"A quarter mile, perhaps a bit more."

"What happens if you go farther than that?"

"I disintegrate."

"Does it hurt? It sounds like it would hurt."

"No."

"What does it feel like?"

"Like disintegrating."

"Yes, but what does *that* feel like?"

"Cold."

"Right, but—"

He realized that she was not going to give up and wracked

his brain for a description that would satisfy her. "Like a dream where you are falling and jerk awake again. Except that I awaken closer to the sword."

It wasn't all about being a sword, either. It was about *everything*.

"So you have sheep in the Weeping Lands?"

"They have sheep everywhere, Lady."

"But what are yours like? Are they the same color?"

"They are brown. And very short."

He helped her across a patch of rough ground, where something, probably pigs, had torn up the earth and then it had frozen into a stiff, treacherous landscape. It was only when he reached down to take her hand that he noticed the deep blue smudges under her eyes, and saw that she was favoring her right foot.

I'm an idiot. She's asking questions to distract herself from how uncomfortable she is.

His men had done the same thing, in various forms; not questions, per se, but endless talking. Vetch has told the very worst jokes. Not even dirty jokes, just interminable puns. And Bo, who had a bard's tongue, would spin out impossibly long stories about everything from the enemy to last night's dinner, until a simple overcooked bit of venison became a three thousand-year-old victim of a god's curse, slain at last and sent to its final resting place in the stomach of a dozen mercenaries.

Fisher, the crossbowman, had made up his own songs, but the less said about that, the better.

Apparently, Halla asked questions.

He should have realized that Halla was doing something of the sort. His only defense was that she was a civilian, and you didn't expect them to cope with things like a normal person.

You're her commander, or close enough in this situation. Do your job. Help keep up morale.

I'm not her commander, he argued with himself. *Quite the opposite. I serve whoever wields the sword.*

He glanced back at her. Halla's eyes were on her feet, picking her way through the cold ground.

Her cheerful expression had faded. Her shoulders slumped and the corners of her mouth sagged with weariness. Her large gray eyes were half-closed, fine lines radiating from the corners.

As soon as she looked up and saw that he was watching, she straightened and forced a smile, like...like...

Like every recruit you've ever had who was determined to die before they complained about anything.

Angharad Shieldborn had been like that. You could chop off her feet and she'd grit her teeth and march on the stumps.

He'd been Angharad's commander. He had to tell her when she was too damn tired, because she'd never admit it. Sometimes the Dervish had done it for him, which was why the two of them had worked well together.

His men were long gone now. He had not seen his two captains since the day that swords had been thrust through their hearts. Presumably they hated him now, which was their right. He had failed them all.

Halla, however, was right here. And if he wasn't her commander, exactly, he was damned close. Which meant that there was only one thing left to do.

Sarkis tried to think of something to say about sheep.

He'd never thought about the animals much. Thinking of the Dervish reminded him, though. "One of my captains came from a land where they bred sheep with thick tails that drag the ground."

"Really!" Halla's eyes lit up with genuine interest. "That sounds like they'd have a lot of problems, though. Sheep get into enough trouble with their regular tails."

"I can't say, I've never seen one. But the fat of the sheep's tail was a delicacy, he said."

"On my husband's farm, we had goats," said Halla. She frowned. "I can't say I miss them."

"I've never kept goats," said Sarkis, doggedly determined to keep up his end of the conversation.

"No one really keeps goats, do they? They just *have* goats. Like having in-laws, if your in-laws climbed on the roof and kicked."

"I have had in-laws that did both those things."

"What, really?"

"Primarily when drunk."

She laughed. Her stomach growled loudly in counterpoint and she thumped herself. "Quiet, you."

After a moment, she said, "My in-laws just seem to want to marry me off. Are you married?"

"I was, once."

Halla stilled. He glanced back and saw her eyes were filled with sudden sympathy.

"I'm sorry," she said.

He shook his head. "It's not what you're thinking. I did not leave her behind when I went into the sword. She decided years before that she did not want to be wed to a man who might be gone for years at a time, and she cut the ties. It was for the best."

"Oh," said Halla. And then, "I'm still sorry. That must have been hard."

He shrugged. "She was strong. Strong enough to know what she did and did not want. And there were no children to bind us."

Strong enough to cut the tie and say to my face that love was not enough.

And a good thing, too, in the end. Enough people paid the price for my mistakes without a wife to suffer as well, or great god forbid, children.

No, when he died at last, if he was ever allowed to truly die, the world would forget the name of Sarkis of the Weeping Lands. He had neither son or daughter to carry on his line.

And thank the great god for that.

CHAPTER 11

They slept that night in a tangle where a hedgerow had run into a band of trees and turned into a dense thicket of brush. It was cold, but it was out of the wind.

"Tomorrow, an inn." Sarkis frowned. "You will need to sheathe the sword, though. I expect our description has been spread about. Do women travel alone in your country?"

"Often enough," Halla said, wrapping the cloak tight around her shoulders. "It won't draw a great deal of comment. If I were younger or better looking, someone might care. As it is, they might think I'm being foolhardy, if anybody notices me at all."

He scowled at her. "You are a fine looking woman. If your countrymen cannot see that, it is the fault of the decadent south, not you."

Halla blinked at him, then felt a smile spread helplessly across her face. "That's...that's very sweet. Thank you."

"I am not sweet. Did I mention that I've fought dragons?"

"Yes, but you also mentioned that it was mostly unsuccessfully."

Sarkis grunted. "At any rate," he said, "if anyone asks, I trust you'll simply do that thing you do."

"What thing?"

"You know." He waved his hand irritably. "Begin asking unexpected questions until everyone in the conversation starts doubting their senses. It's a talent. Like some strange form of diplomacy that goes so far in the wrong direction that it comes out the other side."

Halla had to stop and parse that for a minute.

"Was that an insult?" *Well, two compliments in one day was probably far too much to hope for...*

"It was merely an observation. My lady."

He added the last two words perfunctorily. It reminded Halla of the way that her late sister had said, "The gods bless you." There was an implication that saying it took the insult out of whatever she'd said right beforehand, and if you didn't agree to that, then it wasn't her problem.

She tried to get comfortable against the tree trunk behind her. It was a losing proposition. Sarkis handed her the small pack to use as a pillow, but there wasn't much to be done about the cold or the things poking her on the ground.

I swear the ground has gotten harder since I was a small child. Didn't I used to fall asleep out on the hill behind the house?

Sarkis stretched out his booted feet and leaned against the tree beside her, looking as if he slept on the ground all the time.

He probably does.

Probably the ground is harder in the Weeping Lands, too. These are like decadent southern trees or something.

She knew that Sarkis probably held her in mild contempt. *Mild if I'm lucky.* She was slow and weak and she talked too much. And was from a decadent civilization with too many gods, et cetera, et cetera.

It's probably easy to feel superior when you're hundreds of years old and built like a wall. And nobly sacrificed yourself to become a weapon for your people, even if you lost.*

She studied her right shoe. She wasn't sure if she should take it off or not. There was undoubtedly a blister underneath it. She was mostly afraid her foot would swell up and she wouldn't get her shoe back on afterward.

Tomorrow. Tomorrow, I'll sleep at an inn. In a bed. A real bed. With a mattress. It doesn't even have to be a good *mattress. I don't even care if it's got bugs.*

No, the shoe was going to have to come off. She gritted her teeth, unlaced the shoe, and pulled it loose.

The blister was gigantic. It had broken open and now there were loose flaps of dead white skin across her heel, framed in angry red, with bits of lint sticking to both.

Well, that's unpleasant.

"What have you done to yourself?" asked Sarkis. And then, "Ah. Most impressive."

"It's just a blister," Halla muttered. "Not a big deal."

"On the contrary. Men have died of blisters."

"They have *not.*"

"If someone cannot keep up during a forced march and falls behind, they must be left. Often the enemy gets to them before they can catch up or be retrieved."

"Gods have mercy. We're not on a forced march."

"We are, of a sort, but I will not leave you behind, as that would negate the purpose of the march. Perhaps tomorrow we can steal a horse."

"How about socks?" asked Halla hopefully. "A better sock would fix things."

"Great sagas are not written about successful *sock* raids upon a rival holding."

"How do you know?" said Halla, attempting to tear a strip of cloth from the bottom hem of her habit. "You're in the decadent south now. We might have sock raids constantly for all you know."

Sarkis gave a loud snort to indicate what he thought of this, but then robbed it of much of its impact by taking her foot in his hand and wrapping the cloth around it. His hands were much warmer than they had any right to be, given how cold the air was. Halla waited for him to recoil from the admittedly unpleasant blister, but he seemed unconcerned.

"Warn if it's too tight," he said, patting her knee absently. *As if I were a horse he'd just reshod. Except a horse would probably be more useful right now.*

"What, will my foot fall off?"

"Your toenails may."

Halla blinked at him, realized that he wasn't joking, and stared gloomily at her shoes. "Do people die of lost toenails?"

"Less often than blisters."

"Well, that's a comfort."

"When I led warriors, good shoes were considered as essential as a good sword. Moreso, in fact. If one has a bad sword, one can still run away."

"These *were* good shoes," said Halla. *Oh gods, he thinks I'm one of those women who wear uncomfortable shoes to look fashionable.* If she owned any fashionable shoes, it was purely by accident, because she'd owned the pair long enough for the fashion to come around again. This wasn't something she felt like admitting. "It's just that I'm not used to wearing them for days without taking them off."

Sarkis grunted.

Her stomach growled like a bear. Halla sighed. She'd eaten a few handfuls of chickweed and late sorrel earlier, but her body was not happy with such meager fare, particularly not if it was doing the hard work of keeping her warm.

"I'm sorry," said Sarkis abruptly.

She looked up, startled.

It was growing too dark to see much of his expression. He was frowning, or perhaps the scar through his eyebrow only made it look like a frown.

"Sorry? For what?"

"I am doing a poor job guarding you. You are hungry and footsore and I do not know this land well enough to feed you."

"But we're in a hurry," said Halla. "To get to Archenhold, or at least to get away from Rutger's Howe."

"What do you mean?"

"Well, if we weren't in a hurry, then *I* could feed us just fine," said Halla with some asperity. "It's autumn. You've got to *work* to starve in the middle of autumn."

"Do you?" He sounded nonplussed.

She started counting things off on her fingers. "There's acorns, if I had a week or so to leach them...we're getting to end of the season for filberts, but we could probably turn up a few good ones left...persimmons are ripening, though those could be tricky, since the beasts want them too, and if they're close enough to a house that the beasts aren't a problem, the farmers probably are. If we wanted to raid a garden, there's plenty of things still in the ground, everybody stores the roots like that until they need them. Although I'd feel bad, since if we took too much, people might go hungry. But that's true about any food, except acorns." She considered. "And I guess cattail roots, although they'll be woody right now, so we'd have to be *really* hungry..."

"Enough, enough!" She could hear that he was smiling. "I yield!"

"It's just that pretty much anything we might harvest takes time and work and probably cooking supplies."

"I see."

"I'm not completely useless, you know," she said, picking at her skirts.

There was a long silence, and then out of the dark, his voice said, "I never thought you were."

She was glad that he couldn't see her blush.

Since, despite all the talk, there was nothing to eat and not much to be said, Halla arranged her cloak as best she could, huddling to try and get warm. The air was very cold. She could pull her collar up over her face, which was warmer, but then the fabric got damp and hard to breathe through and she felt like she was suffocating.

She would certainly never get comfortable enough to sleep, Halla told herself sadly, and then fell asleep.

She had a vague memory, somewhere in the night, of Sarkis speaking to her, but she couldn't remember a word he said, or if she even answered.

CHAPTER 12

Halla woke, surprisingly warm, with someone's arms around her.

She couldn't remember the last time that happened.

Probably because it's never happened, has it?

Her late husband had not slept in the same bed with her, preferring his own. Her older sister had married first, so she had been sleeping alone for many years.

Maybe when I was very small, and Mother was still alive...

She seemed to be in Sarkis's lap, with her head resting against his shoulder. He had wrapped his arms around her waist to hold her in place.

It wasn't unpleasant. He made a much warmer surface to rest on than the ground. She just wasn't sure what she was supposed to do, if anything.

Respectable widows certainly did not sleep in the arms of their guardsmen, but Sarkis was an enchanted sword, so that didn't count, did it?

She suspected that someone like Aunt Malva would think it very much counted.

"How did I get here?" she asked finally.

Sarkis snorted. She realized that he had his cheek against her head, which she hadn't noticed because her hood was drawn. "You wiggled around in the night. I assume you were trying to get warm, because once you found me, you latched on to my legs."

Halla sighed. "My sister always said I tried to push her out of bed and steal the blankets."

"I eventually picked you up to make things easier. Do you remember me asking if that was permissible?"

"I remember something or other. Did I say yes?"

"You snored at me. I decided that was close enough."

"Oh. Thank you."

She wasn't sure what to do next. Get up, probably, but Sarkis was really very warm and the air was cold. He hadn't let go of her, either.

The arms wrapped around her were hard with muscle. So was his chest. It was like lying against a surprisingly comfortable brick wall. Halla might be a respectable widow but she'd have to be dead not to appreciate that.

"Aren't I heavy?" she asked.

"Both of my legs are asleep. Lady."

"Oh dear."

"It's fine."

"No, it isn't! You can't feel your legs!"

"There is a certain point after which they cannot get any more asleep. Now that they have passed that, it's fine."

"I'm so sorry!" Halla groaned and rolled off him. He released her immediately. The world seemed much colder outside his embrace, and she had a strong urge to return to it at once before she froze.

Don't be stupid. He's your guard, not your pillow. And he's stuck with you. Don't assume...well, anything.

She rubbed her hands over her upper arms, then dug through her pack for her hairbrush. Her wretched hair was so thin that it tangled if someone so much as looked at it, and then broke when she tried to tease the tangles out.

Sarkis watched her combing out her hair and scowling furiously at the knots, and hid a smile.

He had not quite told the whole truth about how Halla had ended up in his lap. She had indeed latched onto his legs in her sleep, but it hadn't stopped there. She had thrown her arm over his thighs and burrowed against his hip.

Sarkis found this amusing at first. Her expression was one of dogged concentration, as if sleep required a great deal of thought. It was...well...*cute* wasn't a word that was used often in the Weeping Lands, but there you were. He tucked her cloak up under her chin, shaking his head.

Then she had shifted in her sleep and rolled partly onto his legs, with her head in a rather indelicate position.

This was a problem.

It was certainly not the first time that a woman had had their face in that vicinity, but Sarkis really preferred them to be awake and enthusiastic about it, not snoring.

"Lady?"

More snoring.

"Lady Halla, I'm going to have to move you."

Definitive snores.

He picked her up and settled her on the ground beside him, whereupon she rolled over and attached herself to his side again.

Sarkis sighed. He'd had plenty of wielders, but this was the first one who had been determined to use him as a mattress.

"All right."

He lifted her into his lap. She mumbled something, eyebrows drawing down.

"Is this all right?"

Snore.

Sarkis gazed briefly at the sky, or what he could see of it through the tree branches.

He drew her head down against his shoulder and wrapped his arms around her. "I suppose I don't have much choice."

She snored agreeably against his neck.

He sighed again, feeling an inexplicable rush of protectiveness. *Which is redundant for any wielder. I must protect them no matter how I feel about it.* He stroked a finger across her cheek. Her eyelids didn't so much as twitch, even when he tucked a strand of hair behind her ear.

The skin along her jaw was very soft. He wondered how far down that softness went.

Well, he certainly wasn't the sort of man to take advantage of a sleeping woman. He even felt a bit awkward about this much contact, but he was simply going to have to deal with it. Halla was warm and heavy, her body pliant...as long as he didn't try to move away.

Glancing over at her now, Sarkis thought she looked much less soft. The severe lines of the habit did not flatter her figure at all. If he had not held her in his arms—and if he hadn't had an involuntary look when first summoned—he would have had no idea at the extent of the curves that lay under the dark fabric.

Woman's built like an hourglass. The sort that measures twelve hours at a stretch.

Had he been younger and not trapped in a peculiar living death inside a hunk of enchanted metal, Sarkis would not have minded checking the time more closely.

...As it were.

Ah, yes, that's a very useful thought when she's starving and half-frozen and you're still waiting for the guards to catch up with you.

Mourning black did not suit her. It showed up the contrast between her skin and her white-blond hair, leaving her pink and blotchy, her nose red with cold.

Jewel tones, he thought absently. *Deep red, dark green. Perhaps warm browns.*

Yes, thinking about what colors would suit her is an even more useful thought. Has being in the blade addled your wits at last?

Well, something better than black, anyway, he argued with himself. *Black is not a good color on her.*

Still, that was probably for the best. A woman traveling alone did not want to attract unwanted attention. And while Sarkis would defend her to his last breath, he'd rather not have to do so.

"Are we ready?" he asked, and she nodded.

They walked for an hour or so, keeping to the side of the road. The only traffic was a swineherd leading his charges out of the acorn wood, and he did not seem inclined to make conversation.

"There's a public house a little way up ahead," said Halla after a time. She shoved pale strands of hair out of her eyes. "I know we probably shouldn't stop, but I guess we'll want to get off the road so nobody spots us."

Her stomach growled again.

"If they are looking for anyone," Sarkis said, "it is for two people traveling together. If your aunt has convinced the constables that I have kidnapped you, then they will not be expecting a woman traveling alone. If you sheathe the sword and go in, you should be able to buy some food."

"Really?"

He'd seen men rescued from certain death with less hope blazing in their eyes. He nodded.

"Real—" he started to say, and then Halla slammed the sword back into the scabbard and the blue fire took him away.

CHAPTER 13

Halla approached the door of the public house with her heart in her throat.

She knew she shouldn't be scared—she hadn't *done* anything, and if anybody asked, she'd explain about Malva and the locked door—but her nerves still jangled. What if they were looking for her, and dragged her back to Rutger's Howe? What if they'd been told she was mad or an accomplice or a criminal herself?

What if Roderick had died and the constables were looking for a murderer?

Stop, she told herself firmly. *You're being ridiculous. You care very much because it's your life, but most people won't care in the slightest about Aunt Malva and Cousin Alver and your stupid inheritance. Everyone's got their own troubles and nobody wants to get involved in yours.*

This was all undoubtedly true, and yet the door of the public house loomed in front of her like a castle gate. The sign over the door was a pig with a mug of ale, and the words 'The Drunken Boar' crudely carved underneath.

She shook herself. *This is ridiculous. How did I get so far outside of my normal life that I'm frightened to go in and buy a meal?*

That was exactly what it felt like, though. As if she had stepped to one side of the world and now her life was running in strange, shadowy parallel. She had been in the normal world where Silas was alive and she slept in her normal bed and got up in the morning and ran the million little tasks of a household, and now she had fallen into a world where she slept in hedgerows in the arms of an enchanted sword, and tried not to be so helpless that he'd hold her in contempt. A world where she listened for constables coming for her, where she was worth more money than she'd even imagined and still only had a few coins to her name.

It's all the same world. And you just have to get through this bit and everything will go back to normal.

She didn't quite believe that was possible. Could the world simply snap back into place that easily?

Why shouldn't it?

She opened the door and stepped inside.

It was early enough in the morning that a few guests were eating breakfast. They glanced up at her as she entered...and then looked away, uninterested.

Halla felt invisible and nearly fainted with relief.

Then the warmth of the fireplace hit her, and she thought she really would faint. It was glorious.

She pulled the door shut behind her and marched up to the counter to order breakfast.

The publican took her order, took her coin, and gestured her to a seat by the fire. "Ye look cold," he said.

"I am *freezing*," she said.

"Brisk out, aye."

"Well, it's that time of year."

"Oh aye, aye. Ye come far?"

"Just out from Amalcross," she lied.

"Long way to walk."

"Ah well. Got no horse to carry me."

"Ah, but it means ye've no horse to feed."

"There's that."

Pleasantries thus concluded, she sank into one of the chairs by the fire.

I may never move from this spot.

She stared into the flames. Red-orange tongues licked the underside of the logs, scaled like a lizard in white and black ash. Her cold feet began to tingle painfully as they warmed. Halla grimaced, but at least it kept her from falling asleep on the spot.

It was only a moment before a serving woman came out with bread stuffed with spiced meat and potatoes and a tankard of cider. Halla forgot her feet, forgot her woes, and fell on the food like a starving dog.

It wasn't even good meat. It was stringy and tough and probably from a milch-cow that had gone too far past her prime. Halla didn't care. It was *amazing.*

Afterward, she slumped in the chair, trying not to fall asleep, aware that she should get up and keep moving, but it was *warm* and the chair was so *soft...*

"Hello...?"

Halla realized her eyelids had been closed and sat up quickly.

The woman who spoke was smaller than she was, not young, with a lined face and gray-streaked black hair. She had dark eyes with wrinkles fanned out from the corners.

"Hello," said Halla. "I wasn't asleep. Um, okay, I was sort of asleep, but let's pretend I wasn't."

"I'm sorry to bother you. I just saw another woman and I... well, you know." The woman glanced over her shoulder at the rest of the room, full of men eating quietly, paying no attention.

Halla nodded. She did indeed know.

"It can be difficult for a woman on the road alone," said the woman.

"That's the truth," said Halla. "My name's Halla."

"I'm Mina."

They sat while the serving woman brought Mina cider. She wrapped her hands around the mug to warm them.

"Have you been traveling long?" asked Mina finally. She looked over her shoulder again, as if expecting pursuit.

"A few days." Halla felt suddenly better about the whole thing. *Traveling.* She'd been *traveling.* Not staggering through hedgerows with aching feet, after a man who probably thought she couldn't find her way out of a paper sack without help.

Traveling. I am a traveler. I will look back on this someday and be worldly and jaded—"Oh, yes, my dears, I was a great traveler when I was middle-aged. I saw many exotic hedgerows and was manhandled into ditches all across this great land."

Mina smiled uncertainly, and Halla realized that she'd been smirking at her own thoughts. "And you?"

"Oh," said Mina, her smile fading. "It feels like a long time. Probably longer than it really was." She stared into her mug.

Halla nodded. Sadly, this reminded her that she, too, had a destination, and she should probably get moving. She started to rise from her chair.

Mina held out a hand. "Ah...Miss Halla? I...ah. Would you mind if we left together?" She glanced over her shoulder again. "I'd rather no one know I was traveling alone. If it wouldn't be too much trouble."

Halla's heart went out to her. "Of course not. Whenever you're ready."

She put the mug down. "Now is fine. I just wanted to stop and get warm. I don't mean to keep you waiting."

Halla got to her feet, rearranged her cloak, and picked up the enchanted sword.

"Is that *your* sword?" asked Mina, her eyes going round.

"Oh, no!" said Halla, and then, "Well, sort of. I guess it's mine, but it's really a friend's." She shrugged herself into it, tugging her cloak free of the straps. It did get easier with practice.

"I suppose if you're waving a big sword around, you're not so worried about someone attacking you."

"If I waved this sword around, I'd probably cut my head off," said Halla cheerfully. "No, I'm just carrying it. It's a long story."

THEY LEFT THE INN TOGETHER, chatting amiably. No one followed them, so far as Halla could tell.

They walked along the side of the road together. Sarkis would have been wary, probably scoping out nearby ditches, but Halla pushed the thought out of her mind. *If anyone is looking, it's for a man and a woman, not two women. Or one woman. Technically, I've been kidnapped, I think.*

Undoubtedly, Cousin Alver would have spun it that way to the constables, since, "My cousin ran off with a strange man rather than marry me," would have been an unforgivable blow to his pride.

She didn't mention any of this to Mina.

After a time, the other woman fell silent. She looked over her shoulder repeatedly, as if she was running away from someone.

"Are you all right?" asked Halla.

"Aye, fine." She sounded curt.

Frightened, Halla thought, a bit sadly. She wondered if it was a man, then snorted at her own foolishness. *Of course it's a man. It always is.*

"Do you need to go your own way?" she asked. "Get off the road a bit, perhaps?"

"Not just yet," said Mina, glancing over her shoulder again. "But...aye, off the road is not a bad thought."

They found a break in the hedgerow, on the far side of the ditch. Halla paused, not entirely willing, but the other woman gestured to her to go first.

I don't know what you're worried about. You've been sleeping in hedgerows. You crapped in one this morning, while Sarkis tried to pretend that he was birdwatching. It's not like you don't know them intimately by now.

Halla shook herself mentally and crossed the ditch.

She'd barely stepped around the hedge when a shadow loomed up before her.

"Mina!" cried Halla, backing away. "There's someone here!"

"Good," said Mina. Her voice sounded different suddenly: sharp and irritated, without a trace of fear. "Took you long enough to show up. I thought I'd have to walk halfway to Archenhold."

The figure grunted and stepped forward.

It was a man. He was taller than Sarkis, though not as broad. He had a very large knife in his hands, the sort used to gut deer.

"Um," said Halla, eyes fixed on the knife. "Mina? Is this a friend of yours?"

Mina gave a loud, derisive snort.

"I'll be having your money now," said the man.

"You what?" said Halla.

"Your money," said the man. "Give it to me."

"My...oh gods! Are you robbing me?" She wheeled around and stared at Mina. "Wait, you came out here with me so you could *rob* me?"

"Not real quick on the uptake, are you?"

Halla flushed with embarrassment. Here she'd been thinking about being a great traveler, and she couldn't even get robbed correctly. *Traveler.* She was a country bumpkin who'd been to a real city three times in her life. What was she thinking?

The man gestured with the knife, and fear rushed in and joined the embarrassment. "Give me your money, there's a good girl," he said, advancing on her. "I don't want to hurt you."

"I don't want you to hurt me either!" said Halla, backing away. "But I don't have much money, and I need it. I'll starve!"

"Not my problem," said the man. He gestured with the knife.

"Get the sword, too," said Mina from behind him. "It's probably worth something."

"No!"

Halla had almost forgotten the sword.

For one instant she thought *Maybe it would be better to be robbed than to let Sarkis see how stupid I just was*, and then good sense prevailed. She grabbed the hilt over her shoulder and tried to claw it free. "Sarkis! Sarkis, help!"

At the same moment, she tripped on a tree root and fell over backward.

The sword struck her across the back, knocking the wind out of her. *Please, gods,* she thought, as the man loomed over her, *please, please don't get knocked back in the sheath—*

"Stop there," said Sarkis softly. The edge of his sword lay across the back of her attacker's neck.

The man froze.

"Step back," said Sarkis. "And you, madam, you may think

you're being very sneaky with that knife, but I'll have his head off if you take another step. Halla, are you hurt?"

"Fine," squeaked Halla. She had no idea if she was hurt or not. She very much wanted all of this to not be happening.

"Please don't kill me," said the man with the sword against his neck. "I wasn't gonna do anything. I swear. I'll go."

"Where the hell did you come from?" hissed Mina.

"Don't care," said the man with the knife, staring straight ahead. "Don't care. I'll leave. Sorry to have bothered you."

"Drop the knife," said Sarkis. "At your feet, not on her."

The man's fingers opened and the knife landed in the leaves with a crunch.

"I'm doing it," he said. "Not going to fight you. Mina, don't do anything stupid."

"That is excellent advice," said Sarkis. "I suggest you listen to him. Drop your knife as well."

"But—"

"*Mina,*" said her partner, in pained tones.

She tossed down the knife, grumbling.

Sarkis lifted the sword a half-inch away from the man's neck. "Now would be an excellent time to back away," he said.

"Yes. I'm going. Sorry." The man kept his hands in front, where Sarkis could see them, without even being told. He began backing into the woods.

"Madam, I suggest you go with him. If I have to deal with either of you again, my patience will be exhausted."

Mina, lips thin and arms folded, joined the man at the edge of the woods.

"You may run now," said Sarkis pleasantly.

They ran.

The pair did not exactly melt into the trees—there was too much loud crashing and stomping and cursing for that—but they vanished in very short order. Sarkis stood over Halla, sword held at the ready, then leaned down and helped her to her feet.

"Are you sure you're unhurt?" he asked.

"I'm fine," said Halla. "I'm fine. Completely fine."

Don't embarrass yourself in front of the magic sword.

She nodded firmly to show him how fine she was, and then promptly, humiliatingly, burst into tears.

SARKIS WAS NOT in the least surprised. Halla had held up surprisingly well, but two attacks in three days was simply a bridge too far.

He swapped the sword to his off hand and sheathed it awkwardly. With his free hand, he pulled her close.

"It's all right," he said. "Shhh. It's okay. They're gone."

She sobbed into his shoulder, fingers locked around the edge of his surcoat. He wrapped his arms around her and waited.

It was not the first time that he'd held someone who was crying their heart out. His mother had done it when his father died. And his troops...well. Fisher was notoriously tender-hearted for a man who put crossbow bolts into people for a living. He bawled after every single battle. Nobody said anything about it because Fisher had saved all their lives twice over. You just patted his back and said, "There, there," until he was okay again.

Angharad had done it once—and only once—when the man she loved had turned out to be worthless. That had been awkward, since she was a head taller than Sarkis and also he had been battling his desire to take a fast horse after the man and gut him like a hog.

He wouldn't have minded gutting Halla's attackers like hogs

as well, but he suspected that would have upset her even more. So he contented himself with chasing them off and now with holding Halla while she soaked the front of his surcoat with tears.

She kept saying something over and over again. It took him a few minutes to make out the words through the sobs.

"But I didn't *do* anything to them!"

Sarkis sighed. "I know. I know."

And that was the problem right there. There was something terribly kind and trusting about Halla. Wherever these people had come from, their impersonal malice had clearly astonished her. She just wasn't used to evil or desperate people turning up out of nowhere.

Well, when you think about it, the greatest threat was people she knew. And she went off with you, trusting as a lamb, without any more proof of goodwill than that you were clearly enchanted. Why are you surprised that she has no proper fear of strangers?

Yes, but that's different. I was getting her away from a bad situation, he argued. *I was clearly the lesser of two evils.*

Sure. When are you going to tell her what the blade says, then?

Sometimes Sarkis hated arguing with himself. He kept being right.

Halla snuffled against him, hiccupped, and mumbled, "I'm sorry."

"It's all right."

"I shouldn't have…I mean, she was at the inn…she talked about how hard it was to travel alone and asked if I'd walk her a little way, just so the men didn't see her leaving alone and that made *sense,* it really did, and I thought of course she was scared, I would be too, so I'd wait to draw you, and then…"

"It's all right. You couldn't have known."

"I was so *stupid.*"

"No," he said. "Just kind. It's all right. It will be all right. I'm here. You're safe now. No harm done."

She looked up at him with her water-gray eyes, now rimmed with red. Her cheeks and nose were swollen from crying.

The urge flared again to go after the people who had done this and kill them. Or possibly just burn the entire world that was so unkind to people like Halla.

A fine thing for a former mercenary to be thinking. You'll be running off righting wrongs like a swordsaint if this keeps up.

Not that he could run off anywhere. He was anchored to the sword and the wielder, whether they were as malicious as a devil or as kind as Halla.

She drew away. He found that he was reluctant to let her go. She still looked miserable, and now she looked embarrassed, too.

"I'm sorry," she said again.

He kissed her forehead. "You don't have to be. They're the ones who did wrong, not you."

Now why in the great god's name did I just do that?

He didn't know. He hadn't even thought before he kissed her.

It doesn't mean anything. He'd only brushed his lips across her forehead, like a brother might. It didn't have to be anything more than that.

Good. Don't let it be anything more than that. Getting involved with a wielder is asking for trouble that would take a great deal more than one lifetime to sort out.

He knew this was true, and yet the desire to kiss her again was much stronger than it should have been.

Stop. You will fail her as you fail all the others who wield you, in time.

"Oh gods," she said, sounding exhausted. "Does that mean we can't stop at an inn tonight?"

Despite the darkness of his thoughts, he had to laugh at that. "We'll stop. We'll just go in together."

"What if they've heard of us and try to stop us?"

Sarkis shrugged. "They can try."

CHAPTER 14

No one tried to stop them.

It took Halla a moment to gather up her courage to go into the next inn. She'd washed her face in a puddle so that no one could tell she'd been crying a few hours earlier. But she stared at the door and thought about other people and other people's malice, and had a sudden urge to turn and run into the fields and never come out again.

Then she realized she'd been standing there for several minutes, with Sarkis beside her, and that he had to guess she was frightened—frightened of an inn, for gods' sake!—and the shame of that lifted her chin. *Don't embarrass yourself.*

She opened the door and went in, with Sarkis standing behind her like a particularly war-like dog at heel. She wondered if the innkeeper would think they were married, then glanced at Sarkis and had a hard time picturing him being married to anyone.

Though he was once, wasn't he?

She didn't want to think about that. *She was strong*, Sarkis had said. The admiration in his voice had been obvious.

He certainly could have no admiration for a woman who

had been foolish enough to fall in such an obvious trap, and who had sobbed on his shoulder like a child. But apparently he was stuck with her so long as she wielded the sword. *Whether he likes me or hates me, admires me or despises me.*

She did not want him to despise her.

How could he not? You're a decadent southerner. Hell, even by decadent southern standards, you're pitiful. You can barely climb over a wall on your own. You were held prisoner by an old woman armed with embroidery hooks. He'd have been well away already, most likely, if he wasn't stuck with you.

No, that was unfair. Sarkis was clearly a decent man, and he wouldn't leave someone so obviously helpless wandering around in the woods by herself.

This was, if possible, an even less comforting thought.

After this is all over, after I've got enough money to set up my nieces—if I can get enough to set up my nieces—I'll hand him the sword and tell him he's free to go find a better wielder. That would be the best thing I could do.

"Can I help you?" said the innkeeper, turning back to her.

"Two rooms for the night," said Halla.

"One," said Sarkis.

The innkeeper looked from one to the other. "Which?"

Oh...oh, of course. I can just sheathe the sword, he doesn't need a room. It'll save money.

Halla knew that she was blushing. "One," she said.

"You sure?" The innkeeper's eyes lingered on hers and she was glad that she had washed the tears off them.

"I will sleep in the stable, if you have one," said Sarkis. "I do not require a room."

"Ah." The innkeeper nodded, apparently relieved. "Good to hear, for I've only one room free in any event."

He took Halla's money and nodded her upstairs. "Last on the left."

She went to the stairs. Sarkis followed. "I will bring up your bags, my lady," he said, loudly enough for the innkeeper to hear.

"Thank you," said Halla.

They went to the room. It was a narrow strip of bed and a narrower strip of floor beside it. There was a chair and a basin wedged in so tightly that using either one would require a great deal of planning. The mattress sagged.

Halla collapsed onto it and made a distinctly unladylike noise of relief.

"I once heard a yak make a sound like that," said Sarkis.

"Are you comparing me to a yak?" She heard the thump as he set her pack down and a rattling as he checked the doors.

"It was merely an observation. My lady."

Halla couldn't be bothered to lift her head. Every muscle in her body was trying to unknot at once. "I'm sure I'd be a very good yak."

She could hear the smile in his voice. "You'd be the best of yaks."

Was that a compliment? An insult? She wasn't sure, and at the moment, she didn't much care.

"Yaks complain, but they're smart. As smart as horses. And curious. And they don't suffer fools."

Halla sighed, rolling over. Her back screamed. "I wish I didn't suffer fools."

"You needn't suffer them any longer."

She opened her eyes. "What? Why not?"

"Because I will dispose of them for you."

Halla started to laugh weakly. "Oh gods! If only you'd come along ten years earlier..."

He sat down in the chair, facing the door, as alert as a guard dog. "Take a nap," he suggested. "I'm here now."

SHE FELL ASLEEP ALMOST at once. When she woke again, the sun was going down and Sarkis was sitting cross-legged on the floor beside her. He tilted his head up at her.

"Have you been awake this whole time?"

"Of course."

She shook her head, bemused.

"Do you wish to go downstairs?"

"Mmm." She stood up, wincing at the stiffness in her joints. She didn't mind being older, she just wished her bones hadn't aged faster than the rest of her. Somewhere in her early thirties, her hips had decided they belonged to a much older body.

There was a privy at the end of the hall with a carved wooden seat. It was a great deal better than attending to business in hedgerows. There were fewer twigs in awkward places.

Sarkis, who presumably did not need to do this sort of thing either, waited at the other end of the hall.

"Err," said Halla, once she emerged. "Do you...uh...?"

"If I stay outside the sword long enough to eat and drink, yes," he said. "But not right now."

She nodded. "I thought I'd be hungry again," she admitted. "But I'm just exhausted. I want to sleep for a year."

"Understandable," said Sarkis, holding open the door to her room.

"I guess I'll just sheathe you?" She looked at the sword, tied open with the dressing gown cords, which were by now much the worse for wear.

"No," said Sarkis. "I should sleep, but I will make a bed here. After this morning's attack, I do not wish to leave you unguarded."

Halla blinked at him. "Um," she said.

Don't be silly. It's not as if you weren't asleep earlier. Hell, you climbed into his lap last night. And you're traveling alone together, so your reputation isn't going to get much more compromised.

There was just something very different about sleeping in proximity in the middle of a hedge and sleeping, at the same time, in the same bedroom. Maybe it was the existence of the bed.

Halla looked at the bed, which was narrow, sagging in the middle, and had bits of straw leaking out from a gap in the side. As a palace of carnal delight went, it was definitely sub-par.

Sarkis rolled his eyes, picked up her pack and set it down in front of the door. Then he stretched out, folded his arms across his chest, and put his head on the pack.

Halla peered over the foot of the bed at him.

"It's fine," he said, not opening his eyes.

"Is that comfortable?"

"Not particularly."

"Do you want a blanket?"

"It's fine."

She wrung her hands. It seemed like the worst failure of hospitality to have blankets when Sarkis didn't. "At least take my cloak!"

He opened his eyes and stared at the ceiling. "Lady, I have slept on stone floors with snow coming in through the windows. This is not a hardship."

"Yes, but you don't have to," she argued. "There's no snow. And we've got blankets! And a cloak! You could even share the bed if you want—I mean, not share it, obviously, not *share*-share it, I'm a respectable widow, or I was before I met you and all this happened, but of course I'm still respectable like *that*, so I would never actually—not that I'm saying you'd *want* to, of course, even if I wasn't respectable, or that I'd want to—not that you're not—I mean, it's nothing against *you*, you're a fine man who's actually a sword and I don't know if swords even—I mean, it would be ironic if they didn't, given the symbolism, don't you think?—but—"

At that point, her embarrassment reached out from somewhere in the center of her chest and mercifully throttled her tongue.

Sarkis had begun staring at her at some point in that recitation, his head tilting farther and farther to one side, like a dog that could not believe what it was seeing.

Halla folded her hands in front of her, took a deep breath, and said "You could sleep on the bed if you wanted. Just to sleep. I wouldn't be a threat to your virtue."

He continued to stare at her.

"For the love of the gods, say something," she begged.

"In...I know not how many years..." said Sarkis, "no wielder has ever been concerned about my virtue."

"If you'd just take the cloak," said Halla, feeling her face burning so hot that it could probably warm the whole inn, "we could stop having this horrible conversation."

"Give me the cloak."

Halla sighed with relief, pulled her cloak off the back of the chair and draped it over Sarkis.

He watched her with an indescribable expression. Halla snuffed out the candle and was grateful when they were plunged into darkness so that he couldn't see her blush.

CHAPTER 15

Sarkis lay in the dark, remembering the last wielder he'd actually liked.

The Young Leopard, the man had been called, until years had passed, and then he was just the Leopard. Sarkis had fought side by side with the Young Leopard, when the man had nothing to his name but his blade and his shield and an enchanted sword.

The Leopard was one of those men who wore his cynicism like a cloak to hide his hope. Sarkis had taken to him immediately. They'd carved out a place together, a little low valley with good pasture.

He had been one of those rare wielders, like Halla, who had let Sarkis out of the sword for weeks at a time. It had been good. But time had passed and he had spent more and more time in the sword, as the Leopard had needed more farmers and less force of arms.

He was the Old Leopard when he drew the sword again, years later, and put a cup of wine into his hand.

"Sarkis, my sword brother," he said. "It has been too long."

"Has it?"

"For me, yes. For you…" The Old Leopard's hair had gone steel gray. He kept it clipped short against his skull. "Drink with me. My children don't understand what we did to earn this place, and I pray that they never have to."

So they drank together, night after night, an old man and an immortal warrior, trading lies and, later, in their cups, the truths they couldn't speak sober.

It was in the Leopard's service that Sarkis came to terms with his immortality. For many years he had been drawn and fought and sheathed again, with little time for reflection between battle and the silver dreams inside the blade. But with the Leopard he had time to think, time to talk out his fears.

"I fear I will live forever," he said once, not knowing if that was a cruel thing to say to an old man. "I fear I will go on and on and on, until there is nothing left of me but silver scars and I have forgotten what it is like to be a man instead of a blade."

"Nothing lives forever, my friend," said the Old Leopard, topping up his drink. "Not even gods or mountains. The day will come when the sword breaks or the magic runs out or a god or a devil passes by and snuffs you out like a candle."

Sarkis smiled. "Is it strange that I hope you are right?"

"Not at all. I am old, brother, and I will die this winter or the next, but I would not trade places with you. It is a hard thing to be dragged beyond your allotted years."

"For my sins," said Sarkis softly.

"There are few sins that should chase a man beyond death. I do not think yours qualify."

Sarkis had taken comfort in that judgment. The Leopard had been his friend, but he had also been a good man. Certainly a better one than Sarkis.

Halla was nothing like the Leopard. The man would have died laughing at her babbling about his virtue.

But dammit, Sarkis liked her.

She was as earnest as a new recruit and she was trying so damn hard. And every now and then, she'd come out with a sly remark and startle him into laughing. There were so few people who kept a sense of humor when they were miserable, you learned to appreciate it. The Young Leopard had been like that. Probably that was why he was thinking of the man now.

Sarkis stifled a sigh. Had he failed the Leopard?

Not quite. Even I can't be expected to guard a wielder against age. His old friend's heart had given out, a few months after that conversation, and his daughter had drawn the sword long enough to inform Sarkis, so that he could attend the funeral. It had been a kindness. He hadn't forgotten that.

The next time the sword was drawn, he was in a place with different mountains, where the people wore different armor, and no one had heard of the Old Leopard. He never did find out what happened to the man's valley, or his family, or why the sword had been passed on.

That felt like a failure to Sarkis.

I can't do anything if they don't draw the sword, he told himself wearily. He'd told the Leopard's daughter that he was there to serve, but perhaps he hadn't tried hard enough to make her understand.

Halla rolled over in her sleep, mumbling to herself.

You won't automatically fail, he told himself. *It's a walk to the next village, not a seven-day siege. Surely you can escort one good-natured woman to a temple without making a miserable hash of things.*

Surely.

Great god have mercy on us both.

"I HAVE PURCHASED A CLOAK," Sarkis announced the next morning.

Halla was still bleary-eyed from sleep and was trying to remember where she was and why there was a large man with a sword in her room. *Right. Sarkis. Enchanted sword. Inn. Right. Okay.* "Oh?"

"It will be a better disguise," he explained. "I have an undershirt as well. The constables are searching for a tattooed man in leather—if, indeed, they are bothering to search at all."

"Makes sense," she said, standing. She had slept in her clothes last night and was trying to press the wrinkles out with her hands. It was a largely futile effort.

"Should you need to sheathe the sword, grab the cloak if you can. It will not come with me."

"Right."

He paused, suddenly frowning. "I have only been downstairs."

"Okay?"

"I did not want you to think that I left you unguarded."

"Err?" Halla tried to rake her hair into some semblance of respectability. "It's fine? I wasn't worried?"

Sarkis stripped out of his leather surcoat and the shirt underneath and stood, bare-chested.

Halla gaped at him, the tatters of sleep fleeing immediately from her mind.

He caught her expression and one corner of his mouth crooked up.

"It's been a few years since my physique struck women speechless," he said, slapping his belly. "Several hundred, at least. But I didn't think it was that bad."

"No! No—I—What is *that?*"

Sarkis glanced down at himself, puzzled. "What?"

Halla pointed to the center of his chest.

He was, in truth, no longer young. His muscles were smoothed by a layer of fat and his figure thickened substantially at the waist. But that wasn't what astonished her.

Across his sternum, written and overwritten like a scribbled line, was a slick silver scar as wide as Halla's hand and at least a foot long. A few of the lines started at his shoulders before trailing down to join the others. One, longer than the rest, ran down the line of his belly and then jerked jaggedly to the left.

"What on earth..." she breathed, reaching out and tapping her finger against his breastbone. She half-expected the silver mark to ring like metal when she tapped it, but it was only skin and scar.

"Ah," he said, catching her hand. "Yes. My deaths. Most of them, at any rate. There are one or two across the back that cut my spine, but this is where most of them end up."

She looked up to met his eyes, astonished. "When you said you died several times..."

"Well," he admitted. "Perhaps more than several."

"There's dozens here!"

"They weren't all fatal. I got back into the sword in time to heal from a few." He traced the line that ran across his side with his free hand. "That one spilled my guts in the roadway. Not an experience I recommend, but I didn't die of it. The sword healed me up. The scars, though...well, I can't do much about the scars."

"It must have hurt so much."

She could actually see the glib answer rise to his tongue, and then he simply nodded.

The contrast between scar and flesh was strangely stark. His dark bronze skin was made even darker by black hair across his chest, running in a line down his belly. The silver marks stood out like wounds...which, of course, they were.

It occurred to Halla that she was standing with her hand

pressed against a man's bare chest for the first time in many years. Had she ever touched her husband this way? Surely she must have, though not for long. He would not have enjoyed it.

Sarkis's hand held hers flat against his chest. She could feel his heartbeat. He still had a heart, then, pumping blood in the usual way, even if he bore the signs of dozens of mortal wounds.

She swallowed and stepped back. He released her hand at once, as soon as she moved, and she told herself that was right and proper and correct and there was no reason to feel disappointed.

She absolutely did not have any desire to keep moving her hand across his chest and feel the texture change from skin to scar and back again, or to move it downward, following the line of hair to...well, regardless, she had no desire to. None whatsoever.

Sarkis pulled on the undershirt and rolled it down over his arms, then shrugged into the surcoat and his cloak. Halla pretended that she wasn't watching.

She hefted her pack over her shoulder. "I suppose we should get moving," she said, giving the bed a longing look. "We're not getting any closer to Amalcross standing here. And I can already smell breakfast."

CHAPTER 16

S arkis was concerned.

Halla had been walking beside him for several hours now, and she hadn't asked him a single question. It was not that he missed her endless chatter, he told himself, but it was certainly cause for concern.

He knew she'd slept the night before. Her breathing had been deep and even and then she'd started to snore. The dark circles were gone from under her eyes and she was no longer limping.

I would think simply that she is no longer talking to keep herself going, except...

When she did not know he was looking, she was gnawing on her lower lip and her pleasant mask slipped. She was chewing something over and by the flat, unfocused look in her eyes, she did not much like the taste.

Yesterday's attack is still bothering her, or I am a pronghorn's uncle.

Well. If she would not ask questions to distract herself, it seemed that it fell to Sarkis instead.

"You have two nieces," he said.

"Huh?" She blinked at him, then smiled. "Yes. Erris and Nola. Good girls."

"Their mother has gone under the earth, though?"

"Well, she's dead, if that's what you mean."

He nodded. Halla nodded in return. "My sister Anatilya was their mother. She died in childbirth a few years after Nola was born."

"Her shade give you strength," said Sarkis politely. "Their father raised them?"

"Yes. He's a good man. I've only met him a few times, though."

She fell silent again. Sarkis, never skilled at small talk, plowed forward. "Do you have no other family, then?"

"Ironic, isn't it? I was the middle of five. There were too many of us growing up, always underfoot and too many mouths to feed, and here I am, the only one left. My two younger sisters died of fever a week apart. My brother went off to the mines after Mother died, and he died in a collapse not long after I married. And I already told you about Anatilya."

"*All* their shades give you strength," said Sarkis. *Well done. You try to distract her from an unpleasant memory, and you plow right into her entire family being dead. Excellent work.*

In the Weeping Lands, her story would not be surprising. It was a hard land, after all. He wondered if it was unusual here, to lose your parents and all four siblings, your husband and anyone else to care for you.

"I'm sorry," he added.

Halla shrugged. "Well, someone's always got to be the last one standing, don't they? I'm good at planning funerals, anyway. And it's awful to say, but I probably handled it better than some of the others would have. My brother would have drunk himself to death before too long, mine or not. Anatilya was always tough as nails, but the twins...gods have mercy.

They'd probably still be crying. Without stopping, I mean. They always cried over every little thing, and if one of them started, the other one would join in, even if she didn't know what she was crying about..."

It took Sarkis very little coaxing to get her talking after that. The picture she painted of her childhood was not an easy one, although she remembered it fondly. Her mother had been a fierce, flawed woman who loved her children very much but was hard-pressed to care for all of them. A string of poorly chosen men hadn't helped in that regard.

When he found out that Halla hadn't even met her father, that the man had fled as soon as he learned his lover was pregnant, Sarkis's jaw muscles ached from clenching.

"In the Weeping Lands, he would have been hunted down by her relatives for such a slight," he said. "And his steading made to pay reparations."

"Well, she didn't have any relatives to do the hunting," said Halla practically. "I mean, she had two children at that point, but you don't put a five-year-old on a horse and tell her to go bring a man back, dead or alive. Or do they do that in the Weeping Lands, too?"

"We try to wait until the child is at least six for that," said Sarkis, deadpan.

"You...oh!" She swatted his arm. "Gods, for a minute there..."

He ducked his head, pleased to have steered the conversation away from dangerous ground.

They went on in silence for a little while after that. Sarkis watched an ox cart approach, but it rumbled past with only a polite nod from the driver.

"Out of Amalcross," said Halla. "We're getting close."

It was only a few minutes later that Sarkis heard hoofbeats on the road, and did not like the sound of them.

It sounded like two horses moving at a gallop. The horses were obviously being poorly used—their hooves weren't hitting the ground evenly, there was a trace of a stumble, and he thought one might even be limping—and of course there were perfectly legitimate reasons why two riders should be galloping hard down a small rural road, but by this point, Sarkis had already thrown Halla into the ditch and leapt in after her, throwing the ragged cloak over them both.

"Ow," mumbled Halla, from somewhere under his right elbow.

Sarkis cocked his head, waiting. Surely there was no reason for the riders to be looking for anyone in the ditches...surely the constables of Halla's town would not still be riding hell-for-leather so many days after the fact...

The hoofbeats slowed, then stopped. Sarkis heard the jingle of tack as a rider dismounted.

Great god's hells.

"You there! Why are you hiding in a ditch?"

"Here we go," said Halla, under her breath.

There was no point in pretending they weren't. Sarkis stood, helping Halla to her feet.

The horses were indeed tired. They were blowing and panting and one was favoring a hoof just a little. Sarkis had a strong desire to yell at the riders for mistreating their beasts.

The riders were odd. One wore light armor, rather like Sarkis, and had a fierce scowl...again, probably rather like Sarkis.

The other, the one who had dismounted, was a lean man with close-cropped hair. He wore rich, dark blue, almost indigo, with an odd silver symbol across his chest—a teardrop shape that seemed to fan out at the top into tendrils.

"Priests of the Hanged Mother," said Halla softly.

Sarkis would have muttered something about decadent southern gods, but it didn't seem like the right time.

The priest narrowed his eyes. He did not look pleased. "Well? What are you doing? Why would you hide from a priest?"

Sarkis opened his mouth to say something—he wasn't sure what—but Halla elbowed him in the ribs and stepped forward. "We are very sorry, your Grace," she said. "We didn't realize that you were of the Mother. We were attacked by bandits yesterday along this road, you see, and when we heard the horses..." She shrugged, looking sheepish. "I'm afraid my nerves are still unsettled. I thought someone was coming to attack me."

The priest's eyes narrowed even farther, turning into chilly slits. "Bandits?"

"I don't know that they were *organized* bandits," said Halla. "A man and a woman, and they seemed a bit desperate. My—husband—stood them off."

Sarkis was faintly surprised at his sudden promotion to husband. He hoped the priest didn't notice the very slight pause when Halla spoke.

"Obviously if we'd known you were priests of the Mother, we wouldn't have hidden," Halla continued. "I mean, you can't really hide from the Mother, can you? And everyone knows the good work that you do, rooting out evil. Which, incidentally, if you wanted to root some out, those bandits could probably stand to be—"

"The Mother does not concern herself with *petty* criminals."

"Yes, of course," said Halla, immediately casting her eyes to the roadway. "I'm sorry. I'm not presuming to tell you the Mother's business, of course. But that's why we were hiding. It's my nerves. It runs in the family, you see. Mother's nerves were—not *the* Mother, I mean *my* mother—I mean, not that the Mother isn't *everyone's* Mother, obviously—"

The armored man made a swift ritual gesture at that, and the priest followed suit, looking faintly annoyed.

"—but my mother, the human one, she had terrible nerves. Why, a thunderstorm left her completely deranged. She'd take to her bed for days and call for brandy. And cauliflower. I mean, I don't know why she wanted cauliflower, I've never thought cauliflower was a particularly soothing vegetable, but it certainly made my mother happier, so we'd cook it up whenever the weather started to turn. Do you have any cauliflower?"

Sarkis did not know whether to laugh, put his hand over his eyes, or draw his sword and kill the two men while they were distracted. He was fairly certain he could get the priest, but the mounted guard might be more difficult. The man had a sword and a horse. There were solutions to both, of course, but Sarkis hated killing horses. There was even a chance the man might run off down the roadway for help, and then they'd be right back to hiding in ditches.

He wasn't sure if Halla was defusing the situation or making it worse, but she had her hand tucked in his elbow and was digging her nails into his forearm, so he let her go on and didn't try to break in.

"Why would priests of the Mother carry cauliflower?" asked the priest, sounding exasperated.

"Well, you never know your luck. I mean, my mother carried it, so I thought maybe since the Mother is everyone's mother—"

The two men grimly made the ritual gesture again.

"—maybe She knew you'd be here and She'd send you with cauliflower. But I don't expect that!" Halla raised her free hand in front of her. "I'm certainly not important enough to merit the Mother's attention! Or Her vegetables."

The priest looked away, clearly disgusted. His gaze settled on Sarkis.

"Can your husband not speak for himself?"

"I can," said Sarkis.

"Then why don't you?"

"My wife talks enough for both of us."

The mounted man snickered. The priest shook his head, turning back to his horse. "I will pray for you."

"I would appreciate that," said Sarkis, deadpan. The mounted man put his hand over his mouth.

"The blessings of the Mother upon you," said the priest, climbing into the saddle. He did not sound as if he meant it.

"Oh, thank you!" said Halla. "That's better than cauliflower!"

"Wife," said Sarkis, putting his arm around her, "quit your nattering about vegetables. These are busy men, and we have detained them too long with your foolishness."

The glance she shot him indicated that Sarkis was going to pay for that later, but he didn't mind.

The priest kicked his horse forward again. It was the limping one, Sarkis saw, and the few minutes standing around had stiffened its legs. He wanted to pull the man from the saddle and thrash him for mistreating his beast, but Halla was stiff as a board under his arm.

She waved as they left, beaming. Sarkis was rather impressed at how genuine the smile looked, when she had been leaving bloody little half-moons in his skin not two minutes past.

As they rode away, he saw that the indigo cloaks had the same teardrop shaped symbol on the back.

When the hoofbeats had completely faded, he said "Now what was that all about?"

"Ugh." Halla dug her hands into her hair. "Priests of the Hanged Mother. Nasty people. There didn't used to be many of them until about five years ago—after the Clocktaur War, you know—"

"I don't."

"Gah!" Halla shook her head. "I forget, sorry. Okay, so some artificers in Anuket City dug up this army of monsters and then Anuket City decided to start sending them out to attack people. Archenhold surrendered immediately. You couldn't not. I saw a column of them go by, and they'd have trampled us all flat and not even noticed. So then they went after the Dowager's city— oh, don't worry about it. They all stopped working one day. Went berserk and smashed each other to pieces. For about a year after that, we had the occasional rogue clocktaur roaming around, but the paladins handled it. Anyway, the point is that Archenhold had surrendered, right?"

"All right," said Sarkis.

"Well, they sort of...un-surrendered...after the clocktaurs stopped working, but no one was terribly happy with the Archon who surrendered in the first place, so he got deposed, and then the new Archon was chosen, and it turned out he really liked the Hanged Mother. So all of a sudden this obscure little priesthood gets a lot of money and a lot of public power and becomes effectively the state religion, not that we have state religions, but if we did, it'd be that one."

"And I take it they are not well thought of?" said Sarkis, who was pleased that he had followed the conversation this far.

"Oh no. Nobody likes them. I mean, they like *themselves*, presumably, but nobody else does. Nasty bunch. Their goddess hung herself with her own hair."

"Why?"

"I dunno. God reasons, I guess. Anyway, they like to root out people they think are heretics or witches and torture them into confessing. Then they burn them. They didn't used to be able to get away with it so much, but now that the Archon looks favorably on the Motherhood..." She shrugged.

"You never mentioned them before."

She gave him a wry look. "It didn't really come up. I wasn't going to ask *them* for help, was I?"

"Have I mentioned that your entire country should be put to the torch?"

"Frequently."

"Consider it mentioned again. What was all that about cauliflower?"

"Oh, that. Hardly anybody kills stupid women," said Halla, starting down the road. "They kick us out of the way, they smack us occasionally, but nobody thinks we're a threat."

"You're not stupid," said Sarkis, remembering that she'd said something similar a few days ago. At the time, he had disagreed with her mostly out of courtesy, but he was beginning to suspect that Halla was in some ways much sharper than he had realized.

"I try not to be. Except when I am trying very hard to convince someone that I am." She grinned abruptly. Her grin made his stomach turn over rather oddly, and he wasn't sure how to feel about that.

Sarkis suddenly remembered her babbling about dragons when they had first met. A suspicion woke in the back of his mind. *A strange swordsman appearing in the middle of her room at night...of course she'd try to defend herself. However idiosyncratic that defense might be...* He eyed the back of her head thoughtfully.

Halla, meanwhile, was scrambling out of the ditch and onto the road. "Not too much farther now. Let's go slowly, though—I don't want to run into those priests again if we can avoid it."

CHAPTER 17

"Tell me about your wife," said Halla, an hour later.

They were walking along the side of the road now. Traffic had picked up enough as they approached Amalcross that they were becoming lost in the crowd. Covered in road dust, the pair did not stand out from any other pair of travelers making their way toward the larger town.

"My wife?" said Sarkis. "Why?"

She shrugged. "You know all about my late husband."

She was rather proud of how calmly she said that, as if it didn't matter at all. They were two people exchanging information. She absolutely was not trying to find out what Sarkis had respected about his former wife in hopes that he would think Halla less useless.

Because that would be strange. And would imply that I care. And I absolutely do not care in the slightest. At all.

She grimaced. She had always been a poor liar, particularly to herself.

Sarkis didn't seem to have noticed. "True enough," he said. He thought for a moment. "She was tall. She had dark hair and she was very tanned."

Halla sighed internally. Even if she'd dyed her hair black, she wasn't going to get any taller and she would probably go to her grave pink and rather flushed.

"She could put an arrow into the eye of a wolf at fifty yards away."

Halla made a mental note to take up archery.

"She ran her farm like a warlord's camp."

"Efficiently?" hazarded Halla.

"Ruthlessly," said Sarkis.

"Mmm." Halla had helped run a farm once. It had not been ruthless. It had been haphazard and everything had always seemed to be on the edge of collapsing and there was always some chore that needed doing. It had seemed like that was just the way that farms were, but perhaps it had simply been that she wasn't very good at it.

Oh, why do I even care if he thinks I'm useless? He's not really a man, he's an enchanted sword. And I doubt he'd be unkind even so. He's been...well, mostly pleasant this whole time. Even if he does still grab my arm when he isn't thinking about it.

Certainly it had nothing to do with the moment where she'd laid her hand against his bare chest, feeling the contrast between the solid muscle and the slick silver scars. His heartbeat under her hand had meant nothing. He was her guard, not her husband.

The thought came unbidden that he would have made a far better husband than her late, not-much-missed spouse.

His wife must have left him for some reason. Such a paragon of virtue wouldn't have just gotten tired of him, would she?

Halla eyed the breadth of Sarkis's shoulders and the heavy muscle of his arms and thought she probably wouldn't get tired of that in a hurry.

Even the thought astonished her. *I'm turning into a dirty old woman in my old age. For all the good it does me...*

Well, at least she knew the way to Amalcross. That had to be worth something. She steered Sarkis away from the main entrance, full of drovers and livestock, to one of the smaller side roads. Unlike Rutger's Howe, Amalcross did not have city walls.

Her uncle's old friend lived in a tall, narrow house on the west side of the town. It was large, but much like Silas's, it was stuffed full of artifacts. She remembered it being a dusty, cluttered place, the two times that she had visited.

People gave Sarkis puzzled looks as they walked down the street. It wasn't the sort of town where you saw a hulking warrior with a sword, even one who was wearing a cloak and trying to look inconspicuous.

The fact that she was carrying a second, even larger sword over her back probably didn't help.

Sarkis, for his part, could feel eyes on them as they crossed to stand in front of the door that Halla indicated. They didn't feel hostile, just curious, but the skin on the back of his neck prickled nonetheless

The tightly packed buildings in the south made for much easier ambushes. There was no earthly reason to think anyone would want to ambush Halla, but he took a step back and half-turned, just in case he had to turn and defend against attack.

Halla, oblivious, knocked on the door....and waited...and knocked...

"Coming..." called a voice finally. "I'm coming!"

The door opened and a reedy older man stood in the hallway, blinking up at them.

"Bartholomew!"

For a moment he looked completely baffled, then his gaze sharpened and he said "Halla? Silas's Halla?"

"It's me."

"I...yes, yes, so it is." The man ran his hand through his hair, making it stand up in irregular spikes. "I...oh dear. Yes. Come in?"

Halla began to follow him, but Sarkis stepped in her path. He paused for a moment on the threshold to let his eyes adjust to the gloom, then nodded to Halla.

She gave him a bemused look. He suspected she was wondering why he was acting as if there might be attackers inside the house.

Truth was, he wasn't sure. Something made his nerves itch. Probably it was nothing—a trick of rooms and angles reminding him of some other, long ago place.

Maybe it was just that people you knew were always the most likely to be hostile.

But the hallway was empty. Sarkis followed Bartholomew past an open door to what was clearly the heart of the house.

The room was simple enough, a long table covered in haphazard stacks of papers, with two benches on either side. A spot had been cleared in the papers for a person to eat dinner. But it was not the furniture that attracted the eye.

The walls were covered in...*things*. Swords and knives, axes and daggers of curious design. Not only weapons, but dozens of objects: strange skulls, the stuffed head of a two-headed calf, masks carved into fantastic shapes, woodwinds with a dozen shafts that no human mouth could possibly have played.

He remembered what Halla had said of this friend. A collector, like Silas. One that she might be able to bribe with strange objects.

When one was oneself a strange object, this took on an unexpectedly sinister life.

"This is Sarkis," Halla was saying. "He's a—"

"Friend," said Sarkis firmly. "Of her great-uncle's."

Bartholomew looked briefly puzzled. "Of course, of course. Though, forgive me, but Silas never mentioned you."

Sarkis shrugged. "It was some time ago. He did me a favor. Probably he thought less of it than I did."

Halla was looking at him with frank astonishment. Sarkis gave her a brief, hard look. *Play along.*

She recovered herself, smiling broadly. "Yes, well. Sarkis heard he'd passed away and came to pay his respects."

Her great-uncle's friend put a hand over his heart. "Yes. I'm so sorry I could not attend myself."

"Fortunately," said Sarkis, "I was able to offer her assistance. And my escort away."

Bartholomew frowned. "Away?"

Halla groaned. "It's a really long story..."

Bartholomew gestured her quickly to a bench. "Forgive me. Please, sit!"

He called and a servant girl came out of the kitchen. She was much more neatly kept than the rest of the building, and Sarkis doubted that she lived there. Certainly she seemed a bit embarrassed to have guests. She wiped down the table in front of them and brought out mugs of cider, murmuring apologies as if the clutter was a reflection on her.

Halla waited until she was done, then told Bartholomew the story, heavily abridged. Sarkis was pleased to see how quickly she picked up on the fact that he did not wish his status as the sword to be known. In her version, he had been a guest in the house and had come to her aid when he heard her arguing with Aunt Malva.

Parts of the story strained credibility, but she put so much passion into the bit about sleeping in hedges that it would have taken a harder man than Bartholomew to call her out on the other bits.

Sarkis liked watching her. She waved her hands a lot and her face was never still. It was an odd performance to find pleasure in, perhaps, but he found himself wanting to smile. He scowled fiercely to prevent any trace from escaping.

"And so we've been on the road for days," she finished. "I'm so sorry to barge in on you, Bartholomew, but..."

"No, my dear, not at all!" He waved his hands fretfully. "Of course not! You're entirely welcome. But how may I help you?" He blanched suddenly. "Ah...you don't wish *me* to marry you, do you?"

"No!" said Sarkis, more forcefully than he intended.

Halla smoothed over the awkward moment by bursting into laughter. "Oh dear! No, no. That's very sweet of you, but no."

Their host looked relieved. "Not that you're not a fine girl, my dear, but...well...I am rather set in my ways, and..."

She giggled. "It's all right. No, I just hoped we could stay with you for a day or two. We were on our way to Archenhold and the Temple of the White Rat. I'm hoping that they can help me to get my inheritance."

"Oh, an excellent thought. Some fine legal minds at the Temple." Bartholomew nodded. "Not that there should be a problem, of course. Oh dear. What was Silas thinking?"

"If you don't know, I'm sure I don't." She propped her chin up on her hand. "Weren't you one of the witnesses to his will?"

"Was I?" He thought for a moment. "Oh, yes, I suppose I was. But I didn't *read* it. It would have been rude, wouldn't it? Like I was asking for something."

Sarkis, who had negotiated mercenary contracts with kings, did not scream *'Always read before you sign!'* and shake anyone by the neck. He was rather proud of that.

"And you had no idea?"

"Not the least in the world," said Halla. "I suppose I thought he'd leave me a few coins. Honestly, I was going to offer to stay on as the housekeeper to whoever he did leave the house to."

T. KINGFISHER

"Oh. Hmm." He stared into his cider as if he had forgotten what it was. "Ah...was there some reason you don't want to marry Alver? It seems like it would solve many of your problems, my dear."

Sarkis had a strong urge to growl like a watchdog and restrained himself.

"It wouldn't solve the problem of Alver," said Halla. "Or of Alver's mother."

"Oh...that. Yes." Bartholomew deflated a bit.

They drank the cider. After a moment, Bartholomew seemed to remember that they had asked to stay with him. He called to the servant girl and asked her to clean out two guest rooms.

"One is sufficient," said Sarkis. And when Bartholomew started to look scandalized, "I will guard her door. I do not require a bed."

"Sarkis, I don't think we're going to get attacked in Bartholomew's house."

"Then I will get a good night's sleep."

"...uh," said Bartholomew.

Sarkis put his arms on the table, crossed at the wrist. He was aware that his biceps were thicker around than the man's neck. It was not a threatening gesture, precisely, but Bartholomew's throat bobbed up and down as he swallowed.

Halla gave him a look that said she was quite aware what he was doing. "Is this really necessary?"

"I am sworn to guard you." And then, somewhat perfunctorily, "Lady."

"Ye-e-e-s..." said Bartholomew. "Uh. Right. One... uh...room."

"If you could get him a pallet for the floor, I'd appreciate it," said Halla, apparently giving up on persuading him otherwise. "Otherwise I feel guilty."

"A...yes. That's fine." The man's eyes darted around the room, seeking a change of subject, and finally settled on Halla. "You've got a sword. Is that the one I traded to Silas years ago?"

"I don't know," said Halla. "It was on the wall of my room. Sarkis—ah—thought I should carry a weapon, since I was traveling, and it was the only one I could find."

"Hmm, yes. You've tied it rather oddly, though. I don't think those cords are original to the piece."

"No. It..um..."

"Sticks in the scabbard," rumbled Sarkis. "This makes it an easier draw."

"Oh, does it?" asked Bartholomew vaguely. "I don't think I ever drew it. Part of a mixed lot of weapons, not terribly valuable. He traded me quite a nice stormpipe for it, though."

Sarkis tried not to take offense at being called, "Not terribly valuable."

"It's been quite useful," said Halla, with such studied innocence that Sarkis had to stifle his laugh behind a cough.

The maid returned a few minutes later to announce that a room had been cleaned. Sarkis, intending to continue as he started, insisted on entering it first, hand on his sword hilt.

"Now you're just hamming it up," muttered Halla under her breath.

"There could be assassins."

"I don't know how they'd fit."

His lips twitched. The room was indeed very small...or more accurately, it was a large room so filled with junk that the livable area was not much larger than the room they had rented in the inn the night before. A wardrobe loomed ominously over the bed and while presumably there was a window somewhere, it was lost behind stacks of books and folded fabrics.

"This is worse than my room at home."

"I'm sorry, miss," said the maid, wringing her hands.

"There's fresh blankets on the bed but the room...I'm not really allowed to touch anything, miss, except to move what was on the bed."

"It's all right." Halla put a sympathetic hand on the maid's shoulder. "My great-uncle was just the same way. We all had to work around his latest treasures. It was terrible when company came over." The maid looked as if she might cry with relief.

She and Halla engaged in a brief, intense conversation involving laundry. Sarkis had not had to do laundry for several hundred years and thus did not feel he had much to add to the discussion.

The maid left. Halla looked at the available space in front of the door. "Will this even work for you?"

"I will manage."

"You'll be halfway under the bed."

"Not the first bed I've slept under."

She started to reply, stopped, and pursed her lips. "Wait. Why were you sleeping *under* a bed?"

"All the space under the table had been taken."

The maid returned with an armload of clothes. Halla took them, then shooed Sarkis toward the hall. "Go. You can guard from the other side of the door."

He put up only a token resistance. "What if there are assassins hiding in all that junk?"

"Then I'll tell them hello for you." She put her hand in the center of his chest and pushed.

Sarkis grinned. Halla was clearly far more in her element now that she was back in familiar surroundings.

Halla closed the door, then came out a few minutes later, wearing...

"What in the great god's name is *that*?"

"One of Bartholomew's nightshirts. The over-robe is ceremonial garb from a death cult that went extinct a few decades back. Silas had about ten of them, too. We mostly used them to do chores in." She wiggled her toes. "And these're Bartholomew's socks."

The socks came halfway up her legs. The same could not be said of the nightshirt. Bartholomew was a narrow-chested man. Halla was a large-chested woman. Sarkis found his eyes drifting below her collarbone and dragged them back up.

"You may wish to...ah...belt that overrobe..." He thought, not for the first time, that women's clothing in the south involved far too few layers.

"Sarkis, you're a magic sword and he's old enough to be my father. This isn't church. No one cares."

"Yes, but it's cold in here."

"What does that have to do with...oh, *damn*..." She yanked the over-robe more tightly around herself. Sarkis bit his lower lip to distract himself from the sight of her nipples, which had been far too visible under the thin fabric.

He had a strong urge to drag his thumbs across them, feel them get even harder against his palms, and then perhaps...

Why am I thinking these things? I haven't noticed a woman's body like this since they put me in the sword.

In fairness, his wielders tended to draw him only when they were in some kind of danger. It had been a long time since he had simply walked and talked, eaten and slept like a normal man. Perhaps it was no surprise that a normal man's appetites would start to return to him as well.

Or perhaps it was simply that there was another man about, even a meek older one, and he was...jealous?

That cannot be it. I would have to be completely lost to reason to be jealous of Bartholomew. And she is not mine to be jealous of, in any event. I am her servant, not her lover.

You could be both, whispered the little voice in his head. *She's a widow, not a maiden. Widows tend to know what they want...*

Sarkis recognized the voice of temptation and squelched it firmly. He'd dallied with a widow or two in his time and they'd both gone away happier for the experience, but they'd been very different women than Halla. Those had been mutual seductions, full of warm glances and lingering touches, flirtations conducted to see if both parties were interested and if so, taken to the logical conclusion.

He had only to remember Halla's offer to share the bed with him last night to know that Halla was not an experienced seductress. Her face had blazed so red that it was probably visible clear back in Rutger's Howe.

Her face was turning red again as she cinched the overrobe tightly. Little embroidered skulls on the shoulders grinned at him. "Is this better?"

"Much, I assure you."

"I'm sorry I keep offending you with the sight of my..." She swallowed. "Well, you know."

"I'm not offended, lady. Merely...distracted."

She turned even redder. Sarkis didn't know whether to feel smug or guilty about that.

There is no honor in embarrassing an easily flustered woman. Control yourself.

He did wonder how Halla had managed to be married for so long and still retain the ability to blush so fiercely.

He also wondered how far down that blush went. Part of him would very much like to find out.

Great god's teeth, what had come over him? Perhaps he needed to go roll in the snow. Except that there was no snow here yet. A plunge in icy water?

As it seems unlikely that Ser Bartholomew is keeping a frozen lake in his garden, perhaps not.

Maybe that was why he hadn't felt this way on the road. He'd been too damn cold.

Halla had been very warm in his arms the second night. He had not appreciated that nearly enough at the time.

Right, he thought crisply. *Out of the sword much too long.* He clearly needed to spend some time alone, which was going to be damned difficult when he was trying to guard Halla from... well, everything.

The maid came back down the hall. Sarkis turned to her and growled "Is there a privy in this blasted place?"

"Y-yes...sir...there's...yes...I'll show you..." She fled down the hall in front of him.

She was a pretty enough slip of a thing. Sarkis made an effort to be attracted to her, just to see if it was specific to Halla or if he was suddenly hopelessly randy. It didn't work. She was much too young and nervous and he mostly wanted to go hammer on her family's door and demand to know why they weren't feeding her enough and then perhaps yell at Bartholomew for not hiring at least five more servants to help her deal with the clutter in the house.

Well, at least I am not lost to all human decency. That's worth something, I suppose.

The maid led him to the courtyard, pointed across the walk to the privy, and then fled. Sarkis pulled the door shut behind him, leaned against it, and finally let himself think all the thoughts he'd been keeping clamped down behind his teeth.

The woman in his fantasy had white-blonde hair and water-colored eyes. And excellent breasts.

It didn't take long, but that was fine. *Style doesn't really count when it's just you.*

He stuffed himself back into his trousers and went to wash his hands under the well pump. Then he shoved his head underneath the cold water for good measure.

Hopefully that will keep me acting like a rational being for a few hours.

He went back inside and found Halla in the kitchen. Bartholomew was wringing his hands. "I'm sorry," he said. "I didn't expect company, you see, and I haven't...well..."

"Bartholomew, it's fine," said Halla soothingly. "I'll go to the market and get the makings of dinner..."

"Not dressed like *that*, you won't," growled Sarkis, immediately abandoning his resolution about rationality.

Halla wheeled around and stared at him. "What are you, my mother?"

"If you were my daughter, you would be wearing more clothing!"

She narrowed her eyes. "I'll put on shoes."

"You're wearing a nightshirt and the ceremonial robes from a *death cult*."

"Yes, but the cult's extinct."

He drew his eyebrows down in a fierce scowl.

"Err...I'll send the girl..." said Bartholomew, wringing his hands even harder. "It's no trouble. I just...err...I'm not sure what to send her for..."

"Leave that to me," said Halla. "I'll cook something. If you don't object to *that*, Sarkis?"

Sarkis inclined his head. "I have no objections."

"Good. You can help me peel the potatoes while we wait, then."

If she expected him to balk at this chore, she was disappointed. By the time she had given the maid instructions on what to purchase and soothed Bartholomew's nerves, Sarkis had peeled more than half the potatoes.

He knew she was annoyed with him. He was already annoyed with himself, so at least this made two of them.

I am not her lover. I am not her kinsman. I am certainly not her mother. I am being an ass.

One of the grimmer realizations of Sarkis's youth had been the discovery that *knowing* you were being an ass did not actually stop you from *continuing* to be an ass.

She can just sheathe the damn sword at any time, you know, and the great god knows what trouble she'll get into if she's afraid to draw it again for fear you'll growl at her. Stop bristling like a damned boar and apologize.

"Well," she admitted, looking at the pile of potatoes, "you're good at that."

"I have a great deal of experience skinning my enemies," he said, deadpan.

"Do you have many enemies among the potatoes?"

"Not any longer."

The corner of her mouth crooked up, although she clearly tried to suppress it. She picked up a potato and a knife and sat down next to him.

"So what *exactly* is your problem with me going to the market dressed like this?"

"Men will stare at you," muttered Sarkis, hunched over the next potato.

"Well, that'd be a first."

"And then I will be forced to beat them."

She nearly cut herself with the knife. *"What?"*

"I am your guardsman." He eyed a dark spot in the potato and wondered whether it was worth digging out. "Lady."

"Sarkis, I'm a widow, not the local warlord's virgin bride. We don't even *have* a warlord. And the Archon's like eighty. I mean, we've got the Senators in Anuket City, I guess, but they can probably afford a better class of virgin anyway."

He scowled at the potato. "Humor me."

She gave him a dubious look.

"...please."

She sighed. "All right, since you ask so nicely. But you're peeling the rest of these while I try to figure out where the pots are in this wretched kitchen."

"As you command," said Sarkis, and went to battle against the remainder of the potatoes.

CHAPTER 18

Halla was forced to give Sarkis credit. He did not balk at any kitchen chores she set him.

He clearly had entirely ridiculous notions about beating men up in the market, but he scrubbed pans without complaint.

Still, between settling Bartholomew—"It's all right, I know we've descended on you and made a mess, cooking is the *least* I can do, no, no, go back to cataloguing, *please*, we don't require you to play host!"—and dealing with Sarkis's unexpected surliness, she was not feeling charitable towards men in general or either of them in specific by the time dinner was ready to eat.

It was not until she placed a dish in front of Sarkis and he looked up at her, startled, that she realized this was likely his first meal in...*heavens, it could be a century, couldn't it? Or more?*

This was an unexpected amount of pressure on a meal that Halla had whipped up in a strange kitchen. She hoped it didn't disagree with him. Still, she couldn't very well *not* feed him.

He took a bite, delicately, chewed for a moment, then shrugged and started eating.

Bartholomew came in, took a bowl, and went back to whatever he was doing in a back room. Cataloguing something or looking up something. He had books propped up around him. Halla made a mental note to go in an hour later and take the bowl away, because otherwise it would sit in his study for the next ten years, a lesson she had learned the hard way from Silas.

"Acceptable?" she asked Sarkis, as he finished the bowl and went for seconds.

"I have been outside the sword long enough to realize I am ravenous," he said. "I am sure it is very good, but I am currently a poor judge." Then he had thirds.

Well, she'd take it.

When he had plowed through three bowls, he did the dishes. He wasn't good at it, but he did his best. Halla leaned against the door frame and watched, slightly baffled.

"In my land, we use sand," he said. "For scouring. It does not freeze, unlike water."

"Well, that would explain it." She took the bowl away from him. "You said you led a band of warriors. I take it you didn't lead them anywhere with a lot of water?"

"Oh, frequently enough. But I confess, once I led the war band, I did not do many dishes. And no one wants to eat my cooking. My jobs were to plan our work, study maps, read orders." He picked up another bowl and tackled it again.

"And the potatoes?"

"My mother required me to peel many, many potatoes."

She left him to it.

"Sarkis?"

Halla's voice came from the dark, slightly above his head. Sarkis had been forced to lie slant-wise across the open stretch of floor, although he wasn't quite under the bed. If anyone did force their way in, they could take him out just by throwing the door open violently.

But they'll break their legs trying to get past the...whatever that piece of furniture is there...ornamental table thing... He had no idea what it was, but it had five legs and a stack of carved whalebone ships piled on top of it.

A far larger concern was that Halla would try to get up in the night and step on him.

"Sarkis? Are you awake?"

"Yes?"

"Why don't you want Bartholomew to know about the sword?"

"He collects rare antiquities. I am, by definition, a rare antiquity."

"Oh. Hmm. You think he'd want to collect you?"

Sarkis shrugged, then remembered she couldn't see it. "He might."

"But you're a person."

"A fact that stops surprisingly few people."

He waited for Halla to leap to Bartholomew's defense, but instead she said "Hmm. He and Silas could get very...oh, *focused*, I guess. I know sometimes they didn't always acquire things completely legally." Sarkis could hear the frown in her voice. "I guess I'd like to think he wouldn't try to take your sword, but I don't know if I'd be sure enough to swear he wouldn't. And if he tried, I don't know if I could make him understand about you. He might not listen. Silas wouldn't, when he got in these moods."

"If he tries to take the sword, you need only draw it. You are the wielder. I will teach him his mistake."

Halla sighed. "When you say it like that, I assume you mean

by stabbing him, and I'd rather you didn't. He's being very nice to put us up for the night."

"I will attempt to keep the stabbing to the bare minimum required."

"What, you're not going to threaten to put the whole countryside to the torch?"

"Not tonight."

"That's a relief."

After a time, her breathing evened out. Sarkis closed his eyes.

It was a relief that the bed was so small. He could not even fantasize about getting up and joining her in it.

You're assuming she'd even have you. She's about to be a very wealthy, very respectable widow, and you're not even human any longer. All you've got to offer is a battered old body covered in scars. No home, no lands, no prospect of either.

Go to sleep, old man. Tomorrow you'll be back on the road again.

It took him some time to realize that he was dreaming, because the world was not silver. He had dreamed inside the sword for so long that it seemed unnatural to have a dream that did not gleam like oiled steel.

Angharad and the Dervish sat across from him, a study in opposites—Angharad tall and powerful and reserved, the Dervish slim, absurdly handsome, every emotion visible on his angular face.

Sarkis knew on some level that they both must hate him now, but he did not see that in their faces.

"You're dreaming, boss," said the Dervish.

"Am I? Yes, of course, I must be." He nodded. "You aren't really here."

"No need to be insulting about it."

Angharad smiled, trading a look with Sarkis. They were both slower, more ponderous creatures than the Dervish. It would have been easy to resent him, but they both knew better.

"Strange job you have now," said the Dervish.

"I don't mind this one."

Angharad raised an eyebrow. The Dervish snorted. "Be careful," he started to say, and then the dream changed around them and the table they were sitting at went away, and all three of them were chained to a wall.

This again, thought Sarkis, unsurprised. He knew what came after. He moved his feet and the stalks of moldy straw on the floor rolled under his heels.

"I miss you both," said Sarkis, looking down the wall where his captains were chained. He would not have said such things before going into the sword, but since then, he had learned not to waste time.

"I know, boss."

Angharad nodded. "We miss you too."

"No." Sarkis shook his head. "You hate me. You must hate me by now. I failed you. It was my fault that you're trapped in the swords. You told me not to do it, Angharad. I didn't listen." He lifted his chained hands.

Angharad shrugged.

"Well," said the Dervish. "I probably do want to bash your head in. But that's out there." He gestured with one hand and Sarkis heard the chain clinking.

"Listen," said Angharad. "*She's* out there, too." She nodded toward the far side of the cell. There was a door, and through the door, Sarkis knew that the sorcerer-smith was waiting for them.

"She's dead," said Sarkis. "She's been dead for centuries."

"So have we," said the Dervish. "It doesn't stop us."

Angharad shook her head. "It hasn't stopped," she told him. "We're still going."

"Yes, but..."

The dream began to fray around him. Sarkis tried to cling to it. There was so much more he wanted to say to both of them, so many things he had to apologize for...

He opened his eyes and saw the ceiling of the crowded room. The only sound was Halla snoring softly on the bed.

Sarkis was glad that she was asleep. It would have been far too difficult to explain why he was so close to weeping.

CHAPTER 19

"My dear, what do you truly know of this Sarkis fellow who travels with you?"

Sarkis froze. He had been returning from an early morning trip to the privy and was padding down the hallway to the main room when Bartholomew's voice came to his ears. He paused outside the doorway, waiting to see what Halla would say.

"He's been wonderful," said Halla staunchly. "He's brave and very kind. I mean, he mutters about burning our civilization down occasionally, but I don't think he *means* anything by it."

Sarkis fought back a smile.

"Yes, but..." Bartholomew coughed. "He's...well, a man traveling alone with a woman and...not that I am implying anything, my dear! But he should have considered how it looked for your reputation!"

"We were fleeing the house by night! Aunt Malva set her guardsman on us to keep us from leaving! What should we have done, knocked on doors until someone answered and agreed to be a chaperone?"

"Well..." Sarkis couldn't see either of them, but he could picture Halla folding her arms and giving Bartholomew her you-are-being-rather-dense look. "Obviously at the time it was impractical, but once you were well away from that woman, he should have given a thought to your reputation."

"He did," said Halla. "He brought me *here*."

"My dear, I care for you as the niece I never had, but bringing a respectable woman to the house of an unmarried bachelor, even one as old as I am, is hardly the most proper thing."

"I'm a middle-aged widow, Bartholomew," said Halla. Now would be the weary one-of-us-is-stupid-and-I'm-pretty-sure-it-isn't-me expression. "If anyone thinks that I am debauched, it would probably be an improvement."

"Halla..."

"I mean it. I've been respectable for thirty-six years, and it got me locked in my own room by a grasping old woman who wanted me to marry her nasty clammy-handed son. I might as well try being less respectable for a while. If that means running off into the night with a man in a sword, so be it."

"A man in a...?"

Uh-oh. Sarkis stepped through the doorway hurriedly. "Man *with* a sword, I suspect she meant."

"Yes, that," said Halla, covering quickly. "Sorry, I'm still angry about Aunt Malva, and it's making my tongue knot up. The nerve of her! Locking me in my room like she owned Silas's house! And you know Silas couldn't stand her!"

"I remember," said Bartholomew wearily. "Oh gods, do I remember." He pushed a stack of papers aside to make room for Sarkis beside him. Sarkis pretended not to see and sat down beside Halla instead.

"Did you sleep well?" asked their host warily.

"Very well indeed. Thank you, Ser Bartholomew, for your hospitality."

"Oh, goodness." The man looked flustered. "It was nothing." He turned back and called for the serving girl. She came out with a mug for Sarkis and refilled those at the table from her teapot.

Sarkis nodded gravely. Halla's thigh was touching his all along its length and he knew that he should move over and give her a little more room, but the bench was not terribly long. She didn't seem to mind.

He found that he didn't mind either. His skin prickled with awareness.

Great god, it made no sense! Insomuch as Sarkis had a type, it was bold women who knew what they wanted. Halla was the farthest thing from bold, and not only did she not know what *she* wanted, she had an ability to make other people in the room start to question what *they* wanted.

Hell, she was doing it to Bartholomew right now. He'd said something about the dangers of a woman traveling alone and she'd just stared at him, baffled, until the poor man trailed off in confusion.

"But I'm not alone. I've got Sarkis with me."

"Yes, but..." Bartholomew obviously was trying to find a way to say that Sarkis might well be one of the dangers, but couldn't figure out a way to do it to his face. Sarkis smiled at him. The Dervish had always said that he had a very unsettling smile.

Halla wrapped her fingers around her mug. "I'm grateful for your concern, Bartholomew," she said. "Really and truly. You're the only person other than Sarkis who actually cares about me, not just my inheritance." She frowned. "Well, and my nieces, I hope, but it's been a few years since I've seen them. I'm hoping if I can sort this whole thing out, I'll be able to help them with dowries."

"That's very kind of you," said Bartholomew. "And of course I care. Silas was a tough old bast...err...bird..." he cleared his throat apologetically, "and you took excellent care of him. He lasted a lot longer than he would have if you hadn't taken him in hand."

He gave Sarkis a look that managed to be both apologetic and faintly hostile. Sarkis could understand the man's position. Though honor did not demand him to stand as Halla's elder male relative, he nevertheless felt an obligation based on friendship. Sarkis was an unknown quantity.

In his position, Sarkis would have stepped in and stood as her honorary uncle, but that was easy to say when one had nothing to lose and could easily best any of her relatives in a fight. Bartholomew was a reasonably hale older man, but he did not have the look of someone used to defending themselves in single combat.

Of course, there's probably not a lot of single combat here...

In truth, there wasn't much in the Weeping Lands either. Some decisions were much too important to rest on who had the superior strength of arms. In practice, everyone pretended that it was an option and then the clan lords arranged matters so that hardly anyone ever actually did it. There was a lot of posturing and holding one's fellows back. Indeed, one of the slang terms for "brother-in-law" translated as "arm-holder."

Single combat or no, Sarkis had to admit that he was glad not to have to stand as Halla's relative himself. It would have been awkward.

Halla shifted position to reach for the teapot and a little more of her leg came in contact with his. He was quite sure she wasn't doing it intentionally.

...awkward. Yes. It would be awkward.

I have been in the sword too damn long if merely sitting next to a woman makes me start to have thoughts like this.

"You will go on to Archon's Glory today?" asked Bartholomew. "Not that I'm trying to get rid of you, my dear—you're welcome to stay longer, of course!"

"I appreciate that." Halla patted his hand as if he was an ancient, doddering relative. "You've been very sweet. But no, we'll go on as soon as I've packed."

The man tried not to look too obviously relieved. Sarkis felt just as relieved to be going. He still wasn't sure why, but the collector made him nervous.

Well, soon we'll be back on the road. And there will undoubtedly be plenty of other things to be nervous about. No doubt we'll be set upon by a cult or rogue magi and Halla will give me a puzzled look and say, "Sorry, I didn't think to mention them..."

He was both pleased and faintly disappointed when she reappeared from the room, clad in her newly cleaned habit. It was not flattering, but at least he would not have to fend men off with a stick.

That Halla had absolutely no idea that men would find her attractive was either a sign that she was just as naïve as he thought or that men in the decadent south had no taste whatsoever. Possibly both.

"Shall we?" asked Halla.

"Let us go." He bowed slightly to their host. "Ser Bartholomew, thank you for your hospitality."

"Oh? Of course. Oh! You're welcome, I mean. Yes."

"Thank you so much," said Halla. "When we've gotten this all sorted, you'll absolutely have the first look at all of Silas's artifacts."

The man's gaze sharpened so quickly that Sarkis was reminded of an adder spotting prey. "I would like that very much, my dear. Very much indeed."

CHAPTER 20

Despite Sarkis's misgivings, the walk to Archon's Glory was a much easier one than the long road to Amalcross. The roads were full of drovers, pilgrims, merchants, and other travelers on foot. A trio of priests wearing the indigo cloaks of the Hanged Mother rode by. Halla could feel Sarkis stiffen beside her.

"Don't attract attention," she murmured. The Motherhood had only passed through Amalcross a handful of times, but Halla knew enough to stay out of their way. The last time, they had reduced the hostelkeeper's wife to tears with their sharp questions, and the general feeling was that she had gotten off lightly. In a battle of wills between the Hanged Mother's priests and the constables, no one believed that the constables would be able to keep the Motherhood from burning anyone they felt like burning.

Sarkis grumbled, pulling his cloak around his shoulders and slouching. As a disguise went, Halla had seen much better. There was simply no mistaking Sarkis for anything but a warrior, no matter what he was wearing.

Ah, well. People will probably be too busy staring at the frumpy woman with the big sword on her back to even notice him.

No one gave them any trouble. The inn that night was very full and both of them ended up sleeping in the stables alongside a dozen other travelers, which was at least warm, if not particularly private. Sarkis glared at anyone who came close to their spread cloaks. Halla just tried not to die from being poked to death by little jabby bits of straw.

The walls of the city were coming into view the next morning when Sarkis froze. "What is that?"

Halla followed his gaze. There was a wall, a few people, a gnole on some business of its own... "What's what?"

"The striped creature."

"Oh! That's a gnole."

"What is a gnole?"

"Errr..." Halla wasn't sure how to explain. Gnoles were small, badger-like creatures that favored brightly colored clothing and did odd-jobs in cities. They had shown up in Anuket City and environs about fifteen years ago, and hardly anyone noticed them anymore. There was even a small burrow of them in Rutger's Howe. Humans treated them with a sort of good-natured contempt, and the gnoles returned the favor. "Well, they look like that...they're nice enough. I mean, they're usually very polite. They show up and do work and keep things clean."

"Are they dangerous?"

This was a complicated question. Halla had to think about it. "Are humans dangerous?"

"Very."

"Then probably, yes. But I've never heard of a gnole attacking anybody. Or, I mean, I've heard of it, but usually from really drunk people who were probably attacked by their own feet, if you know what I mean, and tried to pin it on a gnole.

They don't bother anybody and they leave the world cleaner than it was, so most people don't have a problem with them."

Sarkis looked unconvinced. "We do not have them in the Weeping Lands."

Halla privately thought they didn't have a lot of things in the Weeping Lands, but it didn't seem diplomatic to say so. "They migrated in years ago. We didn't see them in the outlying towns much, but they were already in Archenhold by the time I moved here." She considered for a bit. "Errr...have you not met non-human people before?"

"A few. The Thinnang—the rabbit folk—have a dwelling in the Weeping Lands. And one encounters a minotaur from time to time near the sea, of course." He shrugged. "There are always stories of shapechangers and forest-folk, but I don't know how many are true."

"There's rune in the Vagrant Hills," said Halla. "At least there's supposed to be. I've never seen one. Mostly, though, there's gnoles."

The gnole in question was long gone. The crowd had begun to grow thicker as they approached Archen's Glory.

"A defensible city," said Sarkis, eyeing Archen's Glory with approval. "At least the core. The rest would be burned during a siege, of course."

"Well, Archenhold's right on Anuket's doorstep," said Halla, shrugging. "They have to maintain their independence or they'd get swallowed up. So they keep the city walls maintained and their standing army is no joke. Young men from Rutger's Howe would go join up if they wanted to impress young women."

"Did it?"

"Did it what?"

"Impress the young women."

"I'm not sure. It didn't impress *me*, anyway, when I was young."

Sarkis actually laughed. Halla had grown to appreciate his laughter all the more for its rarity. "Wise girl. In the steading, they said the foolish girls sighed after warriors, but the smart ones married the farmers."

"The steading?"

"Where I grew up."

"In the Weeping Lands?"

"Yes."

"What was it like?"

He appeared to consider this at some length, as they approached the outer city of Archen's Glory. Brightly colored banners hung over the streets, flapping in the wind. The houses were no more than two stories high, which gave the outer city an oddly truncated appearance.

"It was...empty," he said finally.

Halla looked at him, puzzled. "What was?"

"The steading."

"Oh! Err...why was it empty?"

"All of the Weeping Lands is empty. The wind howls over the grass and you think you can see for a thousand miles. But you can't. There are folds and hills and clefts in the earth. It is rotten with holes and old places."

"Do you miss it?"

"Very much."

Halla frowned, reaching behind her head to touch the hilt of the sword. "Do you need to go back? I mean, if you're homesick, you should definitely—"

"I am *not* homesick."

"Oh."

The road they were on split into a dozen streets. Despite the earliness of the hour, stalls were already being set up along the streets and women carrying full water jugs streamed past.

"*I'd* be homesick," said Halla.

"That does not surprise me."

"Are you sure you don't want to go back?"

Sarkis stopped so abruptly that Halla continued a pace or two past him before she realized he'd stopped. "Are you asking me to leave your service, lady?"

"What? No! I mean, if you want to go, I'd miss you, but..."

He raised an eyebrow. "You'd miss me."

It didn't sound like a question, but Halla plowed ahead anyway. "Yes! I mean, you're very...uh...there." She waved her hands in the general outline of his body. "Very *there*. I'd notice if you weren't there."

They paused in a large stone courtyard with a well. A pump stood to one side, with a tin cup on a chain beside it. Sarkis filled the cup and handed it to Halla before drinking himself.

"I will not go back to the Weeping Lands," he said. "As long as I do not, then in my heart, they are all still there, still alive, unchanged. If I return, I will see what hundreds of years have wrought, and my heart will know that they are dead."

Halla stared at him, her mouth open.

"I find that I would rather be an exile in my heart than the last survivor. Now where is your temple to your very sensible rat god?"

Halla pointed, then led the way when he fell into his accustomed guard position. She hardly knew what to say.

"I'm sorry," she said finally.

She expected him to grunt, but he said, "As am I," and that was all that needed to be said.

CHAPTER 21

The Temple of the White Rat stood near the edge of Archen's Glory. It was a busy complex, not as ostentatious as the temples of the Forge or Dreaming God, but full of human activity. It was built of pale sandstone with sharply slanted rooftops. Arched doorways set around the main courtyard stood open and people streamed through the doors. Acolytes in white robes carried things from place to place, or escorted the faithful to those who could better serve their needs.

Despite the numbers, there was a pervasive air of calm and order, as if everyone knew where they were supposed to be and what they should be doing to make the system work smoothly.

It reminded Sarkis of nothing so much as a softly humming beehive.

He wondered if it contained a hidden sting as well.

Halla led the way, not to the nave but to a side door that looked like offices. A line of petitioners was already forming.

"We're standing in line," observed Sarkis.

"Well, yes. We're petitioners."

"I would think that we had priority."

"We're not that important. Are we?"

Sarkis looked over the other people in line. It did not seem likely that any of them were also enchanted swords.

"I suspect we may be a trifle more unusual than they are used to seeing."

"Maybe, but we're going to be polite." She nudged him in the ribs. "Anyway, only one of us is getting any older and I don't mind waiting."

He stifled a sigh. "I might age outside the sword."

"Oh! Really?"

"I don't know. I haven't spent that long outside it, all told."

Halla looked suddenly worried. "Should I keep it sheathed more? I don't want you to be aging for nothing."

"No, it's fine. It's been...well, a long time since I ate and slept and walked about. It's been good to remember what it's like to be human."

The woman in front of them looked over her shoulder and said "You can go ahead of me."

Halla blinked. "Really?"

"Sir...ma'am...I'm here because my youngest needs to get out of the house and learn a trade. You two appear to be either enchanted or desperately insane. And in either case, I'd rather you weren't standing *behind* me."

"You're very kind," said Halla.

"And obviously very wise," added Sarkis, bowing.

They ultimately stood in line for about twenty minutes. Three more people looked at the sword, or perhaps Sarkis's expression, and suddenly decided that they'd rather have him dealt with sooner rather than later. They might have gotten past even sooner, but one of the men in line made the mistake of mentioning that he trained guard geese, and Halla peppered him with questions about guard geese until the acolytes came for him.

Eventually an acolyte ushered them through the stone arch and down a corridor.

The priest of the White Rat was a slender person with a pointed chin and long gray hair braided back from their face. Their vestments bore the slender silver stripe indicating the polite form of address. They beckoned, gestured to chairs, and said, "How may the Temple help you, friends?"

Halla sat down and said, "I've inherited a lot of money and a magic sword, and now my relatives want to force me to marry my cousin, so I ran away, but now I don't know how to get back to get the money, or even if I can, and they've told everyone that I was kidnapped."

"I...see." The priest looked over at Sarkis. "And you are...?"

"The magic sword."

The priest had a calm, reserved face but one eyebrow began to climb, very slowly, towards their hair.

"Uh, yes, this is Sarkis. He's been trapped in a magic sword. He serves the wielder, which is me. I was trying to kill myself to get away from my relatives but I used his sword to do it and summoned him. This sword here." She slung it off her back.

The other eyebrow joined its mate in the slow march toward the priest's hairline. They steepled their fingers. "This is...quite a story. Could you start again from the beginning?"

She did. Sarkis watched the priest very obviously not asking questions until the end, when they asked only one.

"May I see the sword?"

"Oh, yes." Halla laid it across the priest's desk. "If you sheath it, he goes back in the sword. Here, I'll show you. Sarkis?"

He nodded.

Halla untied the cords holding it open, and pushed the blade into the scabbard. Blue flame jittered around Sarkis as he vanished.

The priest fell back in their chair with their mouth open. Then they started to laugh. "Oh my! Oh, by the tail of God. Well done. If that's an illusion, I've no idea how you did it."

"It's not," said Halla. "Here, you draw it and..."

"May I? In case you are giving some signal that I cannot see..."

"Sure, go ahead."

The priest drew the sword. Sarkis flickered into existence behind Halla's shoulder.

The priest hastily sheathed it again and Sarkis vanished. They drew, saw the blue fire, sheathed.

After the fourth round of this, Sarkis reached out his hand and said, "Please stop. I'm getting dizzy."

"Oh, yes. Apologies." They sat back with a broad grin. "The sword summons you, then? Are you a demon or a djinn?"

"No," said Sarkis. "I'm a man, or was when I went into the blade."

"He went into the sword centuries ago to help fight a war," said Halla. "By being a weapon. Now he's stuck there."

Sarkis rolled his eyes at this characterization. "It wasn't *quite* like that..."

"How fascinating!" The priest shook their head, chuckling. "Gentlefolk, you are well above my pay grade, though I thank you for livening up my morning. I will take you to the bishop."

Bishop Beartongue was a tall, muscular woman with short graying hair, wearing vestments. She listened to the priest's murmured explanation, raised her own eyebrows, and beckoned Halla and Sarkis into her office.

Other than being larger and slightly more cluttered, her room was similar to the one that the priest had been in. The only major difference was a massive oak desk, over which the bishop stared at them.

"Zale has told me a story I can hardly believe," she said,

"but they are the least fanciful of priests. Suppose you start from the beginning?"

Halla started from the beginning again.

The bishop asked a great many questions, and not only about Sarkis and the sword. Alver's family had no claim on her except by her former marriage? Halla was sincere in her desire not to marry her cousin?

"He has clammy hands," said Halla.

"Avert!" said Beartongue, making a warding gesture. "We'll say no more, then." She continued the questions. Did Halla know the exact amount of Silas's estate? As much as that? Fascinating. She had been trying to kill herself? Why? Did she wish to die otherwise? No? They had run then? Yes, understandably so.

She stopped the polite interrogation long enough to order food and drink brought in, and watched them eat with interest. Then she turned to Sarkis and went through an abbreviated version of the same tests the priest had done, sword sheathed and then unsheathed.

"Would you object terribly, Widow Halla, to leaving the room while I try this? Forgive my suspicion, I mean no offense, but this is so very unusual, and while you do not seem like a liar, I would be remiss in my service to the Rat if I did not take all precautions."

"Oh no, go ahead." Halla pushed her chair back. "Err... Sarkis? It's okay with you, right?"

He nodded. He held the bishop's eyes, though, while he said, "And now *I* mean no offense, but in the event that they try to steal the blade, lady, do not leave the Temple complex. As soon as they draw it again, I will find you. I will not be separated from my wielder except by *her* choice, Bishop."

Beartongue inclined her head. "Fair and more than fair."

Halla took an apple from the tray, stepped outside the room, and leaned against the wall.

She had time to finish most of the apple before the bishop called her back in. Sarkis was sitting in the chair where she had left him, but he had slid down in it, his hands folded together, studying the bishop with unreadable eyes.

"This is truly amazing," Beartongue said. "We are used to artificers coming in from Anuket City, occasionally with marvels, to the occasional relic that someone claims is from the ancient civilizations, but you are something else entirely. A true work of magic." She leaned back in her chair. "Wonderworkers who can do some small feat are one thing, but this..." She shook her head.

Sarkis said nothing.

"But you have come to us to solve a problem," said Beartongue, as Halla sat, "not to have us gawk. So we have several options."

She tapped her finger on the table. "First of all, the Temple of the White Rat, for a tithe, will arrange to help you retrieve your inheritance. It will cost you—oh—twenty percent, let us say, which includes arranging to sell your uncle's house if you wish. I am honor-bound to tell you that you do not need us to do so, that legally the estate is yours and the only barrier is your husband's relatives. But I also understand that family can be..." She pursed her lips. "...trying."

Halla gave a single laugh that sounded high and hysterical in her own ears and clamped it down immediately. "Sorry."

Sarkis reached out and took her hand.

Am I to be manhandled again?

It did not feel like manhandling. It felt like comfort, and that was a very strange thing to be taking from the touch of an enchanted sword. Had his hands always been so warm? She couldn't remember. She looked down at their joined hands, his fingers dark bands across her pale skin. He rubbed his thumb gently across her palm and she glanced up at him, but his face was as hard and remote as ever.

"Mistress Halla?"

"I'm fine," she said. "Sorry. It's been...well, a long week."

"The Temple can make this easier for you." Beartongue smiled. "Providing advocates is one of the Rat's primary functions. We are very hard to bully."

"I'd like that," said Halla. "Err...very much."

"There is also the separate matter of the sword." She picked up the sword, drew it partway out. The steel made an almost silken noise against the scabbard. The etched words that Halla couldn't read winked in the light.

The hand clasped in hers was suddenly gone as Beartongue clicked the sword into the scabbard.

"Now," said the bishop quietly, "we are alone. You may speak freely, Halla. The White Rat is very old and nothing shocks Him any longer. Are you in danger?"

"Danger?" said Halla, baffled.

"Your enchanted companion," said Beartongue. "Do you fear him? Has he harmed you? Does he have any hold over you? We can have you safely away, if you do not wish to stay in his company."

"I...oh!" Halla's hand flew to her mouth. "Oh! You think he might really have kidnapped me, or he's threatened me or something like that? Is that what you're asking?"

"That is indeed what I'm asking."

"Oh no, no. Sarkis would never do anything like that. He's really very kind. I mean, he mutters about burning my civilization to the ground a lot, but that's just his way. Although I don't know that he likes me very much. He counts to very high numbers sometimes."

Beartongue blinked slowly at this.

"Anyway, he saved me from Cousin Alver and got me away when they sent the constables out. And didn't let me kill myself. He wouldn't hurt me. Actually, I don't think he can hurt me. He's supposed to guard the owner of the sword. Although he did manhandle me into quite a few ditches those first few days—no, not in a mean way!" she added, as the bishop began to look alarmed. "I mean, we were being chased by the constables on horseback, because of the stabbing. Did I mention the stabbing?"

"You mentioned that your companion fought a guardsman, yes."

"Right. He got stabbed. Well, both of them got stabbed. Roderick worse though. Oh dear! We'll need to sort that out with the constables too, won't we?"

Bishop Beartongue put her chin in her hand. "This will be substantially more difficult if the guardsman is dead. The Temple will need to make inquiries, but if it is, indeed, merely a...tragic misunderstanding...perhaps we can help to smooth that over as well."

Halla sighed with relief. "That would be good."

Beartongue tapped a finger on the scabbard before her. "If you wish," she said, almost diffidently, "the Temple will purchase this sword from you."

"What?"

"Purchase. It is an artifact of the sort that none of us have ever seen." She smiled abruptly, and looked half her age. "Or you are charlatans of incredible skill, and I will be losing a large amount of the Temple's money to you. But at that point, I would say that you had earned it."

"How *would* someone fake that?" asked Halla, distracted by the notion. "You might be able to do the blue light with phosphor of some sort, but then we'd have to make Sarkis disappear..." She chewed on her lower lip.

Beartongue frowned.

"Sorry," Halla began. "I get interested in things."

"It'd be easiest if he wasn't here to begin with," said the bishop of the White Rat thoughtfully. "If you have very good mirrors, you can do extraordinary illusions, making someone appear to be somewhere else. But if you could afford to get a glass of that size made and silvered, you wouldn't be asking for our help with your estate. And I've no idea how you'd get the glass in here, and your companion moved the chair when he sat down, so someone of flesh and blood is definitely in his place."

Halla leaned forward, fascinated. "How *would* you make a mirror glass that large?"

"I know it's possible," said the bishop. "But only done in a very few places—Anuket City is one, actually—and even then, I'm told that nine out of ten break in the process. It has something to do with the heating point of lead and the impurities in the sand, and they guard the secret jealously. There was a wonderworker, I'm told, who worked with hot glass, and they made amazing mirrors, but that was a hundred years gone and only a few survive."

"What if we had a wonderworker who could turn invisible?" asked Halla. "That would be a lot easier, wouldn't it?"

"If your companion is one, that would explain it," admitted Beartongue. "But I sheathed the sword while he had turned to watch you go into the hall, and he still vanished, even when he was unaware of it happening." She tapped her fingers together. "We would need a way to test for that..."

Halla snapped her fingers. "Bars!"

"Bars?"

"You could do it with bars, or a grate if it was big enough. You summon him in one room, then sheath the sword, pass it through the grate, and unsheathe it. He'd appear next to the sword again, and then you'd know he wasn't just invisible."

Beartongue nodded slowly. "That *would* work. Although..."

She cleared her throat sheepishly, apparently realizing that they were getting rather far from the matter at hand. "Probably an additional few tests would be required before we could pay you. But at any rate, we are prepared to offer you a high price for the sword, if you wish to part with it."

"Sell the..." Halla finally focused on the other part of the sentence. "I can't sell Sarkis! He's not mine!" Halla frowned. "I mean, he's sort of mine, I suppose, but I can't sell him! He's a person!"

Bishop Beartongue nodded. "I thought as much. A shame, but an understandable one."

She drew the sword.

The familiar blue fire swirled upward and left Sarkis standing just behind Halla's chair.

"Well," said the bishop, nodding to Sarkis. "If you will leave your information with my clerk about where you can be reached, we will be in touch tomorrow, when we have an appropriate priest ready to travel with you to...Rutger's Howe, was it? And then we will see what can be done about your inheritance."

Halla nodded and stood up. "Thank you for your help, Bishop Beartongue."

"Of course." Her eyes crinkled at the corners as she smiled. "Thank you. A very unusual situation. I'm glad that the Temple will be able to help. And if I may offer a note of caution?"

Halla raised her eyebrows. "Yes?"

"Be careful who you tell about the sword. Such an object may breed greed. The fewer people who know, the safer you are."

"Oh." Halla frowned, glancing at Sarkis. "I don't think we've told anyone but you and the priest at the front. And some of the people in line may have guessed something..."

"Good," said Beartongue. "Stay safe. And thank you."

They turned to leave. As they neared the door, the bishop said, "Sarkis."

He looked over his shoulder.

"You were right."

CHAPTER 22

"What did she mean by that?" asked Halla, as they left the White Rat's compound.

"I said you'd ask too many questions," said Sarkis, which was not exactly a lie.

She gave him an exasperated look. "She answered them, though!"

"Did she?"

"Oh, it was fascinating. We talked about how to fake a magic sword, and then how you'd test to see if a magic sword was fake. And about mirrors. It was really very interesting."

"Mmm."

"And do you know that she wanted me to sell you to the Temple?" said Halla. She was scurrying to keep up and he slowed his stride.

Sarkis grunted again. After a moment, he said, "What did you say?"

"I told her no! Obviously!"

She sounded indignant at the very idea. He was obscurely pleased by this, and yet he kept poking at it like a sore tooth. "She would have given you a great deal of money."

Halla was getting out of breath following him. "Yes, but—dammit, Sarkis, slow down!"

He stopped and glanced around the streets of Archen's Glory, then caught her arm and steered her through the bustling crowd to the mouth of an alley, out of the way of the crowd. He had known that the White Rat's bishop planned to ask if she would sell the sword. He knew this because the woman had told him outright.

"She will not sell," Sarkis had said.

"Are you certain of that?"

He was. He didn't know *why* he was—he had known the blasted woman for all of a week, after all. She was alone in the world, with very little money until her grasping relatives were dealt with. She could have used the money to set herself up very nicely. It would have been entirely sensible for her to sell.

He also knew that Halla wouldn't do it.

She is far too tender-hearted and you know her feelings on slavery.

Slavery had been the bishop's next question, in fact. "Do you wish to be free of her? I confess, there is no legal description of your current status, but if you are in her service unwillingly, it is within my power to decide that you are being held as a slave. That is illegal, and the Temple will fight to have you freed."

"You will *not!*"

He hadn't realized that he raised his voice until the echoes went clashing around the room. The bishop put up one slow eyebrow at him.

"I am sorry, holy one," he had said, willing to give her the respect due a true priest, even if she served a soft southern god. "I should not shout. I find Lady Halla's service acceptable. Compared to many past wielders, it is...congenial."

She had nodded, and then called Halla back inside.

The congenial wielder in question now looked down at his hand on her elbow, and then pointedly back up at him.

"Sorry," said Sarkis, releasing her. "I forget myself."

"It's all right," she said. "You've been much better about the manhandling." She frowned up at him. "Anyway, of course I wouldn't sell! It doesn't matter how much money they offered me. I mean, you're a person! That's not how it works!"

"You would not be the first to grow tired of my company."

Those gray eyes narrowed. Confusion? Annoyance? "I'm not tired of you," she said. "You saved me. I'm grateful."

Sarkis found his jaw clenching. It wasn't her gratitude that he wanted.

Well, what do you want, then?

He didn't know. Or rather, he knew exactly what he wanted and it was a terrible idea.

I should not want anything. She is the wielder of the sword and I am her servant. I will serve until I am no longer called to do so. That is all that I can do.

He said this to himself three or four times, until it was absolutely clear in his mind, and then Halla reached out and touched his arm, frowning. "Sarkis? Are you all right?"

"The great god have mercy," he said, and kissed her.

SARKIS KNEW that the kiss was a mistake the moment he did it. He kept doing it anyway, at first because stopping a kiss so quickly offended his sense of craftsmanship, and then because it felt too good to stop.

Halla's lips were warm and soft. So was the rest of her. Her hands lay flat against his chest, and then, as the kiss went on, curled to clutch the edges of his surcoat. He pressed closer against her, feeling her body begin to mold against his.

This is a terrible idea, he told himself conversationally, sliding his tongue along her lips until she parted them.

Yes, and?

Well. Just so you're clear.

She tasted like apple and she had very little idea how to kiss, but she seemed to be figuring it out quickly. He slid his hands up her arms and tilted his head, deepening the kiss until she made a small sound—*approval? astonishment? dismay?* He didn't know, and the fact that he wasn't sure made him end the kiss and pull back.

This is why it's a terrible idea. You don't know what she wants. And even if she doesn't want you as anything but a guardsman, she needs your services to get her back home safely. She might be afraid to reject you for fear of her own safety.

Better women have made worse bargains, and will again before the world ends. It's your job to keep her from having to make a bargain like that.

Sarkis might not know what he wanted, but he was damn sure that he didn't want Halla to submit to his desires simply because she needed his help.

She did not particularly look like a woman making a bad bargain. She was flushed and her lips were still slightly parted.

"I'm sorry," he said, his voice clipped.

Halla blinked at him. "Oh," she said. "I...uh. Okay."

"I shouldn't have done that."

"I didn't mind?" she said, and then looked down at her hands on his chest and blushed suddenly scarlet. She dropped his surcoat as if she had been burned. Sarkis stepped back hurriedly to give her room.

"I...uh. Yes. Of course." She nodded to him. "You're a respectable widow. I understand."

Sarkis waited.

"I mean, *I'm* a respectable widow. Me. Not you. Very

respectable." She seemed to have trouble catching her breath. "Not that you're *not* respectable, of course. Which is...err...are you going to do that again?"

"Not without your permission."

"Oh." Sarkis wasn't sure if he was imagining her disappointment. "Right. Okay. Uh."

Now why did I do that?

Obviously because you wanted to. Sarkis occasionally thought that his own mind believed he was an idiot. He only wished that he had evidence his mind was wrong.

He led her from the alley, back into the market. "The priest to travel with us will not be ready until tomorrow," he said. "Are there any errands you need to run between now and then?"

Halla still looked a bit out of breath, but suddenly brightened. "Yes! I need clothes. More clothes. Any clothes, really. They don't have to be good. Just something to wear that isn't this." She fingered the hem of the habit, looking glum. "This was a very nice outfit once and now I think I would like to have it burned."

Sarkis privately thought she should burn it and buy something that suited her better, but he was her guardsman, not her maid.

"Do you have the funds?"

"We will once I sell this jewelry."

The trader who bought and sold gems and metalwork looked at Halla's offerings and grimaced. "This is old-fashioned stuff," he said, picking up a necklace.

"My husband had old-fashioned taste," said Halla.

The trader glanced at Sarkis, who was looming in the background, then over to Halla.

"Not him. He's my bodyguard. My husband's dead."

"Sorry for your loss."

"That makes one of us. Look, I know the craftsmanship's not great, but surely the gold is worth something."

"Well..."

He ended up weighing most of it on a scale and counting out coins. Two pieces were deemed unobjectionable enough to sell, and he counted out more.

"Could be worse," said Halla, pocketing the money as they walked away. "This should get me at least a change of clothes."

"I am sorry you had to sell your jewelry," said Sarkis.

Her gray eyes were amused, if slightly puzzled. "Why? I never wore it. I can't even say I had fond memories, since I'm pretty sure his mother picked it out. But she favored heavy stuff, so she did me a good turn after all, since I had to sell it by weight."

Sarkis offered her his arm while they made their way to the clothier's stalls. She held his elbow. Her hands were small, with slim fingers, particularly compared to his. Had he never noticed that before?

As it turned out, Halla was an excellent haggler. Sarkis didn't know why that surprised him. Clearly she'd been running a household for years, and getting a good price for something was a skill you had to acquire. He had never enjoyed it and had delegated as soon as possible. The Dervish had been much better at it than Sarkis. People were surprisingly willing to give a very handsome man with big, sad eyes a deal. Not so with Sarkis.

"It doesn't help that you say, 'Is that your best price?'" like you're about to beat them over the head," the Dervish had told him once. "Threats of bodily harm lower the price once. After that, they just make people stubborn."

Halla, of course, did not threaten anyone with bodily harm. She just asked questions. Very...pointed...questions. And then the questions led to anecdotes.

"Oh, where is this from? And what's the thread made of? Really! And how long ago was that? I see. This dye is so lovely, but is it waterproof? Are you sure? Because my cousin had a batch almost this color—not as nice, though, yours is better—and the first time she wore it in the rain, she looked like she'd got gangrene. I mean, she did actually get gangrene later when the ox bit her, but that wasn't related to the fabric. Her forearm got all oozy. It was terrible. The smell, too. The leeches couldn't do anything. The Temple of the Four-Faced God did their best, but you know how it is when you take off a limb, everything's very touch and go. She made a full recovery, though! Well, except for the arm. Obviously *that* didn't recover. But it hardly slows her down at all. Can't wear this color at all, though, says it brings back bad memories. Do you have anything like that in brown?"

By the end of this recitation, the shopkeeper was just staring at her with a stunned expression. Sarkis didn't know how much of a discount Halla got on that deal, but she walked away with a brown gown and a pleased expression.

"Do you even *have* a cousin?" he asked under his breath.

"Only on Alver's side, and I wouldn't care if he got gangrene clear up to his nose."

"You made all that up?"

"Heh. You should see me get a deal on candles. I've got a story about a house fire that'll curl your nose hair."

"Does that work?"

"Only on people who haven't heard it before. Most of the people in Rutger's Howe know me, of course. I had to save it for traveling merchants." She smiled slyly, an expression that he wouldn't have thought Halla could manage. "Not that I didn't pull it out occasionally back home, mind you."

Sarkis shook his head, remembering what Halla had said

when they met the priests of the Hanged Mother. *Nobody kills stupid women, they just kick them out of the way.*

His own survival strategies had mostly involved putting a sword into the enemy before the enemy put one in him, but if you didn't have that option, presumably you learned to adapt.

Halla certainly held her own with the merchants. The man who sold socks even tried to flirt with her. Sarkis was fairly certain that Halla didn't realize this, but it was hard to tell how much was an act and how much was just...well...*Halla.*

After the third or fourth statement about how a well-turned ankle deserved a well-turned heel, Sarkis stepped forward and looked at the man very hard. The man turned slightly gray, pressed the socks into Halla's hands, and finished his business with admirable speed.

"That was odd," murmured Halla, as they walked away. "Do you think I did something to upset him?"

Sarkis grunted. "Don't know. Do you have anything else you need to purchase?"

"No, this should cover everything for the trip back." She looked over at him. "Do *you* need anything?"

"I have not needed anything for hundreds of years."

"Well, fine, have you *wanted* anything?"

Sarkis knew she meant equipment for the road—extra socks or scissors or spices, something of the sort that people carried when they travel—but it still took him a moment to quell his immediate thought.

"Nothing they sell at the market," he said. Halla nodded, apparently taking that statement at face value, and he wasn't sure if he was relieved or disappointed.

CHAPTER 23

They stayed at a hostel near the temple. The accommodations were minimalist and Sarkis did not care for the lack of security, but it was free to petitioners of the Rat waiting on the Temple's response. *And as we are all staying ten to a room, even if I do begin to have foolish thoughts, I certainly cannot act on them.*

There was some slight difficulty as the hostelkeeper wished to put Halla in the women's wing and Sarkis in the men's. Sarkis folded his arms and glared at the woman. She was a nun, so she folded her arms and glared right back.

They might have stood there until the air ignited from the force of the glaring, but Halla said, "Look, I'll sleep with the sword right next to me," and elbowed Sarkis in the ribs.

He grumbled. "You will use it at the first sign of trouble."

"I promise."

He suffered the nun to lead him away.

I truly hope she does not decide to go to a nunnery when all this is over. I will probably get her thrown out for arguing with the nuns, if she does not get herself thrown out for questioning them.

Also, it would be a terrible waste of good breas—

He dragged his mind forcibly out of the gutter.

The hostelkeeper showed him where he could leave his belongings, which was a bit puzzling for both of them. "I have none," he admitted.

"Ah," she said. And then, to his astonishment, the old nun's face softened, almost imperceptibly. "I understand. There's no shame in it, my son. We all fall upon hard times. We must lift each other up, that's all."

Explaining would have been far too difficult, and Sarkis did not have it in him to turn down compassion freely offered. The great god knew that the woman was correct. He bowed his head politely, and went to join Halla for lunch.

She had changed into the new clothes—a snug bodice and a full skirt. The bodice did not cover her the way the habit had, and it furthermore was lifting certain...assets...in a way that surely had to be incredibly indecent.

Sarkis looked around a bit wildly, and saw that the nun didn't so much as blink when she saw Halla.

Apparently this is how they dress in the south. And nobody sees anything wrong with it.

He had an intense urge to rush over and cover her breasts. Possibly with his face.

"Is something wrong?" asked Halla.

No, I'm just coming to terms with the fact that I'm a ravening animal, not a man.

Then again, I've been coming to terms with that since I was four-teen, so what else is new?

"It's fine," he told Halla. And then, although it pained him, "You look nice."

Halla beamed at him. Then she blushed. Sarkis suspected that Halla was not used to compliments and now had proof that the blush went...well, quite a long way down.

Settle down, man. You're a warrior, not a rutting boar. You've seen breasts before.

Yes, but these are really good breasts. And their owner is...

"Are you *sure* you're all right? You're staring off into the distance."

"Fine!" said Sarkis, a trifle too loudly. One of the nuns looked at him disapprovingly. This was actually helpful. He sat down hurriedly and fixed his eyes firmly on Halla's face.

Know your place. She is your wielder. You have no rights here. If she chose to wander about wearing nothing but strategically placed lizards, that would be her choice, and you would say nothing. Know. Your. Place.

The hostel served food on long tables. It was plain, filling, not particularly elegant fare, but there was a great deal of it. Sarkis had not thought about eating, but the server brought him a bowl anyway. Some kind of thick wheat noodles, with onion and small salted fish chopped over it. More onion than fish and more noodle than either, but not the worst he'd seen.

He stared at it, then shrugged and began to eat. It wasn't the worst he'd tasted, either.

"What will you do if the priest cannot get your inheritance back?" he asked between bites, still thinking of the nunnery.

Halla blinked at him. "Uh. I...well, I guess I'm no worse off than I was." She frowned. "Except for the bit where I can't hire on as a housekeeper to whoever takes the house. So...well. It could be bad."

Sarkis frowned. "Bad how?"

She propped her chin on her fist. "Bad enough. I suppose I'll find a church to take me in. Without a payment of some sort, I can't hope to join a nunnery as anything but a servant, though. Even a bride of the gods requires a dowry. But...well..." She shrugged. "There's usually work somewhere for someone who can scrub a floor."

He scowled into the noodles for long moments. "You must sell the sword if that happens."

She looked up, startled. "I can't do that!"

He shook his head. "You will have to. I will not allow you to be a drudge somewhere merely for my convenience."

"Sarkis, I can't..."

"The other alternative is that you and I take up work as mercenaries, and that is entirely too dangerous. If I could go any significant distance from the sword, I would do it, but I will not place you in harm's way."

Halla blinked at him, apparently trying to imagine life as a mercenary. Sarkis tried to picture Halla working a contract and wasn't sure if he wanted to laugh or break out in a cold sweat. *We're supposed to guard this caravan? All right. Why? Oh. No, I just thought you might have an interesting reason. I had a cousin who guarded caravans, but then a horse stepped on him and then his foot fell off...no, no, the two were actually unrelated. But he got out of the business after that. Oh, hello there mister bandit, now why did you go into this line of work...?*

No, it didn't bear thinking about.

"Do...do you want a different wielder?" Halla asked after a moment. There was an unexpectedly fragile look in her eyes.

"No!" He didn't know if he was reacting to the question or the look, only that he didn't want her to look like that. "I just don't want you to suffer because you think you have to keep me around."

He went back to his meal, shoulders hunching. The thought of no longer seeing Halla was an unexpectedly sharp knife in his gut.

Don't be foolish. You've known the woman for less than a week.

She smiled at him abruptly. The knife twisted.

You will only fail her in time, as you have failed all your people. If she sells the sword, perhaps you can avoid that somehow.

"Well, hopefully the Temple will take care of all that," she said.

He grunted.

"Well," said Halla, sitting back. "It is somehow only the middle of the day. I have a thought about what we could do next, but...err...I don't want to offend you..."

Sarkis had a brief, mad hope that she was propositioning him and stared at her. *Surely not.* "What?"

"There's a library in Archen's Glory," she said. "A pretty good one. I thought we could go dig around in there, maybe find a scholar who's willing to talk, and maybe we can work out how long you've been in the sword."

Sarkis blinked at her. It had been so long since a wielder had cared where he was from—had even seen him as a person with a history, rather than a weapon—that he had almost lost sight of the question himself.

"Oh," he said, a bit faintly. "I...Yes. I would like that."

"Great!" Halla pushed back from the table. "Let's go."

THE LIBRARY WAS a testimony to civic architecture—large, clean, set back off a courtyard with a fountain. Friezes of scholars engaged in debate gazed down on them benevolently. Halla had visited once before with Silas, and was pleased to see that nothing much had changed. She walked up to the attendant just inside the doors and said, just as Silas had years ago, "Is there someone who could assist us with a historical research question?"

She was just congratulating herself on handling this like a competent person and not a yokel from a tiny backwater town when the attendant gave her a weary smile. "There are many kinds of history, ma'am," he said. "Can you narrow it down a bit?"

"Uh...hmm..."

"Military," put in Sarkis.

The attendant nodded. "Go straight back and turn right, then take the second left. There's a woman back there named Morag who can probably put you on the right track."

The path was not quite so clear cut as the attendant had suggested. There were about five possible places to turn right, and Halla was briefly distracted by an enormous statue of a minotaur with improbable endowments—*my goodness, that can't possibly be to scale, can it?*—and then Sarkis very clearly noticed her noticing the minotaur and she blushed scarlet while he grinned.

Why did the man make her blush so easily? She was a respectable widow, for the gods' sake.

This made her think of the fact that he'd been kissing her not two hours earlier. And then that led to other thoughts about Sarkis, possibly in comparison to the minotaur, and that only made her blush harder. She put both hands to her burning cheeks and muttered something about it being hot.

"Well, if our bull-headed associate is any indication, it certainly isn't cold in here."

"You are a *wretch*."

By the time they had located their historical scholar, Halla had finally stopped blushing. Morag was a dark-skinned, heavyset woman with her hair in narrow braids, the whole mass pulled back from her face with golden cords. She looked from Sarkis to Halla and back again. "My specialty is military history," she said. "What can I help you fine people with?"

Halla had been trying to work out the best way to ask questions without revealing Sarkis's secret. She had had an idea at last, and was rather proud of it.

"This is my friend Sarkis. He's from...ah...well, a long way away. We're not sure how far away. His people tell a great many stories about battles, and we're wondering if you can help us figure out where and when some of those battles took place, so we can work out his people's history."

Morag put her chin in her hand. "Now that's an interesting request. How specific are the stories?"

Halla glanced at Sarkis, who was looking at her with surprise and approval. "Very specific," he said. "I can tell you at least the local geography and what the people involved called themselves."

"A good start," said Morag. She gestured for them to follow and went deeper into the stacks, eventually stopping in front of a map cabinet. "Start with one, and let us see if anything rings a bell."

"The lord called himself the Leopard..." Sarkis began.

IT TOOK HOURS. There were false starts and false leads. But at last Sarkis was able to point to a place on the map and say "There. That is where the Weeping Lands must have been."

"Modern Baiir," said Morag. "You're a long way from home." Sarkis inclined his head.

"And this battle, here..." he said, tapping his finger on the map. "The fortified keep held by mercenaries."

"Four hundred and fifty years ago, give or take," said Morag. "A lot of messy battles around that period. The civil war took the kingdom apart, and even the victor only held it together for about five years before it fragmented again."

Sarkis kept his face blank. It would not do to let this woman see his reaction.

Five years. My troops dead, my captains chained in enchanted undeath...all so a cold, vindictive king could hold on to power for five more years.

Because I failed them. Because I played the odds and lost.

And I have paid for that gamble for nearly five hundred years.

"Thank you," said Sarkis gruffly. He felt an unexpected tightness behind his eyes, like unshed tears. "Thank you, Wisdom Morag. I have no money—not even any possessions save the clothes on my back—but you have given me a great gift. If I can ever repay you..." It occurred to him as he spoke that perhaps *Wisdom* was the wrong term of address, but he did not know any others to use.

The scholar looked up at him, her face unexpectedly somber. She reached out and clasped his forearm, wrist to wrist.

"I know what it is to lose your connection to the people before you," she said, and he heard the heaviness of that knowledge in her voice. "To come unmoored in history. It's why I became a historian in the first place. We must help each other find our place again."

Sarkis did not trust himself to speak. He bowed to her, very deeply, and went to find Halla.

CHAPTER 24

She was sitting on a bench near the front of the library, leaning back against the wall. She was obviously napping, so he sat down beside her and waited for her to wake up.

"I'm not asleep," she said thickly.

"Of course not."

She rubbed her eyes. "Did you find what you were looking for?"

"I did. More than I expected to find." He had also learned the fate of the Leopard's valley, and though it was a tiny thing to set against nearly five hundred years of failure, he took a small comfort from it. They had known peace there for many years, and even now, absorbed into a larger empire, it was a prosperous place. The Leopard's daughter had not drawn the blade because she had had no need to do so.

"And did you learn how long...?"

He told her.

Halla's eyes went round, and the last traces of sleep fled her face. "Four hundred and fifty years!"

"Yes. And I would not have known where to look, if you had

not thought of such a clever way to ask." He reached out and took her hand. "That was well thought of."

"Oh," said Halla. "I didn't...well, I mean, you and Morag did all the work. I just thought how I'd do it, without explaining about the sword, and...you know." Sarkis saw that she was blushing again.

He had a strong urge to kiss her again, but the taste of centuries spent in a sword lay on his tongue, and he knew it would be a mistake. "Come on," he said instead, tugging her to her feet. "We should get back to the hostel before it gets too dark."

It was already late evening. There were lamps lit around the courtyard, but the shadows were very thick. Sarkis saw several women leaning against walls, in a pose that hadn't changed much in five hundred years.

"Halla? Mistress Halla?"

Sarkis heard the voice from an alley and turned, putting one hand on his sword. Who could be calling Halla's name here? Did she have friends in the city she hadn't mentioned?

Halla looked as puzzled as he did. "Yes?" she said.

The speaker stepped forward. He had been standing at the corner of a building that faced onto the courtyard outside the library. He was tall and pale, with a seamed face and a short shock of red hair. "Most recently of Rutger's Howe?"

"Do I know you?"

"I've been sent with a message," he said, beckoning to them.

"Oh!" Halla stepped forward. "Did the Temple send you?"

"Indeed. It's a somewhat sensitive matter, so if we could... ah..." He glanced at the open courtyard, then back at Halla, raising his eyebrows.

Sarkis's danger senses twinged. There was something suspicious about the situation, but Halla was already walking toward the red-headed man.

He seems respectably dressed, but what do I know of clothing in this land? And fine clothes may still conceal a blade.

"Is something wrong?" asked Halla.

The red-haired man took a few steps back. "Yes, but this isn't the place to discuss it."

The space between the buildings was barely more than a glorified alley. It was much darker. Sarkis put out a hand to catch Halla's arm, while his eyes adjusted to the gloom.

That pause saved him a great deal of trouble.

When his eyes adjusted, he saw that there were three more men in the alley, including one that was trying to lurk behind a chunk of the decorative façade. Unlike the redhead, these men did not look particularly respectable, and they also had weapons in their hands.

"...um," said Halla, her eyes growing wide. "What *exactly* is the problem?"

The redhead tried, Sarkis would give him that. "I'll be happy to discuss it once we're somewhere more private."

"I think we'll discuss it now," said Sarkis, drawing his sword and pushing Halla behind him.

The redhead sighed. "Dammit," he muttered, to no one in particular. And then, "Mistress Halla, please hand over the sword and you won't be harmed."

"Err...why don't you leave instead?" said Halla. "And then neither of us will be harmed?"

"I've no desire to shed blood," he said.

Sarkis rather suspected that the men with him did not feel the same way. There was a fourth coming from the end of the alleyway now.

"Oh good," said Halla. "Because I don't want bloodshed either. So if you leave, we could both get what we want."

That's a novel negotiating tactic, I'll give her that...

"I'm afraid that won't be possible. Hand over the sword and we can be done here."

Sarkis decided that negotiations had gone on long enough and simply threw himself at the redhead, shouting "Halla, *run!*"

He was half-afraid that she'd stay to discuss the problem of running, where exactly to run, and perhaps relate an anecdote about a cousin who had run somewhere and dropped dead of running-related causes, but Halla bolted like a hare. *Thank the great god for that.*

The redhead cursed and backpedaled. His men started forward, then stopped, because there was a rather large quasi-immortal warrior in the way.

The narrowness of the alley worked to Sarkis's advantage. None of the men could get past him without risking a foot of steel in the belly. None of them seemed particularly inclined to do so.

"Go after her, you idiots!" snapped the redhead. This order was robbed of some of its effectiveness because he was trying to get away from Sarkis as he said it.

One footpad backed away from Sarkis, then turned and ran. "On it, boss!" he called over his shoulder. Sarkis wondered idly if that was to prevent the redhead from thinking he was simply running from the fight. *Not that it matters, since I'll have to kill him anyway if he's going after Halla...*

Two footpads left was easier to deal with. Sarkis didn't bother with finesse. Finesse was overrated. He simply swung forward, giving the men the option to block, duck, or get out the way.

The first one had a long knife, and sensibly chose to duck. The second one was not expecting his ally to duck, and was a bit too slow in reacting to the sword that was suddenly coming at him. He threw his forearm up to protect his head, and the blade sank into it with a wet, meaty sound, and quite a lot of screaming from the owner of the forearm.

The first footpad decided to stab Sarkis while his sword was bound up in the second man's arm. Sarkis kicked him very hard in the knee, and then in the head when he went down.

There was an unpleasant moment where both Sarkis and the second footpad were united in their desire to get Sarkis's sword out of the man's arm but had very different ideas how to go about it. The blade had gotten hung up in the bone, and Sarkis very much wanted it back, so he grabbed the man's shoulder and shoved hard, while hauling backward on the sword. The man screamed a bit more. The first footpad, on the ground, tried to stab Sarkis in the ankles, which Sarkis did not approve of, so he stomped on the man's wrist a few times to make his disapproval known.

And then, as so often happened, the fight was mostly over. The first footpad rolled out of the way, clutching his wrist, and the second one had turned gray and was holding his slashed arm, and the redhead looked at them, looked at Sarkis, and said, "So sorry for the trouble."

Sarkis watched him turn tail and bolt down the alleyway, and wished for a crossbow or a throwing knife or *something*. For a moment he thought about charging after the man, catching him, and beating him until he spat out who had hired him.

But he had bigger fish to fry. Halla was out there somewhere with the third footpad still after her, and the great god only knew what trouble she would get into. Sarkis backed out of the alley, sheathed his sword, and went to go see if any of the ladies of the evening had noticed which way she'd gone.

THE LADIES of the evening proved...less than forthcoming.

"Did a woman run by here?" asked Sarkis. "About yea tall, with pale blonde hair and big gray eyes? Wearing a green bodice and dark brown skirts?"

The prostitute he was speaking to gave him a sour look and turned her back.

Sarkis was a trifle surprised by this. He tried the woman across the street from her.

"No," she said, before he even opened his mouth. "I didn't see her."

Sarkis looked around the courtyard. If Halla had come charging out of the alley, it was hard to imagine how anyone had missed her. "Are you certain?"

"Yes."

The woman spoke with obvious dislike. Sarkis wondered if she thought that Halla was another prostitute, and was annoyed at her for taking business.

"She might be in danger from—"

The woman held up her hand. *"No,"* she said. "I have *not* seen her. I *will not* have seen her. And you can ask every woman here and *none* of us will have seen her. Understand?"

"No," said Sarkis, after a long moment. "I suppose I don't."

She shook her head in disgust. She was a pretty woman, certainly younger than Sarkis—*particularly given that I am now nearly five hundred*—but for a moment Sarkis felt like a callow youth being lectured by a wisewoman.

"Do you think that there's any woman here who hasn't run from a man with blood on his hands?"

Sarkis looked down at his hands. The footpad's blood had spattered across him, even run down his chest in a few places. He stared at the red streaks. He'd already forgotten they were there.

I am barely a man, only a weapon.

"I see," he said. "And if I told you that I was her guardsman, that I only wanted to keep her safe...?"

The woman folded her arms. "Then I'd say that's all very nice, but I don't know you and I don't trust you and I won't hand over a woman just on your say-so."

Sarkis lifted his hand, unthinking, to rub his face and the woman flinched back, almost imperceptibly.

She expects to pay a price for her silence. And she's standing up to a man with bloody hands and a bloody sword nevertheless.

He was not impressed with the warriors of this decadent southern land, but their women were tearing the heart out of him with their courage. And their compassion.

Sarkis bowed to her and said "I respect your reasons." And then, hoping that Halla would have the good sense to make for the hostel, he moved past her and began to jog.

He was four streets over when he caught sight of the footpad. The man did not see him, at least at first.

Sarkis put his arm around the man's neck, held his sword against the man's throat, and gently suggested that perhaps he wished to consider a different line of work. The footpad agreed that this was a very good idea and that he would very much like to get started on that immediately.

Sarkis released him. The former footpad ran off, presumably to start a new life somewhere far away.

He was standing in the alley, listening to receding footsteps, when Halla said "Sarkis?"

"*Where have you*—" Sarkis roared, then heard himself and clamped down his voice hard, so that "—*been?!*" came out in a strangled whisper.

Halla goggled at him. "Are you all right?"

Great god, what was wrong with him? He was yelling like she was the one at fault. Had he been that afraid for her?

Of course you were. If you can't find her, you can't protect her. Perfectly reasonable.

Perfectly.

"I'm fine," he said. That came out more clipped than she deserved, so he tried again. "Sorry. On edge."

"Being attacked would set anyone on edge," said Halla, putting her hand on his arm. "It's all right."

She thinks I'm upset because I got in a fight. Great god have mercy. He patted her hand because he had no idea what else to do. "Where did you go?"

"Oh! I ran back to the library and hid there. I thought they wouldn't come after me with all those witnesses."

"Sensible." Too sensible. He hadn't even thought to look there.

"Then the nice woman on the corner told me which way you'd gone," Halla continued cheerfully. She beamed at him.

"Of course she did," said Sarkis, through gritted teeth.

CHAPTER 25

That night, Sarkis lay on the thin mattress and brooded.

The attack by footpads did not bother him overmuch. He suspected it would trouble Halla a great deal more. She was not used to having people assault her for no reason except that she had something they wanted.

Odd that she could reach adulthood and still hold such an innocence. Perhaps it was this decadent land, or perhaps she had simply never had anything that anyone wanted before.

He grimaced. He knew that he should hold such softness in contempt, and yet...and yet...

Consulting the maps had been kind. He had not thought to do it. He was used to being displaced in time, over and over. He was used to being thought of as nothing more than a weapon, not a man who might wish to know the fate of his country.

He had almost come to think of himself as such as well. Right now, with the memory of the fight still singing in his blood, he still felt very much like a weapon. And a bit depressed at how much he enjoyed being one, from time to time.

It had taken Halla and her endless questions and inability to take anything at face value to see him as a man again, and then to search out how such a man, isolated in time, might find a marker.

It had been kind. Yes. Kind and soft and damned decent of her to do, when she had her own troubles to worry about.

But he should not have kissed her. That had been a mistake.

He rolled over, restless. Perhaps, but it had been a glorious mistake. He could still feel the way she had pressed against him, her body molding against his. He could easily imagine how much better it would be without armor and cloth between them.

And for all you know, she was squashed up against you because you were pushing her into the wall, he told himself grimly. *And if you do not stop these thoughts, you will have to beat your own ass for disrespect.*

He had kissed any number of women in his life, and by his own standards, that had been a very chaste, respectful kiss. He did not know why it had felt so shockingly intimate.

She had not wept or broken down over the attack. He would have held her if she had, and Sarkis did not *think* that he would have taken advantage of her weakness to kiss her again, but...well, if hundreds of years in a sword had taught him anything, it was mostly that he was not half the man that, in life, he had thought that he might be.

It would be easier when there was a priest traveling with them. One did not have lustful thoughts around a priest if one could avoid it.

Although they'll be a priest of one of these decadent southern gods, Sarkis thought glumly. *So for all I know, they'll be as randy as a rooster in a henhouse and call it a sacrament.*

That thought would have killed the libido of far stronger

men than Sarkis. He rolled over again and wrapped the blankets around himself.

His last thought before falling asleep was that neither he nor Halla had mentioned Rutger's Howe while they stood in line. How had the footpad known where she was from?

———

HALLA, too, had difficulty sleeping, though for largely different reasons. The bed was very narrow and the fact that she was sharing it with a mostly-sheathed sword did not help.

She reached out and touched the embossed sheath, running her fingers over the pattern. Sleeping with a sword in her bed. Gods, her life had taken quite a turn since she left Rutger's Howe.

The attempted robbery had been unsettling, but she was not as shaken as she had been after Mina had tried to prey on her. The sword was valuable, someone had overheard that, so they had tried to take it. It did not feel personal the same way.

And if I'm being honest, I only saw a few seconds of it before I ran like a rabbit.

The library had been closing, but the desk clerk had still been there. If she'd screamed, people would have come running. She didn't, because Sarkis had clearly had the situation well in hand, and she wasn't quite sure she wanted to explain about magic and swords and risk spreading the word to even more potential thieves.

She was not at all concerned that the priests of the White Rat had betrayed them. They didn't *do* that sort of thing.

Still, if someone tried to break into the hostel and take the sword, they'd have to get past the guard, past the nuns, find her, then wrestle it out from under the blankets, and all she'd have to do was yank the cords off, sheathe it and draw it again, and Sarkis would appear, large as life and twice as angry.

He had seemed irritated after she'd found him, but probably that was because of the robbery. Of course, he'd seemed irritated after he kissed her, too...

She rolled over, trying to get comfortable. The sword banged against her back.

No one had ever kissed her like that. The miller's son, who'd courted anything in skirts when Halla was sixteen, only *wished* that he could kiss that way. Her husband had never even tried.

Sarkis's kiss had been as fierce as the rest of him. He'd tilted his head to cover her mouth with his, holding her against him, and...well, it had been wonderful. Her initial surprise had warmed into something else entirely, as if her veins were full of...oh, not fire, but something kinder. Melted butter, perhaps. Yes. She'd felt as if she were melting against him.

But then Sarkis had stopped, which was bad, and apologized, which was even worse. She must have done something wrong, or more likely, not done the right thing. There was probably something obvious, something that any other woman would know to do, but she hadn't, so Sarkis thought she must not be interested.

Which I am. Very much.

She'd felt like her insides were turning to honey. She hadn't wanted it to stop. If she had her way, they'd still be leaning against the wall of the alley together.

She rolled over again. The sword dug into her hip and she had to move it so she wasn't lying on top of the damn thing.

Which was the problem, ultimately. The sword was one thing. If Sarkis had been in her bed, instead of the hunk of steel he was entrapped in, he'd want...well, what the miller's son had wanted and hadn't gotten, and what her husband had never wanted, but had done anyway, usually while staring into the middle distance with an expression of bemused concentration.

Halla had a feeling that Sarkis would not be staring into the middle distance while he bedded her. Hell, if the kiss was any indication, she might not be staring in the middle distance herself.

But after bedding came the consequences of bedding. Like pregnancy and childbirth and assuming she lived through that —her family's history wasn't great—suddenly the thin shield provided by being a respectable widow would vanish.

She didn't quite dare.

But oh gods, how she wanted to...

CHAPTER 26

The priest arrived at the hostel the next morning.

"It's you!" said Halla, sounding surprised and delighted.

Zale, the priest they had first met at the temple, sketched a bow. "It is, indeed."

The priest was dressed for travel this morning, their hair pulled back, and had exchanged the white robes of the Rat for more sensible dark brown. There was still a line of white embroidered rats on the sleeve, rather more charming than religious, but Sarkis wasn't going to mention it.

"I didn't know you'd be the one the Temple sent," said Halla.

They smiled. "Ordinarily, I wouldn't be. But I requested it. I fear that I am quite fascinated by your case, and given the chance..." The priest spread their hands.

"And you have the legal skills to assist Mistress Halla?" said Sarkis.

"I have some small experience in that direction."

"How small?"

Zale tilted their head modestly. "Five years as a clerk before

I was called to the Rat's service. Since then, I have frequently assisted in legal cases on behalf of the Temple. My rank is that of advocate divine. I will not lie, inheritance is not my particular field of study, but I have as much knowledge as anyone serving at this Temple and more than many." They paused, then added, almost apologetically, "And—forgive me—while every case is important to those involved, I fear the most skilled of my contemporaries, the solicitors sacrosanct, are reserved for cases with far higher stakes."

"That's fine," said Halla. "I'd much rather *not* be high stakes."

Zale nodded. "The Temple has provided me a wagon. It will be a slower return to Rutger's Howe, but a more comfortable one. You will have ample time to acquaint me with the details of your claim along the way."

The wagon in question was a tall, narrow affair, on oversized wheels, drawn by a single laconic ox. It was brightly painted with an image of the Rat, haloed by the sun, holding up His paw in benediction.

Sarkis grunted when he saw it. "Subtle."

"The Temple prefers that anyone we encounter know exactly who we are. Priests are often granted passage where clerks and warriors are not."

He grunted again. *Decadent southern gods...but in this case, practical.* Even in the Weeping Lands, one did not trouble priests.

One of the striped creatures he had seen earlier sat on the wagon seat. Zale nodded to the gnole. "This is Brindle. He will handle the ox and care for it, since I fear I have little skill with such."

Brindle nodded back to them. He had badger-like stripes running down his face, but the dark fur between the stripes was mottled with brown. *Hence the name,* Sarkis assumed.

"Hello, Brindle," said Halla. She introduced herself and Sarkis. "Do you work for the Rat?"

Brindle shook his head. "Priests work for gods. A gnole works for priests."

Zale smiled. "Gnole theology is admirably straightforward. They have one god. They do not seem interested in adding more."

"This strikes me as enormously sensible," said Sarkis. He bowed to Brindle. Brindle nodded back.

They climbed onto the wagon. Brindle took up a long ox goad, tapped the beast's flank, and clucked his tongue. The ox began ambling down the street, so slowly that Sarkis groaned.

I could walk to Rutger's Howe and back in the time this beast will take...

Well, it's not as if I have any pressing engagements anywhere. My only job is to act as a bodyguard to a woman and now to this priest of a...

"Why a rat?" asked Sarkis.

"Hmm?" said Zale. Their braid pulled the top layer of hair back away from their face, and the long, dark gray strands looked pewter-colored in the sunlight.

"Your god. Why a rat?"

Zale shrugged. "Why not a rat? Rats are smart and they travel with humans, but they are neither our servants nor our prey. They eat the food that we eat, they live within our homes. Who better to understand us?"

Sarkis raised an eyebrow at that.

Zale chuckled. "That is a priest's answer, at any rate. Would you like a scholar's answer as well?"

"I would!" said Halla, to the surprise of no one.

Zale nodded. "So far as we can tell, the Temple of the Rat originated some eight hundred years ago, in the west. A plague was decimating the cities of the old empire there. They knew that rats carried the plague, and a cult sprang up, attempting to appease the rat spirit. From there, the faith evolved and reformed." They grinned slyly. "Of course, our understanding of treatment for the plague certainly did not hurt."

"A moment," said Sarkis. "You *know* the origin of your faith? You can point to it like this? And yet still you worship this rat as your god?"

The priest laughed. "Why does knowing the origin of a thing make it less holy? Do you know your grandparents?"

Sarkis gave them a narrow-eyed look. "I did, yes."

"And did you love your parents less for knowing where they came from?"

"I did not worship my parents."

"Some parents practically expect that, though," muttered Halla.

Sarkis started to say something, then frowned. "There are places I have been," he admitted grudgingly, "where one's ancestors are worshipped. One of my men came from such a place, and she swore by her grandfather's shade."

"There you have it." Zale waved their hand. "We know that the Rat exists. We know He is kindly inclined toward humankind. If we forget His name, He will creep back into the walls of the world, but He will not cease to exist. A day will come when humans remember His name again. So it is, and so it has been, and so it will be."

Halla bowed her head as if receiving a benediction.

"Decadent southern gods," muttered Sarkis, and Zale laughed aloud.

THEY WERE BARELY an hour out of the city gates when they

passed a tiny, nameless town on the ox-road and saw where a burning had taken place.

Zale's thin lips curled back when they saw the smoke rising from the square. The pyre was ringed by men in indigo cloaks. The fire was out now.

"Motherhoods," the priest muttered. "The gods be merciful."

"All the gods?" asked Sarkis. "Not just the Rat?"

"The Rat's mercy is a given. It's the other gods we need to worry about." They craned their neck. "Ah. Possessions only. Books. Not a person, thank the Rat."

"They burn books, too?" asked Sarkis.

"Oh yes. Herbals, bestiaries...sometimes merely books in foreign tongues. In case they might be spellbooks." They shook their head, looking pained. "The loss of knowledge alone... Those people are a menace."

"And here comes one now," said Halla. She wondered if she'd be able to put them off with a saga of cauliflower a second time.

An indigo-cloaked man approached them on horseback. He had a crossbow slung over his back and a sword at his side.

"I can take him," said Sarkis softly, "but the others will be on us right away."

Brindle gave him a look. "You think an ox can outrun horses, sword-man?"

"I'm not sure this ox could outrun a *dead* horse."

"Don't insult an ox. An ox is good at what an ox does. Like to see *you* pull a wagon any better."

"Stand down," said Zale, watching the horseman approach. "I'll handle it."

The Motherhood warrior halted alongside the wagon, eyes flicking over the paint job. "A Rat priest, eh?"

Zale inclined their head.

"Where are you traveling?"

"On the Rat's business," said Zale. Their voice was pleasant enough, but there was a hard note under it.

"And where does the Rat's business take you?"

"Wherever the Rat sees the need," said Zale. Halla rather admired the priest's flat refusal to answer the question. She'd be burying the man in information, herself, with every relative she had in every town along the way, including some made up on the spot. Still, Zale had a certain authority and could get away with defiance.

The warrior's eyes narrowed. He looked over the wagon and passengers again, gaze lingering on Sarkis.

"It might be wise to inform someone where you are going," said the warrior. "In case of...accidents."

Well, that wasn't even subtle.

"I assure you, the temple of the Rat is aware of both our whereabouts and when we are expected to return."

"The Motherhood would appreciate being extended the same courtesy."

"I'm sure they would."

Brindle had not slowed the ox. They were beginning to pass out of the square by this point. Halla held her breath to see if the warrior would continue pacing them.

He drew his horse up. "Be careful, priest," he said. "The roads are dangerous for those not under the Mother's protection."

"I will inform my superiors of your concern."

And that was it. The ox plodded onward. The warrior turned his horse back.

Sarkis opened his mouth to say something and Zale shook their head warningly. "Later."

It was beginning to turn to early evening when the plume of smoke faded in the sky. Zale pulling their robes tightly around their thin shoulders. "Damnable Motherhood," they muttered.

"We tangled with them briefly on the road," said Halla. "But they were a lot more persistent with you."

"There is a rivalry between the Motherhood and most other faiths," said Zale. "A largely one-sided one. The rest of us manage to get along tolerably well, why can't they?" They grumbled something under their breath.

The sun set early in autumn. Sarkis saw the distance they had travelled...or more accurately, failed to travel...and stifled a sigh. The ox moved at half the speed of a human walking, if that.

Still, it's not as if you have anywhere to be. That clammy-handed fellow does not seem like the type to destroy a house he lives in. And if time were of the essence, the Rat temple would likely have provided us with a swifter transport than the great god's slowest ox.

The wagon had two beds that folded down from the sides. Zale took one that night, and then looked helplessly at Halla and Sarkis.

"I shall guard outside," said Sarkis firmly. Halla's presence while asleep was already costing him rest. Lying on the floor less than a foot away from her would be entirely too much.

Zale frowned. "There are extra blankets, but are you sure? It is cold out."

"It is no hardship. I have slept on stone with snow blowing in—"

"Don't get him started," said Halla. "Just make him take extra blankets." She paused. "Err—wait, does Brindle need a bed?"

"Brindle stays with the ox," said Zale. "I've traveled with him two or three times before, and he won't leave his charge for anything less than a blizzard."

Sarkis paused, one hand on the door. "Is he trustworthy?"

"Who, Brindle?" Zale looked surprised. "I have never had cause to doubt him. The temple employs a small group of gnoles who appear to be related, either by blood or family ties. They have a complicated caste system, and I don't believe humans understand it as well as we think we do, but Brindle is a job-gnole, though a low-level one. The high-level job gnoles are traders and negotiators. One of them negotiates the contracts for the entire group. I suppose if one of the higher job-gnoles planned to hand us over to bandits or some other group for ransom, Brindle would likely go along with it, but they've never done anything like that, and we have employed them for years now. Since not long after the gnoles arrived, in fact."

Sarkis nodded, and stepped outside.

It was a cold, clear night. He burrowed into the blankets, feeling the sharp bite of the air in his lungs. The temperature had dropped in just the few days since he and Halla had been sleeping outdoors.

The moon was cut down to a half-smile on the horizon. Sarkis could hear the ox breathing, and Brindle talking softly to it in what must have been his own language. From inside the wagon came the sounds of two people moving around in an enclosed space, which was mostly occasional thumps and apologies.

He felt a brief qualm about leaving Halla alone with the priest, but squelched it. Should Zale prove untrustworthy, Sarkis was less than three feet away. If Halla so much as yelped, he would be through the door and ready to skewer the Rat priest first and ask questions later.

But she did not yelp. The stars moved in the cold sky, and Sarkis slept as if he were home in the Weeping Lands and woke with frost on his beard.

CHAPTER 27

"Now *this* is traveling," said Halla, holding a cup of hot tea between her hands to warm them. Zale had already cooked bacon, and was now frying slabs of bread in the grease. The air was still cold, but she had slept in a bed rather than on the frozen ground.

Sarkis's lips quirked as he looked at her across the fire. "What, sleeping in hedges and ditches was not to your liking?"

Halla rolled her eyes at him, licking bacon grease off her fingers. Sarkis's gaze locked on her mouth, and it took her a moment to think why.

Oh. Uh. Licking my fingers. Yes. Men get very interested in that. Should I try to flirt? Or am I supposed to lick something else?

She was out of bacon and probably nobody found licking a tin cup sexy. Licking the wagon was right out.

Dammit, I'm bad at this.

"The company was excellent," she said to Sarkis. "The hedges, not so much. I like this much better."

"As do I," said Sarkis. He looked as if he might say something else, but then Zale began handing out pieces of toast and the moment, if there had been one, was lost.

"So you heal inside the blade," said Zale, after they had started down the road and the ox had lumbered into what was, for it, a good pace.

"I do."

"How much do you heal? If we cut your hand off—not that I'm proposing that!— "

"Thank the great god. I would object."

"—but would that heal as well? Would you have a new hand or a healed stump?"

"A new hand," said Sarkis.

"Oh. Has it happened, then?"

"Not my hand. One of my wielders liked to cut out my tongue."

There was a brief, horrified silence. He looked up to see both Halla and Zale staring at him. Zale had brown eyes and Halla gray, but their expressions were identical.

"It grew back."

"Sarkis..." said Halla, eyes huge with sympathy. "That's horrible!"

"I did not enjoy it," Sarkis admitted. It had been a great deal of wet fumbling and gouging pain, with blood and spit pouring out of his mouth, and the knowledge that he would live through it had not been much comfort in the moment.

Zale made a gesture over their chest, whether a benediction or a warding, he did not know.

Halla reached out and took Sarkis's hand. He looked down at it, then squeezed.

And which of us is comforting the other is anyone's guess...

"Forgive me," said Zale. "This is indelicate, but...what happened to your tongue?"

"What?"

"The tongue that was cut out," said Zale. "Did it cease to exist? Did it go back in the sword?"

"I have no idea. I was not exactly paying attention!"

"Completely understandable," said the priest in soothing tones. "Who would be? But I must wonder what happened. That might be important to understanding how the blade works."

Sarkis exhaled. "I...can see how that would be useful. But I don't know the answer."

"Hmmm," said Zale. They looked at Halla. Halla chewed on her lower lip thoughtfully.

Both of them looked at Sarkis.

He groaned, recognizing twin lights of curiosity in their eyes. "Fine. Would you like to cut off my little finger to test it?"

Zale looked genuinely shocked. "Oh dear! No, no, we shouldn't start there! What about...oh! What happens when you urinate?"

Sarkis's mouth fell open.

"Oh, that's a good question," said Halla. "We could test from there, couldn't we?"

"Test...what are you...?"

Great god, they were both still looking at him! As if they expected an answer!

He cleared his throat. "Well, I take my cock out in the usual way and aim somewhere and try to relax..."

Zale burst out laughing. "No, not that bit!"

Halla's shoulders were shaking. Sarkis appreciated that she wasn't laughing in his face.

"Does the urine dematerialize? Into blue light, as you do?"

"No," said Sarkis. "Definitely not. I'd notice."

"Hmm," said Zale. "And of course, by definition, you're never around to see what happens after you dematerialize..."

Halla leaped down from the wagon. Sarkis looked after her, not sure what exactly she was planning.

And if I'm being honest, a little afraid to find out.

The wagon door creaked as she opened it. The ox never looked right or left, plodding along. Neither did Brindle.

Halla was back a moment later, holding a crockery jar. Sarkis recognized it as having held the jam they used at breakfast.

"Here!" she said, holding it up. "You can go in this!"

Sarkis stared at her, then at Zale, then back at her.

"It would be a good way to check," the priest said. "We'll put you back in the sword, and then we'll know if it vanishes or not."

Sarkis looked around for help. Brindle glanced at him, shook his head, and said, "Ask somebody else, sword-man. A gnole isn't getting involved."

Defeated, Sarkis took the jar. "I...uh. In front of you?"

It wasn't that he hadn't answered the call of nature with his men any number of times, of course, but there was a difference between simply living in close proximity to others and having two people staring at you with intense interest, waiting for...

"I'm not going to be able to do this with you staring at me."

"You can go in the bushes, if you like," said Halla.

Zale nodded.

Sarkis counted to seventy-two, slid off the wagon seat, and went to go further the pursuit of knowledge.

"Yay!" said Halla, when Sarkis handed her the jar.

"No one," said Sarkis wearily, "in my entire life, has ever said, 'yay,' when I handed them a jar of piss."

"Well, there's a first time for everything."

Zale peered into the jar and wrinkled their nose. "This should do fine. May we sheathe the sword now?"

Sarkis lifted his hands and let them drop. "Sure. Of course. Why not."

"I don't think he's really getting into the spirit of this," said Halla.

"He does seem a bit dour, doesn't he?"

"...I'm still right here, you know."

"Well, we'll fix that," said Halla cheerfully. She slung the sword off her shoulder, unpicked the cords, and sheathed the sword the final inch.

Sarkis dissolved into blue fire. At nearly the same time, so did the contents of the jar.

Zale laughed delightedly. "Look!" They flipped the jar over and nothing came out.

Halla let out a cheer. "It worked!"

"It did!"

"That's amazing!"

"I know!"

"Now what does that mean?"

"I have absolutely no idea!"

They looked at each other for a long, long minute, then both dissolved into laughter.

"Did you see...the look...on his face..."

"And when he tried to explain how he...!"

Zale couldn't finish. The ox flicked back an ear at the strange howling noises coming from the wagon seat, but didn't turn. Brindle looked at both of them and shook his striped head. "Humans," he muttered under his breath. "A gnole does not understand humans." This only made Zale laugh harder.

It took nearly five minutes for the two to get their hilarity under control. When Sarkis re-materialized, he couldn't figure out why Zale and Halla were carefully avoiding looking at each other.

"Well?" he said.

Halla burst out laughing again. Sarkis stared at her, swung around to Zale, and saw that the priest had put their hands over their face, and was making truly bizarre noises.

"Are you both *well?*"

"Fine," gasped Halla. "Wonderful."

"Never better," croaked Zale, through their fingers.

"What the hell did you two do with my jar of piss?"

Halla fell off the wagon seat. Sarkis had to go pick her up. She appeared unhurt, but was sitting in the dust, giggling uncontrollably, unable to stand up under her own power.

"I'm fine," she croaked, when he set her on her feet. "Fine. Perfectly...heh...fine..."

He slapped dust off the back of her skirt. "Are you drunk?"

"No!" She leaned on him as he helped steer her back to the wagon. "Just...ah...heh...look, you had to be there."

"I *was* there!"

"You had to be there and not be you?"

He handed her up into the wagon and looked over at Zale. "Are *you* going to fall off now?"

"I think I'm okay," said the priest, lips twitching. "Mostly. But oh, Sarkis! This is fascinating! The jar empties itself when you go back in the sword!"

Sarkis narrowed his eyes. "Are you telling me that anything I...err...leave out here goes back in the sword with me?"

"Makes sense," said Halla. "I bet it normally dematerializes when it gets far enough away from the sword. It's just nobody noticed. And of course you wouldn't notice."

"I don't often stay out of the sword long enough to have to eat," he admitted. "But are you telling me that my sword is full of shit?"

Halla opened her mouth to say something, received a death glare from Sarkis and meekly closed it on whatever remark she was about to utter.

"No, no," said Zale. "No more than it's full of severed tongues, I imagine."

"What a marvelous image," said Sarkis, putting his face in his hands. Really, he didn't know why he ever bothered to take his face out of his hands. He should just have them permanently attached to his forehead, the way his life was going.

Zale started to say something else and then their mouth snapped shut with a click. Sarkis looked up.

Two figures in indigo cloaks rode down the road. Sarkis narrowed his eyes, recognizing the two Motherhood priests who had harassed them on the way from Archen's Glory.

"Priest," said the first one, nodding to Zale.

Zale inclined their head, all their amusement gone. Their face looked as cold and angular as a hunting fox's.

"Have you had any trouble on this road?"

"Not so far," said Zale acidly. "Am I going to, do you think?"

Sarkis wondered how great the Motherhood's sins were, to rouse such ire in the mild-mannered priest. Halla had stilled, her large gray eyes the color of a clouded sea. Brindle drove on, not looking at any of the humans, eyes fixed on the ox's ears.

"Only the Mother knows the future," said the Motherhood priest. He had short reddish hair and an angular, sallow face. His companion was heavyset, with a scarred complexion, and he carried a sword with the ease of a man comfortable with its use.

Red looked over at Scar and tapped his gloved fingers on his reins. "I am curious as to what you are carrying in your wagon."

"Food," said Zale. "Bunks. Clothes. The sort of things that go in wagons."

"I think I've got a pot of glue," volunteered Halla.

"You've got a rather large sword for a woman," said Scar, looking over at her.

"Yes, but I'm told it's not the size of the sword that matters," said Halla. She frowned. "Although my husband used to say that, and do you know, he never told me what it meant?"

Red blinked once. Sarkis put his hand over his mouth.

"Anyway, it's really more long than it is heavy. It's actually quite light. I can handle it quite well, except that it's a bit too long. My husband should probably have said that the size of the sword doesn't matter unless it's too long to handle, but—"

Scar's face flushed. Sarkis suspected that he thought Halla was making fun of him. Sarkis himself wasn't entirely sure. Surely even Halla couldn't be that naïve...could she?

Nobody kills stupid women, they just kick us out of the way...

As a system, he didn't have to like it, but it had obviously worked for her in the past. But these days she had a servant of the sword, and if someone tried to kick her out of the way, Sarkis was going to take their leg off at the knee.

"*Why* do you carry a sword?" grated Scar.

Halla blinked at him, her eyes round. "Um, for the same reason you do, right? So people leave me alone because they think, 'Oh, she's got a sword, she must be dangerous.'"

"I protect the innocent and punish the guilty," growled Scar.

"Oh," said Halla. "I guess not the same reason, then. I mean, I like to think I'd protect the innocent too. It hasn't really come up. But I don't punish the guilty. Not that I wouldn't, if I found one! I would punish them like you wouldn't believe! But I don't know how to find guilty people. I guess they don't just walk up and say, 'Hi, I'm guilty, punish me!' do they?"

Red and Scar stared at her. Scar looked as if he was becoming angry. Red looked as if he couldn't believe what he was hearing.

"We are escorting Mistress Halla to her home," said Zale, massaging their temples. "There is a legal issue with her inheritance and she has engaged the Rat's services. There is absolutely nothing of interest to the Motherhood in our mission, our wagon, or our possession."

"Then you'll not mind if we take a look," said Scar. Sarkis was probably imagining the note of relief in the man's voice, as if they had returned to a script that he understood.

"Yes, of course I'd mind!" snapped Zale. "You have no right and no call to do so! I'm a priest of the Rat on Temple business!"

"And we are priests of the Mother, on Temple business," said Red smoothly. "Surely you do not wish to interfere with ours...just as we have no desire to interfere with yours..."

Zale folded their arms. "Your business ends where the Rat's begins. You know as well as I do that your Temple must seek permission from mine before you conduct any kind of business that may infringe upon the Rat's. That law has been standing since before *your* goddess had two stones atop each other to call a shrine."

Halla, clearly worried, put a hand on Zale's sleeve. "Now, Zale...the Mother is *everyone's* mother..."

Red and Scar made the ritual gesture.

"And the Rat is everyone's lawyer!" snapped Zale. "Which is why I know that the law is on my side. Now, if you two gentlemen would cease crowding my ox..."

Brindle grunted agreement.

"You talk like a guilty man, priest," said Red.

"And you talk like a petty tyrant," Zale shot back.

There was a moment when the whole situation balanced on a knife edge. Sarkis waited to grab his sword and throw himself at Scar's throat. He just hoped that he could take them both out before any of the others got hurt.

Zale's probably got a trick up their sleeve, if I'm any judge. No idea about the gnole...Halla, of course, is Halla...

Halla chose that moment to defuse the situation by bursting into tears.

"Rat's balls," muttered Zale, putting their arm around Halla.

"I don't...understand...why they're being so mean...we're just traveling...we didn't do anything and I was told...sniff...the Mother loved her children...and we're all her children..."

Red and Scar made the ritual gesture, looking deeply disgusted.

"...and...and...I just want to go *home*..."

Sarkis didn't have to fake the glare he turned on the Motherhood men. Halla buried her face in Zale's slender shoulder.

"Well, now you've done it," said Zale. "My client just lost her beloved uncle and mentor and she's had to make a long trip to make sure his last wishes were honored, and now you've upset her. I hope you're happy."

Red groaned and reined his horse in. "Go with the Mother," he muttered. Sarkis suspected that he didn't mean it.

Halla continued sobbing for several minutes, then said, quietly, "Are they gone?"

"Yes, and out of sight." Zale released her.

"Whew. I wasn't going to be able to keep that up for too long." She sat up.

"Masterfully done," said the priest.

"Eh, men like that usually panic when a woman cries." She dabbed at her eyes with her sleeve.

"Good job, fish-lady," said Brindle.

"Thank y—wait. Fish-lady?"

The gnole glanced at her. "*Hala* is being a fish. You know?"

"I don't."

Brindle set down the goad and gestured with both hands. "Long. Lives in rivers. Big teeth. Eats the other fish."

"A pike?"

"Don't know *pike*. A gnole calls it *hala*."

"Fish-lady," muttered Halla. "Well, it was just my luck."

Zale grinned broadly.

"Halla?" said Sarkis.

"Yes?"

"Do you really not know why people say, 'It's not the size of the sword that matters'?"

A flush began to creep up Halla's neck. "Of course I know! I'm not a—I've—I'm a widow, not a virgin!"

"But a *respectable* widow," said Sarkis mildly.

She elbowed him in the ribs. The flush reached her ears.

"It's fine," he said, trying to hide a grin. "I just didn't know if you needed it explained."

"What a fascinating explanation that might be..." said Zale. "Please, feel free to do so."

"Oh...well..."

Halla was still bright pink, but her expression changed from horror to sly amusement. "Yes, Sarkis, why don't *you* explain? After all, they might mean something different by it in the Weeping Lands..."

He held up both hands. "I'm sure it's fine."

"No, no," Zale said. "Priests must always pursue knowledge."

"And I of course have such limited firsthand knowledge," said Halla. "I've only ever had the *one* sword." She still blushed when she said it, but apparently she'd decided it was worth it to make him squirm.

Sarkis had led a mercenary company and was certainly not going to be out-euphemismed by a priest and a sheltered widow. "Well, I do have *quite* a large sword," he admitted.

Zale dropped their eyes to the blade at his waist and said, "Eh, I've seen bigger."

Sarkis reeled back on the seat. "Ouch. That was cold, priest."

"A gnole thinks humans have lost their damn minds," muttered Brindle.

Sarkis was grateful for the reprieve. "Your people aren't worried about the size of their...ah...swords?" He wasn't sure if the gnole understood the euphemisms or not.

Brindle gave him a sidelong look. "A gnole's ox is bigger than a human's sword."

The three humans sat blinking at each other.

"Was that..."

"Did he just..."

"Look, do you want be the one to try and figure out if he means..."

Brindle said nothing, driving the ox forward with a small, entirely satisfied smile.

CHAPTER 28

"Brindle?"

"Eh?"

"Does your ox have a name?"

Zale had gone to buy food at an inn, and Sarkis had gone with them. Halla and Brindle were left sitting on the wagon together, and Halla was attempting to make conversation.

Brindle was silent for so long that she started to fear that asking about names was a terrible faux pas in gnole circles and he was now trying to decide whether to forgive her ignorance or declare a blood feud against her family unto the seventh generation. *Oh dear. That would be just my luck, wouldn't it? I embark down this road to get dowries for my nieces and I end up with a gnole family pledged to slay them all, except I don't think gnoles do that, do they?*

"Yes," said Brindle, giving her an appraising look. "An ox has a name."

"Ah."

The moment stretched out even longer. Halla wondered if she was allowed to ask what the ox's name was.

Then: "An ox is named in a gnole's language." Brindle

said...something. Halla wasn't sure if she was even hearing it all. His ears were up and his whiskers forward, and she knew gnole language involved a great deal of whiskers, so probably that was part of it, too.

"Oh dear," said Halla. "I don't think I can say that, can I?"

"No," said Brindle. "Humans don't have all the parts to talk right." He patted her arm, much the same way that he patted the ox, and it occurred to Halla that the gnole thought humans were laboring under terrible handicaps and were presumably bravely making the best of it.

Well, he may be right. The gods know I can't seem to tell Sarkis what I want to tell him. About kissing, for example.

Brindle pointed to the ox. "An ox has very good hooves. See?"

Halla dutifully looked at the ox's feet. She had never kept oxen on the farm, only an elderly donkey, so she wasn't sure what she was supposed to be looking for, but the ox did indeed seem to have clean, solid hooves, without cracks or irregularities.

"In a gnole's language, that's an ox's name."

"Good Hooves?"

Brindle pulled down one corner of his lip in a frown. "No, *good*." He arched his whiskers as he said it. "Mmm. Beautiful, maybe?"

Halla stared at the hooves in question, which were brown and muddy. *Beautiful* seemed excessive, but what did she know?

"Prettyfoot?" she said.

Brindle broke into a smile, canines gleaming. "Yes. Close enough. Good name for an ox."

Halla agreed, and made a mental note to never, ever tell Sarkis.

———

THEY SAW the Motherhood riders again the next day, although the men did not speak to them at any length. They merely rode past, giving Zale a hostile look, and kept riding.

"Crying won't keep them away forever," said Halla.

"I wish I knew why they were so obsessed with us..." muttered Zale. "Or perhaps this is simply how they treat all religious travelers."

"Some men do not like defiance," rumbled Sarkis. "It eats at them like poison."

"I didn't defy them *that* much," said Zale.

"Has your god?"

The priest opened their mouth, then closed it again, their dark eyes thoughtful. After a moment: "We have. Whenever they overstep themselves, the other temples stand against them...and I will be honest, it is usually the Rat who supplies the law clerks. I had not thought of our Temple as the face of defiance, I confess, for it is the Forge God who opens their coffers, and the Dreaming God and the Saint of Steel whose paladins often stand guard. I had viewed our position as one of practicality, not of great courage. But it is often the Rat's lawyers that they *see.*"

Sarkis nodded. "The spokesman for the enemy becomes the focus of hate. I would guess they harry you for that reason as much as any other."

"Ugh." Zale scowled. "I feel like I should offer you a discount for having to put up with this."

"You could take a nineteen percent commission instead of twenty?" said Halla hopefully.

"Consider it done. And now let us talk of happier things."

"Does this end with me pissing in a jar again?"

"I believe we have reached the limit of what we can learn from you and the jars."

"The great god be praised! Halla, I know you're laughing, you don't have to strangle yourself trying to hide it."

"I'm laughing *with* you...mostly...and you're not actually laughing..."

Zale snickered, then sobered. "I have been contemplating how the magic maintains itself," they explained. "The power to fuel the sword must come from somewhere. The power to fuel a normal body comes from the food we eat, whether we are horses or humans or rats, but the process is...not efficient, let us say. I suspect that your process is far more efficient, in its way."

"It's magic," said Sarkis.

"Yes, but even magic does not last forever. It wears away eventually, through use and time."

"You mean eventually the sword might run out?" asked Halla, her voice rising with concern.

Zale leaned back against the wagon seat. "In the normal course of events, I would have expected it to do so long since. Few wonderworkers have a power that outlasts their death. I know of very few that might outlast centuries. Whoever your sorcerer-smith was, Sarkis, she was either unimaginably gifted, or she knew how to bend her talent to her will."

"She was as mad as the mist and snow," said Sarkis grimly.

Zale looked unconcerned. "As are a great many people," they said. "Many madmen walk among the sane, and the lines are blurred beyond all recognition. And many people who we would consider sane wreak unimaginable harm in the world, so people call them mad."

Sarkis grunted, but inclined his head in acknowledgement. "Fair enough."

"Humans use the wrong words," said Brindle unexpectedly. "Say *crazy* when they mean *head-sick*. Crazy means *crazy*."

"It is a difficult word to translate," admitted Zale. "The temple of the Many-Armed God wrote the definitive treatise on gnole-language. I fear that Brindle has a much more extensive vocabulary than we do for this, and we are but fumbling in comparison."

"Eh. Humans can't smell," muttered Brindle, with the air of one making allowances.

"*Zeth,*" said Sarkis.

"Beg pardon?"

"*Zeth.* Damn, Brindle's right. Your language is wrong."

"Told you, sword-man." The gnole nodded to him.

"Can you explain?" asked Halla.

"Look, I'm speaking your language now. I know it quite well, because of the magic. If Halla stops wielding me, though, I'll stop knowing it. It's in my head, and most of the words translate automatically, but some don't, and some are trying to, but they're the wrong words. Shit, this is coming out wrong." He scowled. "*Zeth.* It's a word in my language, but not in yours, except yours is trying to make it a word, but I don't think it's the right word."

"I'm with you so far," said Halla. "What's *zeth* mean? Or can you not put a word on it?"

"Ah...a type of wickedness. Your language wants to use 'insane' but that's not right. To go *zeth* is to lose all conscience, but *zeth* people still have all their reason." He raised his hands, let them drop. "A madman should not be punished for being mad, and may still feel horror and guilt at what they do, but the *zeth* know better, they simply don't care."

Halla rolled the word around on her tongue. "So it's like evil."

"Well...yes. Except that you can do something evil and know it's evil and care that it's evil and do it anyway and feel guilt for it. If you're *zeth,* you just do it and the fact it's evil doesn't bother you. But you're still sane. If it is a sickness, it is of the soul, not of the mind that houses it."

Halla frowned, but Zale was nodding. "Yes," they said. "That is the sort I spoke of earlier. They do great evil in the world, those people."

"And was your sorcerer-smith *zeth?*" asked Halla.

Hearing a word from the Weeping Lands on her tongue made him smile, even such a word as that. "Perhaps. It is easy for me to say so, now. Who could possibly prove me wrong? But it has been so long, and I knew her for only a day, so I cannot say for certain."

The conversation was veering toward dangerous places. Sarkis knew that he would eventually have to tell Halla all the truth about the sword and how he came to be in it, but it did not seem like the time.

After she is safe. After she has her inheritance and her own place again, and she can spurn you if she wishes. To do so now would either force her to forgive you when she should not or abandon you when she dares not, and neither option is fair.

And you're afraid. If she does abandon you, even if it is no more than you deserve, you will lose her.

She looked over at him and smiled, and Sarkis wondered what he would promise her, to keep her from abandoning him, and did not know the answer.

CHAPTER 29

The next day passed easily enough. The day was cold and frost lay on the leaves long past noon. It was not until early evening that trouble struck them.

Zale inhaled sharply, looking ahead. Sarkis saw the flash of indigo cloaks and his heart sank.

"Them again," he said.

"They are persistent," muttered Zale. "Like flies returning to a turd."

"Making us the turd?"

"Well..."

"Halt!" said the man in the lead, the one Sarkis was thinking of as Red.

Brindle did not halt, but given that the ox was moving only slightly above a dead stop at any given time, the Motherhood men didn't seem to notice.

"We must insist that you allow us to inspect your wagon for contraband," said the one Sarkis called Scar.

"And I must insist that you do nothing of the sort," said Zale, drawing themselves up to their full height. "We have been over this. You have no authority here."

"The Motherhood is charged with rooting out wickedness," said Scar. "We have the authority of our goddess."

"The Hanged Mother has no authority over the Rat."

"On this road, the Mother has authority over *everyone*," said Red. He crowded his horse closer. "The Archon trusts to our discretion."

"This is tyranny!" Zale fumed. "You overstep yourself!"

"If you have nothing to hide, then you have nothing to fear," said Scar.

Sarkis had heard that line before, usually in the mouths of men who had a great deal to hide themselves. He ground his teeth.

Attack and you can probably take them both. Neither has a bow. But they're mounted and you'll only get the advantage of surprise on one. There's a chance Halla or Zale could get injured.

And supposing you do kill them, what then?

He doubted that anyone would cry for the priests, but the others of their Motherhood might come looking. And as far as a speedy getaway was concerned...well, perhaps if they all got out and pushed.

Zale's thin hand closed over Sarkis's wrist. He hadn't realized that his hand had been drifting toward the hilt of his sword. The priest looked him in the eye and clearly made a calculation.

"Fine," grated the priest. "Look all you want. Brindle, stop the wagon."

The gnole guided the ox to a stop by the side of the road. "Haw!" he called, and then, finally, "Whoa!" The ox obeyed, deeply unimpressed.

There was a secret compartment in the wagon. Sarkis found out about this when one of the Motherhood men went straight to it and pulled it up out of the floor.

They knew there was a compartment. Probably they've seen

wagons like this before. Sarkis kept his hand away from his sword, eyes locked on Zale, waiting for a signal.

"And what have we here?" asked Scar, hefting a small bag.

"Money," said Zale, not at all perturbed. "You carry it to buy things with."

"Why are you hiding it?"

"Are you really asking why I keep my money in a safe place in the wagon rather than dangling it off my belt where any bandit can see it?"

Sarkis's hand moved to the hilt of his sword again. Zale gave him a warning look.

Scar seemed annoyed at this response. He searched the wagon in a somewhat perfunctory fashion.

"If you told me what you were looking for, I could probably be more helpful," said Zale, in a not at all helpful voice.

Red reached under the wagon seat and pulled something out.

"Can you explain *this*, priest?"

"It's a crossbow," said Zale, as if speaking to a rather dim child. "You shoot it at things."

"Why are you carrying one?"

"Because we might get stopped by bandits," said Zale. "Or other people intent on mischief. As I'm sure you're aware, these roads are simply *full* of people who like to harass innocent travelers."

Red scowled. So did Scar.

"You've found nothing," said Zale, folding their arms. "Because there is nothing to find. *Now* will you stop pestering us?"

"We are watching you, priest," said Red, tossing down the crossbow. It was unloaded, but Sarkis and Zale both flinched when it struck the wagon seat anyway.

"And I'm watching you," grated Zale. "And the eyes of the

Rat see farther than those of the Mother. For one thing, there's a lot more of them."

Red curled his lip, stalked to his horse, and mounted without a word. He kicked his horse into a trot before Scar had finished mounting, and the two vanished in a cloud of road dust.

"Petty tyrants," muttered Zale. They grabbed their pewter braid and twisted it irritably.

Halla shook her head. "The miller back home was like that," she said. "He had a little bit of power and he lorded it over everyone. Although there's less damage you can do with a mill than with a religious order."

There was a brief pause while everyone gave this statement the consideration it deserved.

"I am going to compile a book," said Zale. "Wit and Wisdom of Mistress Halla. With occasional interjections by Ser Sarkis of the Weeping Lands and Brindle the Gnole."

"Humans talk too much," said Brindle. "There's a wisdom for a human's book, rat-priest."

"That probably deserves its own chapter." Zale shook themself, looking not unlike a gnole as they did it. "Well. To turn to more important matters...Before we were so rudely interrupted, I was thinking about the enchantment on the sword. I believe your sorcerer-smith had a wild talent of some sort, but she built on that foundation. Do you know what happened to your body when you died?"

"Eh?" said Sarkis. He'd still been thinking about the Motherhood men. "What?"

"The first time," said Zale patiently. "When you were trapped in the sword. Did your body dematerialize into the blade or did it simply die?"

Sarkis blinked at them.

"How would he know?" asked Halla. "I mean, if he went into the sword right away..."

Zale sighed. "I suppose you're right. It's a pity, that might tell us more."

"Not me," said Sarkis slowly. "But I saw Angharad and the Dervish run through."

He could see it far too clearly suddenly: the dim, stinking forge, the smell of iron and charcoal and burning flesh.

"Angharad was first." He picked at the seam of his armwraps. "I watched them quench the sword in her heart's blood. She didn't cry out. She was always strong and silent as an ox. The Dervish screamed, though. I remember his scream. I still hear it sometimes, when I'm dying."

Halla clutched his hand. He looked down at it, puzzled, then squeezed.

This makes hard listening. I should have thought.

"Forgive me," he said. "I didn't mean to upset you."

"No!" she said, exasperated. "I'm not...oh, dammit." She tucked his hand under her arm and bumped her shoulder against him, awkward and sincere.

Zale had gone pale. "I should not have asked," they said. "I find a thread and pull it, sometimes, and I forget that there may be genuine emotions attached."

"It is all right," said Sarkis. *How much did I give away, when I was talking? I know I did not weep or scream...* He cleared his throat. "The bodies fell. They did not turn into fire or vanish into the sword. At least, not that I saw."

Zale looked, if anything, more uncomfortable. "I see." They took a deep breath. "Then, Sarkis, I fear I must inform you that you are probably dead."

Sarkis stared at them for a moment, then burst out laughing.

"Of course I'm dead!" he said. "I've died more times than I

can count. I just don't stay dead for more than a fortnight at a time."

"Oh good," said Zale, with clear relief. "I was afraid that might be a shock to you. You never know how people will take this sort of thing."

"He's not dead, though," said Halla. "I mean, he's warm. And he's got a pulse. And he eats and drinks and then…err…"

"Yes, we've been through what happens after the drinking once today already," said Sarkis.

"To go back to that—" Zale began.

"Oh, by the great god. Am I to be required to fill another jar?"

"No, no. Well, probably not. Tell me, if you have a full bladder and then go back in the sword, do you still have one when you re-emerge?"

"I…" Sarkis had never given this much thought. "I do not spend centuries having to piss, if that's what you mean."

"Thank the gods," muttered Halla. "Can you imagine? That would be dreadful."

"No, no. But when you re-emerge, do you still need to? Or does the sword make all of that go away?"

"Oh, of course!" said Halla. "That's a great question! If you eat out here, when you dematerialize, the contents of your stomach obviously go back in with you."

"They do?"

"Well, think about it," she said. "They must. You've been eating food for the last few days, but when we put you back in the sword, there isn't a pile of half-digested potatoes suddenly hanging in midair, is there?"

Sarkis removed his hand from her arm and inched away from her on the wagon seat. She rolled her eyes at him.

"We'll have to test it," said Zale firmly. They grabbed a waterskin. "I'm going to need you to drink this."

"Of *course* you are."

Sarkis drank the water, even though he wasn't remotely thirsty, and lowered the skin to see both Halla and Zale watching him closely. "I haven't had anyone this concerned about my bladder since my mother trained me out of split pants."

"Sorry," said Zale, clearly not remotely sorry.

"But think how much we're learning!" said Halla.

"The two of you are like kindred spirits. Horrible, horrible kindred spirits." He took another swig of water.

The ox plodded down the road. The air crackled with frost. Brindle ignored them all with the air of long practice.

His companions were far too obviously waiting for his bladder to fill. Sarkis cleared his throat uncomfortably. "So I'm a ghost, you say?"

"I hope not," said Zale. "If you're a ghost then we might be practicing necromancy."

Halla blanched.

"Is that a problem?"

"Necromancy is anathema in every civilized nation," said Zale.

"Is it?"

"People do frown on monstrous evil," said Halla.

"Not nearly often enough if you ask me," Sarkis said. He drank more water, not with much enthusiasm. "We don't have necromancers in the Weeping Lands. At least, not that I have ever heard of."

"Fortunate land," said Zale. They rubbed the back of their neck. "Necromancy is honestly more legend than reality here. But there is at least one well-documented case a century ago. A healer who could not bear failure, and had the gift. He chained the souls of the dying to their bodies, until, he said, he could find a way cure death itself." They shuddered. "The records make for grim reading."

"Did they start to decay?" asked Halla.

"Yes. Many of the dead went to great lengths to try to destroy their own bodies. Some lashed out at others around them. It is the blackest of the black arts."

Sarkis leaned back. "What is the punishment?"

Zale shot him a brief glance. "There isn't one."

"What?"

"It's not a thing you punish." The priest shrugged. "It's a thing you stop. It's like...oh, like a rabid dog. You don't punish the dog or the necromancer. It's not like that. You just kill them so that it stops. It was a group of paladins that killed the healer, with the blessings of any number of gods. They had to burn the entire place down to stop the dead. Fortunately, there was a priest of the Many-Armed God in attendance, and he rescued the healer's notes."

"The great god have mercy."

"I don't think He had a paladin there, but presumably that was a matter of distance rather than approval."

Sarkis snorted.

"The Rat calls lawyers and advocates to His service rather than paladins, but I must admit, the ones with swords have their uses."

Halla was clearly working something over in her mind. "Sarkis may be dead, but he's not decaying," she said. "But that might be because the sword doesn't decay. Do you think a necromancer could bind a soul into a sword?"

"You're saying the smith was a *necromancer?*"

"I'm not *saying* anything," said Halla, sounding exasperated. "I'm asking a question!"

"That *is* a skill you have," muttered Sarkis.

Zale tapped their fingers together, brow knitting. Finally,

they said, "It's an interesting question. It would make a certain sense, but it's not a thing that I know how to test. And I've never heard of a necromancer that could make a temporary body out of pure magic, the way that the sword does for Sarkis."

Sarkis set the waterskin down. "Speaking of which, you could probably put me back in the sword now."

"What? Wh—oh!" Halla flushed. "Right! Sorry. Got distracted."

"Believe me, anything that took the conversation away from my bladder was worth it." He shifted uncomfortably on the seat.

Halla clicked the sword into its sheath and the blue fire took him away.

CHAPTER 30

"**R**ight!" said Halla a day later. "We've established that even if you're hungry or thirsty when you go into the sword, you come out feeling neither, at least if you're in the sword for more than about twenty minutes."

Zale was writing everything down in their quick, precise hand, and nodded to her.

"And if you go into the sword with a full bladder, you come out without one."

Sarkis rubbed his forehead in resignation.

"And presumably that applies to other—uh—bodily wastes—"

"We are *not* testing that," said Sarkis grimly. "A man has limits."

"And if you eat until you are uncomfortably full, that, too, goes away."

Sarkis nodded. He hadn't enjoyed that one. The only food they had on hand in quantity was porridge, and he had eaten a truly heroic amount. He wasn't going to be able to look at porridge again for a month.

"We have not tested what occurs if you are drunk—"

"I become sober when the sword is sheathed," said Sarkis. "I know that one."

Zale nodded, making a note, then paused with their hand over the ledger. "Have you ever starved to death?"

"No. I've gotten very thirsty a time or two during a siege, but that's all."

Zale tapped the pen against their teeth. They had excellent teeth. Sarkis had observed the priest scrubbing their teeth with salt and sage nightly, which was undoubtedly a factor. "I do wonder if you'd be hungry if you were starved until it became a form of injury, then went back in the sword for an insufficient time to heal...but I have a philosophical objection to testing that."

"As do I," put in Halla.

"Thank the great god for that."

He stifled a sigh, remembering sieges. He had dealt with more than a few in his time. His company of mercenaries had been good at sieges—making them, breaking them, occasionally even enduring them. Their services had been in high demand.

And now I am riding on an oxcart with two people who are making me eat porridge until I am ill, and who get excited when my urine dematerializes. The great god laughs at man's expectations.

Still, he had to admit that he had learned rather more about the actual workings of the sword in a few days than he had learned in all the years since the sorcerer-smith had trapped him.

I should have listened more closely when she was explaining the process, but it was so clearly impossible, what she was saying...

The beating he'd taken beforehand hadn't helped his concentration. In truth, he'd probably been lucky to have absorbed as much as he had from the woman before she'd driven a length of white-hot steel into his chest.

Even so, he couldn't remember her explaining how it *worked*.

"The smith was a genius," said Zale, as if echoing his thoughts. "If she had been a simple wonderworker, we would expect that the magic would have released you when she died. Whatever she did, she built this magic that gives you a body that seems real...and to use the processes of that body, the food you eat and the air you breathe, to fuel the magic. And because your body is not truly reliant on the same weak, complicated meat that the rest of us are—" they slapped their arm by way of demonstration "—it converts those processes with remarkable efficiency. It's incredible."

"Could you do it?" said Halla, genuinely interested.

"Rat's Tail, no! I can just barely understand *how* it works. The kind of mind that could set that up..." They shook their head so vigorously that their braid whipped from side to side. "That's why I say genius. Most wonderworkers are creatures of instinct. They learn the boundaries of their power by running into them. This smith built her magic like the artificers in Anuket build clockwork automatons, and then used whatever natural talent she had to power it. It is extraordinary." They gazed at Sarkis with something uncomfortably like awe. "Even killing your body only pauses the magic temporarily. In theory, at least, you are nearly immortal."

Sarkis sighed. "I am very tired of being immortal," he confessed.

Zale looked briefly surprised. "Are you?"

"I would like to be allowed to die," said Sarkis.

Halla made a sound of protest and Sarkis reached out without thinking, taking her hand in his. "Not *now*. Not today. Someday, though, before I am nothing but silver scars, before I've forgotten what it was like to be human."

"Is it so awful?" asked Halla.

He glanced over and caught the look in her eyes. It pained him more than he wanted to admit. He squeezed her fingers. "Sometimes. Though these last few weeks have been a respite. I have had to murder very few people and no one has chopped any part of my anatomy off in *ages.*"

She snorted, obviously happy to lighten the mood as well. "Let us know if you start to miss that part."

She glanced away, smiling. He gazed at her full lower lip and imagined running his tongue across it. Increasingly, the only thing he regretted about their earlier kiss was that he had stopped at just one.

Settle yourself, man. It is still a long way to Rutger's Howe.

"Well," said Zale, in a suddenly grim voice, "it seems that you might have someone try to chop parts off you very shortly."

"Problem?" said Sarkis.

Zale nodded ahead. A familiar pair of indigo cloaked men stood in the middle of the road. One was mounted, while one had dismounted and stood waiting.

"Again?" said Halla. "They already searched the wagon. What more can they want?"

"I suspect that it was never about searching anything," said Zale. "The Rat has been a thorn in the Mother's side, and they are acting it out by harassing us. They never expected to find anything. No one really thinks the Rat is smuggling…I don't know, contraband or witchcraft or children or whatever. They simply want to prove that we cannot stop them."

Scar gestured for them to stop. Halla curled her lip back. There was a look in her eye that worried Sarkis.

As it turned out, he was right to be worried.

HALLA WAS sick of the Motherhood, sick of being bullied, sick of men like Scar and Alver and all the rest. She slid down off the wagon before Sarkis could grab her and stomped determinedly toward Scar.

"Halla!" She heard Sarkis's feet hit the road behind her.

"I have had *enough!*" shouted Halla in Scar's face. "You've bothered us and tormented us and yelled at us and we didn't do anything and you searched the wagon for no reason and you *know* it's for no reason and this isn't how the Mother is supposed to behave! It isn't *right!*"

And then she burst into tears.

It was at least ninety percent intentional, as she already knew that Scar panicked in the face of crying women. Ten percent of it was that she was angry, and she always cried when she was really angry. She hooked both hands in Scar's indigo tabard and wailed. Loudly.

"Uh," said Scar. "Uh. Ma'am. No. Uh." He looked around in panic. Red backed his horse away, possibly afraid that Halla would leap into the saddle and begin crying on him instead.

What happened next was mostly bad luck.

Scar shoved Halla away. He shoved her rather hard, to be sure, but if there had not been a rock under her foot *right there*, she wouldn't have fallen.

But there *was* a rock and she did fall, with a yelp of surprise, and Sarkis, presumably, saw his wielder being knocked down and possibly injured. He charged.

Halla herself saw only the underside of the ox, realized that she had rolled beneath the animal, and kept rolling out the other side. Her ankle twinged painfully from the rock. Then she heard the clash of steel.

She climbed to her feet, eyes wide, to find that Sarkis and Scar were sword to sword. The priest looked shocked and Sarkis looked furious. Zale was yelling, "Stand down, *stand down!*" No one appeared to be listening.

Red, who was still mounted, drew his sword. He shuffled his horse from side to side, trying to find a way to strike at Sarkis without hitting his own ally. The ox was in the way.

"Stand down!" cried Zale helplessly.

Sarkis was winning easily, probably because immortal swordsmen can take openings that mortal swordsmen would find dangerously close to suicide.

The horse's rump smacked into the ox. The ox made an irritated noise and sidestepped, making the wagon shudder, then turned its horns toward the horse, dragging the wagon sideways with it.

Something went THWACK.

An arrow sprouted from the mounted warrior's throat and he toppled off the horse, just as Sarkis pulled his sword out of his opponent's chest.

Brindle lowered Zale's crossbow.

The sound of the second body hitting the road was very loud in the sudden silence.

"Well," said Zale, their voice sounding high and strained, "this is going to be a problem."

CHAPTER 31

"It's my fault," said Halla. "If I hadn't fallen…"

"No, it's my fault," said Zale. "If I hadn't been so stubborn about the Motherhood not having the rights to search the wagon…"

"But if I hadn't tried to head them off by crying at them…"

"Far be it from me to interrupt the mutual self-flagellation, but Brindle and I actually did the killing."

"A gnole doesn't mind if a human wants to take the blame for a gnole."

Zale wrung their hands. Sarkis looked over at Brindle. "Good shot, though."

The gnole shrugged. "Shouldn't have annoyed an ox."

"Well, what do we do now?" asked Halla. "Do we…um… hand ourselves in? Or hide the bodies?"

They looked at the bodies. They looked at each other. They looked at Zale.

Zale raked their hands through their hair, twisting their braid. "What? Why do I have to decide?"

"You're a lawyer," said Sarkis.

"And a priest," added Halla. "I think that makes you the closest we have to a legal and moral authority."

"Yes, but I handle property cases, not murder!"

Halla rubbed the back of her neck. "Would praying help?"

Sarkis snorted, but Zale seized on it. "Prayer. Yes. It'll clear my mind, anyway." They slid off the wagon, walked a little way away, and were suddenly, violently ill.

"Sounds like it's clearing something," said Sarkis.

Halla gave him an annoyed look and went to the priest, holding their hair back from their face.

"All right," said the priest a few minutes later, looking pale but resolute. "I've prayed."

Sarkis said, "That sounded more like puking to m—" and then Halla elbowed him in the ribs.

"This was all a very regrettable misunderstanding," said Zale, blotting the corners of their mouth on the back of their hand. "Sadly, the Motherhood is not likely to be forgiving about it. Those men did not deserve to die, but at the same time, neither do we. And nothing we do is going to make them any less dead." They nodded firmly, as if settling the words in their mind.

"So we're hiding the bodies, then," said Sarkis.

"I think it's for the best."

"The ground's frozen," said Halla. "I'm not sure we could bury them. And we don't have a lot of wild beasts in the area to eat them." She chewed on her lower lip. "If the hogs hadn't all just been slaughtered, I'd say we take them out to an acorn wood..."

Sarkis had been expecting Halla to sob, cry, or perhaps be as sick as Zale. Her remarkable calm in the face of two dead bodies was simultaneously heartening and a trifle alarming.

"You're taking this well," he said.

She raised an eyebrow at him. "I've laid out the bodies of

my sisters, my mother, my husband, one of the fieldhands, my great-uncle, and Old Nan the cook, when her heart gave out in the kitchen. Dead bodies don't worry me. It's the live ones that get you." She went into the wagon.

"Well, I've been put in my place," muttered Sarkis.

"Good to be humble sometimes, sword-man. Helps the digestion."

Halla came out with two blankets. "Let's wrap them up and put them in the wagon."

Zale sighed heavily. "Corpses in my wagon..."

"Well, we can't very well put them on top. People would notice."

"Yes, it's just the principle. What do we do with the horses?"

"I'll ride them out of here and strip their tack," volunteered Sarkis. "Once I'm out of range of the sword, I'll get pulled back to it, and there won't be a trail for anyone to follow, if they do come with dogs."

Zale nodded. "Clever."

"I have my moments."

HALLA WAS, in fact, not quite so calm as she was pretending to be. She had seen plenty of dead bodies, she hadn't lied about that, but seeing someone—two someones—killed in front of her had been a shock.

She was grateful that Zale had been so upset, because it meant that she didn't have to be. Most of what she'd said while the priest was throwing their guts up had been soothing nonsense—it's not your fault, it's not anybody's fault, it will be okay—but she found it had soothed her own nerves as well.

This comes of always being the practical one, she thought, a bit wearily. *Nobody will comfort you, so you learn to do it yourself.*

Sarkis had actually rolled the bodies in the blankets. She was grateful for that. Looking at the wounds would have seriously tested her calm.

He and Brindle hauled the two bodies into the back of the wagon and then Sarkis went off on the horses and Brindle drove the wagon onward. Halla kept looking back at the bloodstain in the road, but eventually it vanished around a bend and that was that.

Well, except for the matter of the two bodies.

"What are we going to do with them?" asked Zale. "It would take all day to bury them in frozen ground."

"Can we take them back to your temple?" asked Halla. Zale was clearly out of their depth, but she had a suspicion that Bishop Beartongue was not a stranger to disposing of the occasional corpse.

"It would take days," said Zale. "And they'd be in the wagon...er...smelling. And if the Motherhood stops us again and demands to search the wagon..."

They both shuddered.

Halla chewed her lower lip. "What about frozen water?"

Zale glanced at her, puzzled. "I don't follow."

"Look, we're freezing at night, but the water's still pretty slushy, particularly in the woods where you get a lot of oak leaves. We could chop a hole in the ice easier than we could dig a grave. They'll freeze under it, and probably no one will find them until spring."

Zale considered this. "That...might work. Clearly you have a fine criminal mind."

"I'm flattered. Wait, should I be flattered?"

"I don't know any more," sighed the priest.

"It's not like I've hidden a body in a pond before. It's just that one of the goats drowned one fall and we didn't find the body until spring."

"It's a good idea, anyway," said Zale. "They'll know that they're missing once the horses show up, and they'll probably guess they're dead before long, but there's no reason they'll suspect us over anybody else on the road. And by the time they find the bodies, it'll be months from now and everyone's memory of when they went where will be hopelessly foggy."

They stared at their hands. "Rat's bones, I can't believe we're hiding bodies."

"I'd feel a lot guiltier if it wasn't the Motherhood," admitted Halla. "They were just awful to the hostelkeeper's wife about a year ago. Really nasty."

Zale nodded. "The Hanged Mother attracts a certain kind of mind, I fear. An unkind one. I have met a few among them who were not so bad, but it is a faith for those value power and punishment. And—"

They cut off abruptly as the wagon rounded a corner, revealing a goatherd moving his charges down the road.

"Act natural!" hissed Zale.

Halla plastered a smile on her face and hoped it did not look as horribly strained as it felt. Zale had a much better poker-face, probably because of their legal training, but they gave away so little that they looked more like a statue of a priest.

"Lovely day, isn't it?" said Halla.

The goatherd looked at her, then at the cold drizzle surrounding them, and said, "Eh?"

"I mean, not lovely. Very not lovely. *Lousy* weather."

The goatherd allowed as how it was indeed lousy. Zale sat stiff as a poker, gazing down the road at nothing much.

The sword on Halla's back moved suddenly, hilt clicking down into the sheath. Halla jumped as if she'd been kicked and let out a yelp.

The goatherd inched over to the side of the road to give the wagon a wide berth. The goats eyed them all maliciously, but this probably didn't mean anything, since in Halla's experience, goats eyed everything maliciously.

They vanished around the bend. Zale relaxed. Halla rubbed her forehead.

"That could have gone better," she said.

"I doubt they suspect we've got bodies," said Zale. "They probably just think we're in a cult."

"Is that better or worse than bodies?"

"It's fine as long as they don't want to join our cult."

Brindle stared straight ahead, shaking his head slowly. He muttered something under his breath, fortunately not in a language that either human understood.

Halla looked both ways for observers, then carefully drew the sword, and Sarkis appeared beside her.

"The horses were running when I dematerialized," said Sarkis. "They'll...ah, you two look a trifle tense. Is something wrong?"

"There are rather more dead bodies than I find acceptable stowed under my seat!" said Zale.

"How many dead bodies *would* you find acceptable?"

"Ideally, zero." The priest chewed on their lower lip. "One would be bad, but I feel like I would handle it better. Two is really an excessive number."

Halla made a strangled noise that might have been a laugh or a sob or a sigh. Even she wasn't entirely sure. Sarkis pounded her on the back for a moment, apparently fearing that she was choking.

"Well, at least the horses will keep going for a little bit, I expect." He scowled. "I don't like to spook a horse, but the farther away they get before they stop, the safer it'll be for everyone."

"Better not try it with an ox, sword-man."

"I would not dream of it, Brindle."

"That's the horses sorted then," said Zale. They sighed. "And now to sort out the bodies..."

FINDING a pond was easier said than done.

It had to be far enough off the road that nobody would notice them lugging bodies and close enough to the road that they *could* lug bodies. It had to be a pond that nobody was using to water their stock, because neither Halla nor Zale wanted to risk fouling someone's primary water source. And they definitely had to have some kind of tree cover so that no one would be strolling by and notice a pair of corpses frozen under the ice.

And of course, nobody would have put such ponds on the map, preferably with convenient notes like, "Perfect for body disposal!" or, "Dump unwanted enemies here!"

The bodies stayed in the wagon that night, which meant that everybody else stayed outside. Brindle generously offered the ox's body heat, so there were three humans and one gnole huddled against the side of the large, bemused, but basically good-natured ox.

Sarkis resigned himself to not getting much sleep. Zale curled themself into a neat ball, not unlike Brindle. Halla dropped off immediately and then began trying to wedge herself into the space between his back and the ox.

Well, it's the warmest spot around, I suppose...

He wondered how on earth she'd shared a bed with her husband. Had the man simply brought his own blanket to wrap himself in?

The thought of Halla sharing that other man's bed woke an

unexpected jealousy. He surrendered to it, and gathered her up so that she was across his lap with her back to the ox's warmth.

This was not the best idea, he realized a moment later. It was all too easy to imagine her waking up, turning to straddle his hips, looking in his eyes and saying...saying...

Probably, "Oh no, are your legs asleep again? I'm sorry!"

He stifled a sigh. Brindle reached out and poked his shoulder with one clawed finger.

"Hmm?" He looked up into the gnole's striped face.

"Twisting your whiskers, sword-man. A human should go to sleep."

"A human's trying."

"A human should try harder."

CHAPTER 32

"I can't believe there's corpses in my wagon," said Zale the next morning, hunching their narrow shoulders up around their ears. "I keep thinking about them being right there. Under the seat."

"I'm wondering how we're going to get them *out* of the wagon," said Halla. "Without being caught."

"You know," said Sarkis, "I've killed hundreds of people—possibly by this point thousands—and I've never had this much trouble with two dead bodies before."

"Perhaps you should take this as an incentive to give up killing," said Zale.

"It certainly takes a lot of the fun out of it."

"Who knew that it would be so difficult to find a small pond?" moaned Halla. "There's hundreds of them. I know there's hundreds of them. But where *are* they?"

"One north of here," said Brindle, not turning his head.

"Eh? How do you know?"

"Smell it." Brindle tapped his nose. "Smells like ice."

"Ice has a smell?" said Zale.

"Gnoles say humans can't smell," muttered Brindle, rolling

248

his eyes. "Not just saying. *Yes*, rat-priest. Smells like cold tin." He tilted his head back and sniffed. Halla could see his black nostrils working.

"I'll go look," said Sarkis, sliding off the wagon.

He came back a few minutes later. "It must be farther back than I thought, because I didn't see it. But there's a track into the woods a little way up from here that we can probably get the wagon down."

When they reached the gap, Brindle looked at it thoughtfully, then nodded and steered the ox toward the overgrown track. "Good road," he said after a moment. "But not used much."

"Could be one of the pig roads," said Halla. "I mean, not *made* by the pigs, but this is the acorn wood everybody fattens their hogs up in, and then you have to go get them out again. And if they don't want to come out, you need to get a wagon up there so you're not carrying a slaughtered hog for miles. But you only need it a couple times a year."

"Are we going to be tripping over all the local swineherds?" asked Sarkis.

"I doubt it." Halla shook her head. "It's too late in the season. Everybody slaughtered their hogs already. Any left out now are starting to lose fat." She frowned. "I won't swear there's not a sounder of feral hogs in the woods, of course…"

"There are," said Zale. "We get reports in Archenhold. Somebody tried to bring an action against a pig farmer saying his boar went feral and mauled their son, but without tracking down the boar to check the brand, they couldn't prove whose boar it was. And the army says it's not their job to kill livestock and the paladins won't do it unless the boar's possessed and the Squire here doesn't hunt, so…" They shrugged. "The case was dropped."

"Pond," said Brindle, nodding ahead of them.

"You smelled this from the road?" said Sarkis, impressed. The pond was little more than hollow filled with leaves and slush. Tracks in the frozen mud showed that the pigs had been using it to drink.

"Surprised you didn't, sword-man."

"Well," said Sarkis, looking at the pond, "I suppose it'll work. If the pigs dig them up, they'll vanish just as effectively into a hog as a pond." Zale made a small noise of dismay.

Sarkis had to use the camp shovel to make a hole in the slush. It was normally for digging small, impromptu latrines and occasionally for covering over campfires, but it did well enough. Brindle got out the hatchet and set to work beside him. Between the two of them, they slowly chopped out a corpse-sized hole in the ice, while Halla collected pine boughs to cover over the bodies.

Zale looked slightly green, but unlocked the wagon and pulled the door open. "I am starting to feel like a murderer," they said.

"This wasn't murder," said Sarkis. "It was *killing*. And they started it." He grabbed one of the sheet-wrapped bodies by the head. Brindle grabbed the feet.

"Hold on," said Halla, as they were carrying it toward the ice. She pulled out a knife and slice off a bit of the sheet's hem.

"Eh?"

"There's a dancing rat embroidered in the corner. Bit of a giveaway if anyone finds the bodies."

"Must your Temple put rats on *everything?*" grumbled Sarkis, dropping the body into the trench in the ice.

"Our god is a rat! It's what we do!"

The second body followed the first into the ice, sans decorative rat.

"Right." Sarkis dusted off his hands while Halla dragged pine branches over the bodies. "There's that sorted."

"It doesn't look very well disguised," said Zale dubiously. "It looks like somebody chopped up the ice and then put branches over it to hide something."

"Yes, well. Doesn't your practical rat-god teach you how to hide bodies?"

Zale sighed heavily. "No," they admitted. "Although I am starting to believe that was a severe oversight. I shall bring it up with the bishop."

"You do that."

"I'm sure it'll be better after it snows a bit," said Halla.

They climbed back on the wagon. Brindle clucked to the ox and it began moving, following the track deeper into the woods.

"Don't we want to go back?"

"Can't turn a wagon here, sword-man. Got to find a wide spot."

Halla frowned. "There must be one nearby. You don't make a wagon road without having at least a place to pass. Otherwise if you meet someone coming, one of you has to back up for a long way."

Sarkis grunted. He had never given it a great deal of thought. The supply wagon for his band, once they were big enough to have one, had been handled by the quartermaster. Beyond determining if a road was wide enough for a wagon, Sarkis had little to do with it. He'd always praised the woman as a miracle worker, he just hadn't realized what sort of miracles she'd been pulling off.

"We could cut down some of these trees," he said. "Make a space to turn around."

Halla and Zale both looked at him as if he had casually suggested burning the forest down.

"...what?"

"To cut another property owner's trees without permission

is worse than poaching," said Zale. "Men have been hanged for it."

"If they try to hang me, they'll get a surprise," said Sarkis.

"Yes, but..." Zale looked at Halla helplessly. "Without explaining three hundred years of forestry laws, I'm not sure how to express this."

"You're allowed to collect fallen deadwood," said Halla. "That's everybody's right. But cutting a living tree is like killing a shepherd's sheep. They *belong* to somebody."

"We've already murdered a couple of people. I don't think cutting trees is going to be that big a sin."

"No, but..." Halla waved her hands. "Whoever owns these trees didn't do anything to us! And if it's a tenant, they have to inform the landowner if they're clearing and if the landowner finds the trees cut, they'll think they're stealing and they might turn out the tenant! People have lost their homes for less!"

"Takes a long time to cut a tree with a hatchet anyway," said Brindle. "Lot of chopping. Lot of noise. Lot of noise *next to dead humans.*"

"Fine, fine." Sarkis held up his palms in surrender. "We don't cut down the trees."

"There's got to be a turnaround up here somewhere," said Halla.

The sides of the road began to rise. Brindle shook his head, but kept the ox plodding forward.

"There's *got* to be..." Halla started again, and then trailed off. Her lips were pressed together, the thin upper lip jammed into the full lower one. Sarkis realized, with surprise, that she was angry.

"Of course I'm angry!" she said when he asked. "Someone didn't do their job! You build a road, you have to put a spot to turn around. It's just...it's what you *do*. There's got to be a spot."

There wasn't. The embankment on either side grew steeper and steeper, until it was nearly shoulder-high on Sarkis, even sitting on the wagon. Trees leaned over the road, their bare branches laced tightly across the sky.

"It's a hollow way," said Zale. "One of the old, old roads. People passed here so often that they wore a groove in the earth."

"It looks like a tunnel," said Sarkis, loosening his sword. "And it feels like a trap."

"It's just the acorn wood," said Halla, but she didn't sound as sure as she had a few minutes ago.

"Better hope an ox doesn't meet a hog on the road," said Brindle. "An ox might get...upset."

Sarkis pictured the ox panicking. It took some mental effort. But assuming the ox was like a horse, and tried to get out of the way of a threat, or tried to run...He pictured the high-wheeled wagon tipping over and being dragged sideways through the hollow way by the panicking animal, or getting hung up in the shafts and breaking legs...no, that was not a good thing. And if the ox decided to attack instead of run, the situation wasn't going to be much better. Sarkis didn't want to think about an ox trying to gore a boar that was trying to gore an ox, all while dragging the wagon yoke behind it.

"I see light," said Halla, pointing. "It opens up there."

Brindle urged the ox to greater speed, which was largely an exercise in futility.

They reached the end of the hollow way and emerged, blinking, into the sunlight.

They were no longer in the acorn wood. They were halfway up a hillside, near a drop-off. Hills stretched out around them, blazing orange with fall color, set against a steel-blue sky.

Zale and Halla went very still. Brindle halted the ox.

"We're out, right?" said Sarkis. "We can turn around?"

"Out of a hollow, sword-man," said the gnole. "But into something worse."

CHAPTER 33

"It's the Vagrant Hills," said Zale. "It's got to be."

"But they're south," said Halla. "Much farther south! Days of travel, at least, and there are hills and..." She knew that her voice had a hysterical edge to it, but she couldn't quite seem to control it.

"Not if they don't want to be," said Zale.

Sarkis looked from one to the other. "The what?"

"The Vagrant Hills," said Halla. "They...well, they sort of move around a bit. Sometimes they grab people. But we should have been much too far north for that!"

"Perhaps they made a special effort," said Zale, glancing at Sarkis. "To get a closer look at something that interested them."

"A gnole is not getting paid enough for this..." muttered Brindle.

Halla put her hands over her eyes. Of *course* the haunted Vagrant Hills had grabbed them. Why wouldn't they? Her life had been wildly out of control ever since Silas died. A cranky, if attractive, warrior in a magic sword, random people attacking her...what was one more patch of enchanted geography, more or less?

Quit dithering. Roll up your sleeves and get to work.

"How are we going to get out?" she asked. "Does anyone have any ideas?"

"All my knowledge of magic is abstract," admitted Zale. "I do not even know if the Hills count as magic, in the sense that we understand it, or if they are something else we have no word for."

"A gnole's job is to drive the wagon. You want magic, you find a different gnole."

"Well, I don't know anything much about magic," said Halla. "My family hasn't even thrown a minor wonderworker in generations."

"On your mother's side," said Sarkis.

"...true."

"Of us all, the only one with significant firsthand knowledge is Sarkis," said Zale. "So if anyone is qualified—"

"What?" Sarkis laughed, mostly in disbelief. "My firsthand knowledge is all from the wrong direction. One might as well say that getting trampled by a horse would make you an excellent rider." He waved his hand toward the landscape before them. "And even if it did, this is wildly different than anything I've ever seen. The Weeping Lands doesn't *do* this."

"What, bits of your countryside don't get up and move around to suit themselves?"

"Certainly not."

"It's these decadent southern landscapes, I expect," said Halla. She sighed and slid down off the wagon.

"Where are you going?" asked Sarkis.

"To check the edge," she said over her shoulder. The hillside road was wider than the hollow way, but not by much. "If we can turn around, maybe we can still get out of here."

Her heart sank as she neared the drop-off. It wasn't a sheer cliff, but it was at a nasty angle, and if a wheel went over, they weren't getting it back up in a hurry. Most of the hill was a growth of pokeweed and blackberry bramble, full of fluttering as birds popped up from the tangle and then flew back down again.

She leaned forward, frowning. How the devil had the road been cut into the hill at this angle, anyway? You'd need a great many men with shovels...well, it could be done, of course, but who would come out to the Vagrant Hills to do such a thing? Even if you assume the hollow way was linked up by magic... hmmm. No, the hollow way looked exactly like the rest of the hillside, just with the embankments higher than the roadway, with trees growing on top.

Arms went around her waist, and Sarkis lifted her back from the edge of the cliff.

"*Please* don't stand so close to the drop. I may be immortal but I would rather not die of heart failure just yet," he said.

"I wasn't that close to the edge..." grumbled Halla. She was having a hard time concentrating on being indignant, however, since his arms were still around her waist. His chest pressed against her back, very solid and very warm.

Was he holding her longer than necessary? It certainly seemed like it. What if she turned around right now and put her arms around his neck? Would he drop her, startled? Would he kiss her again? Would—

Zale cleared their throat loudly.

Sarkis dropped his arms.

"I don't think we can turn around," said Halla, feeling a flush rising up her face. "Not without risking a wheel going over the edge."

Brindle nodded to her. "Think the same, fish-lady. An ox is strong, could pull the wagon back, but if an ox goes over..." He spread his hands.

"I suppose we just follow the road, then," said Halla. "Since our other choice is to abandon the wagon. Which at this point will probably just leave us in the Vagrant Hills with no wagon."

"I can't believe the Vagrant Hills reached out that far," said Zale. "The road was put there mostly *because* it was too far north for the Hills to bother with."

"I cannot believe that your people have rogue mountain ranges roaming about and have not dealt with it!"

Zale gave him a wry look. "How do you propose we 'deal' with it? Various churches tried to burn out bits of the Hills ages ago. It didn't go well. There are songs about it."

"They aren't happy songs," added Halla.

Sarkis grunted. After a minute he muttered, "You should have used more fire, then."

"I'll take your suggestions to the bishop if we ever get out of here. Now where do we go?"

"What are our options?" said Sarkis.

"Go forward, sword-man."

"Or abandon the wagon, turn the ox, and go back the way we came," said Zale.

"It's got to be one of those two," said Halla. "Since we can't fly."

They looked at the track in front of them. They looked at the track behind them. They looked at the Hills around them.

"I suspect that the Hills are going to let us go, or not, as they choose," said Zale, dark eyes somber. "I doubt the direction matters a great deal. We cannot be anywhere near where we are, ergo it likely does not matter which way we go."

There was a pause while everyone attempted to parse this.

"What does your god tell you?" asked Sarkis.

Zale blinked at him. "Uh...I'm a lawyer. I serve the Rat, and yes, I'm ordained, but I'm not...ah...god-touched. You want justiciars for that sort of thing. That's...um...our equivalent of paladins. I'm merely support staff."

"There's nothing *merely* about it," said Halla, with some asperity. "A paladin wouldn't do me any good getting my inheritance back."

"I suppose they could chop your relatives into tiny bits, but there would be repercussions. Anyway, justiciars don't chop people up, except metaphorically and in court."

Sarkis stared at them. "You...literally...have god-touched lawyers in your order?"

"Not many. We used to have more, but they're really more of a frontier justice sort of thing. Once you have a legal system in place, you mostly need good clerks and people to make sure that the powerful don't walk all over everyone."

Brindle took matters into his own hands and tapped the goad across the ox's back, clucking his tongue. The ox began to amble forward.

"I guess we're going ahead," said Halla.

"Better than talking, fish-lady."

The path wound on around the hill, flanked by trees. They looked like oaks and maple, familiar enough to Halla, but these were only barely beginning to turn color. A few leaves spangled the hillside, but not many. It might be late autumn in the outer world, but in the Vagrant Hills, it was still the tail end of summer.

"What lives in these cursed Hills?" asked Sarkis. "Do you know?"

"Well, there are plenty of reports," said Zale. "But you have to filter those reports based on the fact that people lie and exaggerate and scare themselves silly. I don't think there's dragons living in here, for example, or giants herding trees like sheep, or kraken."

"Kraken in the *woods*?"

"You see why we considered that report unreliable."

Sarkis ground his teeth in frustration. It occurred to Halla that he probably didn't have to worry about damaging his teeth, since he'd get a new set whenever he came out of the sword. She had not previously envied Sarkis's imprisonment, but having had teeth drawn before...yes, all right, she could see the advantages.

Brindle sighed. "A gnole knows a few," he admitted. "A gnole's cousin went into Hills during a war." He held up his left hand and counted them off on blunt claws. One claw. "Mandrake root. Little, throw rocks." Second claw. "Big stone fish. Doesn't do anything." Third claw. "Rabbit. Talks." Fourth claw. "Rune."

"Brindle's cousin may be more reliable than many of our sources," said Zale. "The Many-Armed God's dedicates report that there are, indeed, rune in the hills."

"What's a rune?" said Sarkis.

"Stag-men," said Zale. "And women, presumably. An intelligent people, though there is no written form of their language, so we do not know much about them. Not necessarily hostile, though they seem to primarily wish to be left alone."

"Do they wear green body paint and carry spears?" asked Sarkis.

Zale was intelligent enough to know what that meant. "Where do you see them?"

"There's one up ahead, in the shadow of that split tree," said Sarkis, jerking his chin forward.

"If you see one, there's probably at least a dozen," said Zale. "Make no sudden movements. Do not draw your weapons unless they attack."

Sarkis, nerves already taut, did not like how this was going at all. He had only spotted the rune in front of him because the creature had flicked his ear. He looked like a deer-headed man, more or less, but with fine green hair feathering his lower legs, and hooved feet. His spear was taller than he was and had the look of a stabbing weapon rather than a throwing weapon.

A spear like that, in the proper hands, could be far more lethal than a sword, as Sarkis happened to know. One of the lower scars in the mass scribbled on his chest had been from the point of a spear like that. The wielder had used it like a staff, blocking Sarkis's sword, and then jammed it directly up under his sternum so that Sarkis's last moments had been spent being lifted several inches in the air, looking down the length of the shaft and feeling the sickening drag of metal *through* him.

Then he'd died. Again. It wasn't a pleasant memory, but at least it had been fast.

A bird trilled in the woods, then another. Sarkis did not know even a tenth of the southern birds, but he narrowed his eyes, watching the deer-headed man's ears move to catch the sound.

His suspicions were confirmed a moment later when the rune lifted his head. His throat pulsed and Sarkis heard another high, twittering call. It was strangely incongruous compared to the size of the rune.

Then another, even larger one stepped out of the trees and onto the track ahead of them. He had a massive rack of antlers coated in soft velvet. Another sign that the seasons were running late in these hills, Sarkis thought, assuming that deer in the south were the same as other deer.

Although I do not believe I would call this gentleman a decadent southern deer. The rune was a good seven feet tall, and that was before counting the antlers. His shoulders were at least as broad as Sarkis's, although his height made him appear almost delicate, with inhumanly narrow wrists and ankles.

He held up a hand, palm out. His fingers were stiff and

strangely jointed, with thick, hoof-like nails. He whistled a high, imperious note.

One did not need to be a genius to know what that meant. Brindle stopped the ox.

They stood in absolute silence for several long moments. The ox got bored, dropped its head, and began to graze. Sarkis glanced at Halla, worried that she might be frightened, to discover her gazing at the rune with her lips parted and an incredulous smile on her face.

"This is *amazing...*" she breathed. "What do you think they eat?"

Well, he should have seen that coming.

The rune cocked his head and trilled. Zale spread their hands helplessly. "I do not speak your tongue," they said to the rune. "I am sorry."

The tallest rune turned and whistled. Sarkis heard the whistle taken up by the others, then by still others farther back in the woods, until it faded out of his hearing.

Calling for reinforcements? It seemed strange—there were already far more of the rune than there were of...*well, me and Brindle, if we're being honest about our fighting capacity.*

The rune squatted down on his long legs and settled in to wait.

"What do we do now?" whispered Halla.

"I suggest we do absolutely nothing," said Zale. "And wait to see what he has in mind for us."

It did not take long. A hornless figure made her way up the steep hillside, accompanied by a large rune. Before she had crested the hill, it was obvious that she was human.

The woman pushed back her hood. She had long gray hair and faded blue eyes that stood out against her darkly tanned skin.

She looked from face to face, then spoke in a language that Sarkis didn't know.

"Damn," muttered Zale. "It's what they speak in Charlock, but I don't know it. Halla?"

"My brother taught me about five words. I can say hello, goodbye, and something very unkind about their goats."

"...let's skip that." They cleared their throat and said "Do you speak this tongue, lady?"

The woman frowned, concentrating. After a moment, she said "Yes, but...small."

Zale relaxed. "Oh thank the Rat. Can you tell your companions that we mean no harm?"

She shook her head, not a negative shake but a confused one. "Too fast. Again?"

Sarkis waited while Zale slowly worked through the words with their new translator. Finally, the old woman turned to the large rune and made a series of noises, like high-pitched trills in the back of her throat. The rune whistled in reply.

"He says...no fight...unless you bring fight."

Zale nodded. "Do you know *how* we came here?" They gestured to the hills around them.

She shook her head. "Here..." she gestured to the Hills as well, "want you come. But how...?" She spread her hands and gave an exaggerated shrug.

"Not even they know how it works," muttered Sarkis. "Of course not."

The rune gave a lengthy twittering speech. The woman nodded. "You," she said, and pointed at Sarkis.

"I am Sarkis," he said, putting his hand over his heart and bowing slightly.

"You..." She pointed to the sword on Halla's back. "You are... with sword?" She frowned and shook her head, apparently not content with that. "Sword is...your house?"

"Yes," said Sarkis. It was as accurate as any other description. "The sword is my house."

The rune whistled. "He says...bad house."

"Yes," said Sarkis, sighing. "He's right. It's a very bad house." Brindle snorted.

She gave him a sympathetic look. He noticed that even when she smiled, she was careful to keep her lips together. Perhaps bared teeth upset the rune.

"He says...do you want...sword house gone?"

Sarkis felt his stomach lurch. Could the rune do that? Set him loose from his prison? Let him die for good? Get him off this wretched chain of battle after battle, life after life...

"Can they do that?" he asked.

The woman shrugged.

"Sarkis?" said Halla.

Reality rushed in. He couldn't very well leave Halla. She still needed him.

No, she doesn't. She's got Zale and Brindle and once you're out of the hills, she's nearly home. She'll be fine. She doesn't need you that badly.

Maybe he just wanted her to need him.

"If the rune can help you," said Halla, "then we should find out more. If they can get you out of the sword..."

She trailed off. Sarkis studied her face, the way her pale eyebrows had drawn down and her water-gray eyes. *Could* the rune help him? Could a group of strange deer people possibly unmake the *zeth* woman's sword?

"It's not that I want you to die!" Halla said, clearly misinterpreting his look. "I don't! I think it's awful! But if that's what you want and it's been hundreds of years and maybe the rune can fix it, then—"

"No," said Sarkis. He felt strangely light, as if he had just shed a heavy load of armor. "No, it's all right. I will see you safely home. And then perhaps, afterward, we can find our way back here. A few weeks is not so long, compared to five hundred years."

He did not say what he was thinking, which was that Halla herself might live thirty or forty more years. *Thirty or forty years is not so long either, compared to five hundred.*

"We might not be able to find our way back," said Zale quietly. "The Vagrant Hills are...unpredictable."

"You don't have to give this up for me," said Halla. She seemed near tears. Sarkis wondered how long it had been since anyone had given anything up for her. Perhaps no one ever had.

"It's all right," he said. "Perhaps they could not help me, and perhaps they can only kill me. I find that I would rather wait until our task is done to take the chance."

"But—"

"And perhaps I am not quite ready to die just yet after all."

The woman watching them nodded. She had apparently followed enough to keen her translation to the tall stag-man, who flicked his ears. He lifted his spear in front of him, crossed his forearm over the shaft in a gesture that clearly carried the weight of ritual, and then turned and walked away. One by one, the other rune melted away into the woods, until the human translator was the only one left.

"Will the Hills let us go?" asked Zale.

She shrugged again. "Here...does what here wants." She seemed to think for a moment, then added "Now is...easy. Once was...not easy." She waved her hands, taking in the sky and the ground. "Some day, maybe not easy again."

Zale nodded. "Do you wish to come with us?" they asked. "I do not know who your people are, but we can take you with us."

"What? No." She seemed astonished by the suggestion. "These—" she keened a note "—they are my people." She lapsed briefly into the language of Charlock, without any of the halting effort of translation, then tried again. "I am here. My house. My here. Yes?"

"Yes," said Zale, and bowed deeply to her. "Thank you, madam."

She nodded and vanished as silently as the rune, and then it was only three humans, a gnole and an ox sitting alone on the hillside.

"Well," said Zale slowly. "Well, well, well. I suppose I can vouch for some of the reports of the Vagrant Hills after all."

"What did she mean, at the end?" asked Halla softly, as they climbed back onto the wagon.

"Rat only knows," said Zale. "But she clearly didn't want to leave, so it's none of our business. Now let's see if the Hills decide to let us go after all."

CHAPTER 34

The hillside began to dim as twilight settled over the Vagrant Hills. Something whooped and shrieked in the distance, causing Sarkis to jerk upright and set his hand on his sword. Brindle's ears flicked back, but he did not slow the ox.

"I don't like that," said Zale.

"You and me both, priest."

"A gnole doesn't like it either."

The shrieking came again and was joined by another one, a series of high sounds like someone laughing.

"Some animal you have here in the south?" asked Sarkis.

Halla shook her head. "I suppose it could be a coyote," she said, a bit doubtfully, but then the whooping modulated until it sounded almost like words. It trailed off into silence.

"*Not* a coyote," said Zale, their dark eyes wide.

"There are hyenas that sound almost like that in the Sunlost Plains," said Sarkis. "Do you have hyenas here?"

"Not that I know of, but in these Hills..." Zale spread their hands helplessly.

Brindle pushed the ox on for two or three hundred yards

more, then stopped. "Here," said the gnole, sliding down from the wagon seat. "An ox can bed down between a wagon and those trees."

"Will it be safe there?" asked Halla. "Can anything get through the trees?"

"Don't know. Don't know how wide a thing in the woods is."

This was the sort of statement that made a little space in the air around it, as everyone's imaginations bent to the task.

None of them slept well that night. The wagon walls did not keep out the sounds of alien laughter. They discussed the merits of a fire warding things off vs. attracting attention, and finally Brindle simply lit one, and said, "Hills already know."

The ox slept practically under the wagon. Brindle and Sarkis sat by the fire, half wakeful, waiting.

It was after midnight, by Sarkis's reckoning, when Brindle murmured, "Things in the sky, sword-man."

Sarkis looked up. For a few moments, all he saw was stars, and then something passed overhead, not solid but transparent, so that the stars swam in his vision, as if seen through a coat of oil.

"I don't like that," Sarkis said.

"A gnole isn't fond of it either."

The whooping sounds stopped. The fire had died down to embers and Sarkis wished that it would die even lower.

The oily sky-swimmer passed overhead again. Sarkis was reminded of the manta rays that swam in the Bay of Sandweight, the same undulating motion. Those had been harmless. This...

"Did your relative ever mention this?" asked Sarkis softly. Brindle shook his head.

"*Nyaaaaa-aaa-ah-ah-ah!*" shrieked something, practically in Sarkis's ear.

He dove to one side, rolling and grabbing for his sword. The ox awoke with a snort. Brindle dropped to all fours, mouth open and enormous teeth bared.

"Nyaa-ah-ah!"

"Where is it?" hissed Sarkis, looking around wildly.

Brindle looked past him, then burst into snickering gnole laughter. He pointed.

An animal about the size of a squirrel clung to a tree near where Sarkis had been sitting. It had huge eyes and short, fluffy fur and vast, ridiculous ears.

"Nya-ah?"

"Think we can probably take him, sword-man."

Sarkis groaned. "How is an animal that small making that much noise?"

"Nyaha-aaa-aaa-aa!"

Another one of the little squirrel-beasts answered from the woods. The ox made a sullen noise and dropped its head.

The wagon door creaked open. Halla and Zale stood framed in the opening. Halla had Sarkis's sword held in front of her, fully drawn, and Zale had the frying pan.

"Sarkis?" hissed Halla. "Are they here? Are you alive?"

"He wasn't alive before," said Zale. "I mean, technically. Not to be insensitive."

"Yes, they're here," said Sarkis, pointing. "They're a strange little animal. I don't think it's going to be a—" and then the oily thing dropped out of the sky and landed on him.

He didn't see it coming. It made no sound. All Sarkis knew was that something gelatinous and disgusting fell over him like a blanket. It was rather like walking through an incredibly thick spiderweb. He pawed at his eyes in disgust, spitting out slime.

Then it started to move.

Sarkis had the horrifying sensation of the slime on his skin squirming and trying to get under his clothes, and then the infinitely more horrifying sensation of the bit still in his mouth trying to crawl between his teeth.

"Gaaaah!" He pawed at his armor, spitting furiously. "Get it off! Get it off! Get it—" and then blue fire filled his vision.

Halla lowered the sheathed sword in her hands. The oily swimmer fell through suddenly empty air and landed on the ground, thrashing.

Brindle hissed like a furious cat, and snatched up a burning branch from the fire. He jabbed at the jelly-like beast and it recoiled, rising in the air. Whatever he said was all in gnole-speech, but Halla got the gist anyway—"Get back! Get away!"

The thing obeyed. Whatever it had been expecting, it wasn't prey that vanished and then stabbed it with fire. It rose heavily, moving more like a sea creature than a bird, and vanished into the trees.

"Naha-aha-haaaa!" cried one of the small creatures.

"It's an alarm call they're making," said Zale grimly. "Isn't it?"

"Think so, rat-priest." Brindle looked over at the ox, who was snorting and trembling, but unhurt.

"Do you think Sarkis is all right?" asked Halla, clutching the sheathed sword tightly. "I didn't know if it was hurting him, but it looked bad."

"I think you did the right thing," said Zale, touching her sleeve. "Draw the sword again and ask, I suppose."

Halla nodded. She felt a whisper of unease as she closed her hand over the sheath, in case it didn't draw and that meant he was hurt or worse, but the blade slid out like silk.

Sarkis reformed beside her. He lifted his hands to his neck involuntarily, shuddering. She could see the hair on his arms standing on end.

"That was incredibly unpleasant," he said. "Is it gone?"

"Flew away," said Zale. "What did it feel like?"

"It was trying to get under my clothes and into my mouth. I don't think it had very good intentions." He looked around, still rubbing at his arms. "Gaaah, that's not a sensation that goes away quickly."

"Didn't like fire," said Brindle.

"Good to know."

He and the gnole built up the fire while Halla and Zale watched the sky from the door of the wagon. Halla tried to step out to help and Sarkis very nearly picked her up and put her back inside.

"I can collect firewood as well as you can."

"And if one of those things lands on you, then what? I'll be trying to defend you from a pile of jelly."

Halla scowled, but had to admit he had a point. "Do you think it would have done something bad?"

"I think when a pile of flying slime lands on you and tries to crawl inside your mouth, it probably doesn't have your best interests at heart."

Brindle's fur stood up in spikes. "Better not touch an ox," he muttered.

"Let's hope the fire keeps it away."

CHAPTER 35

E ither the fire kept it away, or the slimy creature warned off its fellows. They heard no more alarm calls from the squirrel-beasts, and they were on their way at dawn, not even bothering with breakfast.

A little before noon, they saw what Sarkis had narrowly avoided.

A gaunt deer came out of the trees onto the roadway. It didn't seem to see them. It moved slowly, not so much limping as picking each leg up like a bag of stones and dropping it again.

"Whoa," said Brindle, but the ox had already stopped.

A clear coat of jelly-like slime clung to its back and head, over an inch thick. The deer's eyes, wide and rolling, stared out from under the glaze. Ribs heaved under the coating as it breathed.

"Oh sweet Rat," breathed Zale. "It's got one of those things on it."

They watched the deer stumble across the road. If it was even aware of them, it gave no sign.

Brindle reached under the wagon seat, and took out the

crossbow. The sound of the string being cranked back was very loud, but the deer's ears were glued flat against its neck. The ox blew nervously.

The gnole sighted down the crossbow. The three humans sat in utter silence, watching. No one moved to stop him. Halla's only thought, through the blind, screaming horror of it all, was that the poor beast should be put out of its misery as fast as possible, and she was glad that Brindle knew how to do it.

The bolt took the deer in the side, just behind the shoulder. The deer staggered sideways, fell, and did not rise again.

They waited.

The slime shuddered and pulled away from the damp hide. A long moment passed, then the oily sky-swimmer rose off the deer's body and flew ponderously to the trees. It draped itself over a branch, almost like a wet towel put out to dry.

And then it hung there, swaying slightly in the breeze, doing nothing.

"Do we keep going?" asked Sarkis.

"Got to get a deer off the roadway, sword-man."

Sarkis nodded and jumped down from the wagon. He went to the back of the wagon and came back a moment later carrying a sheet.

"The last of my sheets," said Zale, a bit sadly.

"I'm not touching that thing bare-handed."

"No, nor do I begrudge it to you. This journey has simply been very hard on bedding."

Sarkis dragged the deer's carcass off the road, grimacing. He looked at the sheet in his hands, then tossed it over the dead animal like a burial shroud.

"It wasn't going to live much longer anyway," he said, swinging back up onto the wagon. "It had sores all over its belly. Very odd sores."

"Odd how?" asked Zale.

Sarkis gave them a level look. "Have you ever seen a lamprey?"

"I was afraid you'd say something like that."

"There was really no chance that it wouldn't be horrible, priest."

"A gnole really doesn't like these Hills."

"A human isn't too thrilled with them either," Halla assured him.

"Humans can't smell, but a fish-lady isn't completely hopeless." Halla decided that was a compliment, probably.

Brindle tapped the ox's flank with the goad and clucked his tongue. The ox ambled forward, while three sets of eyes stayed fixed on the sky-swimmer.

It did not move, except to sway slightly in the wind. None of them made the mistake of thinking it was dead.

"Maybe they're only really active at night," murmured Zale. "Like bats."

"Perhaps it fed all it could on the deer and it's digesting," said Halla.

Zale and Sarkis stared at her. Halla said, "What? Haven't you ever watched a snake eat something? They lay around afterward and don't do anything." And when they continued to stare at her: "Look, we had a big black ratsnake on the farm and one time she got into the henhouse and ate six eggs and I had to pick her up and move her because she was just going to sleep it off in the henhouse otherwise. She had six big lumps in her from the eggs."

"Farms are far more alarming places than I realized," said Zale.

"You should see when it's time to slaughter the chickens."

"I pray you, do not tell me about the running around with the head cut off. I am aware that they do that, and I would like to not think about it ever again."

"See, I just kill humans," said Sarkis. "And once I kill them, they don't run around or anything. *That's* civilized."

"A gnole hates to interrupt a human's *very important* conversation, but there are more things," said Brindle acidly. "In the trees."

All three humans fell silent.

The trees were indeed full of...things.

They hung from branches like glass banners, strangely innocuous. The breeze moved the leaves and the sky-swimmers, with the same mindless motion. They looked so much like glass that Halla expected them to make a chiming noise in the wind, but they did not.

There were dozens, possibly even hundreds. They lined the road for forty yards ahead. The roadway was still sunken here, like the hollow way, though only about a foot high on either side of the roadbed.

That foot might as well have been a thousand miles high. They could not turn around without abandoning the wagon.

"What do we do?" whispered Halla.

Zale shook their head. "I don't know."

"Forward," said Sarkis finally. "They aren't moving. If they start to move, get in the wagon and...ah..." He looked at the ox. "Brindle..."

"A gnole isn't stupid, sword-man. A gnole will make sure an ox doesn't end up like a deer. That's all."

"Do you think the wagon will keep them out?"

"I don't know."

They inched forward down the roadway. Halla had long since stopped noticing the sound of the wagon wheels, but now they seemed incredibly loud, every rattle like a boulder falling down a hillside.

"Cousin didn't warn a gnole about *this*," muttered Brindle.

"The Hills are very large. There are probably things in it that no human or gnole has ever seen."

"Or lived to tell about," said Sarkis.

"You are a constant ray of sunshine."

Sarkis grunted.

They passed a dead rabbit by the side of the wagon road. It was mostly rags of fur and ribcage. One of the things lay over top of it, like a thick glaze of ice on bone.

Halla twisted in the wagon seat to look behind them. She could not shake the feeling that the sky-swimmers were going to rise up as soon as she was no longer facing them and that she would turn and see a hundred panes of glass hanging in the air behind the wagon.

The sunlight warped a little as it passed through the sky-swimmers, focusing just a little, as if through a pane of glass. It left irregular spots of light on the road. When one of those lights passed over the back of Halla's hand, she moved it, feeling ill.

Look at me not screaming, she thought dreamily. *I am not screaming at all. I am not curled into a ball and crying. I am being very calm.*

Skreek...skreek...skreek... The wheels creaked forward. The trees looked as if they had been caught in a sudden ice storm, with sheets of ice hanging from every branch.

We're going to die. We are going to die a horrible and stupid death and Cousin Alver will get the house and my nieces will make bad marriages because they don't have any money and probably one will end up with a man who spends two minutes in bed with her every fortnight, staring at the wall. And Zale will die and Brindle will die and Sarkis will lay in a sword covered in monsters and no one will find him for a thousand years and even the scholars at the library won't be able to find the Weeping Lands again.

I'm going to die without ever telling Sarkis that I...what?

I want him? I love him?

Do *I love him?*

Halla had always found it easy to love. Love was a patient, exasperated emotion, and she knew it well. She had had so many relatives and she had loved them all, except possibly Alver. She loved Zale and Brindle and even slow Prettyfoot the ox because you could not help but love people who had lived through such stupid, terrible things with you.

What she felt for Sarkis was something wildly different, as if a branch had been grafted on a familiar tree and had grown a bizarre and unexpected fruit.

It would be incredibly stupid to turn to him right now and tell him that I was hopelessly in love with him.

The hollow way was growing together over the top of the road again. The sky-swimmers lay thick on the branches, the sunlight dancing off their bodies in a lovely, deadly shimmer.

It won't be any less stupid if you shout that as you're getting engulfed in predatory slime.

Do you really want to make the last seconds of your life unspeakably awkward?

Well, given that it's me, if the last seconds of my life aren't unspeakably awkward, I'm probably doing something wrong...

Skreek...skreek...skreek...

One of the creatures moved in the trees, a slow, languid stretch, like a pane of glass rolling over in its sleep. All four of them stared at it, while the ox walked stolidly onward.

Skreek...skreek...skreek...

"They're thinning out," whispered Zale.

Brindle pointed.

The hollow way opened up again a few dozen yards ahead, but one of the swimmers hung partway down over the opening. It was tall enough for a human to pass under, but not the wagon.

Sarkis looked at Brindle. Brindle tapped the goad and nodded.

"Go through," he whispered, helping Halla and Zale down. "Brindle, do you wish me to do it?"

"No, sword-man. An ox is a gnole's responsibility."

Sarkis scooted next to the gnole on the seat, clearly ready to throw himself over Brindle if the creature reacted.

Halla and Zale walked single file beneath the sky-swimmer. Halla's heart was pounding so loudly that she thought she might faint. Viewed from the side, it was about two inches thick, and she could see soft variations in color, which might have been organs or markings or the gods only knew what. Every pebble under her foot seemed the size of her fist, ready to roll and pitch her forward, face-first, into the creature. She bent nearly double going under it, ready to crawl on her belly if it would keep the awful thing away.

Sunlight blazed on her face as she stepped free of the hollow way. Halla nearly went to her knees.

She and Zale collapsed against each other, staggering out of the shadows of the hollow. It was impossible to say who was holding the other one up, just that neither of them seemed able to stand alone. Halla could feel the priest's body shaking, but that was fine because she was too.

"I must write this all down," whispered Zale forlornly. "I must write it down and tell the bishop that no one is to ever go into the Vagrant Hills, never ever..."

Halla looked around the clearing. Tall oaks and shaggy-barked hickories murmured in the breeze. The road continued on ahead, but the trees were empty of sky-swimmers. She could tell because they were farther along into autumn than the others they had seen and many had bare branches, while others blazed copper and orange and gold.

There was space enough to turn the wagon around, ironically. She didn't think it would be an issue. She would have abandoned a dozen wagons to never walk through that tunnel again.

The wagon wheels started up. Halla bit down on her knuckles.

The ox emerged from the hollow way and then, very slowly, the sky-swimmer's body began to rise. Halla watched, paralyzed, as Brindle lifted it up on the end of the ox goad.

Will it wake up? It's got to wake up. It'll wake up and then it'll wake the others and then they'll come for us...

The roof cleared the beast by inches. Brindle hung from the side of the wagon, hitching himself along one handed, keeping the ox goad lifted. Sarkis lay flat across the wagon seat. The edges of the swimmer rippled, less like water and more like a horse's hide when a fly walked on it. It squirmed restlessly and then...then...

The wagon creaked free. Brindle clung to the back of the wagon, panting like a frightened dog. The ox, seeing grass ahead and having no driver to stop it, dropped its head and began chewing meditatively.

"Brindle, that was amazing!" whispered Halla.

The gnole gave her a fanged smile. "Didn't feel amazing," he said. He stamped his feet and rubbed the fur of his arms against the grain, shivering.

"I suggest we don't linger," said Sarkis. "I don't want to be anywhere near these things when they start to wake up."

There was no argument. Brindle wiped the end of the ox goad in the grass repeatedly to clean it, then grimaced and took out a knife. He whittled the end down to clean wood with a few rapid strokes. "Don't like that stuff," he said. "Don't want it touching an ox."

They climbed back up. Brindle tapped the clean goad on

the ox's flank and the beast walked forward, reluctantly abandoning the grass.

They made forward progress for perhaps half an hour, while the trees changed color around them.

"Sweet blessed Rat, it's narrowing again," said Zale disgustedly. "Are we doomed to drive through hollow ways forever?"

"The branches up ahead are completely bare," said Halla. "Maybe we're getting back to normal hills. Or at least normal winter."

Skreek...skreek...skreek...

The branches were indeed bare. They formed a familiar lattice overhead.

"I could get to hate this place," said Sarkis, to no one in particular.

Brindle suddenly sat up straight, sniffing. He looked puzzled.

"Great god, now what? More of them?"

The gnole shook his head. "No. Smells...familiar."

"What?"

Brindle shrugged.

They made a few more wagonlengths of progress and the trees began to open up. Halla looked off to their left and saw a small pond, the surface frozen in slushy ridges, and a pile of branches.

"You've *got* to be shitting me," she said.

Possibly because she never swore, the other three gave her the attention this deserved.

"Sarkis," she said, pointing, "will you go look and tell me if that's where I think it is?"

He followed the line of her finger to the branches and said something in his own language that didn't sound like anything anyone would want to translate.

"You don't have to get down," said Zale, twisting their braid around their hand. "I can see a hand from here. Unless people are stuffing dead bodies into identical ponds all over the woods..."

"The Hills turned us around," said Halla. "They let us go."

"A gnole will believe it when a gnole sees it," muttered Brindle.

Twenty minutes later, he believed it. The ox ducked its head under an overgrown set of branches, and they emerged onto the road to Amalcross.

CHAPTER 36

"Halla, you're dreaming. It's a nightmare. Wake up. Halla..."

The wagon creaked. Halla tried to fight her way free of the shreds of sleep, but the dream had been so monstrous and the wagon was so dark that she was not sure if she was out or if this was just another moment of it.

"Halla, wake up!" Zale sounded worried and exasperated all at once. Halla wanted to tell them not to worry but she seemed to be paralyzed.

Cold air rushed in as the wagon door opened and it dipped under Sarkis's weight. "What are you doing, priest?" he roared.

"I'm not doing anything, you daft barbarian! Halla's having a nightmare!"

The realization that she had to save Zale from Sarkis's conclusions broke the paralysis. "Nothing!" she gasped. "Dream!"

"...oh." She saw the faint outline of Sarkis's face as he pulled the door shut, and then he was fumbling for her in the dark.

He found her shoulders and pulled her upright, and

between that and the blast of cold, she felt the dream falling away at last. She drew a deep, grating breath, then another.

"They were following us," she said.

Neither Zale nor Sarkis had to ask what they were.

"I looked back and they were on everything. Like there had been a hard freeze and a glaze of ice."

Sarkis sat down on the bunk, banged his head on the wall, grumbled, and then pulled her into his arms.

"I'm sorry," she said. "I shouldn't be having nightmares. You're the one it landed on. *I* don't get to have nightmares."

"Oh for the great god's sake," growled Sarkis. She could hear his voice rumbling in his chest under her ear. "The person who has nightmares is the one who gets to have them. And if I dreamed like normal folk, I'd have them too."

"You don't dream?" asked Zale, interested.

"I dream in silver. It's like being in the sword again. If I dream at all, which is rare." He began running his hand over her hair.

It was very comforting to lie in the dark and be stroked like a cat. It was probably not respectable, but respectability seemed increasingly useless. What did it matter, when there were monsters in the hills, not just stories to frighten children, but real, honest monsters that hung in the trees, waiting to land on the unwary?

She pressed her face against his shoulder.

"It will be all right," he said. "We're out. We don't have to go back."

"How else will we ever know if the rune can get you out of the sword?"

"We'll find another way. Or we won't. It's been nearly five hundred years. A few more years won't kill me."

"That's the *problem!*"

He laughed, a deep, subterranean chuckle that she felt through the side of her face. "Go back to sleep. We don't need to sort it all tonight."

"Nor are we likely to," said Zale. "And we have survived, and that is as much as the Rat asks of us on any given day."

"Practical," said Sarkis.

"We're known for it," said the priest.

AMALCROSS LOOKED JUST the same as it had when they left it. A gnole squeaked good-naturedly at them as the wagon rolled past. The ox was unimpressed, but the ox had not been impressed by anything so far, and was not about to start now.

Bartholomew looked more than a little startled to see them when he opened the door, then suddenly pleased. He ushered them inside to meet his guest, a short, owl-eyed man with shaggy brown hair.

"A visiting scholar-priest," said Bartholomew, by way of explanation. "This is Nolan. Nolan, my old friend Silas's niece, and her...ah..."

"Guard," said Sarkis.

"...guard, Sarkis. And you are?"

"Zale of the Temple of the Rat," said the priest, smiling warmly. "Brother Nolan, an honor to meet you. What temple do you hail from?"

"No temple, I fear. I am of the Order of the Sainted Smith," said Nolan, glancing across the three of them. When no one seemed to recognize it, he smiled. "It's all right. We are very small and somewhat obscure."

"Are you a sect of the Forge God?" asked Halla.

"It is believed that our founder spent time in the Forge

God's service, but that was some centuries ago, and I fear the actual truth is lost to history." He spread his hands. "We are mostly interested in artifacts."

His presence was immediately understandable. Sarkis glanced around the central room, which was, if anything, even more cluttered than the last time they had visited.

He did notice that Nolan's eyes lingered on the sword over Halla's shoulder longer than he liked.

Is he looking at Halla or the sword?

Well, she is a fine looking woman and it is an old sword. He might be interested in either one.

This thought did not comfort him in any way. He drew his eyebrows down and folded his arms.

Zale had no such concerns. The priest turned to Bartholomew and began outlining the reason for their presence.

"...so you see, it is my concern that Mistress Halla's relatives will attempt to claim that she is not who she says she is, or that she is of unsound mind or moral character. A signed statement from you that she is indeed Silas's niece and affirming her as a citizen in good standing will go a long way toward dispelling such a claim."

"Those vultures!" said Bartholomew, scowling. "Forgive me, Halla, I know they're your relatives and perhaps I should not speak ill of them—"

"Speak as ill as you like," said Halla cheerfully. "I'll join in on the choruses."

Bartholomew blinked at her, then broke into a rueful smile. He glanced at Nolan, then back to her, and squared his shoulders. "My dear, I've been remiss, and I must apologize. You should have been able to come to me for help, instead of having to involve the Rat priests—with no offense to you, Priest Zale!"

Zale shot Sarkis a humorous look. Sarkis wondered how many people told the priest, "No offense" on a weekly basis.

"It's all right," said Halla. "Really, Bartholomew. Things get strange when people die."

"Yes. But my oldest friend made a will and instead of helping to see his last bequest carried out, I sat here wringing my hands. I'm sorry. Please forgive me for my failure."

Halla looked surprised, and even more so when Bartholomew hugged her awkwardly. Sarkis had a sudden, startling intense desire to grab the man by the collar and fling him aside.

It is not just jealousy, he told himself. *It is that she looks uncomfortable. And also jealousy.*

Really, he had no reason at all to be jealous. The man was old enough to be her father.

And I am several hundred years older than he is, so what does that say?

He took a step forward anyway, ready to pull the man aside, but Bartholomew stepped back hastily.

"So." He cleared his throat and glanced at Nolan again. "I will go with you to Rutger's Howe and see that this is all settled."

"What?" Halla blinked at him. "Really?"

"If I can help in any way, it is my duty."

Zale inclined their head. "Indeed, sir, your presence would be even more helpful than a signed document."

"Ha!" Halla grinned, clearly warming to the idea. "Yes! I can't imagine Alver can twist his way out of that one." She paused. "Although—uh—the wagon's going to get a bit crowded..."

"I believe," said Bartholomew, with some asperity, "that I can make my own way to Rutger's Howe. I have done so many times before and I am not so aged and infirm that I cannot do so again for my good friend's niece."

"Sorry," said Halla. "Yes. Oh, thank you! I can't wait to see the look on Cousin Alver's face!"

This time she was the one to hug him, and after an owlish blink at Sarkis, Bartholomew hugged her back.

CHAPTER 37

They rode out of Amalcross in a merry mood. Zale and Halla were full of plans. Sarkis slid down and walked alongside the wagon, keeping an eye out for trouble.

His own mood alternated between light and dark. They were nearly to Halla's home. When she was safely in possession of her inheritance...when their association was no longer so terribly one-sided...then Sarkis could act at last on his feelings.

There was no point in pretending he did not have them. He wanted to run his hands over her body, put his lips against the softest part of her throat, cradle her breasts in his hands. She had absurdly good breasts. The decadent south had fallen down on pretty much every other point, but it got this much right. He wanted very much to make a closer acquaintance with hers.

Nor did he want to stop there. He wanted to be the answer to questions she didn't even know she had. Mostly carnal ones. There was a way that she stretched, and he knew she wasn't doing it intentionally, but it showed off every curve and his mouth went dry every single time.

He was fairly certain that the attraction wasn't all one-sided.

Halla did not exactly cast burning glances in his direction—she wouldn't have known how, and the shock might kill him if she did—but it seemed that their hands touched rather more often than necessary, and when they did, they both paused too long, then sprang apart, as if they expected someone to catch them at something illicit.

This line of thinking was having an effect, which was why he was walking instead of sitting where any of his companions could notice. It was just his luck to be cursed to permanently wear clothes that made it obvious when he'd gotten hard. If only he'd been wearing a codpiece or something when they'd killed him.

At least I was over forty when I died. Back when I was eighteen, I could get turned on by a stiff breeze, and that would have been a hell of a way to spend eternity.

He was pretty sure Zale had a suspicion about why he was suddenly spending so much time on foot, but the priest didn't say anything. Discreet, competent, humorous...Sarkis was still unsure about the Rat, but Zale had been an excellent antidote to some priests of the great god that he'd known in his life.

Halla laughed from her perch on the wagon seat. Sarkis knew that it wasn't a sexy laugh, it was neither low nor throaty nor any of the things that men generally liked in women's laughter, but that didn't matter. It was sexy because Halla was the one doing it, and he was hopelessly enamored. Befuddled. Something. There were words in the language of the Weeping Lands, but none of them translated quite correctly. "Overwhelmed with baffled and lustful affection," was accurate, but much too long. And a perfectly good word like *maraal* kept trying to turn into the word "crush" in his head and that was a very stupid idiom because he did not want to crush Halla and would have to stop anyone else who was trying to crush her.

No wonder the decadent south had so many problems. They couldn't even sort their language out in their heads.

There were other words that kept coming up. *Love. In love. Beloved.* He shoved them all back where they came from. You started to think words like that and then you began to hope for things. Things that disgraced mercenary captains should not hope for. Particularly not with respectable widows, when they had everything to offer and you had nothing but secrets and failure and a body wracked with silver scars.

No, things were going to be difficult enough without words like that. But if Halla could still see fit to forgive him, once she knew what was written on the sword, then perhaps they could have a little time together, before she remembered that she was respectable and Sarkis remembered that she was mortal.

It was all that he dared hope for, and it scared him how much that he was hoping.

He climbed back onto the wagon, after a suitable time had elapsed.

"Not much longer now," said Halla. "At least, I hope."

"Going to be a bit longer, fish-lady." Brindle reined in the ox and nodded to the road in front of the wagon.

There was a man in the road, waving his arms frantically to get their attention.

"Is he hurt?" asked Halla. "He looks like he needs help."

"Decoy," Zale said. "I expect the woods are full of highwaymen. We're about to get robbed." They looked more than a little annoyed by the prospect.

"And you're stopping?" Sarkis put his hand on his sword hilt.

The gnole glanced at him. "Ox can't outrun arrows, swordman," he said. "A gnole won't kill an ox trying."

Sarkis grunted. The ox, indeed, could not outrun arrows. If

you placed an arrow on the ground and walked away from it, there was a decent chance it would still move faster than the ox.

"Robbers?" said Halla. "Really? We're getting *robbed* now?" She sounded less frightened than indignant, as if this really was the last straw. "After all that? We get through the Vagrant Hills, we deal with the Motherhood and now—"

Something punched Sarkis very hard in the side.

Sarkis had taken enough arrows to recognize the sensation. He grabbed Halla around the waist and rolled off the wagon seat, away from the direction of the attack. His side screamed in agony.

Zale scrambled down beside them, followed by Brindle. The priest's eyes were wide. "Normally they try to shake you down for valuables before they shoot..."

"Amateurs," muttered Sarkis.

Halla gasped. "Oh my god, there's an arrow sticking out of you!"

"So there is."

"Does...does that hurt?"

"It does not feel great, no," Sarkis said.

"Should I pull it out?"

"Please don't."

"What should I do?"

"You should keep your head down."

Another arrow slammed into the side of the wagon. Someone was definitely feeling hostile.

"How do we get the arrow out?!"

"It's not in my lungs," said Sarkis calmly. "So at the moment, we don't worry about it."

"I am worrying!"

"All you have to do is sheathe the sword," said Sarkis. "The arrow will fall out then. It will be fine."

Halla grabbed for the hilt of the sword over her shoulder.

"Stand and deliver!" someone shouted from the trees.

"We can't stand!" Halla shouted back. "You're shooting at us! If you'd stop shooting, it'd be different!"

Sarkis rubbed his face. This was not the thing to shout at highwaymen. It was hard to read Brindle's expression, but he thought the gnole was staring at Halla with disbelief.

"I am a servant of the White Rat!" Zale called. "My temple has negotiated for safe passage through this region."

An oath came from the trees. The man in the road, who had been waving his arms, stopped and put his hands on his hips.

"A Rat priest?" Sarkis heard one of the bandits say. "You shot at a Rat priest?!"

Whatever the archer said in his defense was drowned out by the smack of fist on flesh. Someone was very unhappy.

Sarkis shifted, then grabbed for the edge of the wagon wheel as the world went gray around him. He had perhaps been overly optimistic about the arrow.

"Sarkis!" cried Halla, grabbing him to steady him. Unfortunately, she was on the arrow side. He sank his teeth into his lower lip to keep from crying out.

"Oh hell no," Halla muttered.

"We've stopped shooting!" someone called from the trees. "You can stand and deliver now!"

"Just a minute!" called Halla.

"You don't tell highwaymen 'just a minute,'" said Sarkis.

"I just did. Zale, take him." She sounded very businesslike and determined.

Zale took Sarkis's weight across their shoulders. Even that shift made the arrow move in Sarkis's side. It felt strange and cold and heavy.

"You're all over blood," said Zale. "Did you know that?"

"No." He considered this. "Well, it's not the first ti—"

Halla got the cords untied and slapped the sword back in the scabbard, and the blue fire took Sarkis away.

"WAS THAT WISE?" asked Zale. Blue light skittered over their clothes, removing the bloodstain as well.

"He had an arrow in him!"

"Yes, but he was also the only one who knew how to fight. Also the only one who's immortal."

"I'm sure it'll be fine."

"We would really appreciate it if you stood and delivered now!" called the highwayman. "We are extremely sorry to bother a Rat priest, you understand, but if you don't put your hands in the air and come out from behind the wagon, things are going to go very badly."

Zale put their hands in the air. So did Halla. So did Brindle.

The highwaymen came out of the trees. There were about a half-dozen of them, armed with bows. One no longer had a bow and didn't seem to know what to do with his hands. The side of his face was already swelling up.

"Where's the other one?" said the apparent leader.

"You shot him," said Halla. "He ran away."

"Didn't see him leave," said the man who had been in the roadway.

The leader looked at Halla. Halla shrugged as best she could with her arms already in the air. "I don't know what else to tell you."

"Your holiness," said the leader, nodding to Zale. "I'm very sorry for the inconvenience."

Zale shrugged. "People make mistakes," they said. "If you release us, I will see no need to report this to my temple."

The leader sighed. He was an older man with grizzled

blonde hair and beer-colored eyes. "I am afraid that it is your companion that I am after."

It took Halla a moment to realize that the man was talking about her and not Brindle. "What? *Me*? Why?"

He turned his head and shouted "Mina!"

Another figure detached from the trees and stalked into the roadway.

"Oh gods," said Halla involuntarily. "You again!"

"That's her," said Mina to the leader of the highwaymen. The woman's eyes were as cold as frost on a windowpane. "That's the one who makes people invisible."

CHAPTER 38

"Wait, *what?*"

Halla stared at Mina. So did Zale.

"Invisible," said Mina. "That's how you did it. You're a wonderworker, don't try to deny it! You made your guard invisible so he could attack Brett without being seen. You're probably making him invisible again right now!"

"You think he was *invisible?*" said Halla.

"This is fascinating," murmured Zale.

The leader was starting to look uncomfortable.

"How else do you explain him coming outta nowhere like that?" snapped Mina, advancing on Halla. "He just appeared, all fiery!"

Halla thought briefly about trying to explain. Then she thought better of it. As long as Sarkis was in the sword, he was safe, and there was a chance that he could get out and free both her and Zale.

"Invisible?" she said, putting as much scorn as she could into the word. "That's your explanation?"

"It was magic!" shouted Mina. "Don't you try to deny it!"

"It was n—" Halla started, whereupon Mina punched her in the stomach.

Halla fell over, curled into fetal position.

Zale dropped to their knees and threw their arms around Halla's shoulders. "Enough!" they snapped. "This woman is under Temple protection!"

The leader of the highwaymen rubbed his forehead and said, to no one in particular, "This is all starting to seem like a really terrible idea."

Halla sucked in air, trying to get her breath back. The assault had come out of nowhere.

Why is she so angry at me? What did I ever do except try to be nice to her?

"I'm telling you!" said Mina. "It was all fiery! She made him appear! She's got some kinda magic! Brett saw it too!"

Halla held up a hand, wheezing.

"Enough, Mina," said the leader. "She can't very well answer when you've knocked the wind out of her."

Mina scowled.

"Easy," whispered Zale. "Breathe. You'll be fine. The muscles spasm, that's all. It'll pass. Just breathe." Halla could feel the priest's own breath heaving in their lungs, and guessed that they were not nearly so calm as they seemed.

"I haven't got any magic," gasped Halla, once she could breathe again.

"Then where's that man now? The one who attacked us?" said Mina.

Halla couldn't think of who she was talking about. "What? No one attacked you! You pulled a knife on me!"

"Your guard!" shrieked Mina. "Don't pretend you don't know."

Think. What answer takes the focus off Sarkis?

"Him?" Halla feigned disgust. It wasn't hard, with Mina

standing in front of her. "I fired him once I got to Archenhold. He was always grabbing my arm. *Why* do men always grab you by the arm?"

One of the bandits, a middle-aged woman with iron-gray braids, let out a loud bark of laughter and covered her mouth.

The bandit leader rubbed his face. "I'm going to tie you up now," he said. "I apologize, priest, but if my people keep pointing crossbows at you, there might be accidents. I give you my word that you, at least, will be released unharmed."

Zale inclined their head. "I shall include your assurance in my report to my superiors," they said coolly. The leader winced.

The bandit woman was the one who tied their hands. She gave Halla a gap-toothed grin. "In front, so you can do your business later. Wiggle your fingers there, love, make sure you're not gonna lose a hand." Halla obeyed.

Zale, Brindle and Halla were led into the woods. One of the bandits led the ox and wagon after them, down a track carefully disguised by trees.

"Well, this is unpleasant," said Halla, as the bandits propped her against a tree. "Although I guess I'm glad they haven't killed us."

"A gnole is glad too."

"The Temple would be very upset. We have an arrangement with the underworld, you see. We are granted safe passage and criminals may come to us for healing without fear of arrest."

Halla blinked at them. "I didn't know that."

"It is not an arrangement that the Temple advertises very loudly."

"And they all agree to this?"

"The underworld is remarkably good at self-policing, particularly in the vicinity of Anuket City. I suppose there's probably places where it doesn't work."

"Huh." Halla considered this. "You don't really think of criminals as following laws..."

"It's more that they realize that the other criminals will be displeased at them if they lose regular access to healers. And these are the sorts of people who express their displeasure...pointedly."

"Was that a pun?"

Zale considered. "More of an observation, really."

The bandits had a rough camp set up. One kindled a fire.

Halla watched as Sarkis's sword was tossed carelessly down on the ground, alongside Zale's knives. She feared for a moment that the blade might come unsheathed, but it stayed in place.

Just let him stay there long enough to heal from the arrow...

Another bandit came through the trees. "Sir," he said. "We can't find hide nor hair of the other one."

"Because he's invisible!" yelled Mina.

"Because you shot him, so he ran away!" Halla yelled back.

It occurred to Halla that this was not a good thing in what was supposed to be a hired guard, so she added, "And anyway, he's fired! What kind of guard runs away because he's been shot? What was I even *paying* him for?"

The bandit leader rubbed his forehead wearily.

"Didn't see him running away," muttered the one who had been scouting. "Didn't see any trail." He scuffed the ground with his foot.

"Thought I saw some shiny light over by them, before," volunteered another one. Halla's heart sank. "But I don't know for sure."

The leader came and sat down in front of Halla and Zale.

"I am very sorry for all of this unpleasantness," he said to Zale. "But ma'am, if you can, in fact, make people invisible, surely you can see why that is a skill that I would be interested in making use of."

Halla wrinkled her nose. "No," she said after a moment. "I can't."

He tilted his head. "I'm a bandit."

"Yes," said Halla, "but you're a *highwayman*. You want people to believe you have superior numbers so that they give you their money without a fight. Making someone invisible would just mean that they were more likely to fight you, wouldn't it? And you can't very well have an invisible person stop travelers in the middle of the road. They'd just get run down. And then if there's arrows flying around and someone is invisible, doesn't it mean that that person is more likely to be shot on accident?"

The bandit leader blinked slowly at her.

"Really," said Halla, "it just seems like a poor idea all around. Even if I *could* make people invisible, which I can't." She shook her head. "It's all moot anyway. I think you've listened to a really unpleasant person and gotten entirely the wrong impression."

Mina started forward with an oath. The bandit leader twisted around and said, "If you don't want to end up in a shallow grave alongside Brett, I suggest you sit down."

She sat down.

So Brett's dead, then. I wonder if this man killed him, or if he got himself killed doing something stupid.

Halla didn't feel guilty over the man's death, but she found that even as angry as she was at Mina, she could feel a pang. The poor woman was obviously distraught over her friend's death and looking for someone to blame. Maybe she'd latched onto Halla and this wild tale of invisibility.

Which, ah, is not that wild, when you think about it. She's got things wrong, but she did *see Sarkis appearing out of nowhere. It's not a completely farfetched theory.*

The bandit leader squeezed his eyes shut. He looked as if he had a headache. "Do you know," he said, "this is not the way that I pictured this going?"

"Oh, I get that a lot."

He actually winced.

"Um," said Halla. "I'm sorry?"

Zale nudged her. "You don't have to apologize to someone who's kidnapped you," they muttered.

"Oh." That did make sense, but apologizing was ingrained in Halla's nature. She chewed on the inside of her cheek and wondered what to do next.

"So," said the leader, still not opening his eyes, "if I am hearing all this correctly, my men have shot at a priest of the Rat, in order to take a prisoner who is not actually a wonder-worker, and who as near as I can tell, thinks that the entire idea would be stupid even if she was."

"Not stupid," said Halla hurriedly. "I mean, if you were a different sort of person, I can see invisibility being useful! If you were a burglar, say."

She peered up through the leaves of the tree. It was starting to get dark. Had Sarkis had long enough to heal?

I suppose any amount of time I can buy him is useful...

"Invisibility might be very useful for a burglar," she added, nodding to the man. "Or an assassin. Or even a pickpocket. I just think that highway robbery is perhaps not a field where invisibility is called for."

The bandit leader looked over at Zale. "Under the protection of the Rat?" he said.

"I fear so."

"They'd be upset if I kill you both."

Zale somehow managed to look tranquil despite having

their hands tied and a man hinting at their death. "I fear there would be dying curses, yes. And then the Temple would be forced to withdraw their services from the underworld until you had been dealt with. Every man's hand turned against you and so forth." They paused. "Nothing personal, you understand."

"No," said the leader, "of course not." He stood up and walked away.

"Do you think he's going to kill us?" asked Halla.

"I'm not sure he knows yet."

"Is that good or bad?"

"Could go either way." Zale's pewter hair had come loose from the braid and fallen into their eyes. They tossed their head irritably, which fixed the problem for perhaps thirty seconds, and then it fell back down again.

"Oh dear."

Shadows crept under the trees. Halla studied the ropes in front of her. "Are we supposed to try to get out of these?"

"People usually try, I think," said Zale.

"A gnole could chew through them," volunteered Brindle, who had been keeping very quiet.

"It's just that we're in the middle of their camp and I think they'll notice. And that awful Mina person keeps glaring at me."

"Seems like we might not want to do that, then."

"Probably not."

"A gnole would at least wait until dark."

"What *do* we do?"

Zale gave her an ironic look. "I have no idea. I've never actually been kidnapped and tied up before. This is a new experience for me."

"Oh. Really? Because you seemed to be handling it really well, so I thought you must have done it before."

"Thank you. The Temple of the Rat does run us through a fair amount of training, you understand. I know what to do, in theory. It's just the first time I've had to put it into practice."

Mina glared daggers at them from across the clearing.

"What gets me," said Halla, after the better part of an hour dragged by, "is that people are tying each other up and robbing each other when there's those godawful slimy things lurking out there in the Vagrant Hills. I mean, don't they realize we have much bigger problems?"

"I don't think they do, no."

"We could tell them."

Zale leaned their head back against the trunk of the tree. "Somehow I don't think that will help much."

"Probably not. It just seems so short-sighted." Another, more immediate thought struck her. "Oh no! You don't think they'll bother Bartholomew and his friend, do you?"

"Hard to say," said Zale. "I suppose they might."

"This is *terrible.*"

"What, only now?"

"A gnole isn't getting paid enough for this."

The bandit leader came back over and looked at them like a man with a problem.

"You're absolutely certain you're not a wonderworker?" he said.

"Very," said Halla.

"And this light that Mina says she saw?"

Halla lifted her bound hands and let them drop back into her lap, hoping he couldn't read the lie. "I have no idea. You'd have to ask her."

"You have no explanation for it?"

She wrinkled her forehead. "Why do you want me to explain somebody else's hallucination? I really *would* have to be a wonderworker for that."

Did that sound convincing? I hope that sounded convincing.

"What would you say if I tortured you?" asked the bandit leader conversationally.

Halla blinked at him. "Err...'ow,' probably? 'Stop, stop, stop,' something like that?" *What a bizarre question. What does he expect me to say?*

The bandit leader's face took on an expression that Sarkis would have found immediately familiar. "I meant about being a wonderworker."

"Oh. I mean, it's torture," said Halla uncertainly. "I'll probably say anything you want to make it stop. But I'm still not going to be able to make anyone invisible afterward, if that's what you're getting at."

"If you release us now," Zale put in, "I am happy to let bygones be bygones. But my superiors would undoubtedly consider torture to be excessive."

The bandit leader walked away again, muttering to himself.

They continued to sit under the tree. One of the bandits came back with a rabbit, skinned it, and began cooking chunks over one of the campfires. Halla's stomach growled.

"Do you think they're going to feed us?"

"I am not entirely hopeful."

Halla started to reply to that, then noticed that two more bandits had sat down alongside the pile of their possessions confiscated from the wagon.

She bit her lip. She couldn't even say anything to Zale for fear of being overheard.

They examined Zale's crossbow first, with appreciative noises, then set it down. The gear taken from the dead Motherhood priests was next.

"Now where do you suppose they got this?" one of the bandits asked his companion, who shrugged.

Halla watched, holding her breath, as he picked up Sarkis's sword.

He idly drew the sword, examining the blade. "Not bad. Good edge on it, don't you think?"

His companion's opinion was lost to the ages, as a foot of steel slid into his throat.

The first bandit gaped, and then Sarkis jerked the sword free and smashed the hilt into the man's face in the same motion. He fell backward, clutching his face, and Sarkis reversed the sword and chopped down into his neck like a man splitting a log.

The attack was so quick and so brutal and above all so silent that for a long moment, Halla thought that she was the only person in camp who even realized what was going on. Even the crunch of steel into bone sounded like a snapping branch.

Sarkis looked around the campsite.

Halla held her breath for what seemed like an eternity and then someone finally realized what was going on and began to raise the alarm. Suddenly it seemed like everyone else in the bandit camp was rising to their feet.

"Oh dear," said Halla, to no one in particular. "I hope his arrow wound is healed up."

She was aware that this was probably not the right response, given that there were now a great many dead people in front of her. She should be horrified. She should scream her head off. But mostly she was just enormously relieved to see Sarkis again.

He'd take care of things. The man was a hero. These were just decadent southern bandits and anyway he was nearly immortal, so as long as she didn't have the poor taste to die in the interim, he would come for her and Zale. She had faith.

CHAPTER 39

Sarkis had a good deal less faith, but then again, he was the one doing most of the work.

He materialized, saw the two in front of him, neither of which was Halla, and therefore they both needed to die. Possibly they were innocent bystanders, in which case he could put another few deaths on the great god's ledger, but he wasn't worried about it.

They expired before either of them had time to worry about it either.

He looked swiftly around and saw that it was far darker than it had been. Hours had passed while he was inside the sword.

If hours had passed, then Halla could have been hurt. Not killed—he'd know that immediately—but tortured or terrified or god forbid, one of the bandits had taken liberties, and if they had, Sarkis would carve out that man's heart and place it at her feet.

A bandit stood up from beside the campfire, blinking stupidly at him. The man was still carrying a skewer with a chunk of meat on it. This proved very ineffective at parrying a sword.

Finally somebody had the good sense to shout "We're under attack!"

Being bandits rather than soldiers, this did not result in a coordinated defense. A few of them decided to absent themselves from the fight altogether. Sarkis watched a tall woman across the camp hold up both hands and step back into the trees.

A much shorter woman, looking vaguely familiar, leapt to her feet and began shrieking "I knew it! I told you! *Invisibility!*"

Invisibility? What?

"I told you! Wonderworkers!"

She was clearly raving with fever or shock or drink, so Sarkis simply smacked the pommel of his sword against the side of her head and let her drop. Such a blow might prove fatal, of course, but it was certainly preferable to decapitation.

Anyway, it was bad luck to kill drunks.

He looked around wildly for Halla, Zale, and opponents, in that order.

He found an opponent. The opponent had an axe. Parrying an axe with a sword was possible, but hard on the sword, and Sarkis had developed a certain aversion to seeing swords break.

He spat on the ground and shouted an insult. The man looked baffled.

Wrong language. Right. The magic was good, but he did tend to revert for obscenities, particularly ones that didn't translate well.

"Your sister screws wolves because the men of your clan have dicks the size of grass blades!"

This did not endear him to the bandit, but the sudden burst of laughter from off to his right told him that Halla was alive.

Alive. Not dead. I didn't fail her.

Sheer relief made him slow to dodge the axeman's charge. He had to dive out of the way and felt his ankle twinge a warning. He ignored it, put his sword in the axeman's kidneys and yanked it back out again, which pretty much ended the matter.

He looked around the campsite again, listening for crossbow strings. "Anyone else?" he asked.

No one stepped forward. This did not really surprise him. Bandits were in it for a profit, and there was pretty obviously no profit in fighting a very dangerous man who had appeared out of nowhere with a sword. He'd be surprised if half the group hadn't followed their colleague's example and melted away into the trees.

He walked to the tree where Halla was sitting.

She had her hands tied in front of her. Zale and Brindle were sitting next to her. They appeared unharmed. Brindle was busily gnawing away at his ropes, bits of hemp falling out of the sides of his muzzle.

Sarkis grabbed Halla's hands, sliced through the ropes, pulled her upright, and said the first thing which came into his head, which was, "We are never going down this stretch of road again! Never! I do not care if we must go a month out of our way and bribe three kingdoms for passage!"

Halla blinked at him. "Um, we could just take the north road up past the sheep downs next time...?"

"Yes!" roared Sarkis "We will do that!"

She nodded. He nodded.

Great god.

He wrapped his arms tightly around her. He wanted very much to kiss her, but he stopped himself. This far was safe. A friend might embrace her like this, particularly after a frightening experience.

A friend would not have had his lips pressed so tightly against her hair, but she could not see that and did not have to know. His heart hammered in his ears so loudly that it seemed like she had to be able to hear it, but perhaps a friend would feel that, too.

"It's all right," said Halla, patting his shoulder as if comforting him.

He held her at arms-length. She smiled up at him. "I knew you wouldn't let anything happen to us."

Sarkis stared into her face and saw that she was telling the absolute truth.

She trusts you.

She trusts you to keep her safe.

Pride warred with sudden dread. He would fail. He had *already* failed. Everyone who trusted him to keep them safe had already died, most in the space of one single bloody day.

Halla didn't know about any of that. Sarkis felt as if his unworthiness was branded across his face, and yet she was looking up at him without a trace of fear, trusting his competence and his care.

Great god, I must tell her what the sword says. I must tell her soon, before she finds out on her own.

"I wasn't worried."

"You should have been worried!"

Halla relented. "All right. I was a *little* worried. I mean, the one in charge didn't seem angry, just really confused and sort of frustrated, but he did talk about torture—"

Sarkis saw red. "I'll kill him. Where is he?"

"He ran away," said Zale, from the ground. "After you killed the fellow with the axe. Which was quite sensible of him, I suspect."

Sarkis lifted his head and scanned the trees, eyes narrowed.

"Before you charge after him, could you untie me? I mean, when you're done with the hugging."

"Oh dear..." Halla stepped back. Sarkis released her immediately. "Sorry, Zale."

"It's fine. These ropes and I are good friends by now." The rogue lock of hair fell back into the priest's face, and they tried to flip it away.

"A gnole wouldn't mind being untied, either."

Sarkis sheathed his sword and helped first the priest, then the gnole to their feet by way of apology.

He turned to Halla and she wasn't there. His nerves screamed, but she was stepping over dead bodies, nose wrinkled, to their gear.

As he watched, she picked up his sword and slung it over her shoulder, then carefully lifted Zale's crossbow and held it at arm's length, like it was a snake that might bite. "This thing isn't loaded, is it?"

"No," said Zale. "You can tell by the lack of bolts and the fact that the string isn't pulled back. Sarkis, forget my ropes, go take my crossbow away from her before she hurts it."

"I'm not going to hurt it!"

"Just don't...you know, drop it or...breathe on it too hard..." Zale rested their forehead against Sarkis's shoulder in apparent despair.

Sarkis patted the priest on the arm. "Let me get those ropes."

THEY LEFT the bandit camp without any particular incident. Sarkis's arrow wound was still tender. His ankle twinged, but that didn't mean anything. He'd had a bad ankle since before he went into the sword, and not even magic could fix that up.

Halla insisted on looking at Sarkis's arrow wound. It looked...worrisome. Not that there was anything wrong with the way it was healing, but the edges of the wound were silver instead of red and there were thin filaments stretched across it, like spider silk.

"That's *fascinating*," said Zale. Sarkis grunted.

They gathered up their own gear, then stood looking down at the equipment stripped from the Motherhood priests.

"Can we just leave this here?" asked Halla.

"You know, it does make things easier," said Zale. "If it turns up, everyone will assume it was just bandits that got them."

"Unless you decide to confess," muttered Sarkis.

Zale shot him a glance. "If I confess, I'll take the blame myself. It falls most squarely on me, after all."

"A gnole hates to interrupt humans feeling guilty, but an ox *could* be moving now."

Zale started guiltily. "For being a priest of the god of practical things, I am failing rather badly these days," they said to no one in particular, and climbed up on the wagon.

"It's been a long few days," said Halla, patting their arm.

They did not stop until after nightfall, and only because the ox could no longer reliably see his way. Brindle pulled the wagon over by the side of the road.

Halla slid down to go relieve herself in the bushes and discovered that Sarkis was following her so closely that she could feel his breath on the back of her neck.

"Sarkis."

"Yes?"

"I need to pee."

"I'll turn my back."

"Sarkis, if you don't step back at least a foot, your shoes are going to get wet."

He scowled. His back was to her, but Halla could actually

feel the force of his scowl radiating off him. "There may yet be bandits about. And some of them may feel vengeful."

"Then their shoes will also get wet. Are you going to do this to Zale, too?"

"I might."

"What about Brindle?"

"I have a certain amount of faith in Brindle's ability to handle his own affairs."

"And none in mine?" Halla sighed, finishing up and getting to her feet. She washed her hands in the water in the ditch by the side of the road, which had a thin skin of ice over it. "Well, I suppose I haven't given you much reason to, have I?"

"That isn't it," said Sarkis. He sounded almost angry. He took a step toward her, and then another, and then they were entirely too close and she thought for a moment that he might kiss her again.

She wouldn't have minded. She could feel the heat radiating off his body in the cold air and see the starlight outlining his face.

Instead he took a deep breath through his nose and turned away, shouting for Zale to tell them how much longer they would be on this blasted road.

I must have done something wrong again. Or failed to do something right, anyway. Halla didn't meet his eyes as he escorted her back to the wagon.

"*Someone's* in a mood," said Zale, later that night, when they had turned in for the evening.

"He is, isn't he?" Halla sighed. "Because he had to kill all those bandits, do you think?"

Zale, clearly attempting to be tactful, said "Ah…I don't think he's…err…bothered by that sort of thing, much."

"No," said Halla. "He's overfond of bloodshed, and I am

overfond of him and..." She put her hand over her mouth, both horrified and relieved that she'd said it out loud.

Oh god, oh god, I shouldn't have said that, but it was right there in my mouth like I've been wanting *to say it, oh god...*

"Ah," said Zale, when the moment became entirely too awkward and someone had to say *something*. "I suspected as much."

"Don't say anything," said Halla. "I mean, not to him. Please." She knew that Sarkis already had to find her weak and helpless. Pining after him would undoubtedly be the final nail in the coffin of his regard.

"I am a lawyer and a priest," said Zale. "There is probably someone on earth more bound to confidentiality, but I have yet to meet them."

"Right. Sorry." She rubbed her forehead. "I know there's no chance, you see."

The wagon creaked as Sarkis shifted overhead.

"He cares for you," said the priest finally. "Never doubt it."

Halla tried not to show the bubble of warmth that rose under her breastbone at the words. "I don't know why," she said. "He's a swordsman and I'm a housekeeper."

"Far more swordsmen have need of housekeepers than housekeepers have need of swordsmen, I expect."

Halla pushed the bubble back down. "Those swordsmen have to eat and drink and need clean beds to sleep in." She waved her hands at Zale, feeling her own words cut deep. "I can keep house for an eccentric old man and keep a farm running on the edge of disaster. I can nurse someone dying of fever. It's just my luck I'd end up with one that doesn't need any of those things."

She expected the very sensible priest of the very sensible god to agree with her. Sensibly.

Instead, Zale tilted their head, a small smile on their lips.

"Perhaps that's why you like him. It must be very dreary, being needed all the time."

"Oh god," Halla heard herself say. "Oh god, you have no idea."

"I might." The priest shook their head. "Go to sleep. He'll calm down in a day or so, or I will lecture him about it."

CHAPTER 40

Sarkis did indeed calm down after a day when, gloriously, absolutely nothing horrible happened.

The ox was set to grazing. Halla wanted to go to bathe in the stream, out of sight of the wagon, and Sarkis grudgingly allowed that she would probably not be horribly murdered.

"But you must sing," he said.

"Sing? What?"

"I will not stand guard over you while you bathe, but if you're singing, I will know immediately if something happens."

"I...uh...don't sing very well."

"This is not a test of your musical ability."

"It's your funeral," she muttered, picking up the soap, and went toward the stream. A moment later, her voice raised into a song about bringing in the harvest. It might have been pleasant if she had been anywhere in the vicinity of a note, never mind the tune.

Sarkis winced, but at least he had no doubts about where she was.

"Zale, I must ask you a question in private," he said, as soon as she was out of earshot.

The priest looked up, their expression quizzical. "Oh?"

He took a deep breath. This was going to be awkward, but there was nothing else for it. "Is your order sworn to celibacy?"

"Oh dear sweet Rat," said Zale. "Are you propositioning me?"

"No!" And then, because his haste might have been a trifle insulting, "Err, not that you're not a fine figure of a priest, but... no. That is not where I'm going."

"Oh thank heavens." Zale rubbed their face. "Not that you're not a...fine figure of a sword...but no. I prefer my men somewhat less cursed to inhabit magical steel for eternity. And also a bit more intellectual and a bit less likely to break people in half."

Brindle looked at them both, rolled his eyes, and went to go sit with the ox.

Sarkis nodded. "So—ah—may I guess that you are not interested in Halla?"

"Halla is lovely, and we are far too much alike. If it was left to us, we would still be sitting tied up under a tree discussing whether it would be too unforgivably rude to escape, and possibly what species the tree is." Zale raised an eyebrow. "Also, she's been mooning after you since before we met, so even if I were so inclined, I would be wasting my time."

Satisfaction warred with alarm. Halla? Mooning after him? Had she told the priest something?

It doesn't matter! You have to tell her what the sword says! You can't let her go around thinking you're a hero.

...but after she gets her inheritance back. Because if she took it badly (and how could she not take it badly?) Sarkis wanted to be damn sure that she was well set up first. If she decided to throw him out on his ear after that, she'd be able to do it safely.

"I was afraid of that," he muttered.

"You don't want her to be interested in you?" said Zale. Over by the stream, the singing was punctuated with splashing and occasional swearing.

"I do. Very much. That's the problem."

Zale steepled their fingers. "Do you want to talk about that?"

"Not particularly."

"All right. But you know, I *am* a priest. It's sort of what we do. Talk to people. Take confessions. That sort of thing."

"I thought you were more concerned with legal matters."

"The law is only talking and confession writ large. With occasional fines and time spent in the stocks."

Halla went for a high note, and Sarkis listened to make sure the song was the only thing being murdered.

"I gather it's at least a mutual attraction, then?" said Zale. "Because I must warn you, I do quite like her and I will be more than a little disappointed if you plan to marry her for her money and then abandon her."

Sarkis blinked at him in astonishment. *"What?"*

"I mean, you don't *seem* like the type...."

"I'm immortal and live in a sword. What am I going to do with money?"

Zale had to stop and think about that for a few minutes. "Well...hmm, I suppose metal polish isn't that expensive, is it? Err...a nice whetstone, maybe?"

Sarkis stared at him until the priest threw their hands in the air. "Fine, all right, I accept you're not interested in her money."

"I most certainly am *not.*"

"It's just...sheltered widow from the south...um...immortal warrior from the Weeping Lands..." Zale made vague hand gestures. "I grant you, they say that opposites attract..."

Sarkis rubbed his forehead. "She is lovely and kind and

generous of spirit and someone has to keep her from walking off a cliff."

"And they say romance is dead."

Sarkis snorted.

"Do you often fall in love with your wielders?" asked Zale.

"Never. Hell, most times I don't even respect them very much."

"Ah, but do you respect this one?"

"...not her singing voice, certainly," said Sarkis, as Halla attacked a chorus as if it had personally offended her.

"You brought *that* on yourself."

"Indeed I did. Well. At first...no, I did not. I thought her another decadent native of this weak, decadent land. Ah...no offense intended, of course."

"I have added it to all the other offenses I am not taking, given that you are a barbaric northerner and cannot be expected to understand civilized behavior."

Sarkis inclined his head to the priest.

"Later, though?" said Zale, who sometimes reminded Sarkis more of a terrier than a rat.

"Later..." Sarkis spread his hands. "Well. Yes. I have begun to. She is not a warrior, but...I don't know. Sometimes I simply want to see what ridiculous question she will ask next."

"Ah, the questions..." Zale laughed. "I admit, I find that delightful. It is so rare that I meet someone who asks questions because they want to know the answers."

Sarkis frowned at him. "What? Why else do people ask questions?"

Zale began ticking off possibilities on their fingers. "To be seen asking the question as if they do not know...to get a specific answer which they desire...to force someone to answer the question publicly...to be given a chance to lecture on the subject...to—"

"I yield, I yield!" Sarkis held up both hands, laughing. "Yes, I know the sorts of questions of what you speak." He had a memory of the Leopard holding a knife to a rival's throat, saying, "If I search this house, will I find something that makes me angry?" (The man had said, "No." He had been wrong about that, and had not lived to answer any more questions.)

"Which is not to say that Halla does not sometimes ask questions to throw people off. But she is, I think, like many children born in poverty. Intelligent...curious...but never given beyond the most basic education. In boys, that sort of thing is valued, in girls..." Zale shook their head. "Had she come to the attention of the Rat, we might have made a scholar of her. As it is, she has learned to be quiet and agreeable and to appear quite stupid when it is convenient. But the curiosity still comes through."

"That's part of it," said Sarkis. "Despite everything, it seems the world has not broken her. We hid *bodies,* for the great god's sake, and still she is...I don't know how else to explain."

Zale smiled. "The world tries to break everyone," they said gently. "But sometimes when it fails, it fails spectacularly. Why do you not say something to her?"

Sarkis groaned. "Because I have too much power over her fate right now."

Zale raised an eyebrow. "You'll have to explain that one for me."

"For a number of years, I was a mercenary captain. And there were jobs where I could say yes, and jobs where I could say no. And then there were jobs where, if I said no, I made sure that we were on the way out of the country when I said it."

The priest had never been slow on the uptake. "You don't think she'll feel safe saying no to you?"

"I am not willing to risk it." He poked the fire, raising a flare of sparks. "A few more days, and she is safe in her own home, and a wealthy woman. Then I'll know that she is not weighing whether I will still get her home safely if she rejects me."

Zale nodded slowly. "It would be the same for me, I admit. A breach of professionalism, until the job is done."

Sarkis let out his breath in a gusty sigh. "I hope this job is done quickly," he admitted. "Because I don't know how much more of this I can take."

HALLA FINISHED WADING in the stream and emerged, clean but freezing. The water was cold. It wasn't quite as bad as fresh snowmelt, in that her bones did not ache, but it wasn't pleasant.

She'd run out of most of the ordinary songs she knew and had started in on hymns. The Four-faced God had excellent hymns about the harvest and the planting and so forth. She wished she knew some hymns to the White Rat, for Zale, but then again, she was also aware that her singing wasn't the sort of thing any god would desire. Anyway, the Rat never seemed to go in much for hymns.

Halla wondered vaguely if Sarkis's great god liked hymns. He didn't seem like the type, but that might have more to do with Sarkis than with the god.

She toweled off, trying to use the rough cloth to rub warmth back into her skin. It wasn't entirely successful. She realized she'd stopped singing and started up again, before her watchdog could come running.

Not that I don't want to see him, but I'd prefer to be dressed.
I think.

Halla stifled a sigh. She had very little to offer anyone in that department, she knew...or rather, she had entirely too much of it, in all directions. Men were only interested in hips like hers if they wanted heirs, and she was fairly sure that Sarkis didn't.

He'd said some very kind things, but presumably he was being just that—kind.

And I must be practical. I must always be practical.

When he'd had his arms around her earlier, she had not felt particularly practical. He was as solid as a stone wall and he radiated heat and he had held her so tightly that she could hardly breathe.

It felt wonderful.

She had to tell herself that Sarkis was her guard, nothing more.

Probably nothing more.

The kiss in the marketplace had felt like a great deal more, but he hadn't repeated it.

Which is for the best, Halla told herself grimly. She had nothing to offer except kisses and men generally wanted a bit more than that. Or they were like her late husband and didn't even want that much.

God, why couldn't she have met Sarkis fifteen years earlier?

Well. Might as well ask why the sun couldn't rise later in the day so we could all sleep in.

She was getting an inheritance she had never expected. She could provide for her family, what little was left of it, and if she did not do anything completely ridiculous, she would be able to live comfortably on what remained. She should be grateful for that much. She *was* grateful for that much.

Her dreams of running her hands down Sarkis's muscled arms, tracing the path of each silver scar...well, they were dreams, that was all. You had them and you enjoyed them and then you got on with life.

She'd already seen what happened when you gave yourself to unsuitable men. Her mother had been a walking object lesson in loving unwisely. Even her mother would probably have balked at loving an enchanted sword.

Assuming that love is the correct word, thought Halla, a bit dryly. Love might well make your heart race and your pulse pound in your ears, but the one pounding a good deal lower was lust, plain and simple.

Which was...well, not helpful. Hell, Halla didn't even know if she *liked* lovemaking. She didn't think she hated it. Plenty of people enjoyed it. It seemed like it had a lot of potential. She'd have liked the chance to find out with a man who was actually interested, but given the risks, it hadn't been worth it to find out after her husband died.

Well. Maybe when she was past the point of child-bearing, someone would come along who wanted to spend time with a good-natured widow.

I don't want someone, *though. I want Sarkis.*

No. She had to be practical. Other women got to be impractical—young ones, beautiful ones, ones with well-off families to catch them when they did something foolish. Halla was no longer young and had never been beautiful. So, she had to be one of the practical ones.

Sarkis did not make her feel the least bit practical.

All those years of thinking that foolish girls in ballads were simply too dumb to know better, she thought, slogging up the cold riverbank toward the wagon. *And it turns out that you're no better, when it comes down to it.*

She came into the circle of firelight. Zale smiled up at her, and Sarkis gave her the muted scowl that passed for a smile, and Halla realized that she almost didn't want the journey to end.

CHAPTER 41

The next day, Zale taught Halla to use a crossbow.

"Are you sure this is a good idea?" asked Sarkis. In the abstract, he believed that it was good for everyone to know how to defend themselves, but in the concrete, that meant that Halla was holding a loaded crossbow.

She's not notably less competent than most of the recruits you've trained over the years.

...yes, and how often did those recruits nearly put a bolt in you?

"It is the best of ideas," said Zale firmly. "We defeat ignorance with knowledge and training."

Brindle hunched his shoulders up and said, "Better not aim at an ox, rat-priest. Better not aim anywhere *near* an ox."

"Oh dear..." Halla looked at the crossbow. "Should we go to the back of the wagon, maybe?"

"That might be best." Zale took their weapon and led her around to the back. Sarkis followed grimly, determined to be on hand if something went wrong.

There followed a few minutes of the priest explaining what part went where. "You must have a bolt to fire it. If you fire the crossbow without a bolt, you damage the crossbow. All that pent up energy has to go somewhere."

"Like some people I know," said Halla, sighing.

Sarkis gave her a sharp look, but she looked innocently at him. Which meant nothing. Halla's ability to look innocent was a constant source of amazement.

"Now, put the stock up against your shoulder. Wedge it very tight. There's a pad, but it will still kick, and the tighter you have it there, the better." The priest set their long, thin hands over Halla's, moving her into position. "No, a little higher. There."

The ox ambled onward while Zale talked Halla through the act of aiming and firing. "Do not point it at anything that you do not want to put a bolt into. Do not shoot if you do not know what is behind it. Now, this dirt bank will do admirably. Aim and fire."

"What do I aim at?"

"That plant there," said Sarkis.

"Coltsfoot," muttered Halla. "Well, it's a weed anyway..."

THWANG.

"...ow."

Sarkis was actually rather impressed at how little the crossbow had kicked. Fisher had dislocated his shoulder once, shooting his in a hurry, and had said it wasn't the first time it had happened. But that had been a substantially larger weapon, with a great deal more range. This one was...well... cute. But then again, Zale was not over large themself and had little need for a weapon that could kill at a vast distance.

And Brindle also killed a man with that crossbow, so let's not get too hung up on size, shall we?

Halla did not seem to appreciate the relative lack of recoil very much. She rubbed her shoulder. "That hurt."

"It is not a thing to be fired lightly," said Zale. "But you've slain your weed, look!"

Halla grinned. Sarkis's heart lurched, as it always did, and he went to go check on the ox and wagon.

As THEY APPROACHED the gates of Rutger's Howe, Halla shivered. It was cold out, but Sarkis doubted that was the reason. He put an arm around her shoulders anyway.

She cast him a brief look, both startled and appreciative, and said, "I know they're not expecting us, but I'm still half-afraid Alver's going to be waiting with the constables."

Sarkis hated the thought of leaving her to face her cousin alone, but nevertheless... "Should I go back into the sword? I do not wish us to spend our first night back in a jail cell."

"You absolutely should not," said Zale firmly. "We begin as we mean to go on, and we will not act as if you are a criminal. You were defending Halla against a completely indefensible imprisonment."

"Yes, but then we ran away afterwards," said Halla.

Zale straightened their back and lifted their chin. "You did not have a lawyer then," they said. "More specifically, you did not have a priest of the Rat. I will not allow my clients to be imprisoned for fleeing from danger."

For once, it really did seem to be that easy. It was hard to believe that the servant of the Rat sweeping into town, wearing the full vestments of the priesthood, was the same person who had been violently ill in a ditch while Halla held their hair. Zale exuded authority. They even looked a few inches taller. When they raised their hand and beckoned to a constable standing by the gate, the poor man nearly saluted in return.

"Your Holiness?" he asked.

"I require your assistance," said Zale. "This is Mistress Halla, most recently of your town."

The constable looked at Halla, and appeared even more confused. "Halla? I thought you were kidnapped!"

"Hello, Michael," said Halla. "I wasn't."

"No thanks to those...*persons*...claiming to be her relatives by marriage," said Zale. They somehow managed to make *claiming to be a relative* sound like a crime on par with bestiality. "Mistress Halla was forced to flee when they attempted to imprison her in her own bedroom. Can you imagine the depths of such depravity?"

Michael blinked several times and looked around, possibly hoping someone else was going to answer the question.

"Direct us to the offices of your town clerk," ordered Zale. "I wish to settle this for my client as soon as possible, and see those imposters subjected to the full force of the law."

Michael was clearly relieved that all that was required were directions, not any arrests. He waved toward the center of town. "And turn left at the butcher," he said. "The three-story building with the angel on the weathervane."

"Indeed." Zale wrinkled their nose. "On, Brindle!"

The tilt of Brindle's ears indicated that there would be words about this later.

"I could have told you where it was," murmured Halla, as the cart rumbled past Michael, who was standing at attention.

"Undoubtedly," said Zale. "But this way, the accusations have been made—loudly—and the constables will know your side of the story before we are even to the clerk."

Halla looked at Sarkis helplessly. He took her hand and squeezed. "It will be all right," he said. "Zale clearly knows what they are doing."

Zale grinned like a shark that had eaten the cat, the canary, and several innocent bystanders.

"A SERVANT OF THE RAT?" squeaked the clerk. Halla felt bad for him. He was a middle-aged man who had the job primarily because of the neatness of his penmanship and his meticulous recordkeeping. He did not deserve to be caught between Aunt Malva on one side and Zale's inexorable courtesy on the other.

Speaking of which...

"What is the meaning of this?" snapped Aunt Malva, throwing open the door to the office. "What is this foolishness I am hearing about Halla being—*Halla?*"

Her voice went up half an octave as Halla turned to face her.

If she had been a better actress, Halla thought, Malva might have carried the day. If she had thrown her arms around Halla's neck and professed how happy she was, perhaps.

Fortunately for me, she cannot pretend to hold me in anything but contempt.

"Hello, Aunt Malva," said Halla grimly. "Surprised to see me?"

Alver came in behind her, saw Halla, saw Sarkis, saw Zale, and began to back out of the door as if he had wandered into the wrong building by mistake.

Malva drew herself up to her full height and pointed a trembling finger at Sarkis. "You! Constables! Arrest this man!"

This would have been a very impressive statement if there had been any constables in the room. Sarkis looked around, apparently saw none, then looked at the clerk and shrugged.

"What exactly are you arresting my guard for?" asked Zale.

Halla watched Sarkis's lips twitch as he absorbed his new employment status.

"He kidnapped Halla!"

"As my client is standing right here, this appears to be some definition of *kidnap* of which I am unaware," said Zale. Halla had never previously paid much attention to the length of the priest's nose, but the way that they looked down it at Malva was positively inspirational. "Mistress Halla, has this man kidnapped you?"

"Certainly not."

"Perhaps it was some time ago. Try to remember?"

"Nothing's coming to mind."

"Alver!" snapped Malva, turning. "Alver, explain to her what happened!"

"Um, he kidnapped you," said Alver. "It was awful."

"How odd," said Zale. "Since my client made no mention of being kidnapped. I would think she would know, wouldn't you?"

"She's mad," snapped Malva. "Or a fool. It doesn't matter. Alver, go get a constable!"

Zale gave her a look of withering contempt. The clerk looked horribly uncomfortable.

"You might try Constable Michael," said Zale. "He greeted us at the gate and is fully apprised on the situation."

"He seemed pleasant," rumbled Sarkis.

Malva, outmaneuvered, snapped her mouth shut.

"Now," said Zale, turning to the law clerk, "I am aware that this is unorthodox, but as I was not present for the reading of the will, would you be so kind as to go over it again?"

The law clerk grabbed onto this like a life line. "Yes! Certainly!" He went over to a cabinet and pulled out the document. "Here, as you can see, the signatures are all in order..."

"They certainly seem to be," murmured Zale. "Now let us take this line by line."

"Is this really necessary?" said Malva. "We all know what it says."

Zale brushed their hand through the air near their ear, as if

T. KINGFISHER

to wave off a buzzing insect. "Let me see...yes, this appears in order. The house and possessions inside it, along with all properties, are to be left to Mistress Halla. Is this your reading too?"

"Yes," said the clerk, nodding vigorously.

"He was not in his right mind when he wrote that," snapped Malva.

"This would appear to be quite straightforward," said Zale. "Is there any reason why my client cannot take possession of her property at once?"

Halla held her breath.

The clerk looked once or twice at Malva, opened his mouth, then forced a sickly smile. "Well, not exactly, but I'm afraid that there's been a...a challenge to the will..."

"I *see*," said Zale. "And the challenge was brought by?"

"Alver," said Malva.

Alver, who had his shoulders up around his ears and had been staring at the floor, looked up, startled. "Yes, mother?"

"Tell them why you've brought this challenge to the will!"

"Uh...I...uh...that is...well, the old boy can't have been in his right mind, can he? To leave it all to his housekeeper instead of his family..."

"You were eager enough to marry that *housekeeper* a few weeks ago," said Halla acidly.

"*Not* of sound mind," repeated Malva. "She was clearly manipulating him. Might even have been..." Malva looked down her nose, "...*carrying on* with him."

Halla's jaw dropped. "Carrying on with—he was *eighty-six*!"

"Not the first old goat to be made a fool of by a young woman, is he?"

"*Young*? You told me that I was so old that I should be grateful for any offer!"

The clerk was looking back and forth, eyes round. Zale cleared their throat. "The age of my client is not relevant. Very well, if a challenge is being brought to the will, we will require a judgment. I assume that the house has been sealed in the meantime?"

The clerk gulped. "Ah...well...no, I..."

Zale's voice grew clipped. "And why not? In the event of a contest to the will, it is accepted legal practice to seal the property to prevent theft, is it not?"

"Yes, but...well, that is..." The clerk glanced at Malva, then took a deep breath. "No, you're absolutely right, your honor. I will order the constables to seal the property at once."

"But that's where we're staying!" cried Malva.

"Then let us hope that irreparable damage has not already occurred," said Zale.

Malva began to turn blotchy and red.

Halla coughed. "Someone will need to feed the chickens," she said. "And the servants—well, if there's any still working there—oh dear, they shouldn't lose wages for this..."

"I am certain that provision can be made for the chickens," said Zale gravely. Sarkis, who had been as silent as a statue, coughed. "Should the servants wish to speak with Mistress Halla, please inform them that we will be staying at the Temple."

"But where will we—"

"Now," Zale continued, nodding to the clerk, "as regards the challenge, I would ask that judgment be delayed until the deceased's friend Bartholomew arrives. He is heading here directly from Amalcross, and should be no more than a day or two behind us. He is the witness on this will and can speak to the mental state of the deceased at the time of writing it."

"Certainly," gasped the clerk, sensing a reprieve.

"Tomorrow, I will wish to go over the extent of the property named in the will with you, if that will be acceptable?"

"Yes, yes of course." The clerk stood up straighter. Property records, at least, he understood.

"Then we will leave you to your duties," said Zale, inclining their head. "Thank you for seeing us on such short notice."

"Where are we to stay?" shouted Malva in the priest's face.

Zale looked at her, then removed a handkerchief from their robes and silently wiped their face, as if removing flecks of spittle. Malva's flush deepened.

"*That,* madam," said Zale, after folding the handkerchief into a precise square, "is not my client's concern."

They swept out of the room. Halla would likely have stayed, rooted in place, but Sarkis put a hand on her shoulder and steered her out in the priest's wake.

"Zale," she started to say, but they raised a hand for silence. Halla, brimming with incredulous laughter, could barely climb onto the wagon. It was not until Brindle had brought the ox to a halt outside the churchyard that the priest exhaled and slumped back against the seat.

"*That,*" they said, grinning, "was *fun.*"

"You were amazing!"

"She is not wrong. I have been on battlefields with less mayhem."

"Ah, well." Zale waved a hand. "I so rarely get the chance for a full dramatic legal scene. The Rat cannot blame me for taking the opportunity now and again." They sighed, putting their hand to their heart. "Tomorrow, I fear, will not be nearly so exciting, though a good deal more essential."

"Do you need me there?" asked Halla.

"You may certainly attend if you wish, but it's dry business," Zale said. "We will go through deed records and maps to determine the extent of your great-uncle's holdings, and thus precisely what will come to you. It may be that there is something in there that we could offer to those wretched people, something you would not miss, and get them to simply go away...though I confess, after that scene, I am inclined to leave them with nothing at all."

"I would *love* it if they simply went away," said Halla. *With all of Silas's property, I imagine I wouldn't miss any of it, if it meant that they didn't come back and bother me every time the wind blew. Although I suppose that might mean a smaller dowry for my nieces...still...*

"We shall keep that as an option, then," said Zale firmly. "And now, let us go meet your priest and tell him that we are invading his stable for the foreseeable future."

CHAPTER 42

The priest of the Four-Faced God was almost pathetically delighted to see Zale. "A colleague!" he said. "Of course—of course—as long as you like, certainly—please, put your ox in the stable—oh dear, I only have one guest room, I'm so sorry, but we can put the novices out and change the sheets and—"

Zale took his hand and patted the back kindly. "That will not be necessary at all, Father. We have a wagon that travels with us, and I would not see your novices suffer in the cold. A stall for the ox and a meal or two is all that we will impose upon you."

"Oh dear! Are you certain? How long are you staying?"

"Until the matter of the will is sorted out." Zale smiled warmly, the icy legal demeanor gone as if it had never existed. "But if we may eat with you tonight? I fear I will bore you senseless, since all my chatter is of the capital and the Temple politics there, but if you will grant me your patience…"

"Not at all," gasped the priest. Halla realized with a pang how desperate the poor man was for news of the wider world.

Was Rutger's Howe really such a backwater? Well, perhaps it was.

She would think so again, several times in the next few days. It was familiar and comfortable and she was glad to be home, but she kept thinking how much smaller it seemed, compared even to Amalcross. People walked by the stableyard and stared at the painted wagon as if they had never seen one.

They stared at Brindle too, and that really annoyed her. There were gnoles in Rutger's Howe, for the love of the gods, it wasn't like they hadn't seen one before. But somehow the local gnoles were unremarkable, while Brindle, calmly going over the wagon, fixing harness leather and replacing nails, merited staring.

"I'm sorry," she said. "I don't know why people are being so...I'm sorry."

The gnole gave her a look, ears down and back, in what she had learned was wry amusement. "A gnole is a job-gnole, not a rag-and-bone gnole," he said.

"I don't know what that means, Brindle."

He turned back to his work. "Rag-and-bone gnole works in gutters, takes trash. Works hard. Not insulting a rag-and-bone gnole. But a job-gnole works on wagons." He put his claws across his chest. "Fixes. Drives an ox. Human sees a job-gnole, maybe a human doesn't expect it."

Halla knew perfectly well what he *wasn't* saying, about human behavior and human assumptions of superiority. *He's being diplomatic. Because I am, after all, a human, and this is my home.*

And if I try to say much more, I'll make a mess of it, and it won't fix Brindle's problem at all.

"Tell me if I can do anything," she said wearily. "Or if anyone gives you trouble. Sarkis'll set them straight."

Brindle gave her a gap-fanged grin. "A gnole would like to see that," he admitted.

THE OTHER SIGNIFICANT problem was the Four-Faced priest's housekeeper.

Widow Davey lived across the road from the small church, and came over every evening to do the cooking and the tidying up. She was kind, generous, efficient, and when she learned that Widow Halla was going to be setting up her own household, she bustled over, full of helpful advice.

"I've been keeping house for over twenty years," said Halla grimly. "I've told her that. But she still wants to show me the best way to blacken a grate and how to make chicken stock. I have been making chicken stock since I was *twelve.*"

"Do you want me to stab her?" asked Sarkis, who was feeling rather useless now that no one was shooting arrows at them.

"No. I mean, yes, very much, but don't actually do it. She means well." Halla gritted her teeth. "She just won't listen. She's seen me at market since I moved here, but now that Silas is gone, suddenly I need all her advice. God's teeth! Did she think *he* was making the chicken stock?"

Sarkis had only the vaguest notion of what chicken stock even was. Something you fed to chickens, presumably. "Well, perhaps Zale will be done with whatever they're doing soon."

"Bartholomew should arrive tomorrow," Halla agreed.

"How will they make a judgment?"

"Oh, they'll call a triumvirate. Clerk, priest—that's our host, Zale can't do it—and the Squire's bailiff will make the third."

"Will they find in our favor, do you think?"

"The priest certainly will. He's already told Zale as much.

The clerk will probably depend on whether he's more scared of Malva or Zale. The Squire's bailiff, I don't know."

The squire's bailiff, when he arrived, was a large man with the placid air of a contented cow and a mind like a razor. He arrived at the same time as Bartholomew and went to the same hostel, where, ironically, Malva and Alver were also staying.

"Should I be worried about this?" asked Zale, upon learning of the accomodations.

Halla shook her head. "I honestly don't think so. Aunt Malva doesn't really improve upon close acquaintance."

"And your cousin?"

"Alver will agree to anything, mean none of it, and then do whatever his mother tells him."

"A familiar, if regrettable dynamic." Zale nodded. "Well, it is only another two days and then we shall have our decision." They smiled. "And I have a trick or two up my sleeve, in case things go very badly indeed."

———

BUT THINGS DID NOT GO BADLY. In fact, given the sheer chaos of their trip to and from Archenhold, the judgment was almost an anticlimax.

The judgment was held in the church, that being both a large room and, given the proximity of the gods, presumably a better space for deliberation. Sarkis didn't know if it would help, but at least the room was large enough that he didn't need to sit too close to Halla's wretched relatives.

He tried to remember what Halla had said. The priest who served in this church did not necessarily belong to any specific god, as he recalled. That probably explained why the stained glass windows were generic scenes of the seasons rather than any particular deity. The wooden pews were sturdy rather than elegant, with marks on the legs where either small children or dogs had gnawed on the edges.

The stone floor radiated cold. Everyone was wearing at least two layers of clothes. Only Zale seemed unaffected by it, moving rapidly back and forth, presenting the case methodically to the three judges. The priest was finally in their element, and Sarkis wondered that he had ever thought them weak. Their long-fingered hands moved back and forth, sweeping gestures to underscore their words, their angular face by turns solemn and stern and amused.

Halla sat in a pew in the back of the room, clutching Sarkis's hand. He wanted to put his arm around her, shield her from the glare that Malva was shooting in her direction, but he wasn't sure how she would feel about it, or if it would bias the judgment. *A respectable widow.* He hated how much that mattered.

Alver's defense was...well, even to Sarkis's biased ears, it didn't sound good. The old man should have left the property to his family. No, Halla wasn't family. Well, she was sort of family, by marriage, so yes, maybe he *had* left it to family, but not the *right* family.

He tried to argue that Silas had not been in his right mind, whereupon Zale called Bartholomew up from his spot on the pew, and Bartholomew demolished that argument in a few well-placed sentences. Senile? No, he had not been senile, he'd driven a brutal bargain with Bartholomew for a set of old books and a giant snail shell a month before he died. And anyway, the will that Bartholomew had witnessed was six years old, so even if he had been getting on at the end, it didn't signify. No, Halla had not had any undue influence over him. She was a housekeeper and a good one. Efficient, kind, respectable, but not what you'd call a seductress, and he meant no offense to her by saying so.

Halla laughed at that. Sarkis wasn't sure whether to laugh or to go glare at the man until he agreed that she was beautiful.

He was braced for a discussion of the way that he and Halla had left the house, but Alver did not bring it up. Possibly the man had realized that it made him look at least as bad as Sarkis and had decided to simply pretend that it hadn't happened at all.

That hired man can't have died, or they would probably try to have me up on murder charges. Perhaps the dreadful woman turned him out after he could no longer guard her.

Alver fumbled his way through the statement until Malva apparently could bear it no longer, and then she stood up and pushed him out of the way. Sarkis watched the triumvirate's reactions with amusement. The clerk visibly flinched, the priest's lips thinned, and the bailiff's small, bright eyes grew smaller and brighter as he narrowed them.

"Family comes first," said Malva. "Silas knew that once. I don't know what changed that, but clearly that woman had something to do with it!"

"But she *is* family," said the bailiff mildly.

"Her?" Malva dismissed this with a hand. "No one could believe that my dear nephew would have wanted his wife favored above his blood!"

"How long has your dear nephew been dead?" asked the bailiff.

Malva opened her mouth and shut it again.

"Twelve years," called Halla. "Thirteen next summer."

"Perhaps the deceased thought that he was doing a kindness, seeing that his nephew's widow was cared for," said the priest of the Four-Faced God.

"A pension would have been sufficient," said Malva. "No one is claiming that she should be turned out into the cold."

"This from a woman who shouted, 'You're dead to the family,' as I was leaving," muttered Halla to Sarkis.

Sarkis snorted. He might have said something, but then Zale astonished him by saying, "Ser Sarkis, please come forward."

"Ah..." He rose to his feet. "Yes, of course, priest Zale, but I am not sure what good that I will do. I know nothing of the will nor the law."

"You have been a guardsman for Mistress Halla for some weeks now, have you not?"

"I have."

"You escorted her to Archen's Glory and my Temple, did you not?"

"Yes."

Zale smiled with the air of one going in for the kill. "And did she travel in wealth and comfort?"

"We slept in hedgerows. She had to sell her jewelry so we could eat," said Sarkis. "I have nothing of my own but the armor on my back, or I would have forbidden it, but she insisted."

"Not exactly the act of a woman who masterminded an alteration of the will in her favor, was it?"

Sarkis snorted loudly.

"Traveling alone with a strange man is not the act of a *respectable* woman," said Malva.

Sarkis turned toward her furiously. "I have guarded her as I would my sisters. No one will offer her disrespect in my hearing, man or woman, or they will answer to *me*."

He put his hand on the hilt of his sword. Malva slapped Alver's arm. "Alver! Are you going to let him talk to me like this?"

Alver eyed the sword and Sarkis and said "Yes, mother, I believe I am." The bailiff's lips twitched.

"Ser Sarkis," said the priest of the Four-Faced God mildly, "we do not threaten violence within the walls of the church."

"Oh. Sorry." Sarkis inclined his head. "I fear I am not native to these lands." He contemplated how barbaric he wanted to appear. *In for a lamb...* "In my homeland, duels are fought before the altar so that the god may decide the victor." Which was nonsense, of course, but hopefully impressive sounding nonsense.

"That will *not* be necessary," said Zale firmly. "Now, if I may draw your attention, gentlemen, to the wording of the will..."

The process stretched out interminably. Halla shivered in the cold room. But at last, the three judges nodded to Zale and Alver, and everyone filed out of the temple to give them time to deliberate.

It took less than ten minutes. The clerk was sweating and refusing to meet Malva's eyes as he delivered their judgment. "The will is upheld. Mistress Halla is Silas's heir."

"What?" said Halla.

"What?" said Malva.

"Really?" said Halla.

"*What?*" said Malva.

"Thank you, wise sirs," said Zale, and bowed deeply, while Halla dissolved into tears of sheer relief.

CHAPTER 43

"Well, there was really no doubt," said Zale, leaning back in their chair. "Or rather, there was no doubt that the will was valid. And I had a few tricks up my sleeve if they didn't happen to agree with me. The bailiff was the only wild card."

"It was still amazing," said Halla firmly.

"Bartholomew's testimony certainly helped," said Zale, raising their mug in Bartholomew's direction. The group was huddled together in the church's back room, while the priest of the Four-Faced God beamed at all and sundry.

"Will you all come stay at the house tonight?" asked Halla. "I don't know what state the house is in, but if I can't get at least the kitchen and a bedroom or two presentable..."

"We won't put you to the trouble," said Nolan firmly, glancing over at Bartholomew. "You've been through a great deal, you don't need to start cleaning up for us."

"I am intrigued, though," said Bartholomew, glancing at Halla, "by that sword you have been carrying. I fear that I may have undervalued it."

"This?" Halla set her hand on the scabbard. "Oh, it's...um... not available, I'm afraid."

"Our agreement included first pick of the artifacts in the house."

"Yes," said Halla, "but it's not really in the house, is it? And anyway, it's not mine. It belong to Sarkis. I gave it to him ages ago. He just makes me carry it around so that people think twice about assaulting me. Do you know we got set on by footpads in Archen's Glory?"

"Shocking!" said Nolan.

"It was. But Sarkis ran them off. He's good at that sort of thing."

Bartholomew was undeterred. "Would you be willing to part with it then, sir?"

"No," said Sarkis. He wracked his brain for some excuse and took refuge in mysticism. "It is originally a sword of my people's make. It will be...unhappy...if it spends too long among unbelievers."

(This was purest refined sheep-shit. Sarkis's people saw swords as tools, not sentient objects, and found the notion of swords having emotions or preferences faintly insulting, as if a human smith had taken on the role of the great god. He was exceptionally conscious of the irony.)

Bartholomew looked as if he might argue the point, but Nolan said, "If it is acceptable, Mistress Halla, we'll come over tomorrow and begin attempting to catalog the artifacts?"

"Your assistance would be most welcome," said Zale.

"Yes, of course," said Halla. She threw her arms around Bartholomew and he staggered back a step. "Thank you so much! I know Silas would be so grateful."

"Oh, well..." Bartholomew snorted. "Probably he'd be rubbing his hands together in glee that he made me come all this way. But I'm glad to have helped."

After he and Nolan had made their way back to the inn, the priest of the Four-Faced God turned to Halla. "I...ah...have something for you," he said. "I did not want to announce it before the case, because had you lost, I knew that it would belong to that dreadful woman, and...well..."

Halla rose to her feet, puzzled. "Oh?"

"Yes. If you'll follow me...?"

He led the three of them to a tiny cell off one of the side chambers. "Used for meditation," he said. "At least...normally..."

He opened the door and a voice bellowed *"Prepare for the coming of the worm!"* Then it sang, "tweedle-tweedle-twee!" and whistled.

"What the hell is *that?*" said Sarkis, reaching for his sword.

"Oh dear gods," said Halla, sagging against the doorway. "You found the bird."

"I found it in the nave the day of Silas's funeral," said the priest. "It was badly chilled, so I thought I would warm it up, and then it began saying all those dreadful things, and I realized it had been that awful pet of his."

"Rat's blood," said Zale, staring at the little finch, who was hopping about inside a wicker cage. "What's wrong with it?"

"It's not a demon," said Halla. "We had it checked. Silas thought it was probably inhabited by a ghost, but the ghost would have had to be a cultist or something."

"The dead are bound beneath the earth and their tongues stopped with clay but the day will come when they are free to sing the praises of the worm!"

"Perhaps a very tiny god," said Zale, tapping the bars.

"A very tiny *angry* god," said Sarkis.

"Tweedle-tweedle-twee..."

"You'll take it back, won't you?" said the priest hopefully. "I've been keeping it in here, but it scares the novices."

Halla sighed heavily. "Yes," she said. "Of course." Sarkis looked at her as if she had agreed to keep a tame manticore in the house. "Well, I can't leave it here."

"Prepare for the coming of the day of hellfire!"

"What does it eat?" asked Sarkis.

"Anything. It likes chicken. We mostly gave it cracked corn because that was a normal bird thing to eat." She picked up the cage by the handle. The bird whistled happily and then told her that the dead were waiting, and Halla began to feel like things were returning to normal at last.

ZALE OFFERED to stay in the wagon again that night, but Halla wouldn't hear of it. "You're not a guest," she said. "You're family. Which means that I can put you up in a room with a fireplace that doesn't draw and not feel guilty about it." Zale laughed.

"A real bed would be nice," they admitted. "I'm completely out of sheets, as you very well know."

"We have sheets. Acres of sheets. They may be mended within an inch of their lives, some of them, but we've got them. And the bird goes to sleep once you put something over its cage."

To give Malva what credit she deserved, the house was not in bad condition. The compost needed turning and the chickens were indignant, but the garden was asleep for the winter anyway. Halla found the bedrooms largely untouched. Only Silas's room and the two best guest bedrooms showed signs of recent use.

That awful old shrew took Silas's room? Halla found that she was chokingly furious about that. It was one thing to be evil and grasping and lock your potential daughter-in-law in a back room, but stealing a dead man's bed? That was just *petty.*

Presumably a number of the family entourage had gone home after the will was read. One of the guest bedrooms smelled vaguely of lavender water and had no fewer than five quilts piled on the bed, which Halla knew from experience meant that Malva's sister had been sleeping in it.

I suppose she's back at the inn, then. Well, she wouldn't have been much good at the trial, particularly if Malva was trying to convince everyone that her side of the family was a bastion of sanity and Silas was moving to senility.

"Can I help?" said Sarkis.

"Dishes," said Halla. That was the one thing that had been neglected. The scullery looked dismal. "I know it's a lot..."

"Have I mentioned that I fought dragons?"

"Not recently, no."

"Well, I have. The dishes hold no terror for me."

It took several hours of work, but Halla scrubbed the tables, swept the floor, appeased the chickens, and put fresh sheets on the beds. She was just strewing fresh herbs on the rush mats when she heard the front door open.

"I have brought wine," said Zale. "In celebration. I also had wine that would work for consolation, but fortunately it wasn't needed."

Sarkis emerged from the scullery, looking soggy. "I have defeated the dishes."

"Were there any survivors?"

"The only casualty was some kind of monstrous serving plate with pears on it."

"Oh, that," said Halla with relief. "Dare I hope it's broken past any possible mending?"

Sarkis considered this for a moment, then went back into the scullery. Sounds of breaking crockery drifted through the open door.

"Yes," he said, returning.

"Thank the gods. It was a gift from Malva's mother."

"I see the lack of taste is hereditary."

"I fear I don't have a full triumphal dinner," said Halla apologetically. "Bread and cheese and jam, mostly."

"I have brought a dinner," said Zale, brandishing a covered dish. "I don't know what it is. The widow who lives across from the church pressed it on me and told me to tell you that she'd give you the recipe."

"Good enough."

She found winecups for the three of them and they all sat down at the table. Halla kept looking around the house and thinking, *This is mine*, but the thought seemed so absurd that she had to drown it in sips of wine.

"What will you do now?" asked Zale.

"Oh! Goodness, I...you know, I don't know?" Halla set down the winecup, startled. "I mean, I've been so focused on getting to this point that I barely thought about what comes after this."

"Understandable. You don't need to decide right away," said Zale.

Halla nodded, glancing at Sarkis. "I suppose it will take a few days to sort the house out here. Bartholomew of course will get first pick of the artifacts, and I'll clean out some rooms. After that, I thought maybe I'd go see my nieces, if Sarkis doesn't mind."

Sarkis looked up, startled. "What? Mind?"

"Well, I mean...I assume you'll insist on going with me..."

"I am certainly not letting you go traipsing about the countryside by yourself." His skin crawled at the thought. Halla would probably trip and fall on a bear. She would undoubtedly then ask the bear questions until it forgot to eat her, but he didn't think his nerves could take it.

"Right. So would you mind visiting them?"

"I go where you go. Wherever that may be."

"Which is why I'm making sure you don't mind where we go!"

Zale hid a smile behind their wine.

"It is not my place to mind or not mind," Sarkis said.

"I think perhaps I will turn in," Zale said. "This is most excellent wine, and too much more will go to my head." The priest rose and nodded to Halla and Sarkis. "And it will be good not to sleep in a wagon again."

"I am looking forward to it," said Sarkis.

"You didn't sleep in the wagon anyway," said Halla, as Zale left the room. "You slept on top."

"Yes, and sleeping indoors will be a welcome change."

"I thought you slept on rocks and snow all the time."

"I didn't say I enjoyed it."

The sound of the priest's laughter drifted down the hall after them.

Halla looked suddenly worried. "Oh dear. I didn't clear out a bedroom for you."

"It is no concern. I will guard you."

She grumbled, but rose. He padded after her as she went to the linen closet and pulled out a pile of quilts. "Here. If you plan on sleeping in front of the door again, I'll make you a bedroll."

He accepted an armload of cloth and said, with absolute honesty, "It had not occurred to me to sleep anywhere else."

CHAPTER 44

Halla led the way to her bedchamber, then paused. It was going to be very cramped with Sarkis on the floor.

"Oh," she said, almost to herself. "I don't have to sleep in there, do I?"

"It is your house now," Sarkis said. "You may sleep in any room that you wish. You may sleep in the garden if you so desire."

"That's quite all right. Maybe tomorrow I'll sort something out. I'd want to change the sheets, though." She opened the door to her old room.

It seemed even smaller than she remembered, but so familiar. An emotion gripped her suddenly that she hardly recognized—the opposite of homesickness, perhaps. *Home. I'm back home.*

She stopped in the doorway and Sarkis nearly ran into her back. He was a warm, solid wall behind her and somehow his presence felt like home too.

She lit the tiny lamp by the door and sat down on the bed with a sigh of relief.

Sarkis set down the blankets and the cups.

"You brought the wine," she said, amused.

He smiled as he handed her the cup. "It's important to celebrate the victories. They are too few in life."

She took the cup and their fingers touched briefly. Her heart squeezed in her chest and that was stupid, they touched plenty of times on the road, there was no reason to feel that way about so small a touch.

"Are you sure you don't mind going to see my nieces?" she said.

He gave her an impatient look. "I am your guardsman. I don't mind. I *serve.*"

"But you're not!" she said, frustrated. "Or you're not just—I mean, you're not a servant. You're my friend. At least, I thought we were friends…"

She hated how small her voice became at the end. She hated how much whatever he said next would matter.

She'd gotten back her inheritance. She had everything she wanted…except, apparently one thing.

This is a terrible thing to want.

Sarkis took a step forward and took her face between his palms. His dark eyes were even darker than usual and there was something in them she didn't recognize.

"Halla…"

No one had ever said her name like that. He looked at her steadily. He was too close to her, surely, as close as he had been when he had kissed her, and she wished that he would do it again.

And then it occurred to her that she was a widow, and it hardly mattered now, and without quite knowing how it happened, she kissed him.

Wait.

What am I doing?

What if he doesn't...

His lips were warm and tasted like the wine they'd been drinking. Halla reached out aimlessly with her hand, to push him away or pull him closer, she didn't know. He caught her fingers in his, so she did not get a chance to find out.

Wait, what?

The kiss started tender and undemanding. It didn't stay that way for very long. His free hand slid up the back of her neck and his mouth opened over hers.

What am I doing we can't do this I want *to do this but I can't this is...this is...*

...wonderful.

Heat erupted in her belly and a pulse began to beat between her legs. She could not remember the last time she had felt like this. Or the first time, for that matter.

It was not until he sat down on the bed, pulling her down beside him, that she came to her senses.

"No," she said, pulling back. "No—we can't—*I* can't—"

He stopped at once. She thought she'd startled him. His fingers were still interlaced with hers. "I'm sorry," he said. "I misjudged, clearly. I did not mean to give offense."

"Offense!" Halla groped for her winecup. "Oh gods! No, not offense. You're the first person who's been interested in...well, in a long time. I'm grateful."

"Grateful?" He looked appalled. "Grateful for what? That I have eyes?"

She made a noise somewhere between a laugh and a sob and was so horrified at the thought she might cry that she took a large swallow of wine and choked on it. Sarkis pounded her on the back while she gasped.

"I've been rejected before," he said, once she could breathe again. "You don't need to drown yourself to convince me."

"No!" Oh gods, he had it all wrong. She shook her head violently. "No, no. I'm not rejecting—it isn't you."

"Yes, I've heard that one before, too. Truly, lady, it's all right."

Back to lady again, and not Halla. Damn it all.

"No, no! It's just—my husband—" She put her hands to her forehead. White Rat help her, she was blushing. "I mean, he's dead."

"I'm aware, yes." A line formed between Sarkis's eyes. "I'm sorry. You loved him very much, then?"

"What? Oh god, no!"

Her vehemence seemed to have astonished him. He stared at her, clearly baffled, and then she saw something dark and chill rise in the back of his eyes.

"Did he teach you pain?" he asked softly. "I'll kill him."

"He's already dead."

"Do you think that will stop me? Give the word and I'll hunt him across the great god's hells and tear his soul out through his bowels."

"That should not be necessary." She couldn't help it, she was amused despite herself. The notion of that poor, weak little man deliberately hurting anyone, let alone doing anything that would enrage Sarkis. "Oh dear." One shouldn't stifle a giggle over one's dead husband, but here she was. "No, he wasn't cruel. Truly. Just...um. Not very interested."

The darkness went away. She was glad to see it go. Sarkis lifted her hand to his lips. "A man would have to be half-dead not to be interested in you," he murmured against her fingers.

"Flatterer."

"I am utterly sincere."

"Well." She shrugged. "I don't think it was me in particular. He just wasn't interested in that sort of thing in general. No by-blows, no complaints from the servants. Two minutes in my bed every few weeks, doing his duty."

"*Two minutes!*"

"I don't think it occurred to him to take longer. Or um, that he was capable, really."

Sarkis shook his head. "I don't blame any man for not enjoying bedsports, but why marry and condemn his wife to the same?"

"Oh, as to that..." She topped off her wine. "He had no choice in the matter. Aunt Malva and her sisters were cut from the same cloth. His mother was determined to see him wed someone. I'd no money, but I was..." She trailed off, staring into the wine. "Biddable," she said finally.

"I find *that* hard to believe."

She chuckled. "Well. I was young. And..."

He raised an eyebrow. "And?"

"...young." She took a swallow of the wine. "They knew, I think, that he had problems. I don't think they expected him to consummate the marriage at all, so they were careful to choose someone who wouldn't go calling for an annulment. Someone poor. But on the off-chance that he did manage..." She slapped her hip. "A good breeder. Strong hips."

Sarkis wisely said nothing to this.

"Fertility runs in the family, you see. That's why we're poor. Too many mouths. But nothing came of it." She set the winecup down with a click. "Then the fever carried him off, a few years later. And I haven't dared...not since then. In case I did catch pregnant."

"You didn't want a child."

"And have someone else living as precariously as I did?" Halla shook her head. "Silas would have turned me out. He was a decent old man and he liked his comfort more than respectability, but there were limits."

Sarkis looked at her steadily.

"And I didn't want a child," she admitted. "Never have. Too many around when I was growing up. Five of us, all climbing over each other and making an unholy racket. And you know how that ended up." She shrugged.

"I'm sorry." He pulled her back against him, hand moving on her hair. Unlike his earlier urgency, there was nothing but kindness in the touch. Halla sighed, both comforted and regretting the loss.

More the fool me. A handsome man looks at me for the first time in years, and I panic like a novice nun and kiss him, even knowing better.

"Are there no herbs among your people to prevent conception?"

Halla scowled. "There are. I even tried some once."

"And did they not work?"

"I suppose it depends on your definition of 'worked.'"

He waited.

"I vomited for four days." Halla shuddered at the memory. "In that sense, they were marvelously effective, since I couldn't get far enough away from a bucket to try conceiving anything."

Sarkis's chest twitched against her back as he choked down a laugh. "I *am* sorry."

"It's all right. Years ago." She leaned back against him, relaxing into the sensation of warm muscle against her back.

He was still stroking her hair. It was soothing and yet the spark of desire she'd been feeling steadfastly refused to go out. *Foolish. You should have known better.*

"So you've let no one into your bed since then? For fear of getting a child?"

Put like that, she felt like a coward.

And because no one was particularly interested, she added mentally, but that seemed like an even worse thing to admit.

"Well..."

"Is that the only reason, then? You can tell me the truth, if you find me repulsive. I'm not going to force myself on an unwilling woman."

She sat up, appalled. "Of course it is! I mean I don't! I—otherwise I would—*yes,* in a heartbeat. You're very...very..." She tried to think of a word and failed. "Very," she added, somewhat anticlimactically.

Sarkis smiled. "That was the word I was waiting for," he admitted.

"What, 'very'?"

"'Yes.'"

The kiss this time started as innocent as the first one, but ended a good way from that. His tongue slid along her lips and Halla felt herself shaking.

When they broke apart, he had both hands cupped around her face again. "I'm no longer entirely human," he said. "I doubt you have to fear bearing my children. But as there is a great deal of daylight between doubt and certainty, we won't risk it."

She blinked at him. "What?"

"Two people," he said, sounding amused, "can do a great many things to bring each other pleasure that don't end in children."

"They can? I mean, you do hear things, but it always seems to end with someone catching pregnant."

Sarkis snorted. "Because you mostly hear it from lusty young men who can't keep more than one thought in their head at a time." He drew her down beside him, tracing the line of her neck with his fingers. "Whereas I am several hundred years old, and if being in a sword has taught me anything, it's patience."

His breath in her ear was very warm. She was having a hard time thinking.

"I can show you," he whispered. "If you want me to."

"Really?"

"Really."

No use dithering, thought Halla, a bit dazed. *Roll up your sleeves and get to work.*

Undoubtedly that wasn't what her mother had meant, but at the moment, she didn't care.

"Show me," she said to Sarkis, and he did.

ANYONE LISTENING outside the bedroom door might have heard the following conversation over the next few minutes.

"Sarkis?"

"Do you not like that? I'll stop if you don't."

"No, it's lovely. I have a question."

A sigh. "Of *course* you do."

"Why do you think men like women's breasts? As opposed to—I don't know, shoulders or feet or—"

"Some men like feet."

"What?"

"Feet. Some men are extremely fond of women's feet."

"Really? Like *that*? Why?"

"People are complicated."

"You're not like that, are you?"

"No."

"Because I have ugly feet."

"Everyone does. Human feet are inherently ugly. Your breasts are exemplary, however."

"You really think so?"

"Yes."

"I've never been told that I had exemplary breasts before."

"I maintain that your countrymen are idiots."

"Are you saying that if I wandered around the Weeping Lands, I'd be complimented on my chest? Because honestly, that doesn't sound entirely positi—mmmf!"

Some moments later: "You did that so I'd stop asking questions, didn't you?"

"Yes."

"Sorry. I'm nervous."

"I gathered."

"I don't know why I'm nervous. It's not like the times I lost my virginity."

A long, long pause. Then, wearily: "I'm going to regret asking. I *know* I'm going to regret asking. But...times?"

"Well, you know he had some problems in the bedroom. He couldn't really stay focused, if you know what I mean. So it took him about a week and I think three tries to actually...you're beating your head against the headboard. Are you all right?"

"If he lived, I would burn his lands and sow the fields with salt for the indignity."

"Awww. That's sweet...wait. Was that supposed to be sweet?"

Another, heavier sigh.

"Halla. I need you to do something for me."

"Yes?"

"For the next ten minutes, the only words I want you to say are 'Yes,' 'No,' 'Harder,' 'More,' and 'There.' And if you don't like what I'm doing, 'Stop.' Can you please do that for me?"

"Sure. I mean, yes."

"Thank you."

The conversation after that involved fewer words, and, eventually, more gasping. Halla eventually began crying out Sarkis's name, too, but he didn't mind at all.

CHAPTER 45

S arkis held Halla in his arms, listening to her breathing, and felt well pleased with the world.

He had spent a long time inside the sword, only coming out when his wielder needed an unkillable weapon or an untiring guardsman. It had been a pleasure, these last few weeks, to live as a man again, instead of as a weapon. To eat food and walk as a man, to sleep, however lightly, in the world instead of inside the blade.

And last night, to make love to a woman.

It had been a near thing. He had badly misjudged the shape of her fears. *Which should probably not surprise me. If I have learned anything about Halla at all, it is that she never comes at anything from the direction I expect.*

But this fear, at least, he was able to soothe. And after that...well.

Taking off another person's clothes was generally sensual for about thirty seconds and then devolved into a confusion of hooks and buttons and lacing. Sarkis eventually gave up trying, dealt with his own armor, and let Halla wriggle her way loose.

She covered her breasts with her hands, looking embarrassed and defiant all at once. The bodice had left two long red lines along her sides. He ran his fingers down one and she squirmed.

"You are beautiful," he said.

"Ah...I...well."

"You are beautiful, and if you deny it, you are insulting my good taste and I will be terribly offended."

She looked skeptical about this, but he took her hands in his and kissed each fingertip, which had the advantage of freeing up her breasts.

They were, indeed, excellent. He slid his hands up under them and growled appreciatively at their weight and softness and the way the nipples hardened under his thumbs.

"Sarkis, I...ah..." She cleared her throat, looking down at his hands. "You'll have to tell me if there's something I'm supposed to be doing."

It was such a Halla thing to say. It woke an unexpected rush of tenderness in him, and he was not used to tenderness. He suddenly was half-afraid himself that he'd startle her or leave her feeling shamed. He sat down on the bed and drew her back against him, lips against her neck. "Enjoy this. Tell me if you don't. That's all you need to do."

And she had. More than he'd expected, honestly.

Admittedly, he hadn't been braced for all the questions, but that was his own damn fault. He really should have seen it coming.

Three tries to lose her virginity. Great god's balls. It made him want to beat his head against the headboard even now. The more he learned about Halla's previous marriage, the more he wanted to set the entire south to the torch and start over from the ground up.

As he did not currently have that option, he had made love

to Halla instead, which was more satisfying than setting a countryside ablaze and substantially less messy.

Finally, he thought. He felt as if he had waited years to be able to slide his hands over her rounded hips and down between her thighs, to finally touch her in all the ways he'd imagined doing.

"Ah! *Sarkis—!*" She pushed back against him, gasping, and he thought that she seemed as much astonished as aroused. But not alarmed. That was the important thing. He held her close, murmuring endearments against her neck, and when she stopped trembling in his arms, he started over again.

She had fallen asleep almost immediately after they had finally finished. Well, there was no surprise there. Sarkis might no longer be a young man, but he prided himself that he had learned a few things that made up for it.

Her passion had not surprised him. He had suspected for a long time that his respectable widow needed only a little coaxing in that direction. She had given herself entirely into his hands and her response...*As hot as fire, as sweet as sinning,* as his countrymen would say.

He had been braced for tears if they happened. Halla was not a weeping sort, but southerners mixed shame with their sex like they were making a particularly foul brew. If lust had fallen over the edge into fear or shame, he would have been ready to stamp down his own desires and soothe whatever hurts he'd caused.

Delightfully, it had not been necessary.

In the morning...well, he'd face that when it arrived.

Perhaps they'd be able to sort out something to allay her fears about conception. He would like very much to slide inside her and feel her moving with him, let them both find their pleasure together. He suspected she'd surprise him there, too.

What had surprised him more, honestly, was his own

response. When she'd bucked under his hands and cried out his name, he had felt something stronger and more unexpected than lust.

He had said things to her in his own language that she would have found astonishing if she understood, and foremost among them was, *You're mine.*

Which was ridiculous, of course. If anything, he belonged to her, as long as she chose to keep him, and when she tired of him, she could pass the sword on to anyone she chose.

This did not stop him from a wild desire to claim her as his own, so that the rest of the world knew to step back and keep their hands to themselves.

Which I have neither the right nor her permission to do. And would be foolish to want in any event. I am a weapon; she is the wielder. She will hand me over to another someday.

Or she will die and I will not.

Still.

He had only just stopped himself from covering her shoulders in love bites. She might have enjoyed them at the time, but she'd have had a lot to say about it once she caught sight of herself in the polished steel mirror.

He had refrained. He wasn't a youngster, so insecure that he had to mark his territory on his lover's flesh.

What in the great god's earth has come over me?

He had thought that slaking his lust would be enough. He had not expected it to make things worse.

I know better than to get too attached to any wielder. I'll outlive them all by a thousand years. He had learned that lesson early on. All their battles and wars and causes, no matter how noble, could not stop them from aging and dying while Sarkis lived on in immortal steel.

Halla sighed in her sleep. Sarkis stretched his arm out over her, pulling her close, and she burrowed against him and mumbled something he couldn't make out. It might have been his name.

The thought warmed him more than he wanted to admit.

Oh, this is foolishness. Even if it was your name, it was probably leading to a question about feet or owls or something else. Can't you just be glad that you've got a solid armful of widow in your bed? Take your pleasure and give her hers and leave it at that.

He did not want to leave it at that.

Even if you were in the Weeping Lands and could take her before a priest of your own god, you would have neither land nor wealth nor even a name to offer her. You do not even have a horse that she could ride to the wedding. Assuming she'd have you, which she likely wouldn't. Marriage brought her nothing but grief.

Marriage to you would bring her nothing but more of the same. You are a dead man in live steel. You cannot even promise to grow old with her.

You haven't even told her the truth about the sword.

Some of the pleasure he felt ebbed away. He had always meant to tell her before...before anything like this. But she had kissed him and then he had been so determined to unravel her fears and then...

'Then' nothing. Then you were as randy as a buck goat.

He couldn't even blame that on being out of the sword too long. They had sheathed it a dozen times on the road, as part of Zale's tests, and it hadn't made a damn bit of difference.

He certainly couldn't blame the sword for the fact that he was lying here thinking of marriage, which was complete foolishness. How could any woman live with an immortal? He would stay exactly as he was and she would fade and fail and pass away. Surely she could not help but hate him, in her old age.

The thought nagged at him that Halla wouldn't. That Halla might even be grateful to know that she would no longer be the last one standing, that someone else would pick up the pieces at the end.

Great god's teeth. Did I always get this morbid after sex, or is this new?

Maybe you should just stop thinking, he told himself. He leaned his cheek against her hair and closed his eyes and tried to believe that this moment, at least, would not end for a very long time.

CHAPTER 46

Halla woke in bed, feeling very warm.

That was the first thing she noticed.

Sarkis was curled around her, his chest against her back. One of his knees was between hers, and his hand rested on her breast.

That was the second thing she noticed.

She wasn't wearing a stitch of clothing.

That was the third thing she noticed.

She hadn't slept naked since she was a child. Respectable people didn't. She had a strong urge to pull the sheet up over herself to hide, which was ridiculous. Sarkis had seen every part of her last night.

More than seen. A lot more.

Good heavens.

To think that the first time she'd seen him without gauntlets, she'd thought his hands looked hard and unkind. He'd touched her in ways she'd heard about, but certainly never experienced. For someone who was constantly complaining about the decadent south, it was pretty clear that the north had its own share of decadence.

Unless men and women have been doing this sort of thing around here for years and no one bothered to tell me. Which I suppose is also possible. Even likely.

Gods knew her late husband wouldn't have taught her that sort of thing. Poor man. He'd have been...well, not appalled, perhaps. Baffled, maybe. "He put his mouth where? Why would you *do* that?"

She blushed even remembering. It had definitely been...err...indecent. Yes. That was the correct word. Most of what Sarkis had done had probably qualified as indecent.

Certainly her response had been nothing close to respectable. Respectable women did not claw at the sheets and make noises like that.

Sarkis himself was undoubtedly not a decent or respectable person.

But quite splendid nonetheless.

"Good morning," he said against her hair.

She jumped and squeaked.

"I have been wanting to do this since...mmm. The second day I knew you, I think," he said, caressing her breast.

"You hid it well."

"You were a respectable widow. And trusting and very kind. Throwing you down and ravishing you on the spot did not seem courteous."

She rolled over on her back, pulling the sheets up to her chin. Sarkis's hands were still touching her under the sheet, but she felt less exposed.

"I thought you wanted to strangle me."

"Well, there was some of that too. So many questions! How big is a dragon? Could I fight my way past a half-dozen old women armed with embroidery hooks?"

"It was mutual!"

"What, the embroidery hooks?"

"The desire to strangle you!"

He chuckled. His chest was against her arm and she felt the vibration all the way through her bones. "I'm sure it was."

"The way you were always manhandling me into ditches..."

"I fear I manhandled you worse last night," he murmured, kissing the point of her shoulder.

Halla opened her mouth to say something and blushed again.

Oh, this is ridiculous. I've been wed, bedded, and widowed for the past decade gone. Why am I blushing now?

Sarkis stroked a fingertip over her cheek. "It's all right," he said. "There's no shame."

"I'm not ashamed," she said, even as her blush deepened. "I'm—I'm embarrassed."

"You don't have to be embarrassed either."

"And now I'm embarrassed that I'm embarrassed. You're being kind."

"We could go back to arguing if you'd feel better."

"I might!" she snapped.

He grinned. "Well, to be honest, I'm impressed I managed to make love to you at all without you stopping me to demand to know if I'd done it before, if I knew what I was doing, and how exactly it worked."

"You've obviously done it before," she said, and was horrified to hear that she sounded aggrieved.

"That is true," he admitted.

She folded her arms across her chest, trying not to feel a tiny bit hurt.

"Mind you, it has been a few centuries."

She lifted one of her hands and swatted at his face.

"The youngest of those other women is...oh, about three hundred years old now, I'd say. I don't think you need to worry."

"You are a *wretch*."

"Yes," he said, seizing her hand and kissing the palm. "An unrepentant one. I'm sorry if we went too fast last night. I should have thought it through. That's my shame, not yours."

"No, no! That's not it—I mean, you were lovely—"

He fell on his back with a groan. "*Lovely,*" he said. "*There's* a death knell. Clearly I should swear to celibacy and join one of your decadent southern religions. Is there one that involves stabbing things?"

"The Dreaming God, but only demons."

"I can stab demons. Demons are very stabbable."

"They aren't sworn to celibacy, though. The paladins are rather notoriously...err...not." She thought back to a number of armored men in white cloaks who had passed through Archenhold a few years back...and the number of inexplicable births that had followed nine months later.

"The Dervish was like that," said Sarkis. "You couldn't take him to taverns. He'd have handsome young men who had met him five minutes ago dueling for his honor."

"Good heavens."

"It was exhausting when you only wanted a quiet drink." He captured her hand again and rubbed his thumb over her fingertips. "Well, I shall simply have to find another of your religions to take me, I suppose."

"Leaving your great god already?"

"The great god, I fear, has no use for a man who cannot please a woman. Or a man, as he prefers."

She had to prop herself up on her elbows for that. "That's... actually a tenet of your faith? Really?"

"Of course," he said, as if it was obvious.

"*Really.*"

"Failure to make the marriage bed glad is valid grounds for divorce in the Weeping Lands."

"I don't understand why there's so much weeping, then."

He gazed skyward. "Well, we also murder each other a great deal."

"Why?"

"A question that you would not ask if you had ever seen the Weeping Lands."

"I'm glad I haven't then!"

He shrugged. "It has its moments."

She shook her head, chuckling. "I no longer have any idea if you're making this up or not."

"Never. Do you feel better now?"

"Yes," she said grudgingly.

He kissed her forehead.

After a minute she said, "You probably don't need to leave the great god's service just yet."

"So you were at least a little pleased, then?"

"I was...um. Very much so. As I'm sure you know!"

"I suspected. Also hoped."

"I *am* embarrassed," she said, determined to have it all out, "because you are obviously so much better at this than I am. And I don't know how to do...well, any of that. All my experience was not moving for two minutes every few weeks."

Sarkis winced.

"It's true."

"There are two things," he said finally.

"Oh?"

"The first is that this is a skill like any other, and you are certainly not too old to learn, if that is what would please you."

"And the other thing?"

He slid his hand down under the sheet and set his lips against her neck. "And the other is that your countrymen have clearly failed you in this matter, and on behalf of the great god and men everywhere, *please* allow me to make it up to you."

CHAPTER 47

I t took some time to dress afterwards. The tendency to look at each other and smile foolishly slowed things down. Eventually, though, Sarkis's stomach growled like a bear and they both went down to breakfast.

"I have spent too long out of the sword," he said. "I am starving."

"Well, hopefully my dreadful aunt left some food in the house. If not, we'll go rummage something up."

There was not a great deal, in truth—mostly bread and cheese and the remains of last night's dinner. Zale was already awake, making notes on their ledger. The priest looked up at the pair, a smile tugging at their lips, and Sarkis suspected that they were quite aware of what had happened the night before.

Well, Halla had not been entirely silent. Probably he hadn't been, either. Or perhaps it was the single love-bite he hadn't quite been able to resist leaving on the side of her neck, or that they sat too closely together to be anything but recent lovers.

He regretted nothing.

No, that wasn't true. He regretted that he had not done it sooner. Why had he wasted so much time?

Because you wanted her to have a choice. Because you needed to tell her what the sword says.

The bread in his mouth was suddenly as heavy and tasteless as clay.

The sword.

She still didn't know.

Halla looked over at him, her water-gray eyes alight, and suddenly Sarkis could not take another moment of deception.

I have to tell her. I have to tell her now, before there's any more between us. If I don't, if she finds out—when she finds out—it might poison everything. I have to tell her now, before it goes any farther.

He was afraid that if he didn't tell her now, he would soon do something utterly mad. Fall to his knees and beg her to marry him, perhaps. He had nothing to offer, less than nothing, but that mad part of his mind was crying out that she was his, that they belonged together...

He stood abruptly, catching her hand. "Is the scholar here yet?"

"Nolan?" Zale looked up. "Yes, I believe so. He and Bartholomew came over this morning. Nolan is in the front room, I think?"

"What's wrong?" asked Halla, climbing to her feet.

If he had been able to explain, he would have done it weeks earlier. He led her through the house until they came to Nolan, in the front room, who was writing in a book.

The scholar looked up from his work and shut the book. "Yes? Can I help you?"

"Can you read ancient tongues?" asked Sarkis.

Nolan blinked at him. "Depends on the ancient tongue, I suppose. There's a great many of them. I know a few. Why do you ask?"

Sarkis took the blade off Halla's shoulders, and drew it all the way out. The words on it were etched in his memory as deeply as they were etched in steel, but he could not trust himself to read them aloud.

Coward.

Yes. I will see her face as I recite the words and I will break and I will not tell her all the truth. I know it.

Even in this, I will fail.

"Read these," he said gruffly, tossing the blade down on the table in front of him.

Nolan blinked at him, then at the sword. "This is...oh, hmm, I do know this one. It's an archaic form, but...let me see." He licked his lips, taking the hilt in his hand and tilting it so that the light caught on the blade.

"This is...no, wait...*Here* is...the prison and...judgment? Punishment? of Sarkis of the Weeping Lands. Faithless in life, he will be faithful in death, until steel crumbles and all sins fade away."

The scholar stopped and looked up, his eyes wide. The moment seemed suddenly trapped in amber. Sarkis saw the sunlight coming through the window, the dust motes dancing in it, the fall of Halla's pale white hair over her face as the color drained out of it.

She turned and looked at him. Waiting for the denial or the protest or the explanation.

Sarkis met her eyes and said nothing at all.

That was enough.

I can't believe I've been such a fool.

No. No, that wasn't true. It was all too easy to believe it.

A man who took you away from your troubles. A man who said you were beautiful. Of course you were a fool.

Only a fool would believe such things could be true.

"Halla—" he said finally, when the silence between them had become agony.

"Why?"

"I led a mercenary troop," he said. "I'll not pretend we were good people, because we weren't. There was a war, and we became...well. Indispensable. But our side was losing. At the height of battle, I changed sides."

Halla stared at him.

Sarkis shrugged. "My loyalty was to my men, not to my employer. I was holding a citadel that I knew could not be held for long. The enemy offered me money. I saw a chance for us to survive."

"And?"

"And if I had held out another two days, I would have been a great hero." He smiled humorlessly. "Our allies arrived. They overwhelmed our position. Most of my men were slaughtered. I and my two captains—the Dervish and Angharad—we were dragged before the king who had trusted us."

Halla put her hand over her mouth.

"He had the rest of my men hanged as traitors. A mercenary stays bought, that's what separates them from murderers. But for the three of us, he had a more fitting punishment. Our deaths were bound to the swords, and the will of any who wielded us."

"That is...quite a punishment," said the scholar. Halla had forgotten that the man was even there.

Sarkis sighed, not looking at him. "For me, perhaps, it was just. But the Dervish and Angharad deserved a clean death, not to be bound into magic steel and forced to fight until the end of time. They followed my orders. Angharad told me it was a poor idea, but I overruled her."

"I see," said Halla. She didn't want to feel sorry for him. He was a liar and a criminal and apparently a traitor.

She could all too easily feel sorry for Angharad and the Dervish. They had trusted him too, and look where it had gotten them.

Look where it got any of us.

"So there you have it," said Sarkis. "The whole sordid tale."

"I suppose you didn't lie, did you?" she asked. "You just let me believe whatever I wanted."

Sarkis shook his head. "That's a coward's way out," he said. "I knew full well what you believed."

"I believed in *you*," she said softly. "I thought you were a hero."

"I know."

"I trusted you. I let you..."

She cut herself off. The night they had spent had been like nothing she'd ever felt, and now it was tainted. *Everything* was tainted.

"Halla..." He reached for her hand.

She yanked it away, shaking her head. She didn't want to look at him. She was going to cry soon and be damned if she was going to cry in front of him.

"You could have just told me," she said miserably. "You didn't have to lie. I wouldn't have cared. Why didn't you *tell* me?"

She made the mistake of looking at him, and saw that his face looked as anguished as she felt. "Because for hundreds of years, I have died for wielders who thought that I was nothing but crowbait. An inhuman weapon or at most, a traitor who deserved a traitor's death, over and over again. And then you came along and you...you were..." He lifted his hands and let them drop. "You were you," he said finally.

"I was a fool."

"*No*. You were kind and you were in a very bad situation and you wanted to believe the best of the man who saved you."

"I should have known." Her voice was as dull as a dying woman's. "I should have known better. My fault for thinking a hero would have anything to do with someone like me."

"Halla..."

"Go away," she said tiredly. "Leave me alone."

"I can't," he said. "I am bound to you until you die or sell me or give me away."

"So that part was true?"

He nodded.

"Then you're free," she said. "I give you to yourself. You don't need to serve me any longer." She flung the sword down on the table.

"Halla, I—"

The pommel struck the table and the blade slammed into the scabbard. Blue light splashed around Sarkis and tore him away, even as he reached out a hand toward her.

"It's real," breathed Nolan. "He's really one of *them*. He's a servant of the sword!"

"Later," she said. "Later."

"But—"

"Later." She turned on her heel. She had to get out of the room right now or she was going to cry and she didn't want to cry in front of other people. She had her pride.

Really? And what do you possibly have to be proud of?

You're nothing but a woman past her prime with a dead husband. You can't take care of yourself. You had to hire a priest to get your own inheritance back from your grasping in-laws.

So you had a lover for the space of a night. So what?

Did you think he truly wanted you? Did you think he wanted anything, except to slake his own thirst?

"But Mistress Halla!" said the scholar, rising to his feet. "I have so many questions!"

"I'm going for a walk," she said. Her voice betrayed her and she clamped her teeth down on her lip and stalked away.

CHAPTER 48

Silver faded. The sword was drawn. Sarkis materialized in the room, looking for Halla. He needed to say something—tell her something—anything—anything to fix the hurt he had caused her.

You were ready to spit her relatives on your sword for what they'd done. And you are worse than they ever were. She knew what to expect from them.

She trusted you.

Angharad and the Dervish trusted you, too. At least you haven't left her gutted and trapped in a blade, so there's that much to be grateful for.

The resignation in her voice had cut him more deeply than her tears. She had sounded as if she had given up. As if she had decided that she did not even deserve to feel anger at her own betrayal.

He wanted her to shout at him, to be furious on her own behalf. He wanted her to believe that she was worth enough to be angry.

I wanted a clean slate between us. I wanted you to know so that it couldn't hurt us later. I wanted there to be a later.

Swordheart

He had no idea how to fix any of it.

I could fall on my own sword in shame...and then what? She'd be alone for a fortnight while I healed. And the great god knows what would happen to her in that time.

She was too trusting. She would trust the wrong person and end up bleeding in a ditch or worse.

Could they really hurt her any worse than you did?

He had to apologize. He had to find her. He had to make it right.

She...wasn't in the room. Bartholomew looked at him, fingers wrapped around the hilt, holding the sword a few inches out of the scabbard.

"Where is she?" said Sarkis.

"Halla? I'm sure she's fine," said Bartholomew.

"I have to talk to her. Where did she go?" Sarkis turned away.

"It hardly matters," Bartholomew said. "Her part in this is done."

"What?"

"Her cousin will take care of her. We have other matters to discuss."

Sarkis was halfway to the door when the word *cousin* struck him. "What? That clammy-handed worm? What are you talking about?"

Bartholomew rolled his eyes. "For god's sake, man, you know the woman. She's a twit. She needs someone to keep her from wandering off a cliff, and for whatever reason, her cousin wants the job. You did your part, and now you can get on to better things."

Sarkis saw red.

He was over the table before his sword had cleared its sheath, aiming for Bartholomew's throat. "*He* has her? Where did he take her? Tell me or I'll kill—"

And he stopped.

The sword hovered inches from the other man's face, and Sarkis had an intense desire to twist around and throw himself in front of the blade.

He tried to move the sword, and found himself leaning forward, leading with his opposite shoulder, determined to get in the way.

Sarkis stared at his sword hand as if it belonged to someone else.

He reached out with his other hand, toward Bartholomew's throat, and watched his own sword turn and press against his wrist.

And then he knew.

Bartholomew reached out, put his finger on the tip of the blade, and pushed it aside.

"She gave the sword away," he said. "You heard her. And now I am the one who wields you."

Sarkis went berserk.

The sword cut deep into his forearm, steel grinding on bone, before he flung it down.

Bartholomew jumped out of the way, eyes wide, as the servant of the sword fell down, thrashing violently on the floor. Rage warred with magic and magic had the upper hand. Sarkis clawed at his own throat with his bloody fingers, snarling, then slammed the back of his head against the floor and saw stars.

How far would the magic go to keep him from harming a wielder?

Apparently a very long way.

The world tilted and darkened. His breathing eased as the magic slowly decided that he was no longer a threat to his new master.

A door slammed. He heard footsteps as Nolan raced into

the room. "What is going on here? What—no! *You drew the sword?!*"

"I did."

"That wasn't our agreement!"

"I didn't trust your order to keep your end of the bargain," snapped Bartholomew. "I required insurance. I will hand over the sword when I am paid, and not before."

Nolan cursed.

The scholar knelt over Sarkis, lips twisted in annoyance. "If he dies, it will be weeks before we can draw him again and that will be time wasted. My order will hardly pay for a servant of the sword if they cannot at least see the servant first."

Sarkis blinked the darkness out of his eyes and looked up into Nolan's face.

He's in it with Bartholomew. They planned this. This is why they came to the town. Not to help Halla at all.

He could do nothing to the wielder of the sword, but Nolan had no such protection.

Sarkis lunged.

His hands went around the scholar's throat. Even with blood pouring down his left arm, even with it badly gashed, it was easy. Necks were so fragile, the windpipe right there, the jugular there, all he had to do was squeeze—

Nolan turned purple and gurgled. Bartholomew gasped and somehow had the presence of mind to sheathe the sword.

Sarkis's curse was cut off as blue fire washed over him, freeing the traitor from his hands and taking him out of the world again.

HALLA ENTERED THE HOUSE, feeling weary beyond all measure.

She had walked for hours, out into the lands around the town, and found herself at the same shepherd's hut they had taken refuge in the first night. It looked as if it hadn't been used since them.

She stared at the dark entrance, high on the hill, and thought, *He got you away from Alver. That wasn't a lie. He saw you safe to Amalcross and Archenhold. That wasn't a lie, either.*

He had thrown himself in front of danger, completely heedless of his own safety. Granted, he was immortal, but he still felt pain, yet she had never seen him balk at any injury. Yes, the sword had compelled him...but he could have been free of her at any time, only by asking.

The sword had not compelled him to hold her when she was shaken, nor to joke with her, nor to hold her hand.

You sound as if you are thinking of forgiving him, she said to herself.

It's mostly my pride that's wounded.

Pride is all a respectable widow has left. It was not the sword that compelled him to be kind to you, but it was not the sword that made him lie, either. Or seduce you.

Halla grimaced as she walked toward the door. She had not exactly been an unwilling party to her own seduction, had she?

She knew something was wrong as soon as the door closed behind her. The house was cold. There were no fires lit in any of the grates.

Dread crawled up into Halla's throat. She went from room to room on the ground floor, but they were all dark and empty. The guest bedrooms for her great-uncle's friends were bare, with signs of having been vacated in a hurry.

No Bartholomew. No Nolan. No sword.

No deep-voiced, sardonic swordsman with fierce eyes and gentle hands.

"They're gone," said a voice behind her.

She knew that voice. It wasn't one she cherished.

Dear gods, it wanted only this.

She turned. "Cousin Alver," she said grimly. "How very nice to see you."

CHAPTER 49

"If you're looking for that horrible guard of yours, he's gone," said Aunt Malva. "Gone off with Bartholomew and that scholar of his, and good riddance to him."

"What?" said Halla blankly.

Sarkis? Gone?

Malva smiled. She was clearly enjoying this. "Oh yes. Bartholomew left in a hurry and came by to tell us where you'd be. Very kind of him. Very lucky for you."

He left with Bartholomew? What?

The hollowness inside her began to expand. She'd thought to find Sarkis and forgive him. It seemed he had decided that it was not worth his time to wait around and be forgiven.

And here I am.

Right back in the place I started.

With these *two.*

"Surprised?" asked Malva. "I don't know why. Men like that don't stay in one place."

Halla shook her head slowly. Blood roared in her ears. The events of the past few weeks began to feel like a long, surreal dream. Had she even known a swordsman named Sarkis?

Where was Zale? She had her inheritance back, the clerk had confirmed it, but she was back in her great-uncle's house and her wretched cousin and his aunt were here and she might as well never have left at all.

"Halla…" Alver said, stepping forward.

It didn't matter how disassociated she felt, Halla wasn't letting that clammy-handed little bastard touch her. She jerked back, eyeing him with disgust. "Why are you two here? I don't care if Sarkis left—"

Liar. You care very very much.

"—I still don't want to see either of *you* again."

Something was rushing into the hollowness, filling it up. She did not quite know what it was. It felt like rage.

"Now Halla…"

"I don't even know why you're here."

"Bartholomew told us to come," said Malva. "He knew Alver was the only one soft-hearted enough to still want you."

Halla stared at her, then broke into a high, braying laugh. She knew it was an ugly sound, and that was fine. She had no desire at the moment to be beautiful. "Do you think I *care*? I don't want him."

Malva flicked her fingers, dismissing this. "It hardly matters what you want. You clearly can't manage your own life. You'll come with us, and this will become a family matter again."

"Once you're carrying a child, it'll be easier," Alver assured her desperately. "Then you won't want them to be illegitimate so you'll understand that it's best to marry me. We can put all this behind us. Mother said so."

Halla stared at him for so long that he started to sweat. "Really, Halla…"

She began to laugh incredulously. "Are you *daft*?"

"*You* must be daft!" said Malva. "Carrying on all over the countryside with that—that barbarian! You're lucky my son agreed to wed you at all, with that kind of scandal hanging over you!"

"Carrying on? Oh yes, there was carrying on!" Halla could hardly believe what she was about to say, but she suspected it was her only chance. "We carried on like you wouldn't believe! He bedded me in half the inns from here to Archenhold!"

Alver recoiled, eyes the size of saucers.

"And I enjoyed it!"

"Stop this!" Alver tried to bellow, but it came out as more of a squeak. "I don't want to hear such talk!"

"*And* I'm pregnant!" shouted Halla, throwing caution to the winds.

Aunt Malva stepped in and slapped Halla across the face.

Halla slapped her right back.

"Mother!"

"Are you going to let her do that to your mother?" said Malva, holding her hands to her face.

"No, of course not...err...Halla, I'm very sorry, but you can't carry on like this..." He grabbed for her wrists.

"If you two get out of my house, I won't have to!"

"This is not *your* house," said Malva coldly. The imprint of Halla's hand on the side of her face had left a blurry mark in her makeup. "It belongs to the family. It will not go to you to use like a whorehouse. You will go into the countryside where you cannot shame any of us." She looked Halla up and down, lip curled. "If you are carrying that barbarian's bastard, you'll soon be properly grateful that anyone will have you at all."

Alver managed to get hold of both her wrists. Halla twisted her arms furiously, but he held them fast. She took some small pleasure that he had to work for it, and sweat started to pop out on his forehead. "Halla, stop! I don't—don't want to hurt—stop that!"

"Tie her up," snapped Malva. "Tie her up and put her with the other one!"

Wait...the other one? Does Alver have a whole stable of women here or something?

In practice, Malva did the tying. She wound rope around Halla's wrists while Alver stood behind her, locking her arms in place. The feel of his chest against her back made her skin crawl.

"And you brought rope, I see. So you knew you'd have to tie me up to get me to the altar. Did you plan on gagging me so I can't denounce you to the priest? Tying me to the bed afterwards?"

Alver made a pained noise. Malva just glared. "You'll be grateful soon enough," the old woman said. "After you've had awhile to think about it. I suggest you stop acting like a whore and start thinking about what's best for you. And your..." her lip curled "...child."

Halla fumed while Alver walked her upstairs. She thought about making him drag her, but it seemed like that would result in a lot of bruises to little effect.

He opened the door to one of the unused servant's rooms and pushed Halla inside. "You rat bastard!" she shouted after him.

"I'd rather you didn't take my god's name in vain in quite that way," said a familiar voice from the floor.

"Zale!?"

The Rat priest smiled, lifting their bound hands. They looked a bit mussed, their hair flopped back out of the braid and into their eyes, but none the worse for wear. "We've got to stop meeting like this..."

"What happened to you?" asked Halla, sitting down beside them.

They're the 'other one.' Not a stable of women after all.

Pity.

"Apparently, no one warned your cousin that I was in the attic conducting an inventory. They came in and began discussing how to marry you off to Alver. I came down to tell them that they would not do such a thing, certainly not without your consent, and the next thing I knew, your cousin was stuffing me in the back bedroom." They shrugged. "You were right, too."

"What?"

"He does have clammy hands."

"Ugh, I *know.*" Halla leaned her head back against the wall. The idea of those clammy hands on her body had been bad enough before. After Sarkis had touched her with such passion, coaxed such extraordinary responses from her body... no, it didn't bear thinking about. Like drinking a fine aged whiskey and then having a dead fish as a chaser.

"And you, I assume, did not feel like consenting to this marriage?"

"Obviously not." Halla scowled.

"I am a bit surprised they put you in here with me," admitted Zale. "If they've already stooped to kidnapping, I would expect them to spirit you away to a willing priest, have it done as quickly as possible, and then deal with the consequences later."

"I told them I was pregnant with Sarkis's child," said Halla.

Zale stared at her. "How did you do that?"

"I didn't! I mean, I'm not! We haven't—well, we *did*—err—well, there was some—he and I—but he used his fingers, we didn't—"

Halla was aware that she had turned bright red and stopped talking. She put her hands over her face. Her fingers felt cold against her blazing hot cheeks.

"You couldn't, though," said Zale. "Even if you wanted to.

Could you? He's dead. Dead men don't sire children, except in a few very specific cases."

"They don't walk around and talk, either, but he manages."

Zale considered this. "Yes, but..." They frowned.

"That's why we didn't," said Halla wearily. "I didn't want to get pregnant. I don't want children. Not his, not Alver's, not anybody's."

Zale gave a very unpriestly snort. "*That's* easily avoided. Just sheathe the sword after he...ah...sheathes the sword. As it were."

"What?"

She stared at the priest so intently that Zale, too, started to turn red. "Look, we did the experiments, didn't we? You saw them, too. Just...um. Look, his...uh...that is...his seed is like the rest of him, isn't it? If you sheathe the sword, it should just go back in the sword. Like a severed tongue." They coughed. "If you're really worried, you could test it. Have him...um...you know...in a jar...and then..." They trailed off.

Zale and Halla looked at each other. Then they both carefully didn't look at each other, since they were both beet red.

"So!" said Zale brightly. "How about this weather?"

"Rainy," said Halla gratefully. "Very rainy."

"And these ropes! So...uh...rope-like."

"Yes. With the hemp. And the knots. Very much so."

"Do you think you can untie it? Or that I can untie you?"

Halla put her wrists alongside Zale's. "I think you have a little more slack. Aunt Malva was not happy with me when she tied mine."

"Fair enough." The priest began picking at Halla's knots with their fingertips. "Dear me, yes. You know, after the last time, I started thinking that it would be wise to carry a knife in my boot."

"And?"

"It turns out that is an excellent way to ruin your sock. I got the most fascinatingly shaped blister, too. Now I rather wish I'd dealt with the blister."

"Men have died of blisters," said Halla. "At least, so Sarkis tells me."

"Good heavens. Where is Sarkis, anyway?"

"I wish I knew."

Zale raised a thin eyebrow. Halla sighed and began recounting the story.

She found herself trying to make excuses for Sarkis as she told it. *I'm sure he didn't mean to lie...It was all a long time ago...*

Zale paused in picking at the ropes and glanced up at her. "Did *he* say any of that?"

She sighed. "No. He said that was a coward's way out. That he knew what I believed and never corrected me."

"That sounds more like him." Zale bent their head over her wrists again.

"He should have told me."

"Yes."

"Now he's gone, though. Alver said that he'd gone off with Bartholomew and Nolan and left me here."

Zale met her eyes, frowning. "*That* doesn't sound like Sarkis at all."

Halla shook her head. "I gave up the sword," she said quietly. "He doesn't have to stay with me any more. I always thought he must hold me in contempt, until...well, until last night, then I thought...oh, it doesn't matter." She could feel tears prickling behind her eyelids and tilted her head back. "I told him he could belong to himself now. I guess he took me up on it."

Zale snorted. "And how exactly is he supposed to draw himself?"

Halla blinked at him. "What?"

"How is he going to draw his own sword? If he goes back into it, he's stuck. It's like trying to pick yourself up."

"I...err...but someone else could draw the sword, couldn't they? I don't have to draw the sword every time, but I'm still—I was still—the wielder."

"Right, but he can never be the first person to draw the sword."

Halla opened her mouth to say that she'd given him the sword so it shouldn't matter, and suddenly remembered the first night that she and Sarkis had met. *I can't very well wield myself, lady.*

"I'm an idiot..." she said, and felt tears start to threaten at last.

"You were angry," said Zale. "Few of us are at our best when we are angry." They glanced up at her. "And it is very likely that *idiocy* saved you a great deal of unpleasantness."

"What?"

"We are not dealing with good men, Halla. They moved too quickly to have done so in ignorance. If you had not given up the sword, I suspect they would have made you give it up."

"Yes, but..." This seemed rather less important at the moment than what Sarkis must be feeling. "What if he thinks I hate him? What if he thinks I don't want to see him any more?"

"We will go and find him and tell him otherwise." They got their nails under one loop and managed to tug it upward. Halla winced as the other ropes pulled tighter. "Sorry."

"It's all right. I'd rather have my hand go to sleep than marry Alver."

"He does seem very determined, doesn't he?" The rogue hair flopped into their eyes again and they blew it out of the way on an aggravated breath.

"Or his mother is. I don't know why they care," said Halla tiredly. "Silas wasn't worth that much. They can't possibly think it's worth all the trouble of kidnapping me *and* a priest of the Rat. Even if they can lock me up somewhere and no one will care, your temple will come looking for you."

Zale nodded. "It's odd, isn't it? Presumably they'll have to kill me."

Halla blinked at them. They seemed very calm about it.

"I wonder if it has to do with the mortgages."

"Mortgages?"

"Yes. It's hard to find in the records and I suspect it was quite a shady operation, but I managed to turn it up in the clerk's office when I was digging around to find Silas's total worth. Your outlying properties are mortgaged to the hilt."

"They *what?* But Silas didn't have any mortgages. He always used to brag that he owned everything free and clear."

"Indeed. And they weren't taken out in his name, either. The only way to find them was to go through the land records themselves. Which I did as a matter of course, since the property was in dispute."

Halla stared at them with her mouth open. "Whose name are they in?"

"Your cousin's. If I were to venture a guess—" They got another loop free and Halla grimaced as the hemp scraped across her wrists "—your cousin used the fact that he expected to inherit as collateral for a loan from someone with more money than ethics."

"That ra—I mean, that bastard!"

Zale smiled gently at her correction. "So now he is in a bind. He must lay claim to that property, or suddenly find that he has no collateral for the loan."

"Him *and* his mother. I'll bet she's in this up to her neck."

"That would fit with what I have witnessed of them, yes. Such situations can be resolved, of course, if the various parties are acting in good faith, but I would wager a small sum that the sort of person who would make such a loan is not acting in good faith." They chuckled. "Ironically, your cousin could easily have found himself petitioning the Rat for mediation in such a case."

"And they'd take the case?"

"Well, never say never. Let us say instead that imprisoning one of their priests would not incline the Temple favorably to his case. I was holding this information in reserve in case the bailiff did not decide in our favor, but now...well. Can you get this loop past your fingers?"

Halla contorted her hand until the loop slipped over her knuckles.

"Excellent! Give me a minute, my nails aren't very happy with me."

"I don't care about Alver," Halla said after a moment, wiggling her fingers. "I mean, I care, but we can worry about him later."

"Well, given that we have to escape, we'll have to worry about him quite soon."

"Right, right." Halla waved her bound hands. "But it's Sarkis I'm worried about. Bartholomew could take him anywhere. Or sell him. What if we never found him again?"

"The Rat has many eyes. But yes, it would be much easier to catch Bartholomew now rather than later."

"What if he won't give the sword up, though?" asked Halla. "Sarkis can't force him, if he's the wielder."

"Then I fear that you and I will have to kill him," said Zale.

Halla looked at Zale. The silence stretched out until it was intolerably loud.

"Do you remember what happened *last* time?" said Halla. "When we had to hide the bodies?"

"Yes, but we're bound to get better with practice."

"I've never killed anyone! *You've* never killed anyone! Sarkis and Brindle did all the killing bits! We stood around and wrung our hands!"

"I'm sure we'll figure something out. People manage to kill each other all the time. How hard can it be?"

Halla suspected that it would be quite difficult, but then again, Sarkis had killed a half-dozen bandits in less time than it took to cook a chicken, so maybe the priest was right.

"Anyway, it wasn't the killing part that was hard, it was dealing with the body afterward. And in this case, they're a kidnapper, so we'll just go straight to the constable and explain the situation. Well...part of the situation..."

"Maybe we can get Brindle to do the actual killing," said Halla.

"Err. I wouldn't feel right about that. I mean, defending his ox is one thing, but asking a gnole to kill somebody in somewhat cold blood..."

Halla sighed. "You're probably right."

"Though I do wish we had a Sin-Eater..." Zale muttered, half to themself.

"What? One of those people who eats food off the dead?"

"Well...no. Not exactly..." Zale lifted their bound hands to scratch awkwardly at their neck. "They're...a religious order my priesthood works with occasionally. For things like this. You know, murders, assassination, things like that. I mean, we're practical but we're not *criminals.*"

Halla gave them a look.

"Yes, all right, the law might frown on the hiding bodies part, but the Motherhood started it."

"They did," Halla agreed. She was mostly just bemused at how Zale had gone from throwing up in the bushes to coolly plotting murder.

She was even more bemused that she seemed to be going along with it.

It's for Sarkis. You have to get him back. He's been kidnapped. If you've got to kill the kidnapper, that's just how it is.

No use dithering. Get to work.

"If you're still bothered by it," said Zale, bending back over her bonds, "I'll take your confession afterwards."

"Who's going to take *your* confession?"

The priest gave her a wry smile. "The bishop. And if I did not suspect the bishop would agree with me, we would be having a very different conversation." They slid their fingers under the loops of rope, tugging another one clear of Halla's knuckles. This one went much easier.

"And if I find she does not agree," they added, "then it will all be on my head for leading you astray. As it should be..."

CHAPTER 50

Sarkis materialized outside the sword again in a room filled with packing crates.

Some kind of storeroom, he thought. Not one he'd seen in Halla's house, certainly.

He eyed the men across the room. Bartholomew and Nolan.

"Throw down your sword," said Bartholomew.

"No," said Sarkis.

There was a packing crate in the middle of the room, about waist high, with a lantern on it. He could not throw the lantern at Bartholomew. Nolan stood too far back.

The fingermarks on the scholar's neck were livid purple, going green around the edges. It had been at least a day, then.

How far could Bartholomew have traveled in a day?

How much damage could Halla's cousin Alver have done in that time?

He had no idea how to get a message to Halla, or even where he was in relation to her. He could be five miles away or fifty.

Sarkis had tasted despair a hundred times in his life, but only a few times like this. He felt as if he stood on the battlements of the keep again, looking down at his men, outnumbered, outmaneuvered, doomed...

"Throw down your sword," repeated Bartholomew.

"Come and take it," said Sarkis.

"Perhaps I shall. You can't very well use it on me."

Sarkis curled his lip back. The man was right, loathe as he was to admit it.

He stood grimly while Bartholomew relieved him of his weapon. Even knowing that Sarkis couldn't attack, the other man inched around him as if he were a wild beast on a chain.

"You will behave in a civilized fashion," said his wielder, stepping back. "Or else."

Sarkis spat on the floor.

"I don't want to have to punish you."

"Better men than you have tried."

Bartholomew retreated around the packing crate and looked at Nolan. Nolan leaned over and whispered into his ear.

"If you do not cooperate," said Bartholomew, sounding strained, "I will cut off your hand."

Sarkis slammed his left forearm down on the packing crate. "Do it. Do you think I'm afraid of pain?"

"Fine!" snapped his wielder. "I'll cut off something you'll miss a lot more!"

Sarkis didn't even hesitate. He yanked his trousers open and slapped his cock down on the packing crate. "Do your worst. It all grows back."

Bartholomew's mouth dropped open. So did Nolan's. Sarkis had seen men who were holding their guts in with both hands who hadn't looked nearly as appalled.

Honestly, he was a little surprised himself. Apparently he was much angrier than he'd realized.

The two men retreated to the other side of the room and had an urgent whispered conference. Sarkis wondered if he should put himself away or if it was more menacing if he just stood there with his good bits on the packing crate.

The relatively cold temperature of the storeroom decided him. Some gestures lost their effectiveness when your balls were trying to crawl back into your body to keep warm. He tucked himself back into his pants and stood with his arms folded, glaring.

It was going to hurt like a bear if they took him up on it, but at least everything grew back.

After a moment, Nolan stepped forward, hands raised. Behind him, Bartholomew held the sword in both hands, clearly ready to sheathe it at a moment's notice.

"Ser Sarkis," said the scholar warily, "I feel we've gotten off on the wrong foot here. I am not your enemy."

Sarkis didn't bother to dignify this with a reply.

"I don't approve of how this was handled," said Nolan, glancing back over his shoulder. "You have every right to be angry. My order wanted to purchase your sword legitimately. We did not intend for this deception."

Bartholomew rolled his eyes. "If my procurer in Archen's Glory hadn't failed so spectacularly to acquire the sword, you would have been able to do so."

Archen's Glory. The red-haired man.

He figured out what the sword was when we were at his home, Sarkis thought. *That's why he agreed to come testify for Halla, when he couldn't steal it away.*

"If you agree to cooperate," said Nolan, "when we have returned to my order, I will do my best to make certain that your friend Halla is safe and unharmed."

Damn, damn, damn. Great god's eyes.

It was the one thing that could have swayed him. He had to find a way back to Halla.

Bartholomew snorted. "You're assuming that she wants

anything to do with a war criminal. She's better off with her cousin."

The words slipped between Sarkis's ribs like the blade of a knife. He would almost have preferred to have his hand chopped off.

Nolan met Sarkis's eyes, hands still raised before him. "That is, of course, for Mistress Halla to decide for herself. I am certain Ser Sarkis wishes only to be sure that she is well."

Sarkis knew he was beaten. If they kept him in the sword, he would have no way at all to get Halla away from her clammy-handed cousin.

Assuming she can't get away herself. Assuming that Zale doesn't find a way to help her.

He had to believe that the Rat priest was too clever to be taken in by Alver's machinations. Zale knew exactly how Halla felt about her cousin.

"Please," said Nolan. "We have a great deal to discuss. There is much my order wishes to learn from you."

Sarkis curled his lip and looked away. "Fine," he muttered. "If you give me your oath as a priest or whatever you are that you will send word to Halla immediately."

"You have it," said Nolan, without hesitation. "Tomorrow morning."

Sarkis grunted.

After a moment, he said, "What does your order even want with me, anyway?"

"You're the only person living who met our founder," said the scholar. He smiled nervously, tucking his hair behind his ears. "The Sainted Smith. The woman who put you in the sword."

CHAPTER 51

They heard Alver coming down the hall before the door opened, which gave both Halla and Zale time to snatch their hands back in front of them, wrists together. Hopefully he would not be looking too closely at the ropes.

Alver stepped inside the room. He looked extremely pained.

"Let us go, Alver," said Halla. "You know this is completely ridiculous."

"It wasn't my idea," said Alver. "It was Mother's. I tried to talk her out of it, but...well, you know what she's like when she gets an idea in her teeth..."

He sat down on the edge of the bed and looked at them both morosely.

"You have to let Zale go," she said. "They're no part of this. And you can't just kidnap a priest. You'll be in very deep trouble."

"Ugh..." Alver rubbed his ringed hands over his face. "I know! I panicked. It was very upsetting. I thought the house was empty and you can imagine how shocked I was when your priest friend came downstairs! Mother was yelling to tie them up and...oh, I still have a headache from it all."

It occurred to Halla that he was actually trying to appeal to her for sympathy. She didn't know if she should play along in hopes he'd give in or just kick him very hard in the shins.

Zale just stared at him, one slender eyebrow slowly crawling up their forehead.

"Nevertheless," said Halla, amazed at how reasonable she sounded. "This isn't the way to start a marriage. You have to untie us both. I won't marry a man who kidnaps priests."

For a moment, she really hoped Alver was that easily led. After all, he'd been under his mother's sway for forty-some years, surely he couldn't have that much capacity for independent thought?

But he shook his head at her sadly. "I can't," he said. "You know I can't. The priest will raise the alarm and then everything will be just a mess."

Halla sagged back against the wall. "There are horrible slimy flying things in the Vagrant Hills," she said conversationally. "They drop out of sky on you and then ride you around while they drink your blood. I don't know why anybody is worried about marrying anybody else when there's things like that out there we haven't dealt with."

Alver looked blank. "What do you expect me to do about it?"

It occurred to Halla that possibly Alver would be improved by slime. "Nothing," she said. "What do you intend to do with Zale?"

"I'm afraid we'll have to kill them. Sorry." He nodded to Zale. "It's nothing personal."

"I'm afraid I'm taking it very personally, though."

To Halla's bemusement, Alver actually looked hurt by that. "It's got nothing to do with *you*."

"If you're killing me, then yes, I do think it does." The priest sounded rather tranquil about it, but Halla was getting used to that.

"But..." Alver closed the door behind him, a line forming between his eyes. "Look, I'm not a bad person!"

"You're plotting to murder me," said Zale, "and you're kidnapping a woman who doesn't wish to marry you, to hold her prisoner until she consents to wed you. I feel this does indeed make you a bad person."

"I have to agree," said Halla, nodding.

Alver gave her a hurt look. "It was all Mother's idea!"

"Yes, and you're going along with it," said Halla. "If you were a good person, you'll tell her to do her own dirty work."

Alver stood up and stormed out of the room, slamming the door behind him.

"What an odious little man," said Zale.

"Isn't he, though?"

"Was your late husband so bad?"

"No, no. He was just very...vague. If Aunt Malva had demanded he do this, he'd have wandered off to the garden and pulled weeds for a few hours until he forgot about it."

Zale's lips twitched. "Are you telling me that *you* had to be the focused and responsible one?"

"Well, you can see why the farm didn't do well!" said Halla with some asperity. "And I did fine, I'll have you know. I knew exactly what I had to do every morning and I did it. There was a routine. I do quite well with routines. It's how I took care of Silas." She sighed, offering Zale her wrists again. "Unfortunately, things have not been routine since he died and I drew the sword."

"Well, there is indeed that. If you pull your hand out here, I believe...be careful...oh, very good!"

Halla's wrists were bloody with bits of hemp stuck to them. She suspected that once she had feeling back in them, it was going to be excruciating. Nevertheless, she was free.

She untied Zale's ropes. "It's a damn shame we're not in my room," she said. "There's a knife in the chest at the foot of the bed."

"Perhaps why they did not use it."

"That, or..." Halla stopped what she was about to say. It was probably true that the sheets on her bed were rumpled and smelled like sex and Alver had taken one look at them and turned gray, but she didn't need to bring it up. "Well, and the lock on that door is broken. Sarkis kicked it open."

"Of *course* he did."

Halla burst out laughing. She couldn't help it. "He *is* quite magnificent, isn't he?"

Zale shook their head, but they were smiling. "I am very glad that you two have found each other. I fear I am too fond of my doors and my locks to be envious."

"*Have* we found each other? It seems like we made a mess of it."

"Possibly, but we won't sort that mess out standing here. Shall we?"

They opened the door and crept down the hall. Halla cocked her head, listening for voices, but heard no one at first. After a few seconds, she gestured to Zale, and they went down the stairs to the second floor.

From there, the voices were audible. Alver and his mother were having a row, which mostly meant that Alver sounded put-upon and Malva sounded furious, punctuated by occasional screams from the bird. Was anyone else in the house?

Halla glanced down both halls, but the doors were all closed. Had they been opened recently?

No, they haven't. The scattering of fragrant herbs on the rush mats were fresh—Halla had hastily spread another basket—but they had not yet piled up in narrow lines as they did when the doors were opened and closed. No one had been in or out since yesterday.

"I don't think there's many of them here," she said. "It's just Malva and Alver."

"The fewer family members aware of their deception, the less chance that one will get cold feet." Zale nodded. "Well. So long as one of us gets out, it should be simple enough. We go out as quickly as possible, agreed? If one of us is captured, the other should go for the constables, not attempt rescue."

"Mmm." Halla glanced at them. She knew that she was valuable to Alver alive, but Zale was not. Zale knew it, too.

Well, we'll improvise.

She was not terribly pleased with the way that her life was coming around full circle. Locked in a bedroom, *again.* Breaking out of her own home, *again.*

And while I love Zale to pieces, I really would rather have Sarkis here with me again. He could rescue whoever needed it and I could just come along and provide moral support.

They slunk down the next set of stairs. The arguing grew louder.

"...tell me you don't *want* to marry her! You've been trying to see under her skirt since your fool brother took her to wife!"

"*Mother!*"

"Oh, that's disgusting," whispered Halla to Zale. "I am disgusted."

"I can quite see why."

"They're in the dining room," said Halla. She pointed

toward the back stairs. "Through the kitchen. Mind the third stair, it's loose."

The two of them almost made it. They were so close that Halla wanted to scream in frustration. But Zale was clumsy from most of a day spent tied up and they didn't know the layout of the house. The priest tripped on one of the flagstones —the one with the deep cleft in it, she'd been meaning to have it mortared for years but everyone had just gotten used to stepping over it—and went to their knees.

"Who's there?" shouted Malva.

"Oh blast," said Zale. Halla helped them to their feet.

"Alver, they're loose!"

Alver was a great deal quicker to try to apprehend them than he had been trying to protect Halla the first time she'd left the house. Halla couldn't help but feel a little bitter about that. He grabbed Zale's arm before the priest had even reached the kitchen.

Halla, for lack of any better ideas, grabbed Zale's other arm and hauled. The priest stretched between the two of them, eyes wide. Then they got their feet under them and yanked themselves loose.

Unfortunately, in the time it took to free Zale from the strange tug-of-war, Aunt Malva had barreled into the kitchen.

"The door!" shouted Malva. "Alver, *get the door!*"

Alver shoved Halla into the kitchen table as he ran to obey.

Malva stood in one doorway, Alver in the other. Zale and Halla stood in the middle, looking from one to the other.

"Halla, how could you?" asked Alver reproachfully.

It took Halla a minute to realize that he was actually trying to scold her for trying to escape. She didn't know whether to laugh at the sheer grotesque hilarity of it or just begin screaming and never stop.

"Alver, you'll have to kill them both," said Malva angrily. "It's the only way."

"Kill me and my nieces inherit everything," said Halla, inching toward Alver. Perhaps if she and Zale both charged him at the same time...

"Then Alver will marry your nieces!"

"What, both of them?" said Zale.

"You keep your nasty clammy hands off my nieces, you slimy, weak-willed little shitweasel!"

"Don't talk to my son like that!"

"That goes for you, too, you horrible screeching harpy!"

"Alver, are you going to let her talk to me like that?"

"Halla, you shouldn't..." Alver trailed off, looking so uncomfortable that she was amazed he didn't curl up and die on the spot.

"Ugh!" said Halla, and then, completely out of other ideas, she grabbed the knife off the butcher block and stabbed Alver with it.

She was aiming for his heart, but it turned out that hearts were difficult targets, particularly when one is in a hurry. She ended up stabbing him rather messily in the upper arm, a situation made worse when he shrieked and tried to yank back and dragged the blade much farther through his flesh than he otherwise might have.

"Mother!" he screamed, clutching at the wound, while blood poured down his arm. "Mother, she—"

"I saw, you useless sponge!" snapped Malva. She snatched up a frying pan and charged forward.

I am going to die fighting with kitchen utensils, thought Halla. It seemed dreadfully ignominious. She ducked the first swing and then Zale punched Malva in the nose. They did not seem much better with their fists than Halla was with a kitchen knife, but perhaps it was the thought that counted.

ség fram

Malva reeled back, dropping the frying pan and grabbing her face. "Alvhgher! Arh you goingh to let them doo thgat?"

"She stabbed me! I've been stabbed!"

"Perhaps now would be a good time to go and fetch the constables," murmured Zale.

"Yes, let's," said Halla. She bolted out the door with the priest hard on her heels, took the deepest breath she could, and yelled, *"Murder!"* at the top of her lungs.

CHAPTER 52

"The constables were very nice about the whole thing," said Halla. "At least, I thought so."

"I still wish that they'd arrested Malva, too."

"Well, yes, but she had a broken nose and it doesn't look right if you're arresting old ladies who've already taken a beating. Even a richly deserved one."

Alver was now in a holding cell, due to be taken by the bailiff to face the Squire's justice. His attempt to claim that Halla had set upon him and stabbed him without provocation had floundered to a halt when Zale had silently presented their wrists to the bailiff, rope burns and all, and told him, in grim, precise terms, about the mortgaged properties.

"I regret we cannot stay and testify," the priest said, "but we are very concerned for our friend Bartholomew. Alver mentioned him several times and we fear that his associate may have led him into a difficult situation. He is...well, very sharp in the field that he is interested in, but not at all worldly, if you understand me."

The bailiff laughed. "I know the sort very well, my legal-minded friend." His gaze flicked from Zale to Halla. "And the large, dour fellow who was with you before?"

Halla silently cursed the intelligence of the bailiff, but Zale never faltered. "Accompanying Bartholomew and the associate in question. He is why we are hopeful that no attempt will be made on Bartholomew's life, but we still do not wish to dally."

"Then good luck," said the bailiff, and the next morning they were on the road at cock's crow, sitting behind Brindle, who was tapping the ox's flanks with the goad and murmuring gnolish encouragements.

Zale waited until they were out of the town gates to say, "They weren't being nice about the whole thing."

"What?"

"Halla, my dear client, they were waiting for you to become extremely angry about the fact that they hadn't protected you from your relatives. The clerk should have spotted the issue with the mortgages, the priest and the bailiff should have realized that they might not let things go so easily, and they should have at least had a constable make sure they left the town. Failing that, they should have closed up the house and not let those two make free with your inheritance *and* familiarize themselves with the layout of the house. They have, in fact, failed you rather dismally. You'd be well within your rights to complain to the Squire."

"Oh," said Halla, rather astonished by this. "I...oh. Hmm." It hadn't occurred to her to be angry. "Well. I'm sure they meant well."

"You are sure that everyone means well," said Zale, clearly amused. "Which is why I think you are perhaps well matched with Sarkis after all. He's sure that everyone is determined to kill everyone else in their sleep. Between the two of you, you average out to a nicely functional outlook."

"Assuming we get him back," said Halla.

"I have faith. It is, by definition, part of what I do."

THE TRIP TO AMALCROSS...AGAIN...WAS slow. *Again.*

"Can't we go any faster?" fretted Halla.

"Faster!" said Brindle scathingly. "A human always wants an ox to go faster. Ox goes as fast as an ox goes. Like to see a human pull a wagon any faster."

"They do not know that they are being pursued," said Zale soothingly. "Indeed, they have no reason to believe that you will be capable of pursuit, or even that you might wish to do so."

"But they've got horses!"

"Horses are not magical and they cannot run for hours at a stretch. Particularly not when ridden by an elderly, sedentary scholar."

Halla was forced to acknowledge the truth of this. They had stopped at an inn, asking for information, and found that, while three days ahead of them, Bartholomew and Nolan had stopped very early in the day.

"Three of 'em," said the innkeeper, when Zale had pressed her. "Old fellow and a young guy, and their bodyguard. Face like thunder on that one."

"But unhurt?" asked Halla. *Oh, it's a stupid question, he can't be hurt, at least not for long.*

The innkeeper cocked an eyebrow at her. Halla could read her thoughts easily enough—*is this woman a jilted lover, come looking for the man who did her wrong?*

"He's an...uh...family friend," said Halla. "The older man. We heard he got into some trouble with bandits, you see, and I worried..."

The woman's face cleared. "He looked fine. Young fellow had taken a beating recently."

"Oh dear." Halla tried to keep her face composed. She could venture a guess who had administered that beating.

So Bartholomew is the wielder, then.

Somehow that made her angrier. Bartholomew knew her. He had been Silas's great friend. He'd even helped her. He knew how much she hated Alver, he knew what Malva was like, and he'd still abandoned her to their mercies without a second thought to get his hands on the sword.

She sat on the wagon seat as they drove on, mile by mile, and fumed.

"Twisting your whiskers, fish-lady."

"What?"

Brindle gave her the annoyed-but-patient look that he usually did when a human was failing to understand something obvious. "Twisting your whiskers. Hurts and doesn't help, but a gnole keeps doing it."

"Oh." Halla sighed. It did feel a bit like that, now that he said something. "You're right. I just can't seem to stop."

To her surprise, Brindle leaned over and licked her cheek. "A human will get her mate back. Be easy."

Halla flushed, as much in surprise as embarrassment. "He isn't...I mean, I don't know if he's...not that I wouldn't like him to be, but..."

Brindle rolled his eyes. "Humans can't smell."

Halla waited politely, but apparently this was a complete thought, and Brindle lapsed back into silence.

They stopped that night near the Drunken Boar inn, far too late to worry about cooking dinner for themselves. Halla looked up at the sign and thought grimly that she had once been so excited to see that sign, several weeks and an eternity ago. Now it seemed like she was cursed to follow this road back and forth until she died.

"I'm not dead, am I?" she asked Zale. "This isn't the afterlife and we're following this road forever, are we?"

"I don't think so," said Zale. "I must believe that the Rat would intervene. At least on my behalf, and I'd put in a good word for you, too." Halla grunted, then thought, *I sound like Sarkis,* and then tried very hard to think of something else.

She and Zale went inside to pay the innkeeper for use of his pump and fodder for the ox, and to purchase what was left of the evening meal. Potatoes and pork drippings, which were delicious even when lukewarm.

"Na' worries," said the innkeeper. "No rooms tonight anyway, thanks to these gents." He nodded across the common room, to where three "gents"—one of them a woman—were sitting at a table. They were all tall and well-muscled and they radiated a sense of purpose and something else...Halla couldn't quite put her finger on it, but she felt like she was standing near a stove.

"Oh, *paladins*," said Zale, sounding affectionate and resigned all at once. One of the gents lifted her tankard.

Halla looked more closely and saw the closed eye symbol on the tabards. Paladins of the Dreaming God. Of course. That would explain why all three were rather relentlessly pretty in a chiseled heroic-statue sort of way. The Dreaming God was well known for His taste.

Zale approached them as if they were colleagues, which, Halla supposed, they were. The three paladins pushed out a chair for the priest and another for Halla. She took it, feeling a bit embarrassed. Widowed housekeepers from Rutger's Howe did not usually sit down with demonslayers.

Zale clearly felt no such compunctions. The priest introduced Halla—"My client"—and then the four launched into a discussion that sounded less theological and more like temple gossip. Halla drank her small-beer and ate her food and did not try to contribute until the talk turned to things she understood.

"It's been a mess," said one of the paladins, leaning back in his chair. "Since the Clockwork Boys got turned off, all the demons that were running the damn things jumped...well, you know. Five years and we're still cleaning up the mess. The last one got into a swineherd, near as we can tell, and then his own pigs killed him. Then it jumped to the biggest sow and went off and had babies. Of course, nobody called *us* in until there was a whole army of demon-led pork on the hoof."

Zale and Halla both winced.

"The demon was just smart enough to open doors. Or the sow was, anyway." The paladin flipped his cloak back to reveal his arm in a sling. "We got her, finally, but she gave as good as she got. Don't suppose you're a healer, priest?"

"Lawyer," said Zale apologetically. "Advocate divine, technically, but I mostly deal with property cases. Halla?"

Halla grimaced. "I can take a look," she said, "but most of the medicine I've done was on goats, and that was a decade ago."

The paladins laughed. The injured one worked his arm out of the sling and laid it across the table.

Halla looked at it, eyes going wide, and then up at him. "How are you not screaming right now?"

"It's only pain, Mistress Halla," said the paladin. "The Dreaming God kept me from worse."

"He could have done a better job," she said tartly, bending over the wound. The pig had stepped on his arm, it looked like, gouging the flesh and grinding mud and grime into the injury. The bone wasn't broken, but it had already swollen and the red taint of infection was starting up around the edges.

Still, from having treated goats a decade ago, she knew this kind of wound. It did not require any great skill so much as patience. She called for hot water and clean cloths and sat down to clean it out. The paladins called for another round of ale.

"You're good at that," said her patient, watching her.

"You move less than a goat," she said absently, picking a bit of gravel out with tweezers.

All three paladins roared with laughter at that one. Halla grabbed the man's arm to keep him from moving—*here I am, acting like Sarkis again*. The paladin's upper arm was as thick around as her neck and she had absolutely no chance of holding him down by force, but he submitted meekly.

It took nearly an hour, and her patient was more than a little drunk by the time she finished. He caught her hand as she stood. "Thank you, Mistress Halla," he said.

"It was nothing," she said.

Her patient tapped her wrist with his finger. She looked down and saw him studying the red scabs where Alver's ropes had abraded the skin.

"I think perhaps you have some troubles of your own," he said, glancing from her to Zale. Halla said nothing. Zale inclined their head, a gesture that agreed without giving away a single word of information.

He kissed the back of her hand. The number of men who could get away with kissing a woman's hand, in Halla's experience, were exactly zero, but now she had to change the number. Apparently if you were six feet tall and chiseled and capable of killing demons, you had the presence to pull it off.

Unaccountably, she blushed. Dammit, the paladins were pretty, and yet...and yet...

You're reading far too much into it. And even if you weren't... All she wanted was a grim, scarred man with silver lines cut through his skin.

"Leave off, Jorge," said the female paladin, elbowing her cohort. "You're in no shape for it and she's in no mood."

"Can't blame a knight for trying," said Jorge. "Well then, I'll show my appreciation some other way. Innkeeper! Put these gentlefolk's bill on the Dreaming God's tab, will you?"

The innkeeper grunted.

"That was well done," said Zale, as they walked away from the inn.

"He probably wouldn't have lost the arm, but you never want to risk it with infection," said Halla.

"Not quite what I meant. It never hurts to having the Dreaming God's folk on your side. They're dumb as posts and single-minded to the point of suicide about demons, but if you want someone with a very large sword to stand between you and the enemy, they truly have no equal." They paused, then added, a bit dryly, "Relentlessly good-looking, too. It's almost annoying."

"I didn't do it for *that*," said Halla.

Zale smiled. "I know."

CHAPTER 53

The morning came and Sarkis wrote a letter to Halla. It was short and to the point, because he had far too much to say.

"*I am alive,*" he wrote, and then stared at the paper, his thoughts clattering in his head like bones.

What do I say? I'm sorry? You deserve better?

For the love of the great god, don't marry Alver?

That last one made him shudder. She hated Alver, he knew that. But the look in her eyes the last time he had seen her, the resignation...that terrified him. What if she decided that she wasn't worth more? What if she was so hurt by Sarkis's betrayal that she simply...gave up?

The thought of that clammy-handed worm taking advantage of her, of Halla dull-eyed but dutiful in his bed... Sarkis's fist clenched and he leaned his forehead against it, gut churning.

And how much of that is jealousy? he taunted himself. *Even now, you're a possessive ass, when you have no right to be. Less than no right. At least he never lied about who he was.*

He stared at the paper some more.

Nolan cleared his throat. "We must leave soon," he said.

Sarkis scrawled *"I'm sorry. Please stay safe."* and folded the paper in half. "Here," he said hoarsely.

Nolan took it from his hand and Sarkis had an immediate desire to snatch it back. Had he really just written, *"Please stay safe"*? As if she were a chance acquaintance met on the road?

She'd be in her rights to wad it up and serve it back to me on the point of a dagger.

What else could I say?

I love you.

I will always love you, as long as this cursed steel endures.

And if he had written that, then...what? They would still be apart. He would still be in Bartholomew's power. He would still be unable to reach her. He would still have betrayed her and he would still have no power to make amends.

Except that you would have found a way to reach out and cause her pain one last time. She is probably cursing your name and glad that you're gone. Leave her with her anger. It will make this easier for her.

Nolan nodded and went to the innkeeper. "This must be delivered to Mistress Halla in Rutger's Howe," he said. "As soon as possible. Is there anyone that will be going that way?"

The innkeeper frowned. "No mail coach out here," he said slowly. "Could send it with one of the lads, maybe."

"Do that, please," said Nolan, setting coins on the counter.

Sarkis looked away. The scholar was keeping his end of the bargain. Honor demanded that Sarkis keep his, and tell him all about the strange, twisted blacksmith he revered.

At least someone will be glad of my company, he thought bleakly, and then grimaced at himself in self-disgust.

And here you thought you had gotten over wallowing in self-pity after the first hundred years. No one's cutting out your tongue, are they? Suck it up and deal with the mess you've made.

Are you a warrior or a worm?

At the moment, he felt more akin to a worm.

"That's all done, then," said Nolan cheerfully. "I believe Bartholomew is outside with the horses."

Sarkis grunted and rose to his feet. Perhaps once Bartholomew relinquished the blade to Nolan, he could convince the man to return to Rutger's Howe. He had to make sure that Halla had not been forced into marrying Alver.

Zale will protect her, he thought. *Zale knows.*

He knew that it was true, and yet the priest's slender shoulders seemed too slight to trust with such a weight.

And yours would be better? How badly have you managed this? All of it? How badly have you hurt a woman you love?

I must find a way back to her. I must not fail.

This time, great god, please do not let me fail.

HALLA WAS deep in a dream where she was trying to do something and Sarkis was not helping—was standing around making completely unhelpful comments, in fact, and it was very annoying, and she still hadn't quite forgiven him for not telling her that he was a traitor—and then the door of the wagon burst open and somebody dragged her out of bed.

It was the sort of situation where screaming would have been entirely appropriate, but at first she wasn't sure if she was really awake, and then there was a lot of blankets in her mouth, and then she was standing out in the cold outside the wagon's door and it seemed a bit late for screaming.

There was a strange man wearing the robes of the Hanged Mother and carrying a very large sword. Bigger than Sarkis's sword. Halla wondered if he was compensating for something.

Zale was dragged out right after she was, by a pair of men

with much less impressive swords. The priest looked as bedraggled as she felt, but they didn't scream either.

"*Where is your spirit?*" roared the indigo-cloaked man.

Halla said, "Whuh?"

He pointed the sword at her. It was quite a lot of steel to be looking at at this hour of the morning. "I'll ask again, woman, and you'd best answer! Where is your spirit?"

"Uh..." Halla wracked her sleep-addled brain. "I guess... probably somewhere in my chest, isn't it? Although when I think of *me,* I usually think of something inside my head..."

The man stared at her. So did the other two. Zale put their face in their hands.

"What?" the Motherhood priest said finally. He had an insignia on his collar that probably meant he was a captain, or whatever the theological equivalent was.

"You know," said Halla. "Right behind your eyes? That's always sort of where I thought the soul was."

"Not your *soul,*" said the man, lowering his sword a few inches. "Your *spirit.*"

"Is there a difference?" asked Halla. Then, realizing this was probably not the time to be arguing, "I'm sorry! I'm not really very theologically minded. If you say there's a difference I'll believe you, of course. You'd know better than I would."

"Your *demon,*" said the man. "Your tame spirit. Your...I don't know what it is! Familiar! The thing that does your bidding!"

"Nobody does my bidding," said Halla, a bit sadly. "I mean, sometimes I ask the cook to make something in particular, but half the time she says it can't be done and I'll take meat pies and be glad for it. So we eat a lot of meat pies. She's very proud of them. Oh dear..." Halla pinched the bridge of her nose. "I'm going to have to see if she's still available, aren't I? You *know* that awful Malva didn't pay her..."

The man in indigo was starting to get flushed, although

with frustration or rage or embarrassment, Halla wasn't sure. "Stop babbling!"

"If I may," said Zale gently. "Brother, wherever did you gain the impression that Mistress Halla had a tame spirit that served her?"

"I'm not your brother, Rat priest," spat the man. He turned a broad glare on Zale. "I have been tasked with finding our brothers who went missing on this road. We encountered bandits two days ago who spoke of you and your witchcraft."

Butter would not have melted in Zale's mouth. "I'm sorry to hear about your men."

"The bandits said *you* undoubtedly killed them."

Zale's eyebrows went up. "And you believed them?"

The flush climbing up the man's face grew redder and more mottled. "They described your wagon! They said you were a priest and a woman and a gnole—and a tame devil!"

"We did run into some bandits," said Halla. "But I'm not sure about the tame devil bit. We had a guard. He fought like a devil, I'll grant you that much, but he's pretty human."

The mention of the gnole made her glance around. She couldn't see Brindle anywhere, which was unusual. She would have expected him to stay close by his ox.

"Where is he now?" The man turned his attention back to her, holding the sword up again.

"Uh..." Halla's eyes nearly crossed as she stared down the blade. "I don't know? I only hired him to get me back to Rutger's Howe, and then he did, and then he left. I mean, I wasn't going to hire him to guard me in my own house. That seemed a little excessive. I wish he'd stayed around, actually, then I could have hired him again for this trip..."

"We are visiting a close family friend," said Zale, stepping into the gap. "He lives in Amalcross. He was kind enough to

416

help Mistress Halla with a legal matter, so we were stopping there."

"His health isn't good," improvised Halla. "And he was so helpful. He was one of the witnesses to the will, you know." She beamed at the man in indigo, on the principle that it couldn't hurt.

His rage was definitely giving way to bafflement. She just hoped that he wasn't one of those men that became angrier when they got confused. "And you know nothing of these missing men?" he demanded.

"If they're the same ones that we saw on the road, we saw them...what, eight days ago? Nine?" Zale looked at Halla. Halla shrugged helplessly. She'd lost any sense at all of how much time had passed. "But I don't know if those are even the same men. They didn't leave their names."

"The bandits described you," said the man stubbornly.

"Yes, but they're *bandits*," said Zale. "I don't think they're going to admit to servants of the Mother if they killed their priests, do you?"

"Where were our men, when you saw them last?" put in one of the other men, with a sidelong look at his leader.

"Errr..." Halla glanced over at Zale. '*In a shallow pond under some pine boughs*' was definitely not the right answer. "I suppose if you had a map we could narrow it down. Before Amalcross, wasn't it?"

"Was it?" Zale rubbed their forehead. "I've been on this road too much, it's all starting to blur together."

"It had to be before Amalcross, because we got that lovely bit of pork in Amalcross, remember? And we had it for the next two nights."

"That *was* a nice bit of pork," said Zale, clearly willing to go along with the saga of the entirely fictional pork, in case Halla was going somewhere.

"And I'm sure we couldn't have had it when we met those Motherhood fellows, because you know I would have offered them some because I made biscuits to go with it and of course I needed to use Bartholomew's oven to bake the biscuits which is how I know it was Amalcross and you know I always make too many biscuits so we had plenty of extras."

"You do make far too many biscuits," Zale agreed.

"And the bandits *stole* them!"

The three Motherhood men were looking back and forth between Zale to Halla with indescribable expressions.

"Can you believe it?" Halla demanded. "If they'd just asked for biscuits, I would have given them some! It's not like they stay fluffy past the second day! You have to eat them up, or they get hard as rocks. Well, *you* know."

Judging by the look on the Motherhood captain's face, he did not know.

"I don't—" he started to say, but Halla had the bit between her teeth now.

"And it was my grandmother's recipe! My grandmother's! They stole my grandmother's biscuits, can you imagine? What kind of depraved mind steals a woman's extra biscuits?"

"Truly shocking," murmured Zale, casting a long-suffering look at the Motherhood priests.

"No, no," said Halla, waving her hand. "No, I know. You've got bigger things to worry about than bandits stealing a respectable widow's baked goods. It's all terrible, the way the rule of law has gone, that's all. I hope you find your missing men. If you do, bring them by, and I'll make you all biscuits."

There was a long, teetering moment when Halla thought it might work. She'd stonewalled better men than the Motherhood captain. Such men hated to look foolish, and if you could appear so absurd that bothering you made *them* look equally absurd...

"I don't have time for this," snapped the captain. "Bind their hands and bring them."

And then, like a miracle, like...well, like divine intervention...Halla heard a voice say, "Excuse me, but is there some problem here?"

CHAPTER 54

The three paladins were almost a head taller than the Motherhood captain, and all of them had broader shoulders. Each carried an enormous demonslaying sword across their back. There was something about the way that they stood that made you really notice the swords.

To give the Motherhood captain what credit he deserved, he tried. "There's no problem," he snapped. "This doesn't concern the Dreaming God."

"Oh, good," said Jorge, the man she'd patched up the night before. "The Dreaming God owes this woman a debt, you see. But if it doesn't concern us, we can all be on our way. Are you nearly ready, Priest Zale?"

"It will take us a few minutes to sort out the wagon," said Zale pleasantly, as if they had always planned to make an early start and weren't currently standing wrapped in a blanket on a frozen road with men pointing swords at them. "Is Brindle with —ah, yes, of course."

"A gnole thought big men would like to know that a priest was ready to leave," said Brindle, from behind the paladins.

The Motherhood captain ground his teeth. "We won't

detain you," he said. "We only have business with the priest and the witch."

"Witch?" said Jorge. "What witch?"

"That woman!"

The other male paladin burst out laughing. "Mistress Halla, are you a witch?"

"I don't think so," said Halla. "I'm not actually sure what a witch does, but I assume you don't just fall into it sideways. I'm mostly a housekeeper."

"And she can patch up injured goats," said the female paladin, sounding very amused. "And occasionally injured paladins."

The other Motherhood men quietly sheathed their swords and inched away, looking as if they'd rather be somewhere else.

"We are told she consorts with demons!" said the captain.

This was a tactical error, as even Halla could have told him. If there was one word guaranteed to suddenly focus the attention of a paladin of the Dreaming God, it was *demon*. The entire order was dedicated to demonslaying. It was all they did, all they wanted to do, and they were very, very good at it.

"Are you claiming that Mistress Halla is possessed?" asked Jorge. His voice was almost silky.

The Motherhood captain thought about it. Halla could *see* him thinking about it.

"Such a claim would place this entire area under the Dreaming God's jurisdiction," said Zale, examining their nails. "Anyone present could be conscripted to assist in their inquiries. Both the Temple of the Rat and the Hanged Motherhood have agreed to this, as you undoubtedly are aware."

"Demons," said the other male paladin, "are *everyone's* problem."

The captain inhaled sharply through his nose. His eyes flicked from Jorge to Zale and back again.

Then: "Perhaps my informant was mistaken," he ground out. "You are, of course, the authority on demonkind. If you do not believe that this woman is a threat..."

The three of them looked at Halla, then back at the captain.

"I believe," said the female paladin gently, "that the three of us together can probably take her in a fight."

The Motherhood captain let out a brief, bitter curse, flung himself into the saddle and rode away. His men scrambled to follow, one or two casting apologetic looks over their shoulders.

"Well, that was unpleasant," said Jorge, watching the Motherhood men ride away. "How'd you get on their bad side?"

"They're Motherhood," said Zale. "They don't have a good side. Their goddess hanged herself with her own hair so that she could punish a murderer who had been declared innocent, and frankly, I'm starting to think that poor soul *was* innocent and their whole religion is founded on persecuting unlucky bystanders." They spat in the roadway, which was, for Zale, as savage a display of temper as Sarkis casually slaughtering a few bandits.

"Well, you're not wrong." The female paladin tapped her mailed hand on the pommel of her saddle. "Your gnole friend came and got us. Good thing, too."

"A gnole knows when a priest is in trouble," said Brindle.

"Some of their other priests were pestering us earlier," said Zale. "And apparently they went missing, so now these fellows are convinced we're hurling magic and demons and probably artifacts of the ancients in the bargain."

This was, Halla thought, a remarkably edited view of the last week or two. On the other hand, as pleasant as they seemed, it probably wasn't wise to inform a trio of paladins, protectors of the faith and servants of good, etcetera, etcetera, that they'd accidentally murdered two men and dumped the bodies.

The paladins rode alongside the wagon as they set out.

Well...they tried.

In actual fact, the ox moved slower than a walking horse and only marginally faster than a completely stationary horse, so they went back and forth for about two hours and then the woman—Halla had gathered that her name was Mare and she was nominally in charge—said, "Did you say you had to get somewhere in a hurry?"

"We're trying to reach Amalcross," said Zale. "We are merely...um...hampered by our ox. No offense to the ox."

"An ox has other qualities," said Brindle. "An ox went through the Vagrant Hills and didn't panic *once.*"

"Ah." Mare turned back to her comrades and held a brief conference with them out of earshot. "Amalcross, you say?"

"That's the plan."

"At the current rate, it'll take you...ah..."

"At least four days," said Zale. "We know."

"Believe me, we know," said Halla.

"Well." Mare dismounted and walked alongside the wagon. "We, too, have to be somewhere. But I don't much like leaving you to the Motherhood's tender mercies. If that captain runs across you and we're not here, I don't think he's going to be in a very good mood."

Halla and Zale nodded glumly.

"So," said Mare. "Would you like to get there much faster?"

Halla's heart leapt at the prospect, though she wasn't exactly sure what the paladin meant. "We'd love to," she said. "But what did you have in mind?"

Mare grinned. "Have you ever ridden a horse?"

Sarkis would have sworn that he remembered his few hours

spent with the Sainted Smith—he grimaced even thinking the name, but knew no better one—far better than he liked.

After a few hours of answering Nolan's questions, he realized just how much he had deliberately forgotten.

"Give me a little time," he said finally, his voice clipped. "I have answered many questions. This is not a memory I cherish."

"Oh," said Nolan. The scholar tried to hide his disappointment. "Yes, of course. I'm sure it was physically quite painful."

Sarkis wanted to laugh or scream or grab the little man by the throat and shake, but he did none of these things. He had to get word to Halla, and cooperation was his only chance for now.

He closed his eyes and rubbed at his forehead with his knuckles. The wagon rattled along under him.

Behind his eyes, he saw firelight and the shadow of the Smith. She was perched on the edge of the table, a lanky woman with heavily muscled arms. Her eyes were lit with flame from without and with a frantic glitter from within.

"It will be glorious," she promised him. "I know this is a punishment, but if it works, you will live for all time! You will see kingdoms rise and fall, you will see history!"

"I've seen enough kingdoms fall," he'd replied, hearing his chains rattle as he moved. "I've helped a few of them along. It's all a lot of blood and screaming."

She didn't listen to him. Sarkis got the impression that the Smith did not listen to many people. The forge light blazed off to his right, where her apprentices were hammering the steel. Three swords, three smiths, the rhythm just slightly off between them, like a faltering heartbeat. "It will be glorious," she said. "If it works."

"What if it doesn't work?" asked the Dervish, in his light,

amused voice. There was a mask of dried blood over his handsome face, but his voice was still the same.

"Oh, you'll die," said the Smith. "At least, I hope you'll die. The alternatives are worse. I'll try to get you out of the sword, of course, if you're trapped in there and can't come out." She chewed on her lower lip.

"That happens?" asked the Dervish.

"Oh yes." She nodded vigorously. "It's happened to two people so far, I'm afraid. But I'm sure I'll be able to get them out. Eventually."

"Eventually?" The Dervish's voice was no longer quite so amused.

"I've been *busy*," said the Smith petulantly. "There's so much to do. And once they've gone mad in the blade, it's not as if they're going to go any madder, are they?"

One of the apprentices called to the Smith. "Time."

"Right!" The Smith slid off the table. "You first," she said to Angharad Shieldborn. "You first..."

SARKIS STRAIGHTENED. The scene was too vivid. He could even smell the stink of burning flesh as the dull red sword sank into his captain's breast. Angharad had grunted, but she had not screamed. The metal had hissed like a serpent and he knew it should not work, it was too uneven a tempering, there were too many bones, the blade should warp or break, but the Smith pulled it free and it was straight and fine and charred black with Angharad's blood.

He'd shouted until his throat was raw, thrown himself against the chains, but Angharad was dead, body falling to one side, as dead as the rest of his men, all those brave, cranky, valiant souls who had looked to him to save them, he had failed them all and they hung from the walls of this cursed keep and now Angharad's lifeblood was burnt onto a piece of metal and the Smith was looking at him with her *zeth* eyes...

Stop. Think of something else. Stop.

He tried to drown the memory in something else. Anything else. The way the Weeping Lands looked in high summer, when the grass had turned golden and wind rushed over it in glinting waves, and the smell of grass came to him on the wind...the ocean, moving like the grass had, while he stood on the deck and smelled salt and heard the roar of the waves and also the Dervish being violently seasick over the side of the rail. That was before Angharad had joined them, a few months before, and he still hadn't been sure about the Dervish, but he went over and pulled his hair back anyway and said, "It gets better," and the Dervish said, "Yes, it'll be better when I'm *dead.*"

The Dervish, who had died at the hands of the Smith, screaming as the sword slid into him...

Stop.

He thought of Halla. Not of bedding her—that felt too much like betrayal still—but the way she had slept in his arms afterward. They had fit together so well. It had been so comfortable, the way his arm slid into the hollow of her waist so that he could tuck his hand up between her breasts, the tops of his thighs against the backs of hers. He hadn't even minded that she tried to burrow under him in her sleep.

Bedding was easy, compared to being able to sleep comfortably against someone. Hell, among his men, nobody'd bed down next to Fisher except Boll. Boll could sleep through the end of the world, and Fisher flailed and fidgeted like he could see the end coming. Fisher was always on the end, if they were jammed into tents together, and Boll was always between him and the rest of the troops. He'd even taken to sending them on scouting missions together as if they were a couple, even though there was nothing between them. It was just easier that way.

Fisher had retired before the end. He hadn't thought of that in years. All the rest of his gallant troops, Boll and Kithrup and Ceri and everyone, had fallen with him at the end. Angharad and the Dervish had fallen even farther than the rest. But Fisher had said he was old and he was done and he'd gone back to his little fishing village to live with his daughter.

Perhaps his daughter had had a daughter of her own. Perhaps somewhere still, there was a clan who could put a bolt in a man's eye from a hundred yards and weep and draw the string back and do it again.

The thought gave him a strange peace. He took a deep breath and straightened and turned back to Nolan, ready to sell his memories for bargaining power once more.

CHAPTER 55

Halla had never ridden a horse. Halla had ridden a donkey, and she had always assumed that it was mostly the same thing.

It was not.

The gait of a horse was smoother, no question. And the donkey could not possibly have carried two riders, particularly not at any speed. But she also had never ridden the donkey for hours and the horse was a great deal larger and also Halla was now fifteen years older than the girl who had climbed on the back of the donkey and her hip joints let her know it.

"We can't gallop to Amalcross," said Mare, who was, ironically, riding a gelding. "The horses would drop dead under us. But we can make good speed, particularly compared to...ah..."

"A gnole doesn't want to hear it."

Brindle stayed with the wagon, of course, and Jorge stayed with him. He'd grumbled a bit, but Mare pulled rank and told him he wasn't going to be exorcising anything with his arm in a sling. "Your sword's a fancy paperweight right now," she told him. "You can't swing it. Guard the wagon, and keep those blithering idiots from the Motherhood from impounding it or setting it on fire or whatever they feel like doing."

"I thought I couldn't swing a sword," said Jorge.

"You don't need to stab the Motherhood. Just glare at them and rattle your armor a bit. They'll back right off."

"Fine, fine..."

So they did not gallop to Amalcross, but they trotted frequently and then they walked and the humans walked alongside the horses, and then they trotted again. Halla rode behind Mare on her sturdy gray gelding. Mare was wearing a great deal of armor, more than Sarkis wore, and every time they broke into a trot, Halla's face bashed into Mare's mailed back. The paladin was wearing a wool tabard, which was the only reason that her face still had any skin on it.

But they did move a great deal faster. Zale was riding with the other paladin—Halla still hadn't caught his name and was now at the point where it would be too embarrassing to ask— and they made it halfway to Amalcross in a single day.

Zale spent the Rat's money recklessly, and rented a room at the inn with a bathtub.

"Only one bed," said the innkeeper.

Zale and Halla looked at each other.

"I just don't care any more," said Halla. "You?"

"Rat's teeth, no. As long as there's a mattress, I'd share a bed with the Hanged Mother herself right now."

"Tactful. Very tactful."

"Tactful Zale was jostled to death somewhere a few miles back. Now you get tired, cranky Zale."

"Do you want the room or not?" asked the innkeeper.

"We'll take it."

They took turns using the bathtub behind a wooden screen, and Halla's only consolation was that the priest made just as many noises of wincing agony as she did.

"I'm old," said Zale, staring up at the ceiling. Their narrow face seemed to have more lines than when the day started. Halla doubted she looked any better.

"...we're old."

"I'm older than you."

"Don't make this a contest."

"Sorry. Lawyer, you know."

"Do you ride horses a lot?"

"Never if I can help it."

"We have to do it again tomorrow."

"We do."

Halla joined them, stretched out on her side of the bed, and made a noise that Sarkis would have likely compared to a yak.

"Couldn't have put it better myself."

After a long minute, Halla said, "What are we going to do with the paladins tomorrow?"

"I told them to drop us inside the city gates," said Zale. "Since I think there's a good chance we'll have to kill some people, I'd rather not get them involved. They are...um...not so good at making a virtue of expediency."

The story they had concocted was straightforward, if not terribly original. Family friend had visited, accompanied by scholar. Family friend had left in a hurry, having taken several valuable artifacts. They weren't particularly worried about the artifacts, but they were very worried that the scholar had some undue influence over him and wanted to make sure that he was not in any danger. The paladins had nodded and not asked any further questions.

Halla propped herself up on one elbow and looked at their gear. She had a small travel pack with a change of clothes, and Zale had much the same. The crossbow, however, lay atop the two packs, unstrung but exuding quiet menace. "Are you sure we'll even be able to kill them?"

"No. If we're lucky, we won't have to find out. Unfortunately, I don't think this is the sort of case that lends itself well to binding arbitration, so I'd rather be prepared." They rolled partway over, a pained look on their narrow face. "Ah...Halla, I don't know how to say this...I am not trying to shuffle this off on you, I promise. But all else being equal...it will be easier if you are the one who does the killing, should it come to that."

Halla lifted both eyebrows.

"I am a better witness in your defense than you are in mine," said Zale. "Priest and lawyer and all that."

Halla nodded. The thought had occurred to her. And she could not suspect Zale of trying to save their own skin—not after they had told her to run, knowing that Alver was far more likely to kill them than her.

"I'll do my best," she said, and closed her eyes.

THE NEXT DAY WAS WORSE. Halla stopped even trying to make conversation, and now clung silently to the paladin's back, hoping that her hip joints did not grind away to powder before they arrived. When Mare halted her horse and said, "We're here," it took Halla several long seconds before the words penetrated her private misery.

She had to be helped down out of the saddle, where she stood, legs trembling, while Mare took her pack down from the horse's back and offered it to her. "You don't look so good," the paladin said.

"I'm used to riding donkeys," Halla admitted. "Only donkeys. Actually, only one donkey. His name was Sugar." She wasn't sure why she felt the need to offer the donkey's name, but Mare nodded gravely, as if this was indeed vital information.

Zale looked better than she did, but not by much. They had their cloak draped over their crossbow, which made it look a great deal more suspicious than if they'd just been carrying it normally. Still, presumably it was the thought that counted.

The paladins waved to the guards at the gate, who saluted. Halla abandoned any idea of sneaking into the city unnoticed.

"Thank you," she said to Mare, grabbing both of the paladin's hands. She was wearing gauntlets, so this wasn't much fun, but never mind that. "Thank you for getting us here. Maybe now we can get to Bartholomew before this scholar does something...well...regrettable."

"Glad to be of service," said Mare, smiling. "And you did us a good turn, too. Jorge would never have agreed to stay out of a fight with demons. The half-day we might have lost bringing you here is more than made up for by not losing Jorge."

She waved to her comrade, tossed a casual salute in Zale's direction, and mounted her horse. The last Halla saw of them was glints of light off armor, riding away into danger.

SARKIS SWAM UP OUT of the silver sword-dreams, and discovered that he was looking at a corpse.

More specifically, he was looking at Bartholomew's corpse. There was quite a large knife buried in his back, and he was face down on a cluttered table that Sarkis recognized from their previous visits.

"I gather you're the wielder now?" he said to Nolan, studying the corpse dispassionately.

"I didn't want to do it," said Nolan defensively. "He left me no choice! He kept changing the terms of the bargain."

"You'll hear no complaints from me," said Sarkis, shrugging. If anything, the scholar had saved him the trouble. "Refused to sell, did he?"

"It's been a nightmare," said Nolan, collapsing on the bench opposite the body. "First he contacted our order saying he had one of the Smith's swords. I nearly killed myself getting here, only to find that his story had changed and now he just knew where the sword was and *expected* to have it in his possession. Then your whole entourage showed up, and Bartholomew was all for stealing the sword in the middle of the night, even though I told him that wouldn't work, and anyway, you didn't spend the night, so then we would go to Rutger's Howe and take it as part of the bargain with Mistress Halla, even though it was blindingly obvious that if you were the sword, she wasn't going to part with it. And I still didn't have any proof that you *were* the sword."

Sarkis nodded, folding his arms. "I suppose he was working with her relatives, then?"

"Not at first," said Nolan. "Dreadful woman. I'd have stabbed *her* if I thought I could get away with it. Once we had proof you really were a servant of the sword, he said it would be the best way to keep Mistress Halla from following after and claiming he'd stolen the blade. But he wasn't supposed to draw it! The bargain was *never* that he'd be the wielder."

Privately, Sarkis suspected that had bought Bartholomew several days more life. Nolan, for all his whining, was clearly not above a little murder to get what he wanted.

"So what happens now?" he asked.

"We'll be returning to my order's compound," said Nolan. He looked over at Bartholomew's corpse, lip curling. "I've already been away far longer than I intended. Smith's grace, this has been *miserable.*"

He sounded so much like an ordinary person complaining about travel delays and unreliable merchants that Sarkis would have felt a pang of sympathy for him, if it wasn't for the dead body.

"So what are you doing with the corpse?" he asked. *Why is so much of my life these days related to corpse disposal? It never used to be. I used to just leave them where they dropped. I could really get to hate the south.*

Nolan smiled. There was a shine in his eyes that reminded Sarkis of something...something bad...

Ah. Yes. Of course. The *zeth* eyes of the Sainted Smith.

"There's so much junk in this house," he said, waving a hand casually toward the ceiling and the second floor. "I expect it'll go up like a torch, and take anything else in the house with it."

Sarkis said nothing. The house shared a wall on either side with its neighbors. Presumably Nolan wasn't concerned or didn't care that the fire might not limit itself to the contents of Bartholomew's back bedrooms.

He wondered how much the sword would let him get away with, in terms of stopping a wielder bent on arson.

He did not have to find out. The front door opened. Sarkis heard footsteps in the hall and turned to face the intruders.

"The door is locked!" hissed Nolan. "What the hell is going on?!"

"Bartholomew's kept a spare key in that gargoyle for the last twenty years," said the intruder, stepping into the room. "Hello, Sarkis. Hello, Nolan. Hello, Bar...oh. I see."

Nolan was making demands. Nolan was cursing. Sarkis had eyes only for one person.

"*Halla,*" he said.

CHAPTER 56

"You!" said Nolan. "You're here? How the devil are you *here?*"

"Mostly luck," admitted Halla. "Or, since it was paladins, maybe grace. Zale? Was that grace?"

"I'm willing to call it grace," said Zale, who was standing behind her in the doorway to the dining room. "Whether divine or simply human kindness, which is its own form of grace. Hello, Sarkis."

Halla stepped sideways, until she was standing in the portion of the kitchen that adjoined the dining room. She was carrying a cloak slung over one shoulder, hanging down past her hips, and limping a little. The notion that she might have been injured sent mingled rage and shame slamming through his veins.

"Are you hurt?" he said.

"Just saddlesore," she admitted, not meeting his eyes. "We rode very fast. Or what felt like very fast, anyway."

It was terribly stupid, he realized, to be trying to work out if she was furious at him based on how she was looking at him when there was a murderer directly behind him and a corpse sitting at the table. Nevertheless, the fact that she wouldn't make eye contact seemed like the worst of signs.

"Well," she said. "You murdered Bartholomew, then?"

"I had no choice," said Nolan. "He was the wielder and refused to give up the sword. I knew he always intended to double-cross me."

"He was the one who sent the footpads in Archen's Glory," said Sarkis.

"Ah. Yes. And left me to Alver's tender mercies. Still, I'm sorry he's dead." She sighed. "I suppose it is you I must negotiate with, then."

"What?" said Nolan.

"I will buy the sword from you," said Halla, in a clear voice. "I never meant to cast it aside, but I realize that things have become muddled." She looked at Zale. "How much is my inheritance worth?"

Zale wiggled their hand back and forth. "My inventory is nothing like complete. Based on what I have catalogued so far, I would say at least fifty-three hundred, give or take, including the house. The outlying lands are not included."

The realization of what Halla was doing sent Sarkis a step forward, hands outstretched. "Halla! No!"

"Fifty-three hundred, then," said Halla, ignoring him. "There may be more in the outlying lands, but I have recently learned that they were mortgaged without my permission, so I can't speak to their value. Will that be acceptable?"

"Halla, you can't do this!"

A small, unworthy part of Sarkis was overcome with relief. She did not hate him. Indeed, she had chased down his captors and was offering everything that she had to get him back.

A much larger part was screaming that yes, she was giving up *everything* she had—her home, her newly acquired fortune, the future dowries for her nieces that Sarkis had not even met —to buy him back from the scholar.

"Halla," he said, trying to sound calm. "I'm not worth this. Don't do this."

"You're my friend," said Halla, not looking at him. Sarkis did not know whether to crow with joy or writhe in shame.

His captor snorted. "Don't be stupid. A relic of the Sainted Smith is beyond any price."

"Are you certain?" said Halla.

"Very certain. Quit wasting my time, woman."

Halla nodded. "I was afraid of that," she said, a bit sadly. "I really hoped you'd be reasonable."

She pushed her cloak back and swung the crossbow she'd been concealing up to aim at Nolan.

Oh great god, she's going to shoot at him. Sarkis didn't know whether to be amazed, horrified, or both. *Can she hit him? Did Zale teach her enough?*

Zale was leaning against the doorframe with a polite, interested expression on their face. This did not fill Sarkis with confidence.

Nolan, meanwhile, stared at the bolt, then back at her. "You won't kill me," he said.

"I won't?" said Halla. "Why wouldn't I?"

"You're not a killer," said Nolan, although he sounded a bit doubtful.

"Well, obviously not *yet*," said Halla. "But I can start with you, and then I will be. I think that's how this works, isn't it?"

Nolan started to back up. Halla made an apologetic sound. "Please don't move. I've never shot at anything but trees, you see, and while my aim's not bad for an amateur, if you move, I don't really know where I'll hit you. It could be anywhere. And then what if it wasn't fatal?"

"I don't want it to be fatal!" yelled Nolan.

"Oh, but you do," said Halla. "You really, really do. Because if I hit you somewhere that doesn't kill you, but it just hurts a whole lot, then I'll have to finish you off, right? And I don't have any idea how to do that, so I'll just be stabbing you in random places with a knife until I hit a good one."

Nolan's jaw dropped.

The great god have mercy. She's found a way to weaponize ignorance.

"I'll feel very bad about it," Halla assured the scholar, gesturing with the crossbow. Every time the tip of the bolt moved a quarter inch, both Nolan and Sarkis flinched. "I don't want to hurt anyone. That's why it would be best if you held very still, I think?"

"Servant!" said Nolan. "Servant, defend me!"

Sarkis winced. He had known all along that he was going to have to get involved. The magic of the sword left him no choice. "Halla," he said, "I'm afraid if you try to kill him, you'll have to go through me. I'm forced to defend him as long as I'm alive."

"You can't fight it?" she asked. "Not even a little?"

I'm trying. I'm trying.

He tried to set his feet. Compulsion dragged him forward anyway, one step at a time.

"Please," he said. "I don't want you to get hurt."

He dragged his sword out of the sheath as if it were made of mud.

"Quit talking!" shouted Nolan. "Kill her!"

"I will do nothing of the sort!" Sarkis shouted back. And to Halla, his voice cracking with strain, "Please. This isn't safe."

She took a step back. She didn't look frightened, just thoughtful.

Oh great god, don't let her trust me. Please don't let her think that I'll pull off some miracle.

"I thought you were used to betraying people," Halla said.

The cut went deeper than a physical wound. He'd honestly rather that she shot him.

Still...

"I deserved that."

"You did." She took another few steps back, putting the kitchen table between them. A kitchen was a very stupid place to have a battle, but apparently this was where they were going to have it.

"I'm sorry," Sarkis said. "I wanted to tell you sooner, but I kept thinking we had to sort the inheritance first because if you were angry and wanted nothing to do with me, you'd sheathe the sword and then I couldn't protect you and then..." He raised his free hand, let it drop. "That doesn't matter now. I'm begging you. Please run away or back away or drop the crossbow, or *something*. If I have to kill you defending this bastard..."

He trailed off. He didn't know how to finish.

It will destroy me. It will gut me. Every time someone draws the sword, I will look for you, and when you aren't there, I will remember that you're gone and that I failed you twice over and I will pray for the great god to grant me a quick death.

The words choked him. He stared into Halla's gray eyes and hoped that she understood a little of what he could not say.

She shoved the kitchen table at him with her free hand. He caught it, set it down. The magic wanted to flip it over, slam her against the wall, defend the wielder at all costs.

She's no threat, he pleaded with the sword. *She won't shoot. Let her go. This isn't a danger I need to defend against. Please.*

Halla feinted to the right, swung the crossbow up over his left shoulder. It was so transparent that he wanted to scream. The magic wouldn't let him ignore it. It wanted him to strike out with his sword, but Sarkis would be damned to the great god's lowest hell before he did that.

He shoved the table instead. The edge struck her stomach,

driving the air out of her. Halla grunted. The big gray eyes that lifted to his were full of surprise—and pain.

"Stop dancing!" screamed Nolan. "Finish her off!"

Sarkis felt something snap inside his head.

He could not kill his wielder. He had to defend his wielder against all threats.

His wielder would make him kill the woman he loved.

I will kill him, thought Sarkis. *I will destroy him. I will pull him apart, joint by joint, bone by bone. I will carve him up into a thousand pieces to make the dying last.*

I will hurt him until he hurts like I hurt.

The magic pounded in his temples like blood.

He had never hated a wielder like this before. He had loathed them and he had held them in contempt, but even the one who cut out Sarkis's tongue had, perhaps, been no more than he deserved.

Halla did not deserve it.

The magic would never let him kill his wielder. That was the one power that it had, above all other. He would throw his own body between Nolan and any threat. He had no choice.

I will kill him. I will end him. I will find a way to destroy him.

I am the greatest threat.

The magic wavered.

He had only a moment, but a moment was all that he needed.

Sarkis flipped his sword around, set the point under his sternum, and threw himself at the ground.

CHAPTER 57

Halla's first thought was, Oh, I guess that's what they mean by falling on your sword.

Her second thought was, *Dammit,* and then her thoughts dissolved into a wordless scream of horror.

"*Sarkis!*" She dropped to her knees, the crossbow held out awkwardly to one side. Shooting him or herself wouldn't help. "Sarkis, you idiot, you didn't have to do that! *Why did you do that?!*"

He was on his knees, both hands grasped around the hilt of the sword. A foot of steel protruded from his back, slicked with red.

"...had to..." he rasped. Blood coated his lips and began to run over his chin. "...couldn't...couldn't let you...get hurt..."

"I wasn't going to get hurt!" She wanted to scream. Possibly she *was* screaming. She was furious and horrified and if she let either emotion slip for even a second, guilt was going to rush in and swamp her.

With agonizing slowness, he unlocked his fingers from the hilt. He put his hand against her cheek and wiped the tears away with a bloody thumb.

She clasped his hand with hers. "You wouldn't have hurt me."

"Couldn't take...the chance..." he said. "Not...not with...*you*..." and then he died.

She stared at her fingers, watching the blood turn into a faint blue iridescence, and then it was gone.

Nolan stared at the place where Sarkis had been. The hilt of the sword in his hand met the scabbard with a soft, final *click*.

Halla stood up. She had not dropped the crossbow. It seemed very important that she had not dropped the crossbow.

"I'm very angry," she said to Nolan. Her voice was quiet. Her siblings, had any of them been alive, would have recognized that voice and run for the door.

The scholar, foolishly, did not pay attention.

"How did he do that?" breathed Nolan. "Did the Saint not prevent the swords from suicide? Why would she not? Was it too difficult, or—"

Halla shot him, inexpertly, in the leg.

Nolan screamed and fell down, clutching his thigh. Blood bloomed through the cloth around the bolt. He rolled back and forth, shrieking.

Zale started forward. Halla handed the crossbow to the priest, her face still extremely calm.

"Give me the sword," she said to Nolan.

"Ahh! No! *No!* I can't—not the sword, not one of the Saint's relics—"

"I'd rather not torture you," said Halla. "I'm not really a person who does that. But you've killed Bartholomew and kidnapped my friend and I think I could probably figure out how to be that sort of person very quickly."

She reached over and plucked a knife from the kitchen table. Nolan's breath came in gasps as he clutched his leg, staring at her.

"Well, it actually helps that he killed Bartholomew," said Zale thoughtfully. "We'll just say that we came in and found that, and it'll be the word of a priest against him. Honestly, this will make it much easier."

Nolan's eyes got huge.

"On balance," said Halla thoughtfully, "I think I'd rather kill you. Then I don't have to be the sort of person who tortures people. And I don't think I'll feel guilty about it, either."

Zale set down the crossbow.

"Stop her!" screamed Nolan at the priest.

"No," said Zale. "But I'll hold you down for her. I think that will make it easier for everyone, don't you? It'll be over faster that way. I don't think any of us want to draw this out, do we?"

"You're both utterly mad!"

"We are both very practical," said Zale. "It's the world that's gone a bit mad." The priest caught Nolan's shoulders.

The scholar searched Halla's face, then Zale's, then Halla's again. Whatever he saw apparently changed his mind because he sagged suddenly.

"Take the sword!" gasped Nolan. "Take it, take it!" He pried a bloody hand loose from his leg and shoved the scabbard at her.

"You release the sword to me? You renounce all ownership?" Halla wasn't sure what words he had to say to make it official.

"Yes, yes! All of it! It's yours, I release it!"

"Thank you," said Halla, lowering the knife.

"I don't think you have to thank him," said Zale. "Since he stole the sword to begin with."

"Seems rude otherwise."

"Well, Rat forbid we be *rude.*"

"On the other hand, he did murder a family friend," said Halla. "Of course, that was after Bartholomew stole the sword, so...I don't know. Does that one equal out, do you think?"

"I think I'm bleeding to death!" screamed Nolan.

"And if you'd do it faster, it would solve a great many problems," said Zale. "Ah, well. I suppose we should resign ourselves to him living. You seem to have missed the big artery."

"You taught me to shoot at trees. You didn't teach me to hit specific *spots* on trees."

Zale opened the front door. "Excuse me!" they called. "You —yes, with the goat! Excuse me! Will you go to the constabulary and ask them to please come at once, there's been a murder?"

Halla didn't hear the neighbor's response. She leaned against the kitchen table, watching Nolan.

"I'm going to lose consciousness," threatened the scholar.

"Perhaps we'd have some quiet, then." Halla's hands were shaking with adrenaline and she buried them in her skirts.

In fact, the scholar did lose consciousness a few minutes later, and then the constables arrived. Halla was not looking forward to explaining things, but Zale immediately took charge. The story they told had nothing to do with any sword being missing, but a great deal to do with an elderly friend of the family, a bit befuddled, being taken in by a smooth-talking scholar who planned to kill him and steal the most valuable parts of his collection. It was a greatly embellished version of what they had told the paladins. In this version, after Bartholomew had come to Rutger's Howe to aid Halla, both priest and widow had been suspicious of the way that Nolan had treated the old man and had followed them back to try and put a stop to it.

They were aided by the fact that one of the constables had seen them on the way into the city, accompanied by paladins, and that Bartholomew was already cold. The word of a Rat priest carried a great deal of weight as well. By the time that a healer was sent for to bandage Nolan's leg and remove the bolt, the man was already being treated as a criminal.

"If he lives, he'll likely hang," said the Amalcross constable. "Pretty clear what he intended. I'm sorry you didn't get here sooner."

"An hour or two," said Halla, wiping away tears. They were genuine enough. Bartholomew had been kind to her, before greed went to work like a poison in his mind. It was easier to think of him as two people, and to mourn the kind one even as she had hated the greedy one. "If we'd only been a little quicker on the road..."

"Now, now." He patted her shoulder. "Wasn't meant to be unkind. You stopped him from robbing the next old man. Sorry you had to shoot him, mistress. Hard thing to have to do."

"I hardly knew what I was doing..." she murmured, falling instinctively back into her protective shell of foolishness. "I saw that Bartholomew was dead and all I could think to do was grab Zale's crossbow. Oh dear! I hope I didn't kill him."

"He'll be dead either way," said the constable. "You did a fine job, and don't you feel guilty for doing what had to be done." He gave Zale what he probably thought was a subtle look over Halla's shoulder. Zale nodded to him, face grave, and then when the man turned away, the priest rolled their eyes at Halla.

And then there was only the sword.

CHAPTER 58

S he lasted until that night in a strange inn, before she finally burst into tears.

Zale put their arms around her, as if they'd expected it. Probably they had.

"Shhh..." the priest whispered. "Shhh, it will be all right. He's only in the sword. He'll come back."

"Will he?" she cried. "But he killed himself!"

"And he may have done so in the past as well," said Zale. "Sarkis has not been terribly forthcoming about his life as a sword, has he?"

That wrung a watery laugh from Halla. "N-no. No, he hasn't." She wiped her eyes on her sleeve. "But how can I...I mean...I was so stupid he had to *kill* himself to save me. How can he ever..."

She trailed off. How could Sarkis possible think of her as anything but a hopelessly useless burden? She'd come to his rescue, and failed so spectacularly that he had to fall on his own sword to fix the mess she'd made.

Zale took both her hands in theirs. "It will be all right," they said again. "You saved him. Dying isn't the same for him as it will be for us. It is only a...a temporary embarrassment." They smiled faintly. "When you draw the sword in a fortnight or so, I am quite certain that he will yell at you for having put yourself in danger. But I doubt he will even stop to consider that he died himself."

Halla heaved a sigh. "Will you come home with me?" she asked. "Back to Rutger's Howe *again*? I know you have duties and I've kept you from them so long, but..."

Zale smiled. "I fear you're stuck with Brindle and I until we sort out exactly how much your inheritance is worth. And then you will probably be stuck with us even longer, albeit at a remove."

"What?"

Their smile grew, although the edges of it twisted. "Bartholomew left everything to Silas and never updated his will. They haven't read it officially, but the clerk here took me aside and told me. So I fear you've inherited *his* estate, too. I assume you'll want me to sort that out as well?"

Halla put her face in her hands and began to laugh, and if it turned into tears and back again, the Rat priest was kind enough not to mention it.

IT WAS NOT the longest fortnight of Halla's life, but it was close. The only thing she could compare it to was the grim fever season when her twin sisters had died. There was nothing to do but wait and see if tragedy would strike or not.

Tragedy already struck, she thought wearily. *He gutted himself to save you. What more do you want?*

In the songs, men always say they'd die for you. I suppose there's something to be said for the fact that you found one who actually did.

447

Surely he'll come back. Surely it's just another mortal wound, and after a few weeks in the sword, he'll come out again.

She wished that she was certain of that. It seemed like death by one's own hand should make a difference somehow, as if the magic should cease to work once it had been so used.

They spent three days in an inn in Amalcross, until Brindle and Prettyfoot the ox arrived. Jorge the paladin was extremely glad to finally hand them off. "It's not Brindle," he said. "A fine fellow, that gnole. I feel we really got to know each other. But I don't think I've ever moved so slowly in my life."

"Don't insult an ox, god-man," said Brindle, and then grinned at Jorge, who grinned back.

They made the long, long trek back to Rutger's Howe, blessedly untroubled by either bandits or the Hanged Motherhood. Halla saw the sign for the Drunken Boar yet again, and stared at it. "I don't know if I should simply rent a room permanently or burn this place to the ground," she said.

"A gnole would object to burning."

"A priest would, too." Zale patted her shoulder. "I'll go in. We'll stay somewhere else."

They camped in the wagon at a wide spot in the road. Halla ate the meat pies from the Drunken Boar. The meat had the thin dampness of rabbit this time, but that was the only difference.

"I don't know, after this is over, if I never want to leave the house again, or if I will itch to be on the road within a week," she said.

Zale snorted. "First one, then the other. You will want to be home, but then you may find that your home is no longer quite large enough to hold you." They shrugged. "You could hold off selling Bartholomew's house, see if a larger town suits you."

Halla shuddered. The flagstone floor had soaked up Nolan's

blood. It could be cleaned, certainly, but she'd always know that the spot was there.

And yet perhaps Zale was right. Silas's house did seem smaller than it should have. She had been thinking, in the back of her mind, that she would sell the house, buy a small cottage that one woman could keep easily, but she found herself pacing restlessly through the house, wanting to walk and keep walking.

Not to leave, she thought. *Not to get away from the house, but to get away from myself.* In the open air, her mind did not seem so cluttered. Here, it felt as if her own thoughts echoed off the walls and jangled in her brain like keys.

She took to walking down the lich road, but it was so cold that her nose was frozen by the time she got back. Probably the priest thought she was a bit daft. Then again, he was a priest, and he knew how people acted when they were mourning and troubled and nervous.

But somehow, the days passed, one by one, and then it was nearly a fortnight gone and then the day was upon her when at last, she could draw the sword.

IT WAS A COLD NIGHT. She sat in the great bedroom with the fire burning, staring at the sword.

It had been...what, a little over a month? Five weeks since Silas died? Everything was hazy, as if she'd stepped out of time. She couldn't fit the last few weeks into the same place as the years before. The time before Silas's death seemed as distant as her childhood or her marriage...a thing that happened long, long ago, to a different Halla, who had been impossibly young.

She ran her fingers down the scabbard. Still the same worn pattern, barely raised under her fingers. She wondered if the scabbard had been old when the sword was put into it, or if the smith had to make it new herself.

Then she'd have to be making scabbards as well as forging swords and trapping souls. Busy woman.

Her fingers closed on the hilt. She had not dared, in the last few days, to even test the draw. She had been too afraid that it would work, that she would draw the blade and find Sarkis before her, and she did not know what she was going to say.

Nolan's dead. I'm the wielder again.

I messed everything up.

I'm so sorry.

She had spent days thinking of everything that she could say, or would say, or might say. She had stripped the master bedroom bare and whitewashed the walls, replaced the sheets and the quilt, evicted dust that had lived underneath the bed for decades. Words beat in her head: apologies, expressions of love, anger at Sarkis for lying, anger at herself for still caring about that, anger at herself for not caring enough about that. It was like a wagon wheel in her head going around and around, skreet...skreet...skreet, carrying her nowhere.

But she had made a decision at last. She would draw the blade and see what happened. If he was cold or aloof, if he held his death against her—and how could he not?—then she would give the blade to Zale. The Rat priest would see far more clearly, would take Sarkis back to the Temple and find a way to free him, or to give him work as a Temple guard where he would be treated as a man and not as a convenient enchantment.

Halla herself...well, she would still have her inheritance. Two inheritances, apparently. She would go to her nieces and see them settled, maybe bring one back to stay with her, if the girl was unhappy on the farm.

Or perhaps it wouldn't come to that. Perhaps his lie and her foolishness would cancel out and they could start over again.

Halla swallowed hard and drew the blade.

Sarkis appeared in a cascade of blue light, one hand already going to his sword. He spun around, searching the room for enemies, and then saw her.

His eyes fixed on her face. She held her breath, waiting for whatever came next.

"*Halla,*" he said hoarsely, and buried his face in her shoulder.

CHAPTER 59

"You're alive," Sarkis said, against the side of her neck. "I thought I'd never see you again. I was so afraid I'd lost you."

It occurred to him, belatedly, that he *had* lost her. He'd been a fool and she'd cast the sword aside. She'd been right to do so. He should let go, step back, accept the judgment that he had due.

He did not seem to be doing any of these things. He seemed to be holding her so tightly that he had lifted her a little off the floor. And she was pressing herself against him, her body molding to his, and if he had lost her, she did not seem to know it.

"It's all right," she said. "I'm fine. Are you—have you—"

"Healed," he said. "It's nothing. It's fine. Are you safe? Alver, Nolan, are they...?"

"All dealt with. We're back home."

He leaned back then, arms still around her waist, so he could search her face, terrified of what he'd find. *Fear? Anger? Impatience? Is she waiting for me to stop mauling her so that she can tell me she's giving the sword to her niece and I can go to hell?*

She smiled at him, and his heart turned over.

"Halla..." he said, and pulled her mouth to his.

He kissed her hungrily, still not quite believing it was real. All the fear that had been coiled in his gut shuddered into passion. He wanted her here and now, on the floor in front of the fire if need be. He wanted to sink inside her and feel her heat around him and know that she was his, as surely as he was hers.

Can't. Can't do that. It's the one thing she really is afraid of.

"Halla," he said, his voice thick. "I need you. I know we can't —but—"

"No, it's all right," she said, surprising him, and then she was off on a complicated tangent about being tied up in a room with Zale and telling Alver she was pregnant and how Zale had worked out that if he just went back in the sword afterward...

He tried to follow this, but his mind got stuck on the bit where Alver had tied her up. He would kill the clammy-handed louse. He'd use his bare hands so as not to waste good steel on him.

"Oh dear," said Halla. Apparently he'd said that out loud. "I stabbed him, you see, and...oh, not very well!" She held up her hands, as if apologizing. "In the arm. He screeched like a chicken laying a particularly large egg, and then I know I was probably supposed to stab him again, but there didn't seem to be much point."

Rage at Alver had dampened his libido somewhat, but Halla's cheerful expression, and the mimed stabbing, woke it again. Great god, but he loved her. She was so absurd and so dear, and also it seemed she was capable of stabbing kidnappers and then being matter-of-fact about it.

Also, he could apparently make love to her without fear.

Sarkis picked her up in his arms—she squeaked—and carried her to the bed. "Yes?" he said, searching her face again.

She reached up and pulled him down beside her. "Yes," she whispered in his ear.

He knew that he should go slowly, that it had been a very long time for her, but he couldn't. He tugged at her clothes, slid his hands across her breasts, and then he was lost to a kind of frenzy. Her warmth and her softness filled his senses. He needed her desperately, needed to take her and be taken until all the fear and horror of the last few weeks was a faded, distant memory.

It was not until he had entered her on one hard thrust that he fought clear of the haze. "Halla." He pressed his forehead against hers. "Am I hurting you? Is this...?"

"No, it's fine," she said, sounding a bit faint. "Truly. Err...are you done?"

He resisted the urge to beat his skull against the headboard. "No. I'm not done. It goes on for awhile yet, unless you don't want it to."

"That's fine." She wiggled under him, adjusting her position, in a way that tested his self-control enormously. Just the feel of her breasts against his chest was probably going to kill him.

At this rate, it may not go on for much longer at all. Although if it goes on for more than two minutes, I'm already ahead of the game.

Besides, I'd like to see how any other man would manage, after a few hundred years of celibacy...

In the end, he did not last nearly as long as he'd like. When she gasped in his ear, he came completely undone.

When he could manage coherent thought again, he propped himself up on his elbows. "I could have managed that better," he said.

"I'm just glad you're here," she said.

"So am I, but it was not my intent to...ah...manhandle you."

"As long as you don't intend to throw me into a ditch." She

chuckled, which did interesting things to various muscles and focused Sarkis's attention immediately.

"No ditches," he said. He slid his hand down between their bodies and began to touch her in ways that did even more interesting things. "But it would be unforgivably rude to take without giving back."

"If you say—so!" The last word came out as a squeak, and Sarkis set out to make sure that both of them were well pleased.

IT WAS the middle of the night. The fire had burned down and the bird had woken in its sleep to shout loudly about death and the worm, then gone back to sleep. Halla was half-asleep against his chest, and Sarkis stared down at the fine lines etched across her eyelids and the corners of her eyes.

Great god, he'd almost lost her. No, he *had* lost her. It was by Halla and Zale's doing, not his, that she was here in his arms. He had failed her. How could he keep from doing so again?

She opened her eyes and frowned. "You're upset."

"How can you tell?"

"You're scowling. The sad scowl, not one of the others."

He filed the notion that he had different types of scowl away for later.

"Forgive me," he said. He freed one hand and brushed the hair out of her eyes. "I've failed you. I didn't protect you, and I didn't tell you all the truth. I don't deserve...this. I don't deserve *you.*"

"You didn't deserve to be stuck in a sword for five hundred years, either," she said tartly.

"Well, perhaps not." He flopped back down on his back, staring at the ceiling. "So...err...now what?"

Halla considered this. "Well. I suppose you are stuck with me, now that I'm the wielder again."

He smiled up at the ceiling. "So I am."

"And as I am now a wealthy enough widow to be automatically respectable, I do not need to worry about having a very handsome lover lurking around the house."

"I'll kill him," said Sarkis.

"I meant *you*, wretch."

"I am not very handsome. I am scarred and irritable and, unfortunately, immortal."

"Yes, but you carry it well." She propped herself up on one elbow. "I mean it, though. The neighbors will gossip, but...well, it's not fair, but there you are. I will be eccentric instead of a pariah."

He scowled at her, clearly deep in thought, then said, "Marry me."

Halla blinked at him, not sure if she'd heard correctly.

"If you marry me, you won't be eccentric. No, dammit, this is coming out wrong. Marry me to marry me, not because of your neighbors. I'll kill your neighbors."

"I'd rather you didn't," said Halla, focusing on the one bit that she could make sense of. "I like most of them."

"Fine, then I will glare at them. But you should still marry me anyway. I mean, you shouldn't, really, you can do much better, although given what I've seen of the men in your land..." He trailed off, muttering something under his breath, in which Halla caught only the words *decadent* and *torch*.

"Are you *asking* me to marry you?"

He gave her an exasperated look. "Yes. Of course. Because— oh, great god's balls, I don't even know how to marry you in this country."

Halla felt her lips twitching. He sounded so distraught, she didn't want to laugh at him. "Well, we go before a priest...Zale would probably be happy to perform it...and say vows and then..."

Sarkis shook his head. "But you have no family to set your price. And even if you did, I could not pay it."

"Price?"

"The marriage price. What your husband pays your household, to make up for your loss."

Halla raised her eyebrows. "We do it the other way around. The woman provides a dowry so that the husband will take her."

The resulting mutter was louder and sounded a bit like Silas's bird. "How barbaric."

"Well, I haven't got a family and you haven't got any money, so can't we just ignore that?"

He bristled. "I will not steal you!"

"Err...but I'm agreeing to it?" Halla did not know whether to laugh or cry. "Sarkis, I've chased you from pillar to post and then you had to fall on your sword and—and—can't this all just cancel out?"

She could tell by his scowl that it did not, in fact, cancel out. He got to his feet and stomped around the bedroom, dragging his hands through his hair.

This is just my luck. I worry that he'll hate me, but instead he wants to marry me except that he can't because...because...

"All right," she said, tucking her feet up under her on the bed. "Explain this to me so I understand."

———

IT WAS, she had to admit, rather fascinating. It made sense, in a land where you lived and died by social standing. *Not like this one*, Halla thought wryly, *where if you have no standing, you go work as someone's housekeeper, and if there's a hint of scandal, he turns you out and you end up scrubbing floors in a nunnery. Hmm, yes. Wildly different, those.*

Hell, maybe Sarkis's people have the right idea. Put a material price on people so everybody knows what they're worth.

"Why does somebody need a high price? Aren't you just bankrupting your husband before you marry him?"

"No, no. A high marriage price means higher standing for both husband and wife. The wife because her family values her highly, the husband because he can afford to meet it. Most of the goods will go with the couple. If land is offered, they may live on it, or it will be held in trust for their children." He shook his head. "If it isn't...well, we have fought clan wars over less."

Halla rubbed her forehead. "What if her husband can't meet her price?"

"Then they do not wed."

"What? *Seriously?*"

He looked uncomfortable. "Well...she can agree to be raided away. It causes a great deal of upheaval, but if two people are obviously in love, sometimes their families will turn a blind eye, or...ah...pursuit will be symbolic. But she still has her price, you understand. Everyone knows her status. That is not lost. And her children cannot then inherit her husband's wealth, because she is still a member of her parent's household, in absentia. Her children are fatherless, to all intents and purposes, though they may know their fathers well."

Halla rubbed her temples. "What if two men or two women wed?"

"Whichever one is being taken from their household must be paid for. If they are both leaving a house, then they will each set a price and their families will negotiate. Between two women of high standing, for example, particularly if one or more has proven that they can bear children, negotiations can stretch on for months. Frequently both families will cede land, or one will cede land and the other build a house on it, and feel that both have gotten off lightly."

"So how do we figure out my price?" she said, "I run my own household now, so do I get to name my own?"

"Absolutely not," said Sarkis. "No one names their own price. You can't determine what you're worth to other people." For the first time since bringing up the price, his scarred face cracked into a smile. "Besides, I know you. You'll undervalue yourself terribly."

Halla didn't know whether to be flattered or annoyed by the accuracy of this observation. "Well, my family's dead."

"Only the first family is blood. The rest are made by time or love or battle." He frowned, tapping a nail against his teeth. "Zale. Do you value Zale?"

"I'd jump in front of a charging horse for them," admitted Halla.

"Then they will set your price." He nodded firmly. "They are a crafty negotiator. They will drive a hard bargain."

"But you said you can't pay it!"

He leaned his forehead against the bedpost. "There's that. Perhaps I could work as a mercenary for a time, or..."

"Oh no!" Halla glared at him. "I just got you back! I'm not losing you again! And anyway, maybe you don't age, but I don't want to waste any more of the years I've got left."

Sarkis sat down on the bed and wrapped his arms around her. "Are you certain you wish to marry me at all? You'll grow old, and I will not. Will you hate me in time?"

She gave a very loud and un-ladylike snort. "I spent the last decade tending an old man," she said. "The fact I won't have to do that again is not a hardship." She tilted her chin up to look at him. "Will it be too hard for you, watching me age?"

"It will gut me," he said calmly. "But everyone watches the one they love age. At least I can know that you will not be alone. And I would rather be here, for as long as you live, than out in the world, worrying about you." He smiled abruptly. "Besides, I know you. You'll still need someone to pull you out of trouble when you're ninety."

Halla let this bit pass because he had just said something unexpected.

Everyone watches the one they love age.

The one they love.

"Love?" she said.

"Yes?"

His tone of polite inquiry was so at odds with what Halla expected that it took her a minute to sort out the reason. *He thinks that was an endearment. Is the magic in his head translating things strangely?*

"Sarkis, this is important. I don't know if the words are coming out right. You said...well, implied, I guess...that you love me."

"Oh. Did I?" He pulled back so that he could look her in the face. "Is that a problem?"

"No, but...I..." She rubbed her forehead and decided that all this hedging around was making her head hurt. *And what's the point anyway? To not be the first person to admit you're in love so that you don't feel like you're pathetic if the other person doesn't love you back?*

"Sarkis, I love you. Or I'm in love with you. Or both. Both seems likely?"

"That *does* explain why you want to marry me, given my obvious flaws."

"Flaws? What flaws?"

"Immortality. Manhandling."

"You've got better about the manhandling."

"I try." He frowned. "Ah—I'm in love with you, too. Did I say that already?"

"No, you didn't."

"Oh. Well, I am. For quite awhile now. I don't just gut myself for any wielder, you know."

Halla winced. "Hopefully you won't need to do so again."

"I am looking forward to a long stretch of being human, married to you, and not acquiring too many more scars. And perhaps—oh great god, you're crying."

"It's all right," said Halla, wiping the tears away with the heel of her hand. "It's fine. It's really fine. Yes, I'll marry you. We'll work out the rest somehow."

He kissed her then, and for a little while, neither of them worried about prices or the future at all.

CHAPTER 60

Zale listened to Sarkis's explanation of marriage price, nodded seriously, and proceeded to ask most of the same questions that Halla had. Then they steepled their fingers and considered.

"On the face of it, it seems obvious," they said. "Halla has considerable wealth, so her price should be quite high. You, on the other hand, are an itinerant swordsman and also dead."

Sarkis inclined his head to acknowledge both of these points.

"On the other hand, you come attached to a magic sword, the value of which is considerable."

"That shouldn't matter."

"Hush. You ask the Rat to stand as kin, and the Rat will do so in his own fashion." Zale frowned. "Now, what constitutes a fair price among your people? You have been expressing things in terms of land and trade goods, but the relative value of trade goods to your people may be different than ours, depending on scarcity and distance to sources. We do not even have an agreed upon exchange rate between our respective currencies." They rolled their sleeves up. "I am afraid, my dear Sarkis, that we are going to have to do a great deal of math."

Sarkis put his head in his hands.

"You gentlefolk enjoy yourselves," said Halla. "I'm going to go feed the chickens."

SARKIS AND ZALE spent three days negotiating, arguing about comparative values of precious metals, and during one particularly exhausting period, comparing the trade routes of spices to determine their relative cost between Archenhold and the Weeping Lands. Since Halla also had Sarkis carrying heavy furniture and beating rugs, this meant that much of the negotiation was shouted across the house.

"Clove oil is not that expensive!" shouted Zale from the front room, where they were working on the catalogue.

"It's worth its weight in gold!" Sarkis shouted back, dragging a particularly hideous nightstand out of the bedroom.

"Not here, it isn't! We've got a direct trade route with the Devilspine Islands. In your day, it had to go overland through about eight kingdoms and was marked up accordingly!"

"Decadent southern trade routes!"

"Behold the worm that chews upon the throne of the gods!"

Halla put her face in her hands, and wondered if she actually did want to marry Sarkis that badly after all.

I must, to be putting up with all this...

On the fourth day, he stomped into the kitchen, slammed a small, clinking bag down on the table, and said "There!"

"There what?" said Halla.

"The marriage price. Zale negotiates like each coin is a childhood friend, but we've agreed."

"All right," said Halla, gazing dubiously at the coins. "What do we do with it?"

"If you accept it, then we can be wed."

"You know I don't need this," she said.

"*I* need this," he said. "Because otherwise I will never feel that I have done enough to deserve you." He scowled. "I'm still not sure..."

"A good marriage is one where both parties feel that they got the better deal," said Zale from the doorway.

A thought struck Halla. "Wait—where did you get the money?"

"Courtesy of the Rat," said Sarkis. He scowled. "I've agreed to talk to some of their scholars."

Zale coughed. "And to a dedicate of the Many-Armed God."

"Gods," said Halla. "You'll have earned it, talking to one of them. Obnoxious people." She prodded the bag with one finger. It clinked. "So now what?"

Sarkis took both her hands in his. "Will you accept me as a husband now?"

"Yes?" said Halla. And then, realizing it sounded like a question, "I mean, yes. Definitely. Yes."

"Then we'll be wed."

———

THE PRIEST of the Four-Faced God performed the ceremony in the end, because Zale said that they could stand for the bride's family *and* the groom's family, but not if they were also expected to lead the vows.

"You *should* ride to the priest on one of my horses," said Sarkis, as they approached the church.

"You haven't *got* any horses," said Halla practically.

He considered this. "Perhaps we still have time for me to steal one..."

Halla laughed and took his arm. "And afterwards you can put the countryside to the torch."

"Naturally."

Zale, walking behind the couple, rolled their eyes.

The ceremony was short, simple, and dignified. The priest beamed at both of them as he tied the red cord around their forearms, binding them together. In theory, a representative of each of the families was then to take one end of the cord and unwrap it at the same time, but since Zale was standing for both, they had to take an end in each hand and loosen the cord rather awkwardly.

"It's a good thing I have a lot of experience with being tied up recently," they muttered. The priest of the Four-Faced God looked worried. Halla laughed. Sarkis scowled, but in a genial fashion.

Brindle was pressed into service as a witness, which he bore with aplomb, and signed his name to the parchment by dipping two claws in ink and swiping them across the page.

As soon as they left the church, the Widow Davey rushed up and soaked Halla's collar with happy tears. "Oh, my dear! My dear! You'll be so very happy together!" Halla patted the woman's shoulder and gave Sarkis a helpless look. The priest of the Four-Faced God moved in and gently detached her.

"She cornered me in the kitchen during the wedding supper," said Halla that evening. "And she tried to give me motherly advice about the wedding night."

Sarkis, who was lying on his back next to Halla, enjoying the warm afterglow of his wedding night, choked and had to sit up and grab for the mug of water on the table beside the bed. He nearly knocked it over and Halla pounded his back enthusiastically while he wheezed.

"She *what?*" he gasped.

"I know, I know." Halla shook her head. "I kept telling her I'd been married before, but she was determined to have her say. You'll be happy to know that while it may be uncomfortable at first, you *want* to please me and it's just a matter of nudging you in the right direction."

"I'm going to put my pants on and go stab her."

"That's your solution to everything."

"It's worked for five hundred years."

"Well, you'll have to come up with a different one. I thought maybe we could give her Silas's bird."

Sarkis laughed. "Diabolical," he said. He pulled his wife's head down against his chest. "The great god has clearly sent me to keep your wickedness in check."

"Oh dear. And here I thought I was so very respectable."

"It is a very respectable wickedness."

She chuckled. He kissed her forehead. "I much prefer you sleeping here," she said, "instead of in front of the door."

"It was not a hardship. I've slept on stone with—"

"Snow coming in the window, yes, I know." She poked him in the ribs. He laughed again. He seemed to be doing a lot of that lately.

He would not be Sarkis if he wasn't scowling at everything, but if I can keep him laughing too, I think we'll manage. Mortal flesh may not last as long as immortal steel, but it will last long enough to be happy.

"I love you," she said.

At first she thought he hadn't heard her. Then he kissed the top of her head. "And I, you. The great god has sent me a reason to go on."

Halla smiled, wrapped in her husband's arms, with her cheek cradled against the silver scars.

EPILOGUE

Spring was returning to Rutger's Howe, and Sarkis was more than ready for it. He could smell the thaw in the air and it made him feel itchy and skittish, like a horse too long in the stable. Halla was already talking about visiting her nieces, once the roads were clear.

Oddly though, he felt a pang at the thought of leaving Rutger's Howe, even for a few weeks. The great god help him, he had come to like a number of the neighbors. They had no idea what to do with him, but he had married "their" Halla, and that made him theirs.

He suspected that Halla had vastly underestimated how much the townsfolk liked her. It was also possible that having a large, angry man with a sword glowering at them made them realize just how much they liked her. This was fine with Sarkis.

Still, it was only a few weeks, then they'd be returning home.

Home.

The Weeping Lands would always be his homeland, but for a time, at least, he had a home. Even if it came with a strange bird that screamed evil prophecy (the Widow Davey had declined the gift), and a cook that quit twice a week and then showed up again the next day with meat pies (they didn't actually need a cook, but the cook needed employment and Halla had a keen sympathy for her situation), and a house where, despite having sold off a number of the stranger antiquities, one might at any moment open a little-used closet and have a manticore skull fall on one's head.

The front door opened and Halla came in, looking puzzled. She had a piece of paper in her hand, with a broken wax seal.

"This was sent to us, in care of the clerk," she said. "It's from Zale."

"Zale!" Sarkis, who had been sharpening the kitchen knives, straightened in his chair. "How are they?"

"They're well," said Halla, "but that's not why they wrote. They went back to Amalcross, you know, to deal with Bartholomew's estate, and...well. Huh."

Sarkis had been married long enough to recognize the world of concern contained in that *huh*.

"What is it?"

"They went to see Nolan in prison, and he said something odd." She read aloud from the letter. "'Odd enough, my friends, that I felt I should inform you. When I asked if his order had sent anyone to defend him, he said that it was not their way, and '*It does not matter that I have failed. They will have the second sword soon enough.*' When I pressed him, he refused to answer any more. He died in prison two nights later. I have informed the temple, and they are looking into it, but I wished to see that you knew as well.'" She folded down the page.

"The second sword..." said Sarkis slowly. "The second one she made? I don't know who that would be. Or the second one they found? Again, that could be anyone."

Halla shrugged helplessly. "I don't think we know enough.

And I wouldn't necessarily count on him telling the truth, either."

"True," said Sarkis. He set down the whetstone and wiped off his hands. He had a sudden urge to hold his wife and feel real and solid and not like a ghost of a sword. "True."

"The Temple of the Rat will tell us when they know more," said Halla. She put her arms around him, and for a long time, Sarkis could not have said which of them was offering the other more comfort.

AUTHOR'S NOTE

It was almost exactly a year ago from the time of this writing that my husband and I were in the kitchen and I was ranting about how much Elric—Michael Moorcock's Elric—whined about everything. "If you ask me," I said, "the real victim was his sword Stormbringer. The sword had to listen to him whine and couldn't leave. But does anybody ever ask the magic sword's opinion? Noooo."

I did not need another book idea. I have too many. But somehow the notion of a beleaguered magic sword saddled with an inept wielder stuck with me. I had already written a short story called "Sun, Moon, Dust" about a gardener who inherited a magic sword with warriors who lived in it and I thought that had been my last word on the subject, but the idea kept nagging me.

Finally I sat down to write just a couple of sentences, and Halla and Sarkis more or less barreled onto the page in front of me. I churned out nearly a third of the book in that first month, despite deadlines and other projects that I really should have been working on. The book wanted *out*. Also, it wanted to be a trilogy, and I am already working on Angharad's book, because...well, apparently I have a lot to say about magic swords.

Thanks go, as always, to my intrepid proofreaders, Cassie, Jes, and Andrea, and to my editor K.B. Spangler, who puts up with a lot. Huge major thanks to Andrea (again) for lengthy treatises on ox behavior, geography fact-checking, and for cheerleading *Swordheart* when I was convinced that nobody would want to read it because it wasn't like *Clockwork Boys*, my previous duology. And extra thanks to some enormously kind non-binary folks who read through it at the eleventh hour to offer thoughts on how to make Zale ring true.

And, as always, to the love of my life who keeps *me* from stepping on bears (and who muttered, at several points, that he was really feeling for Sarkis) my husband Kevin. I could maybe have done it without you, but it wouldn't have been nearly as fun and I would have lived on frozen pizza for several months straight and nobody wants that.

ABOUT THE AUTHOR

T. Kingfisher is the vaguely absurd pen-name of Ursula Vernon, an author from North Carolina. In another life, she writes children's books and weird comics. She has been nominated for the World Fantasy and the Eisner, and has won the Hugo, Sequoyah, Nebula, Alfie, WSFA, Cóyotl and Ursa Major awards, as well as a half-dozen Junior Library Guild selections.

This is the name she uses when writing things for grown-ups. Her work includes horror, epic fantasy, fairy-tale retellings and odd little stories about elves and goblins.

When she is not writing, she is probably out in the garden, trying to make eye contact with butterflies.

You can find links to all these books, new releases, artwork, rambling blog posts, links to podcasts and more information about the author at www.tkingfisher.com

 twitter.com/ursulav

House of Diamond

Mountain of Iron

Digger

It Made Sense At The Time

For kids:

Dragonbreath Series

Hamster Princess Series

Castle Hangnail

CPSIA information can be obtained
at www.ICGtesting.com
Printed in the USA
LVHW061153090723
751849LV00001B/16

9 781614 505228